P9-CKG-430

MURDER AT THE WAR

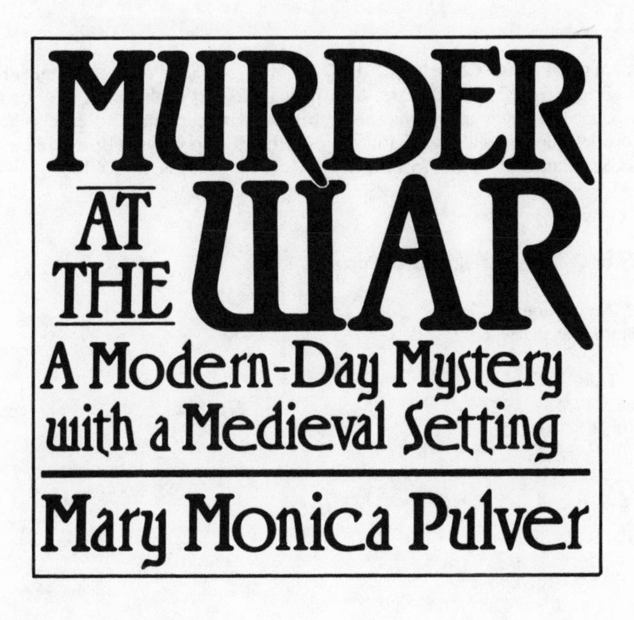

St. Martin's Press
New York

 For information, address St. Martin's Press, 175 Fifth Avenue, New York, N.Y. 10010.

Design by John Fontana

Library of Congress Cataloging in Publication Data

Pulver, Mary Monica.
Murder at the war.

I. Title.
PS3566.U47M8 1987 813'.54 87-4480
ISBN 0-312-00622-5

10 9 8 7 6 5 4 3 2

Author's Note

There really is a Society for Creative Anachronism, whose members hold an annual War at a campground in western Pennsylvania. But Miller's Pond is not the name of the campground, nor are the other SCA place-names correct, except Forgotten Sea and the kingdoms. The Dark Horde is real, and the knighting ceremony. The courts are a lot bigger nowadays—more royalty in attendance—and last year they tried letting both sides defend a banner in the Woods Battle. I make the standard author's assertion that the characters in this novel are fictional, but those of you who have browsed through a dictionary of saints or the Norse sagas may be amused.

This book is dedicated by Margaret of Shaftesbury to Einar Lutemaker, and is for all the members of the Society, especially Fiona, Andrew, Svea, Solomon, Koshka, Bertram, and Dur.

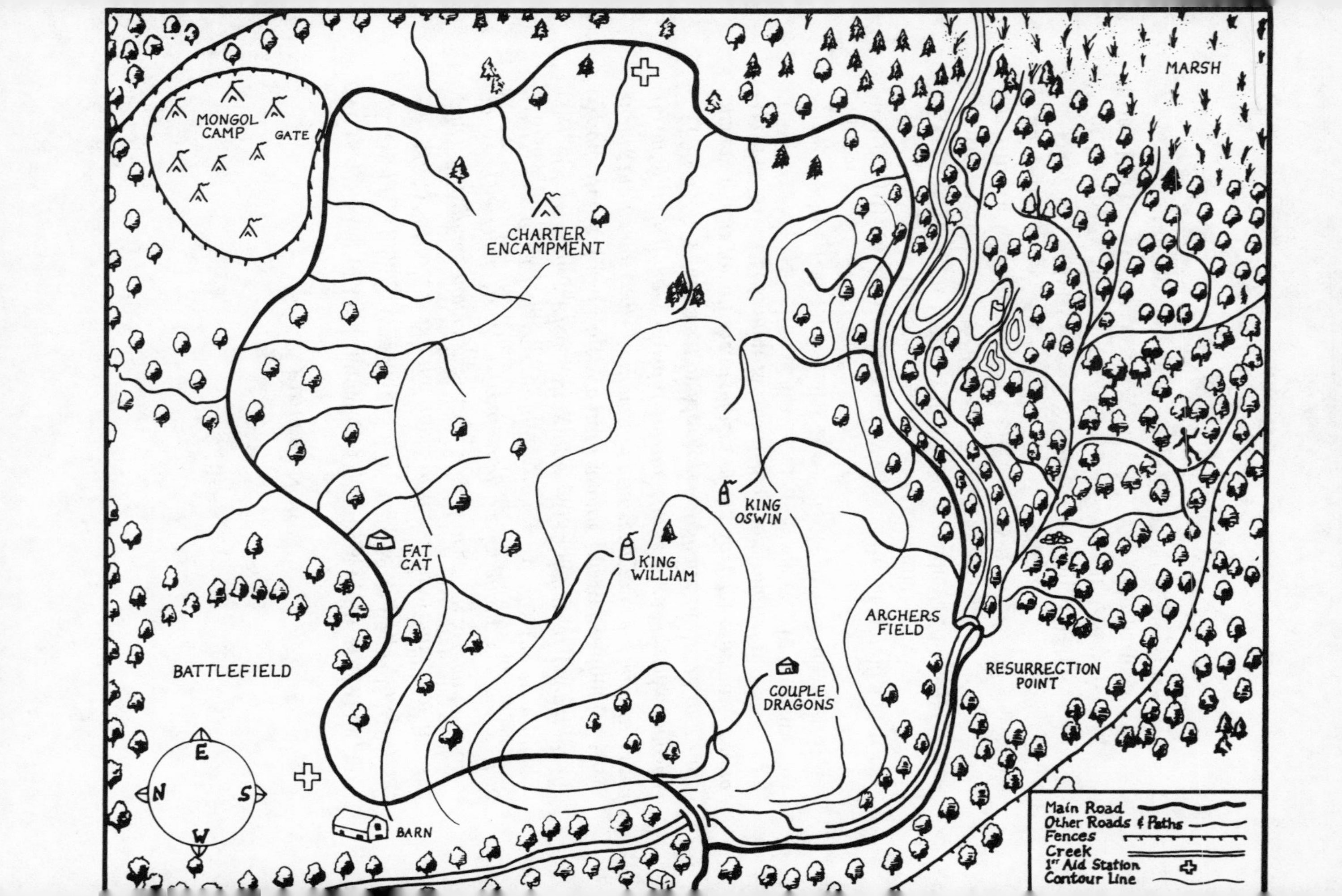

MONGOL CAMP
GATE
CHARTER ENCAMPMENT
MARSH
FAT CAT
KING OSWIN
KING WILLIAM
ARCHERS FIELD
RESURRECTION POINT
BATTLEFIELD
COUPLE DRAGONS
BARN
E
N
S
W
Main Road
Other Roads & Paths
Fences
Creek
1st Aid Station
Contour Line

Cast of Principal Characters

William: King of the Midrealm, a ceremonial title within the Society for Creative Anachronism he sometimes thinks is real.

Oswin: King of the East. He wants a nice, safe, friendly War.

Mistress Radegund d'portiers: The fretful Autocrat who can run the War any way she likes.

Master Wulfstan: Khan of the Great Dark Horde, an honorable man who prefers his wishes obeyed.

Thorstane: A drunken bully who should have stayed at home.

Sir Geoffrey of Brixham: Both in and out of costume, a very perfect, gentle knight.

Lady Anne of the Snows: Geoffrey's wife. She considers the Great Dark Horde to be the motorcycle gang of the SCA.

Lady Katherine of Tretower: A wealthy horsebreeder in the real world, assault victim and murder suspect at the War.

Lord Stefan von Helle: Katherine's husband. He must use his real-world talents as a police investigator to save his wife from arrest.

Sir Ignatius of Antioch: King William's Royal Herald and drinking buddy. He has a secret motive for murder.

Master Petrog: A lover of things truly medieval, he would have loved to use a real medieval weapon on the victim.

Sir John de Capestrano: A handsome sword jock with an eye for the ladies.

Sir Daffyd O Mynyw the Welshman: Called Taffy. A maker of Poacher's Stew and Katherine's mentor in things Welsh.

Lord Rocco the Italian: Called Roc, he is a Hordesman wrongly scorned at home and out to even things up at the War.

SIR HUMPHREY THE VIGILANT: Polearm fighter and leading ambush-layer with Geoff, Stefan, and Taffy in the woods.

LADY FREYIS: Dark Horde official whose green eyes shine like her many knives.

LORD HREIDER: He fails in his task as k'shaktu (guardian) of the victim.

TROOPER HARVEY HARRISON: Thinks he has discovered a nest of cultists.

TROOPER VINCE BEAD: He wants to know what really happened.

LORD CHRISTOPHER BRIDGEMAN: Everything about him but his armor vanishes.

LORD SABAS THE GOTH: Shaman whose runes say Katherine holds the key to the puzzle.

AND A SUPPORTING CAST OF THOUSANDS.

"Gold is for the mistress—silver for the maid—
Copper for the craftsman cunning at his trade."
"Good!" said the Baron, sitting in his hall,
"But Iron—Cold Iron—is master of them all."

—RUDYARD KIPLING

MURDER AT THE WAR

1

THE two kings sat shoulder to shoulder at the picnic table, across from the autocrat. William had pushed his heavy brass crown to the back of his fair head; he was a big man, uncomfortable in the early September heat. He glanced at Oswin, a skinny dark man in a bright orange tunic who wore his copper circlet more properly around his forehead.

The autocrat, a very slender young lady in pale green, said, "First, there's a problem with Archer's Field." Her voice was hard and brittle, as if the effort of keeping this vast gathering under control had begun with herself.

King William sipped from his can of Bud. "I hope they got us some new bales of straw. The old ones had grass growing out of them." He slapped impatiently at a mosquito trying to bite him through the tight sleeve of his purple tunic.

"Yes, they've replaced the bales. The problem is, it's only Wednesday and there are nine hundred here already. At this rate we'll have over five thousand in camp by the weekend. And the only way to make room for that many is to let some camp on Archer's Field. I talked with the owners, and they say the archers can use their cornfield across the road. The corn's already been cut. The field isn't pretty, but it's certainly big enough."

King Oswin asked, "Is it okay for the crossbows? Mine is pretty powerful; if a bolt misses, there's no telling how far it will travel. What's on the other side of the field?"

"Miller's Brook and some trees to the north. To the west—"

King William interrupted. "We won't be shooting to the west. You set the archery competition for four, which means it probably won't start until five, and that means, by the end, the sun will be well down. You can't hit a target if the sun's in your eyes." He took another drink of his beer.

The autocrat made a note on her clipboard with a hand that had already developed a fine tremor. "Thank you, Your Majesty," she said.

Poor lady, William thought. Didn't realize what a logistics problem the War was. He'd fielded a steady stream of complaints all day. The Porta-John people had delivered only half the needed additional units. The water spigot in the Mongol Horde camp wasn't working. The two chief judges of the Arts and Sciences Competition had already had three major quarrels over criteria. Thank God he was only king; he could wave a hand and say, "See the autocrat." The autocrat, Mistress Radegund d'Portiers, looked about ready to shatter into tears. *And it's only Wednesday. Poor lady.*

She asked, "I take it you both agree to move the Archery Competition to the cornfield?"

William nodded and said, "Looks like we have to."

Oswin said mildly, "Cornstalks are no fun to trip over, and if it rains, they'll whine about the mud."

"What's the forecast?" asked William.

"Scattered showers," the autocrat said humbly.

"Surprise," he said with a sarcastic grin, lifting his drink.

"Aw, it always rains at Pennsic," said Oswin. "Go ahead and use the cornfield, my lady, since they were nice enough to offer it to us. No extra charge, I hope?"

"No, Your Majesty." She made a note and turned a page over the back of the clipboard.

William asked, "Has the Khan arrived yet?" He wanted to talk to him. The Great Dark Horde comprised the biggest subgroup in the Known World; they included Vikings, Mongols, Huns, Visigoths, and undifferentiated mercenaries. They lived in all the kingdoms, called none home. Each year their Khan negotiated with the two War kings, accepting trinket gifts, negotiating overt and secret bribes, and attending a feast or other ceremony designed to please and impress him, before deciding on which side his warriors would fight. It was shtick but serious shtick: His fighters were skilled and numerous enough to affect the outcome.

''I understand he'll arrive later today,'' the autocrat said. ''There are nearly seventy-five Hordesmen here already. Which reminds me . . .'' She consulted her clipboard. ''What are we going to do about Thorstane Shieldbreaker?''

William asked sharply, ''He's here?''

''Yes, Your Majesty. He arrived an hour ago.''

William felt his face grow red. ''You sure?''

''I saw him myself, at the gate, paying his fee.''

''I thought the Khan was going to make him stay home this year!''

The autocrat said, ''The Khan is not a king, Your Majesty; he can only suggest that his brothers do what he wants.''

''Goddammit, if I'd known Thorstane was coming, I'd've told the gate to turn him away! He still hasn't satisfied me about that incident at the Crestfallen Tourney!''

''What happened?'' Oswin asked. Oswin was King of the East; Thorstane lived in the Middle and was William's problem. But Oswin had undoubtedly heard the rumors, and on this battlefield, East met Middle. Like William, Oswin wanted a nice, safe, friendly War.

William said, ''The story is, he hit Olaf Stiklesland from behind in the melee.''

''Isn't Olaf a Hordesman too?''

''Yeah, but I don't think Thorstane was paying any attention to who he was hitting. He said afterward Olaf knew he was swinging, but no witness will back him. He's done stuff like that before, you know; remember Pennsic Twelve? I say, if he won't obey the rules, he don't play the game!''

Oswin suggested, ''How about we scare up a few of our guys and heave him out?''

''Hell, he's in the Horde camp now; you want to go walking in there and lay hands on a brother? They must be as mad at him as I am, but he's one of their own, and they won't let a kingdomer touch him. We'd have the whole household down on our necks!'' William rubbed his face with a pink hand. There was a time when he'd have done as Oswin suggested, and damn the consequences. But that was when he was young and hotheaded, when his roar of laughter had less of a forced quality to it. He was going to be forty next month, too old for impulsive imperiousness. This was going to be his last reign, and he had decided to exit in a somewhat dignified manner.

He sighed. ''There could be some problems if we don't think of something. He's got no idea of what it means to behave decently, much less chivalrously. Hell, I wish King Basil had gone ahead and called a Court of Chivalry on him; we could've tossed him out of the Society a year ago.''

''If he's that dangerous, maybe the Horde will do something themselves,'' said Oswin.

''I've asked to be told the second Wulfstan arrives,'' offered the lady.

''Let me know what he says,'' ordered William. Wulfstan was the newly elected Khan, and reputedly a cool head. William eyed the clipboard. ''What's next?'' he asked.

The autocrat turned another page. ''As you know, there will again be two inns on site this year, the Fat Cat and the Couple Dragons.'' The inns were sponsored in part by the respective kingdoms; the emblem of the East was a tiger and the emblem of the Middle a dragon. It was thought when they started seven Wars ago they'd be rivals, but it quickly developed that hungry people went to the Cat and thirsty people went to the Dragons. ''This county voted itself dry last November,'' Radegund said. ''The Couple Dragons sells ale.''

''No, they don't,'' said William. ''Well, not exactly.'' He grinned. ''Now, I admit, their imported well water has an unusual taste, just like homemade brown ale, in fact. It may well be that the water is treated in some way, maybe by adding yeast and flavorings before it's bottled; but after all, it's legal to bring alcoholic beverages into the county."

"But it's not legal to sell them," said Radegund.

"And they don't. They sell souvenir tickets for a quarter. If you find you bought more tickets than you meant to, they allow you to exchange them for sandwiches and beverages, including 'well water.' But they don't sell anything except the tickets. It's legal; I know a church back home does the same thing so they don't have to buy a liquor license."

Oswin nodded. "Me, too. I checked with the owners; they said they didn't mind the Couple Dragons' setup. This is a private party, remember; no mundanes allowed."

William grinned, and the autocrat sighed. She crossed something off on her clipboard and folded back another sheet.

"I'm not a fighter," she said, "so may I leave the organization of the battles to Your Majesties and your Earl Marshals? I've set the order: Woods and Bridge battles on Saturday, Field and Champions battles on Sunday."

"Thanks, my lady, we'd enjoy taking all that off your shoulders," said William sincerely. Nonfighters could definitely mess up the organization of fighting.

"I'll second that," said Oswin. "Want us to run the Archery Competition as well?"

"I'll direct the members of the Royal Archers' Guilds to arrange a meeting with you."

"Swell," said Oswin.

"Wonderful," said William, taking a deep drink of his beer. "Now what?"

"That's all I have, for now," the autocrat said. "Oh, wait. I recommend you order all participants in the Woods Battle to wear boots. Sir John de Capestrano was scouting around in there this morning and almost stepped on a copperhead. He says he saw two more on his way out, and he was in a hurry."

"Holy cow!" said Oswin.

"Holy *shit*!" said William.

The lady rose and so did the kings. "If you will excuse me," she said, "I have another meeting to go to, with the chirurgeons, who don't like where I've stationed their first-aid tent. I thank you for your patience with me." She curtsied deeply, and they bowed their heads at her. She turned and marched out into the bright sunlight, her long hair in a single straight braid down her narrow spine.

"Poor kid," said Oswin.

"Yeah, I think she thought autocrating the War would be like doing an extra-big tournament. Listen, I got more beer in my tent. Want one?"

It was eleven o'clock in the morning, but Oswin said, "Sure. How's your queen taking things so far?"

Just before the last Midrealm Crown Tournament, William had, as customary, asked his then-girlfriend to be his queen if he won the crown. But being queen involved real work, and the lady declined. So William's queen this reign was a young newcomer. There had been doubts about her ability to face up to the challenges and politics of the position, but the lady had proved sturdier than anyone expected. William, still miffed at his former lady, had also discovered that his new queen, while awed by His Majesty, could not be seduced by him. Everyone was amused, even, after a while, William.

"Aw, she's all right, if you don't mind the mess," he said.

Oswin hid a grin behind a thin hand. He'd already paid a courtesy call at the Middle's Royal Pavilion, and the mess he'd seen consisted of William's armor, William's tabard, William's Oreo cookies, William's mantle, and the royal greatsword. "Takes a while to break them in," he said politely, and the two, who would be mortal enemies after Opening Court Friday morning, walked off together.

• • •

The Khan arrived very late that afternoon, and agreed to speak with the autocrat, if she could talk to him while he and his wife and two daughters set up their tent.

The Horde encampment, which was the biggest single encampment at the War, was marked off with a canvas fence. Inside, members in their colorful, comfortable, and not always historically accurate costumes were setting up tents, gossiping, or sorting out armor. All wore somewhere on their person the braided black-and-red cord that was the household badge.

The autocrat found Wulfstan the Fearless of Iceland setting up his tent in a central place within the Horde enclosure. It was an authentic Viking tent, a broad inverted V of black-and-red canvas. He greeted her politely, but did not stop work. "That pole needs to be set closer, hon," he said to his elder daughter. "You were saying, my lady?"

"Thorstane is here after all," she said. "And King William is not pleased. He was sure you'd persuade him to stay away."

"I tried, Mistress," said Wulfstan. He was a short man of medium build and great dignity, even in plaid flannel shirt and painter's pants. His thick hair was iron-gray and his bandit's mustache grew down even with his jawline. "Marta, please help your sister with that pole." His tone was gentle, but the younger girl immediately set down the kindling she'd been collecting and went to help the older.

"Lord Wulfstan, I'm sorry, but I do wish you had let me or His Majesty know Thorstane was not going to listen to you. There is great concern about his behavior, especially during fighting."

"My brothers and I will speak to him about his behavior," he said, tugging experimentally at the canvas. "Got it on that side?" he called to his wife, invisible behind the rising tent.

"Yes, love!" she called back.

"Perhaps you should know that His Majesty is of the opinion that Thorstane should be thrown out of the Society."

Wulfstan said coolly, "Until that happens, he is permitted to take part in all SCA events, including the War." He began to pound in a tent peg.

The autocrat said, "Please, my lord, try to understand my difficulty. Thorstane is perceived by many people, including myself, as a menace. The owners of Miller's Pond rent us this site year after year because we're relatively neat and well behaved. Beyond the legal ramifications, if Thorstane hurts someone, we may lose our War site. People will remember it was a Horde brother who was responsible."

Wulfstan stopped pounding. "You speak well, m'lady, and I

respect your feelings. But you and His Majesty can leave this matter to the brothers.'' His voice turned hard. ''And, never fear, we will handle it.''

Satisfied, she thanked him and left the camp.

• • •

Wulfstan finished setting up the tent, then changed into a brown knee-length tunic with three narrow bands of yellow ribbon around the skirt. He saw to it there was enough firewood to cook supper, tucked his good knife with the antler handle into his belt, and went to find Thorstane's tent.

From the voices, there were two men in the tent, laughing over a salacious and probably untrue story of a revel held after a recent event in Strange Sea. Wulfstan listened only long enough to identify the voices, then touched the cluster of brass bells outside the entrance.

''Who is it?'' called a drunken voice.

''Wulfstan. Is that you, Thorstane?''

''Yeah, it's me, Wulffy; whatcha want?'' growled Thorstane.

''I'd like to speak with you for a few minutes,'' said Wulfstan.

''Sure, come in,'' said Thorstane.

The Khan pulled aside the entrance flap and stooped to enter the orange tent. The other man was about to leave. He nodded to Wulfstan and said to Thorstane, ''Come over to my tent tonight; it's more than my turn to buy.'' He departed, giving the Khan a speculative glance. Thorstane was seated cross-legged on an Indian blanket. He was a big man, with long, tangled dark hair, and wearing a distorted idea of Viking garb: vest and diaper of brown fake fur, with his braided Horde cord as a headband. He had a shaggy beard; there were suds in it. He lifted the lid on a handy ice chest and said, ''Want a brew?''

''Not right now, thanks,'' Wulfstan said. ''Thorstane, I need to have a serious talk with you.''

Thorstane rummaged noisily amid melting ice cubes and came up with a can of beer—an imported brand, Wulfstan noted. ''I don't know if I got time to listen,'' he said sullenly, pulling the tab.

''You were going somewhere?''

"No, but that don't mean I've got time to listen to a lecture."

Wulfstan seated himself on the dirty blanket. "I thought you weren't coming to Pennsic this year," he said.

"Aw, hell, Wulffy; you know how much fun the War is! And I ain't been anywhere away from home all year! How could I pass up a chance to come?"

"Lady Freyis spoke to you, didn't she?"

Thorstane ducked his shaggy head. "Yeah." Lady Freyis was Thorstane's Tar-Khan, head of the Horde district that included Thorstane's barony, and noted for her sharp tongue.

"And I spoke to you as well. Perhaps we didn't make clear to you the trouble you are in, and the need for you to lay off your offensive behavior, at least until things cool down. Frankly, I'm surprised you weren't summoned before a Court of Chivalry after Crestfallen."

"But Olaf's not mad at me anymore! He came to me at Dragon's Day and said so. He's willin' to let bygones be bygones. So the king can go suck a toad for all I care."

"I want you to pack your gear and go home, Thorstane."

"I won't!"

"Why not?"

"For one thing, I don't have to. For another, I hitched a ride here with some kingdomers, and they're how I'm getting home, too."

"But I told William you weren't coming, and your showing up diminishes me before him. There's a bus station in Slippery Rock. I'll give you a ride."

"You gonna buy my ticket, too? I don't have but seven dollars on me. Look, I really want to be at the War. I got lots of friends here I don't see nowhere else. I'll behave, I promise."

Wulfstan studied the barbarian, who was looking very earnest. It would strain his pocketbook to have to buy a bus ticket for Thorstane—and there was no guarantee the man wouldn't get off the bus at its first stop, cash in the remainder of his ticket, and turn up back here. "On your honor as a sword brother?"

Thorstane drew a big X on his hairy chest. "I swear."

Wulfstan nodded. "Okay. I want you to go light on the booze, and stay away from the kingdomers. And if one brother—man or woman—comes to me with a complaint about you, you'll wish you'd stayed home. Do you hear me? Consider yourself on probation and under watch at all times."

Thorstane nodded solemnly. "I hear you."

2

IT had just grown light when the van entered Courthouse Square in the little city of Charter, Illinois. Geoffrey Collins was driving. He was twenty-seven, a tall, muscular man with dark auburn hair and close-cropped beard. In the passenger seat was his wife Ann. She was combing her streaky-blond mane and smiling to herself.

"Penny?" he asked.

"Oh, I was just thinking that the Society for Creative Anachronism is actually very much like the old Norse myth of Valhalla: You can fight all day, get killed any number of times, and still be in great shape for the feast that night!"

Geoff chuckled. "Bruised but whole, yes. It helps that the armor is real and the weapons only thick sticks of rattan." They came around the corner, ducking and peering out the windshield. "See him, Kori?" he asked the other passenger. He pronounced her name with the accent on the second syllable, because it was from the Greek word for girl, a nickname given her when she was a child.

"No." She leaned forward from her seat behind him to scan the sidewalk ahead. She was very slender, small-boned and muscled like a whippet, with clear gray eyes, translucent pale skin, and a lot of unruly black hair already beginning to escape from its two braids. She pointed a small hand and said, "There he is."

Geoff pulled the van to a halt at the curb. A man in a rumpled corduroy suit hustled up the sidewalk toward them. Kori opened the side door and he got in. "Good morning," he said. "Did I keep you waiting?"

"No," Geoff said. "We just got here ourselves."

The man sat wearily in the swivel chair behind Ann. He glanced in the back, where armor mingled with wooden chests, sleeping bags, and dismantled tents. "Have we got everything?" he asked.

"I think so," Kori said. "I got Geoff to check your list with me before we left the ranch."

"That's fine." He rubbed his eyes and yawned. He was about five-ten or -eleven, narrow like Kori, but knobbier, with thinning no-color hair.

Geoff put the van in gear and they drove off.

"Hard night, Peter?" asked Ann.

"Yeah. I didn't even get a chance to shower and change before I had to come meet you. Jesus, I'm beat."

"Well, sleep all you like," said Kori. "We three can share the driving."

"No, wake me at noon; otherwise I won't sleep tonight."

"All right. Good morning, Peter."

"Good morning, *fy'n galon,*" he said. They kissed lightly and he sat back. In two minutes he was sound asleep.

"He's turned into such a lamb since he married you," said Ann, turning around in her seat to look at him. He was nearly thirty-four, and sleep couldn't soften his features much: the thin wide mouth and long narrow nose in a face wide at the back of the jaw.

Kori smiled at him and said, "I think he always was a lamb."

"That's because you didn't know him before he met you," said Geoff without thinking.

"If that's an example of how your mind is working at present," said Ann, giggling, "maybe you should let me drive."

"Naw, it's just War fever," Geoff said. "I'm all right. But Ann's right, Kori; Pete has lightened up a lot since he got married; he's no longer the police department's annual nominee for Mouth of the Year.''

''I hope he put some of that saved energy into fighting practice,'' said Ann.

''He did; he and I are going to tear them up on the battlefields this year.''

''You, maybe,'' said Kori. ''But this is the first War Peter will be fighting in; he was only authorized as a fighter last Christmas.''

''You'll see,'' said Geoff. It was true Peter still didn't look like much. He had taken up sword and shield to impress his lady, and he was a cool-headed, careful fighter, without the flash and brilliance that impressed the crowd. His armor was more workmanlike than beautiful, but he'd made most of it himself—a good sign. It had been a pleasure to see Peter's surprise when Geoff offered to make him a squire, and perhaps Geoff had been a little surprised when he agreed, accepting the red squire's belt and taking the oath of fealty as Lord Stefan von Helle, now esquire. Stefan promised to serve Sir Geoffrey, honor his lady, and support him in battle; and Geoffrey promised to help Stefan complete the rigorous training that led to knighthood. Kori had been very pleased.

Geoff slowed the van, turned a corner, and accelerated up a ramp that put them on the freeway.

''Geoff, tell me how the War got started,'' said Kori, like a child asking for a favorite story. She was the youngest member of the quartet, and though all of twenty-three, sometimes she seemed even younger. Perhaps it was her flattering assumption that nearly everyone around her knew more than she did about nearly everything.

''Well,'' he began, ''twenty-three years ago in Berkeley, California, a group of college students, history majors, threw a party with a medieval theme. Everyone who came had to dress medievally and behave chivalrously. They did their research, learned some authentic dances which they danced to authentic music, served a feast with authentic recipes. And some of the guys put on a display of foot jousting with wooden swords. The winner was crowned king, and he knighted some of the other fighters. Everyone had so much fun, they did it again. And again. Pretty soon they were a club—and now we're a non-profit, educational, international organization of people who research and selectively recreate the Middle Ages. By selectively, I mean we leave out fleas, dirt, and intolerance. There are fifteen thousand members in Canada and the United States, which is divided into twelve kingdoms.

"Now, once upon a time, back in the sixth year of the Society, there were only three kingdoms—West, Middle, and East. Phillip the Archer was King of the Middle. That's us. He looked eastward and saw lands sparsely populated and decided to give the King of the East a hand at developing them." Geoff signaled and pulled out to pass a slow-moving semitrailer.

"He wrote a letter of intent to the King of the East. It was in simple language and all capital letters, and he wrapped it around a handy arrow and gave it to a messenger to deliver.

"The messenger duly appeared at a big court being held in the Eastern Kingdom, and handed over the arrow. Algernon, King of the East, read Phillip's note and he waxed wroth. He ordered his herald to read it out loud, and the whole court waxed wroth! So Algernon broke the arrow in three pieces and threw them at the messenger's feet. 'Thus shall we do to any Midrealm fighter who dares set foot on one inch of Eastern territory!' he declared, which is pretty good, coming from an Easterner on the spur of the moment. Some members of the court began pounding with their fists on the table and calling for blood. 'Ladies, ladies!' said King Algernon"— Geoff had to pause while Kori laughed—" 'I'm sure when this messenger carries our sentiments back to King Phillip, he will give up his foolish idea.'

"It's a funny thing, but many people, some of them actually present at the event, claim the messenger bore a strong resemblance to King Phillip. Perhaps they were related. At any rate, the messenger was invited to sit at the head table during the feast that night—a whacking great honor for a lowly messenger—and King Algernon shared a bottle of Solomon ben Jacob's '70 cherry wine with him. That was a better honor. I had a goblet of his '82 apple mead once, and I couldn't stand the taste of any other wine for a month afterward. He has a magic way with fermentation. . . ." He sighed and shook his head.

"Anyway, that was the end of the thing, everyone thought. Then King Phillip got transferred to Baltimore by his mundane employer. He had to resign his crown to his successor when he moved, because Basketweave—Baltimore—is in the Eastern Kingdom. Shortly after his arrival Phillip entered an Eastern Crown Tournament and, because he was simply the best fighter in the Known World at the time, won it handily. After six months' apprenticeship as crown prince, he was crowned King of the East. While going through some old papers, he came across a tatty, insulting message from a certain old ex-King of the Middle and *he* waxed wroth. 'This means war!' he shouted. He called Alphonsus de Liguori, then King of the Middle, on that strange-fangled device we call a farspeaker. Within half an hour the broad outlines of the first War were drawn, and sometime in September seventy people met at a campsite on the Pennsylvania border. About forty-five of them donned armor and fought it out in the rains of the First Pennsic War, and we've been doing it annually ever since. Rain and all."

"We won that first War, didn't we?" asked Kori.

"Of course. How could we deny King Phillip the singular honor of being the first king in history to declare war on himself—and lose?"

Kori laughed and asked Ann, "How much of that is really true?"

"Well, it's all sort of mostly true. Duke Sir Phillip the Archer, as King of the Middle, sent that war arrow, and as King of the East declared war on the Midrealm. And lost." She had wrapped her tawny hair around one hand and now began pinning it into a knot on top of her head. "Those seventy participants are a long way from the five thousand they're expecting this year. I read in *Tournaments Illuminated* that we added twenty-seven hundred new members last year. Sometimes I think the Society is growing too fast. We don't get to the newcomers fast enough, and they don't know how to act or dress at events. At the Queen's Ransom event in Talltowers, I saw someone in jeans and a big-sleeved shirt he bought in a department store. He kept trying to borrow pieces of armor so he could try out the fighting. Disgraceful!"

"Now, he'll be all right," said Geoff. "I took him aside and filled him in a little bit, warned him about his garb. I suggested he try a monk persona to start with, since monk's robes are easy to make and don't call for expensive trimmings. And I told the shire's knight marshal about him, and he promised to take him under his wing, get him started at fighting practice and armoring. He's just new. He's a bright young man; he'll be fine."

"Yes, but there are hundreds like him, and more coming all the time. And a marshal is only for fighting; these people need lessons in all things SCA-ish."

"So let's do what we always do when we need to develop new talent: start a guild. A Newcomers' Guild. Organize lectures, give a few lessons."

"Well, maybe. The Dungeon and Dragon players need to unlearn as much as they learn. I'm going to talk about the problem at the War. Get some ideas. Some shires and baronies have chatelaines who run loaner-garb closets, I hear."

"I was grateful you'd loaned me that red bliaut for my first event," said Kori. "I felt right at home, right from the start. Everyone was so kind."

"It wasn't the garb, m'lady," said Geoff. "It was because you're young and lovely and no one knew Pete had already staked a claim on you."

"That and because she volunteered to help with cleanup after the event," said Ann, "which to a tired autocrat made her price above rubies."

• • •

"I agree, Master Petrog; we should give high marks to entries that are accurate reproductions in style, materials, and method. But I think we should give higher marks to entries that are originals, provided they are also medieval in style and material." The speaker was Sir John de Capestrano, a very large and handsome man with curly golden hair. He and Master Petrog of Devon were standing in the old barn's hayloft, site of the Arts and Sciences Competition at the War, and Sir John was near the end of his patience.

"Bullshit, my lord, bull-shit," said Master Petrog. "The only way we can get most of these turkeys to do medieval work is to make them try to copy the real thing, and give the prize to the one who comes closest.'' Petrog was a tall, dark man of forty with thin, beautiful hands. He was a surgeon and an amateur scholar and collector of some repute even outside the Society. ''If we don't, they embroider cute baby unicorns on their banners, treat Prince Valiant as a historical figure in their research, and make Tudor garb of polyester double knits—and expect us to hand out prizes for such garbage!''

John watched him stride angrily up and down the dusty room, slapping his long brimless cap into one palm. His ankle-length houppelande was two colors, blue on the right, green on the left, the skirt split fore and aft, so that when he walked one could see that his hose were also two colors. The long cap and his soft leather shoes were dark green and set with aquamarines. It was an extravagant costume to be wearing this early in the event, but Petrog had an authentic medieval love of display. He gestured at the dozen items on the long table in the middle of the room, and the dagged ends of his enormous sleeves fluttered. ''Look here, a tunic that purports to be Welsh, but the dragon on it is Chinese! And here, someone's entered a stainless-steel helm. Very pretty, but stainless is modern, dammit!''

John sighed and walked over to the table. The sun streamed through a dusty window and picked out the brass trim on the scabbard of his broadsword. His simple tunic was sky blue, and his white belt, gold spurs, and the gold chain around his neck marked his status as an SCA knight. He picked up the helm, a gorgeous, gleaming thing. ''All right, this won't do, I agree. It's not for SCA contests; stainless steel isn't period. And there isn't room inside for padding, so it couldn't be used in combat, either; it's neither authentic nor functional.'' He put it down and picked up a tabard, a long piece of cloth with a head hole in the middle, and read the four-by-five card attached. ''But look at this. The card says it's hand-woven and it's linsey-woolsey material, both of which are authentic, and there's three citations for the embroidery as being real Celtic style. See, the animals' necks and tails are stretched out and interwoven. But here's the nifty part—'' He held the tabard up before Petrog's offended aristocratic nose. ''One animal's a dragon, and the other's what medieval Europe thought a tiger looked like. The dragon and the tiger, emblems of East and Middle. This is a War tabard, and I think it's a clever idea!''

Master Petrog turned away. ''Bullshit—'' he began, but stopped short, and Sir John turned to see why.

Standing at the top of the stairs was the autocrat, looking thin and imperious. ''I beg your pardon, Mistress Radegund,'' said Master Petrog, as both men bowed; ''I did not hear you come up the stairs.''

''With all the shouting you two are doing, I'm not surprised,'' she replied. ''I take it you have not come to an agreement about contest points?''

''I am afraid not, Mistress,'' said Sir John humbly. He stepped into a patch of sunlight, and his hair glowed like a mass of fine brass wire. He bowed.

She strode into the room, and John, straightening, saw the look in her eye and thought, *Ah, she's really wearing her autocrat hat now—and about time*. ''As I understand it,'' she said calmly, ''you, Sir John, believe there should be an equal distribution of points for creativity, complexity, workmanship, quality, functionality, and—what is the last?''

John thought. ''Authenticity, Mistress.'' This wasn't altogether true. John was primarily an armorer, and as such more concerned with what worked than what looked authentic. He'd been asked to serve as judge at the War by the King, and it was not courteous for a knight to say no to the King. He'd talked to a few people about judging, picked up this attitude about creativity over authentic replication, and now was stuck with it. On the other hand, a lot of people didn't like Master Petrog, so John didn't mind being found at odds with him.

Mistress Radegund continued, ''You feel the artisan should be free to work as he or she wishes within the constraints of medieval knowledge and culture, right?''

''Yes, Mistress.''

''And you, Master Petrog, wish there to be a skew in weight to emphasize authenticity, specifically replication of authentic artifacts. Am I correct?''

"Yes, Mistress."

"And you have been quarreling about this for thirty-six hours. The War officially starts tomorrow morning. I have many tasks to accomplish and I don't have time to arbitrate your fight. Therefore, I am going to sit on that rather dusty barrel over there, and you two are going to agree in five minutes, or I will call off the Arts and Sciences Competition."

"You can't do that!" said Master Petrog, astonished.

"Yes, I can," she said, walking to the barrel. "I'm the autocrat, this is my War. I can run it any way I want."

Sir John hastened to dust the barrel with a blue sleeve. Master Petrog begged her pardon and flapped at the barrel with his cap. Both helped her to seat herself.

"You have four and a half minutes left," she said sweetly, her blue eyes flashing.

"Please, we need more than four minutes to solve this," begged Petrog. "Give us two hours—one hour!"

"I'm sure we can find a compromise in an hour," agreed John.

"Bullshit, if you'll forgive me, Master Petrog. I assure you, I will not yield on the time limit, so you had better start talking."

The two men withdrew to the other side of the loft and began conversing in swift undertones that quickly rose heatedly.

"By these ten bones!" shouted Petrog at last, throwing up a hand. "Have you no ink in your pen, you ballocky, club-fisted calf's head? Oh, what's the use!" He stormed to the head of the stairs. "Have it your way this time, but it's going to be different next year, you hear?" He went rapidly out of sight down the stairs.

"I think I've been insulted," said John, turning, bemused, to Radegund.

"I think you have, too, but never mind," she said, slipping off the barrel. "How did you get him to surrender so quickly? There must be thirty seconds to spare!"

John came to take her arm. "Simple. I pretended to see it his way. Then I was struck by the realization that if we did it by his rules, we'd eliminate most of the entrants. There would be whole categories without an entry, and not enough entries in others to make it an official contest."

Mistress Radegund laughed. "Very clever!"

Sir John shook his head. "God, he's hot-tempered! I actually thought he was going to sock me for a second there!"

"All Society purists are like that. But with poor Master Petrog, there's also the additional cross of Thorstane to bear."

"Thorstane?"

"Haven't you noticed that every time their paths cross, Thorstane begins chanting 'Patty-cake, patty-cake, baker's man'?"

"Typical stupid thing for Thorstane to do."

"Well, I found out what's behind that, and it's a surprisingly sophisticated bit of cruelty, considering the source." They began walking across the floor to the stairs. "You see, Petty speaks Latin, and he thinks we all should be able to; it was a sign of an upper-class education in the Middle Ages. Not many of us are willing to expend the time and effort to learn it, but Thorstane has, somewhere and somehow, picked up a Latin vulgarity. *Pathice,* which is close to 'patty-cake' in pronunciation, means the passive one in sexual intercourse, and the one who plays the female in homosexual encounters. I don't know who told Thorstane that, but he's about driven Petty round the bend with it. And it isn't helping that more and more of us are learning what 'patty-cake' means."

Sir John started down the stairs, saying thoughtfully, "If I were Thorstane I'd cut that out. Master Petrog's a funny guy, he doesn't handle teasing very well. And he never forgets an insult. He's no fighter, but he's strong enough to shove a knife into Thorstane's kidney."

"Oh, come on!" said Mistress Radegund, amused. "He's a queer old duck, but a knife? Master Petty? I should think he'd be afraid something might drip on his beautiful period shoes!"

3

THEY had stopped for lunch at a tollway plaza a little past the Ohio border. Kori sliced into her stuffed tomato and asked newcomers' questions. "Tell me about the campsite. How do you find your way around?"

Ann said, "It's not hard. There's only one road. The tents line it on either side, with more tents behind, and paths going back between the tents. Our encampment is at the end of one of the paths this year. You look for an identifying marker along the road so you'll know your path. Some people put up paper signs, like Nunneslane or Wall Street, or hang miniatures of their coats of arms at the entrance, so you know who's back there. When I talked to Taffy last night, he said we should look for kerosene torches at the entrance to ours."

Geoff massaged the back of his neck, stiff from driving, and ruffled his auburn hair. "Let me draw you a map." He reached for a paper napkin and took a ballpoint pen out of his pocket. He drew a big circle with several large wobbles in it, saying, "If the napkin is Miller's Pond Campground, then this is King's Road. It begins at the gate, here, goes up a steep hill and winds down and around, ending up at the gate again. Cutting a diagonal across the campground is a brook, which runs along between the edge of Phillip's Forest and Archer's Field, and empties into a marsh, here. It's been dammed behind the old mill, and there's a good-sized pond you can swim in if you like. The road crosses it twice, near the gate and here, at Resurrection Point, which is a clearing outside Phillip's Forest. The forest is over here, kind of triangle-shaped''—Geoff drew a looped line to indicate trees—''bordered by the fence of the campground here, the marsh at this end, and the road and brook along the other side. Archer's Field is across from the Point, with the archery butts at the east end.

''At the furthest place from the forest, on the other side of the campground, is the big field where we hold the Champion, Bridge, and Field battles. Near it, on top of the hill here, is a big old barn.'' He drew a small rectangle to represent the barn. ''The kings hold court downstairs, and in the haymow are the Arts and Sciences contests. The whole campground takes up what, Ann—two hundred acres?''

''Maybe more.''

''Maybe more. There's just this one entrance. Beside the gate is the owners' house, and by the pond is what used to be a mill but which is now a general store and bathhouse. Go for a shower early in the morning, because the hot water runs out before the line does.''

''It's hard to get really lost if you stay on King's Road,'' said Ann. ''They set up a big map outside the store with important campsites marked, and there's usually a schedule of events beside it.''

''There are replicas of the map for sale,'' said Geoff. ''Maybe we should buy one so you can get an idea of the way the trails in the forest go, since you'll be water-bearing in there.''

''All right.''

''I never realized that the woods are surrounded like that,'' said Ann, leaning forward and looking at Geoff's little sketch. ''The fence in back, marsh at the end, and then the river and road along here.''

''Keeps us honest,'' said Geoff. ''It's impossible to sneak fighters into the place, and the only way out is to die—and even then you get resurrected and sent back in.''

"How do you get resurrected?" asked Kori.

"They fight by standard SCA rules of honor: If you get hit hard enough that a real sword would have put the arm or leg out of commission, you fight without said arm or leg. And if you take what would have been a killing blow in the head or torso, you fall down dead. But instead of staying dead until the battle is over, when you get killed in a Woods Battle you take your helm off and go to one of the designated gathering places. A marshal comes by every so often and marches the dead out to the main entrance. He carries a black flag so anyone he runs into knows not to attack. After about fifteen minutes at the entrance you're declared alive and head back to the action. I was killed and resurrected twice in one Woods Battle a few years back. The third time I died, the thing ended before my fifteen minutes were up, and I was so glad I almost cried. I was completely exhausted. It was after that War I started jogging."

"How many take part in the Woods Battle?" asked Peter, taking a bite of his sandwich.

"I've seen as many as eight hundred fighters, or about four hundred a side, though the woods are big enough that it doesn't seem crowded. Plus medics, marshals, and water bearers, of course. It can be a lot of fun, if you're in good condition. You break into parties and lay ambushes and get lost and throw each other in the river."

"The idea is to capture the enemy's banner and hold it until a cannon shot signals the end of the battle," said Ann to Kori. "I remember my first War, Pennsic Nine. The East was defending that year. They made a fake banner and let our fighters find it, and the rest of the battle was spent fighting over the fake while four Eastern knights hid with the real one. If our people had stopped and taken a close look they'd have seen the tiger on the fake had crossed eyes. But they were too busy gloating over how easily they'd gotten hold of it."

Kori laughed. "Are we defending or attacking this time?" she asked.

"Attacking," said Geoff. "And you can bet we'll look close at any banner we take."

''Do you get together beforehand and plot maneuvers?''

Geoff shrugged and grinned. ''We meet ahead of time, all right; but everyone's too busy giving advice to listen to any.''

''I hope the Horde's on our side this year,'' said Peter.

''Me, too,'' said Geoff. ''And not just because they're good fighters.''

''Why do you say that?'' asked Kori.

''Some of them, the really crazy ones, wear only the armor absolutely required by the rules: a helm, a neck brace, gloves, kidney belt, pads for elbows and knees, and a nut cup. Everything else, arms, legs, shoulders, belly and ribs, all go uncovered. I don't like fighting one of those lunatics. I'm so busy trying not to hit him where he's not protected, I get killed two times out of four.''

Peter smiled his lopsided smile. ''I'm so busy trying not to get killed myself, I don't get time to worry about that. Like you said, they're good fighters.''

''Why don't they change the rules, call for a complete suit of armor for every fighter?'' asked Ann. ''Or, better, tell the Horde to go play its game somewhere else? They aren't medieval at all!''

''Oh, I don't know,'' said Peter. ''There have always been barbarians waiting at civilization's gates for someone to forget to lock up at night. I think they're kind of authentic.''

''Peter, you've been so busy learning to fight, you haven't been paying attention to them off the lists; they're getting really terrible!''

''They're not as terrible as some people think,'' he said, biting into his sandwich, and Kori frowned at him. Under Ann's tutelage she had come, like many mainline SCA members, to dislike the Great Dark Horde. Defiantly rude and unkempt, they swore fealty to no king.

Ann said, ''They spoil the medieval ambience we're working so hard to create. They're—they're the motorcycle gang of the Society!''

Geoff and Peter laughed, but Kori said, ''Roc insists on bringing his dog to feasts and he sits in the doorway like a beggar because we won't let him bring it to the table.'' Lord Rocco the Italian was the Charter group's lone Horde member.

"It's very medieval to have a dog under the table at a feast," Peter said.

"Yes, but modern health laws won't allow it," said Ann. "And anyway, that dog is the size of a donkey!"

"And Roc doesn't bow to anyone," said Kori.

"Lord Roc bows to those he respects," said Peter, with slight insistence on the title due all Society members. "I will admit he is scruffy and irreverent. Like all his tribe, he tempts the noble rest of us into acting unchivalrously, unscrupulously, or unkindly, and sneers at us when we succumb. I've seen him bow a few times. It expresses his honest opinion. Has he ever bowed to you, *fy'n galon*?" he asked Kori.

"No," she said uncomfortably.

"Maybe you've never been introduced to him properly."

"You won't get much of a chance to introduce them at the War," said Ann. "He's not staying with us in the Charter group, you know, but with his sword brothers in the Horde camp."

"Fine; there are some other brothers I want to introduce her to. Maybe you're right, I haven't been paying attention. And my failure has permitted my wife to learn to avoid some damn fine people." Peter stood and went to refill his coffee mug.

"What a terrible thing to say!" said Ann indignantly. "I thought you were teaching him manners, Geoff!"

"He's grumpy when he first wakes up," said Kori soothingly. "You know that."

Geoff said, "I'll speak to him about his tone. But I warned you a long time ago that Pete has friends in the Horde. Lord Roc is one of them. You'd better tell him you know not all Horde members are terrible."

Ann nodded. "Solly, for example. I hope he's there; he's sweet. But we'll introduce her outside the Horde camp; Peter can't possibly be serious about taking Kori in there. Those people are . . . grabby around women, especially pretty young ones. What if she meets up with Thorstane?"

"Now I'll grant you Thorstane. But he won't be at the War; I hear the Khan told him to stay home. Thorstane's in real trouble; there's talk he may be asked to quit."

"That's long overdue," said Ann. "He's been warned any number of times."

"Yes, he's our really bad apple, and a rotten example to the jerks who join to act out their Dungeon and Dragon fantasies." He looked at the man walking back toward them. "Pete, on the other hand, is shaping well. His sense of justice is a little overdeveloped, but if his manners ever catch up, he'll outshine us all."

• • •

King William was sitting at a table in a corner of the big white triple-tent complex that was the Couple Dragons Inn. Beside him was his best friend, short and stout Sir Ignatius of Antioch, royal herald of the Middle Kingdom. Across from them sat Sir John de Capestrano, a new knight, anxious to find acceptance among the peerage. He was William's size, as blond as William was red, and handsomer. He was wearing his good court garb, a short black velveteen gown, belted closed, with overlong sleeves cut open at the elbow so he could poke his arms out, gray shirt and hose and black ballet slippers. His gold chain and white belt gleamed in the dim lanterns of the inn. His black low-crowned hat with the upturned brim was on the table beside him—he'd doffed it on greeting William.

Sir Ignatius wore an old green tunic—green was the herald's color, and the emblem of crossed trumpets was on his long green cape. William was wrapped in a heavy plaid cloak, and his crown was on the grass under the table.

A Renaissance melody played in sharp counterpoint on recorder and lute drifted through the inn. A pair of musicians was entertaining the crowd in the inn's other room.

Some smart aleck had made a banner for the inn showing two dragons—coupling. It hung inside the west room of the inn, on the wall across from William. A few customers had objected, but it was the King's opinion that people who didn't like the banner should sit in the east room, or go over to the Fat Cat and drink lemonade. A breeze walked through the tent and Ignatius shivered. King William pulled his heavy plaid closer about him. "Thor is gonna piss on us for sure," he said.

"I wish he would; at least it would be warm," grumbled Sir Ignatius.

John laughed and said, "The cold will keep the snakes at home. Maybe."

"There aren't any snakes at Miller's Pond!" snapped Ignatius, his voice sharp and ill-tempered. He didn't like being cold, liked even less the thought that he should have known better. This was, after all, his tenth War, and the weather had nearly always been bad. The chill breeze again lifted the roof of the tent and made the lanterns flicker.

"There are too snakes," said William. "Always have been, so I don't know why all the fuss this year. After what Rags told me, I went in the woods myself and scared up a whole one of them."

"That one must be mighty mean," said John. "I heard someone got bit."

"Bull," said William. "The autocrat and I would've been told if that happened, and we haven't. Fighters, of course, shouldn't worry in any case; any snake dumb enough to try to bite through armor will bust his fangs. But just to keep the chirurgeons happy, I'll order that medics and water bearers and scouts stay on the trails or wear boots."

"I don't remember we had snakes before," said Ignatius. When not chilled, he was a humorous man, intelligent, with a vast store of War stories. As Dragon Herald he was a Great Lord of State, and had enjoyed serving on the King's Council in this and most of William's several reigns; his advice had produced some good legislation.

"Sure you do; remember Pennsic Eleven?"

"That turned out to be a garter snake, didn't it?"

"And it's probably that snake's great-granddaughter scaring the chicken hearts this time," said William.

"Remember the mice last year?" asked John. "The grass was alive with them."

Ignatius said, "A mouse ran over my lady's face at the War last year. She sat up with a scream that woke up half the camp, and spent the rest of the night in the car." William chuckled, but

Ignatius went on, "If something scrabbled over my face in the dark, I'd probably yell too. And reach for my sword shouting 'Bear, bear!' "

"Hell, Iggy, if you really thought it was a bear, you would've done your yelling from up in the nearest tree," said William. "And once I understood what you were yelling, I'd've been right up there beside you, with most of the rest of the chivalry."

The three laughed and drank their ale. John said, "And that's why there's snakes this year. There were plenty of mice to eat and so now we're up to our asses in snakes."

"No, we're not!" said William. "Dammit, the next man who says 'snake' to me gets banished from my sight the rest of my reign."

"Between Thorstane and—er, them crawly critters, this is going to be an interesting War," said Ignatius. "It's a good thing you took my advice and told the press to stay away."

"We've had too much publicity lately." William nodded.

John said, "If it gets any worse, they may ask if they can put us on 'Wide World of Sports.' God!"

William's face became dreamy. "Oh, I dunno. Get Frank Gifford to do commentary . . ." Ignatius snorted and William drained his cup. "How about another round?" he asked.

"Sure," said Ignatius, pushing his wooden goblet to the middle of the table.

"I'll buy this one," said John. "Since Sir Ignatius got the last one." He set his pewter mug beside Ignatius' goblet.

"No, it's my turn," said William, digging in his pouch for tickets. "Anybody seen His Highness this evening?" Meaning the Crown Prince; kings are majesty, princes are highness.

"Prince Thomas and his lady are hosting the Khan and one or two others in his pavilion," said John.

"Oh, yeah," said William, remembering, "he told me Wulfstan accepted his invitation. That's good; I think the Khan's leaning our way."

"That's just his good manners," said Ignatius. "King Oswin told me he's leaning theirs." He picked up the tickets and looked around for a server. "Wulfstan's not like other khans."

''Not much,'' said John sarcastically.

''No, seriously; he's more subtle. Trinkets and a keg of beer won't win him.''

''What will?'' asked William.

''The trappings of power. Let him sit with the royalty at court.''

''Ha!'' said John, surprised.

''No way,'' agreed William. ''No one sits up there unless he's got a kingdom, I don't care how many followers he has. That would set a precedent, and who knows who they'll elect khan next?''

John said, ''Can you imagine Sulu the Loon on a throne?''

Ignatius grinned and shook his head. ''Yeah, and they'd do it just to see if we'd keep our word. Okay, Will, how about I let Khan Wulfstan know you want to consult with him on battle strategy?''

''Sounds good,'' said William, then nodded sharply. ''Actually, that's not a bad idea. I'd like to consult with him if he's on our side. I'll serve a bottle of Solly's wine at the consultation, my last bottle of his '81 cherry.'' William really wanted to win this War.

''Pearls before swine, don't you think?'' offered John, but William frowned at him, and his grin died.

''Anyhow, maybe Tommy will win him over tonight,'' said Ignatius.

William agreed, ''He's a good man.''

Ignatius reached for his goblet to hold it up upside-down, signaling he wanted it refilled. ''Of course, he's not as much fun since he started winning crown tournaments. Funny how putting on that crown can change a man.''

''How did it change me?'' asked William.

Ignatius glanced over, but William was smiling, so he answered honestly. ''Sometimes I think you think you're really a king,'' he said.

''You mean I'm not?'' asked William. ''Damn!'' He snapped his fingers and there came immediately the patter of rain on the tent's roof. He looked up, his face blank with surprise. Ignatius started to crow with laughter, and after an instant William joined in.

4

THE van stopped at the gate to Miller's Pond about ten in the morning. Peter was driving; Ann, navigating, was sitting beside him. Geoff and Kori peered around their shoulders. Kori, all eyes, could see a narrow white farmhouse standing on the edge of a large graveled area. Beyond it, on the bank of a little river just beyond a small pond, was a rustic mill whose turning wheel dripped water. Nearer them was a tarp set up on four metal poles, and standing in front of it was a skinny half-naked man in black balloon pants. He had a wispy black goatee, and hanging by its blade on one shoulder was a double-bladed war ax. He saw them, grabbed some papers from a table under the tarp, and started over.

"Looks like Lord Roc's drawn gate duty," said Peter.

"And just look at him!" muttered Ann. "That's a hot thing to see first off at a supposedly medieval event!"

"He looks cold to me," said Geoff. The skies had cleared, but the sun had not yet warmed the air.

"The Beav and I give humble greetings," the Mongol said politely when he reached the van, stroking the wicked-looking ax. He glanced into the van and saw Ann. "Why, it's Lady Anne!" he said. "We've been anxiously awaiting your arrival." He said to Peter, "It's fourteen bucks a head this year. Got your waivers ready?" Peter handed over fifty-six dollars and four slips of paper signing away their right to sue if anything damaging happened to them during the event.

"Beav?" asked Kori.

"Beaver Cleaver," explained Lord Roc briefly, taking the waivers and money and giving Peter the papers he'd brought. "They're doing a survey this year. 'Why I joined the Society for Creative Anachronism,' in twenty-five words or more. No mention of a prize for the best answer." He took the money and waivers to a middle-aged woman in a short blue tunic standing behind a table under the tarp—"Mrs. Miller, one of the owners," explained Geoff to Kori, taking two of the single-page questionnaires from Peter and giving her one. The single question was typed at the top of the page, and there was a request that it be put into a collection box located at the campground store. "I guess if they've started this kind of thing the Society's gotten really respectable," he said, and did not sound happy about it.

Lord Roc came back with a white square of cardboard with "1427" crayoned on it.

"Drive across the bridge and climb the hill," he said. "Campsites are on the other side. Unload and drive it right back out again. Parking's down the road; no vehicles allowed to remain on the site. Welcome to the War."

"Thanks," said Peter. He put the cardboard on the dash and drove on.

"We are the one thousand four hundred and twenty-seventh vehicle," said Geoff with a low whistle. "Figure three or four persons a car, and we already have quite a little crowd here." The van crossed a narrow bridge, then groaned in low gear up the hill. Peter stopped at the top to stare, and the others looked in awe at what lay before them: a city of tents, every shape, color, and kind, from bubble tents to great medieval pavilions, with the thin smoke of countless cooking fires rising between them. A large shaggy barn stood nearby, hung with pennants and the great banners of the fourteen kingdoms. Everyone in sight was wearing medieval costume.

Costume at this early stage of the event consisted mostly of working garb, simple tunics and dresses of knee- or ankle-length, in faded reds, sky-blues, lettuce-greens, and earth-browns. Painted shields, longbows and crossbows leaned against tent poles or hung from tree limbs. Swords and maces, war axes, lances, and polearms were everywhere, as were the duct-taped wooden versions used in actual combat.

Peter raised the clutch pedal and began very slowly to drive down the rutted King's Road. A forge had been set up under a fly, and two men were making its anvils ring. A man in doublet and hose, a lute strapped to his back, strode purposefully by. A bare-legged child in a hooded tunic was leading a greyhound along the verge, its humped back nearly as high as the child's head.

Ann and Geoff stuck their heads out the passenger side window and exchanged greetings with friends.

"Master Petrog!"

"I greet you well, lady."

"Mistress Radegund!"

"Later, if it please you, Sir Geoffrey," said that busy lady.

"Look, Sir Odo's here," said Geoff, pointing to a white shield with a black cross and a red heart on it hanging outside a big gray pavilion.

Kori, all eyes, at last saw someone she knew. "Bless us, Father Hugh!" she called over Ann's shoulder, and a diminutive figure in monk's robes raised his hand in blessing, his homely face alight with pleasure at being recognized.

"There's the Queen of Meridies," said Ann, waving to a small woman with short, very curly blond hair. "Hello, Your Majesty!" she called. The woman turned and waved. She wore a crown made of a tangle of gold wire set with garnets. Her simple blue dress had a white belt that rode low on her hips and hung down long in front.

"See the white belt?" said Geoff to Kori. "Queen Jane's a knight as well as a queen. Lady knights are still pretty rare in the Society. I once saw her defeat her lord in a melee, and King Edmund is by right of arms King of Meridies. She's got the fastest hands I've ever seen. Hey, there's Humph! Sir Humphrey!'' called Geoff, waving a hand. ''Over here!''

''H'lo, Sir Geoffrey!'' A large man in a short green tunic and leather apron waved back. ''Come visit, we're the end of Dromedary Lane!'' He was carrying a piece of leg armor with a dent in the shin guard, and was obviously bound for the forge.

''That's Sir Humphrey the Vigilant,'' said Geoff. ''I've told you about him, Pete. Hang around him in the Field Battle; he'll see you through.''

''Okay,'' said Peter absently, concentrating on his steering. They were at the bottom of the hill now, coming around a long curve marked by Porta-Johns.

Ann said, ''There's the Horde camp.'' Its canvas gate was marked by two poles, one set with red and black streamers, the other decorated with feathers and surmounted by a real-looking human skull. Beside the gate, on a lounge chair covered with a blanket made of rabbit skins, reclined a plump, smirking barbarian. He was wearing a pink kimono a size too small and nodded familiarly at Peter as they drove by.

''He looks like something you'd find after a nuclear holocaust,'' muttered Ann, and even Peter laughed.

''Our path should be just a little further on,'' said Geoff. ''Taffy said to look for a pair of kerosene torches—there it is.''

Like the others, the path here was extremely narrow; Peter had to drive carefully, maneuvering to avoid tent pegs. At its end was a small open space enclosed with rope and already containing two tents, one very small. A campfire was blazing and a slight man with shoulder-length black hair was squatting beside it, slicing a leek into a pot balanced on its logs. He was wearing a long wine-colored tunic with a green tabard held in place by a white leather belt—Sir Daffyd O Mynyw the Welshman. ''Taffy!'' said Kori happily. Her persona was also Welsh, and he was helping her with her research.

The occupants of the van tumbled out to embraces and arm grips and shoulder thumps. ''I can't believe the sunshine!'' said Ann.

''It rained last night,'' said Taffy glumly. ''And the forecast is for more showers tonight.''

"Oh, it always rains at Pennsic," said Geoff cheerfully, going around to open the back of the van. "I'll need a hand with our stuff." Peter immediately went to help. Ann and Kori climbed back in through the side door and began handing out luggage and tent poles to Taffy.

Ann volunteered to drive the van out to the parking lot while the others began setting up the tents. Geoff and Ann had an authentic-looking two-room pavilion of lightweight buff canvas, which took Kori, Peter, Taffy, and Geoff half an hour to erect. Kori and Peter had a four-man tent of green rip-stop nylon that went up in minutes but did not look very medieval.

Ann came back, and the quartet retired to their respective tents to put on their costumes.

"Could we get a pavilion?" asked Kori after a while. She was on her knees, quickly fingering the many silver buttons through their loops down the front of her long violet dress. She had wrapped her braids into a large knot at the back of her neck, then drawn a very fine linen band under her pointed chin and pinned it on top of her head. Her long, boat-necked dress had tight sleeves and fit closely down her slender torso to the hips, then hung loosely.

"Why do you want a pavilion? You just saw how much trouble they are." Peter, also on his knees, was tugging down a yellow linen tunic notched front and back. He was already wearing navy blue hose and soft-soled red shoes with pointed toes. He picked up a navy-blue leather belt. "And they don't fold down small for travel, either."

"Yes, but they look so—real," she said. She turned to look into a small mirror standing on a wooden chest and began fastening a fine white linen veil to the band over her head—medieval married women covered their hair. "And you can stand up in them."

Peter buckled his belt and walked on his knees to his lady. "Well, let's look into it. Maybe we can find one that doesn't take a crew to set up."

She turned to face him, and he lifted her hand to his lips. "My lady Katherine of Tretower, I greet you well."

"My lord Stefan von Helle, we are indeed well met," she said, smiling. For the remainder of the War Peter would be Stefan and Kori would be Katherine.

They brought their shield-shaped cloth banners out and fastened them to the corners of their tent. Lady Katherine's was blue in background with a blazing golden sun in the center; a dish-faced Arabian stallion stood silhouetted on the sun, his mane and tail lifted in a light wind. Lord Stefan's arms were much simpler, a lit white candle glowing against a black background.

"Lord Stefan, Lady Katherine, your meal awaits," said Taffy from beside the fire. He was holding wooden bowls and pewter spoons for each of them.

The food had a remarkable mix of flavors, unlike any stew Lady Katherine had tasted before. "Taffy, this is wonderful," she said. "What are the flavorings? Besides leeks, of course."

"Thyme, oregano, a very small bay leaf, sage, and a pinch of cinnamon."

"Cinnamon?"

"Sure. Use just a little and people keep asking what it is. Hardly ever used in meat dishes today, but it turns up in medieval recipes all the time. But I think it's the meat in this that's fooling you, too. It's three parts rabbit, two parts venison, and a quail."

Lord Stefan's sideways smile appeared. "What do you call it, Poacher's Delight?"

Taffy laughed. "No, but that's an idea. The mix wasn't deliberate. My dad's a hunter, and Mom cleaned out the family freezer last week."

"Have you saved any for us?" asked Sir Geoffrey of Brixham (formerly Geoffrey Collins) as he and his lady, Anne of the Snows (formerly Ann Collins), walked up to the fire.

"There's plenty. Help yourselves," said Taffy.

Geoff took two bowls off the trestle table and went to fill them. He was wearing a short, lightly padded gray jacket called a joupon. An ornamental roll of fabric went around each shoulder. His hose and belt were white, his shoes black. A blunt black conical hat sat atop his auburn curls, and there was a jeweled dagger at his belt.

Lady Anne wore a very dark green cotton underdress with tight sleeves. Over it was a big-sleeved natural linen dress with geometric green embroidery around its hem and sleeves. She had a dark green headband, and her wheat-colored hair hung in two fat braids down her back.

"That's new, isn't it?" asked Katherine.

"Yes, it's tenth-century Saxon maiden. My old grubbies fell apart after the last time I wore them." She took her bowl and tasted the stew. "God, Taffy, this is delicious!"

"Thank you, my lady," he said.

A man's voice came from out on King's Road. "Oy-yea, oy-yea, oy-yea!" he bellowed, and they turned their heads to listen. "Will the owner of the blue Ford pickup, Iowa plates, please remove it from the campground at once!" Pause. "Contest entries should be brought to the barn loft!" Pause. "Armor inspection will be held along King's Road at four o'clock! That is all!" Faint repetitions of the herald's announcements could be heard from elsewhere.

"What's the fighting schedule this year?" asked Geoff.

Taffy said, "Gather with King William at nine tomorrow morning, Woods Battle at ten, Bridge Battle at two, Archery at four. Sunday morning at nine is Champions, followed immediately by the Field Battle, followed immediately by a court to announce the victor."

"The poor champions will be too winded to do us any good in the Field Battle," said Geoff.

"And if things run late—as usual—they'll be shooting arrows by candlelight," said Taffy, whose longbow was hanging on a tent pole. "I wonder when they're going to get this thing right?"

Stefan said, "It's my understanding that they've tried it differently every year since they began. If they try it every possible wrong way before they get it right, we should all go home and not come back until Pennsic One Hundred."

Geoff laughed, then asked, "Where's your belt?"

Stefan looked down, surprised. "Oh," he said. "The red squire's one? I was going to wear it only when fighting. I didn't want to seem to be bragging."

"Steffy, when you can tell me why that's a dumb thing to say, I'll know I'm making progress with you."

"Sorry, m'lord," said Stefan, and he put down his bowl and went to the tent to change belts.

"Why is that a dumb thing to say?" whispered Katherine to Taffy.

"The burdens of being a squire make it no great honor," Taffy whispered back, and said to Anne and Geoff, "Too bad you missed Opening Court. This year when Will presented the War Arrow, Oswin gave it to his queen. She broke it over her knee and said" —Taffy switched to a sweet falsetto—" 'If even I, a weak woman, can break this arrow, so much more will our noble fighters break those nasty Midrealmers.' "

Geoff growled, "Next year we should bring an iron crossbow bolt for a War Arrow. How do we divide housekeeping chores?"

"Cooks wash the pots, but otherwise everyone washes his or her own eating gear," Taffy said. "How about you and I get dinner tonight?"

Anne said, "And I'll get lunch tomorrow, since you boys will be busy in the woods."

"That leaves me to get breakfast, right?" said Katherine.

"You're the only one of us who actually enjoys getting out of bed in the morning," said Anne, "so do you mind?"

"No, of course not. We didn't bring any food; where do I buy what I need?"

Taffy said, "There's sausage and eggs in my ice chest. There'd be bread, too, but I left it open this morning and it's turned into a brick."

Geoff said, "I'll have Stefan get supper tomorrow, and if he does a halfway decent job, I'll let him help with cooking lunch on Sunday."

"If he does a rotten job?" asked Taffy.

"Breakfast *and* lunch," said Geoff, and they laughed.

"Can I buy bread somewhere?" asked Katherine, who wanted to load her husband with carbohydrates at breakfast.

Taffy said, "The Fat Cat promised it fresh and hot first thing in the morning."

"Fat Cat?"

"It's the good-food inn about halfway back up toward the barn on King's Road," said Anne. "Just follow your nose."

"We'll look for it when I show you around in a little while," said Stefan, returning to the fire wearing a wide red belt with a long tongue. He picked up his bowl and sat on the grass beside his lady.

"Any good gossip?" asked Geoff.

Taffy drained his goblet while he thought. "This is now a dry county, but the Couple Dragons is selling homemade ale. I hear they found some tricky way to make it legal. There are copperhead snakes in the woods; everyone's to wear boots. Somebody's been trying to start a peace movement—"

"At the *War*?" asked Anne, laughing.

"Don't ask me, I'm only your faithful reporter. The Arts and Sciences judges went to duke city over the rules. Thorstane's here—I saw him myself—and as soon as he's drunk enough, the kings are going to toss him out."

"You ought to start a newspaper," said Geoff. "Call it the *New Old Times*."

They laughed and Stefan asked Katherine, "Finished?"

"Yes, thank you, m'lord."

"Here, I'll wash your bowl with mine, then we'll take a walk."

"Lovely!" Katherine got eagerly to her feet, and a few minutes later she and Stefan wandered down the narrow lane, hand in hand.

"Are you annoyed at Geoff for assigning supper to you without asking first?" she asked.

"No, Geoff's a lot easier on his squires than some knights."

"Are you proud of being his squire? I mean, you're six or seven years older than he is, and used to being the one giving orders."

"Yes, I'm proud. He's one of the best fighters in the Middle, and certainly the most chivalrous. I never thought I'd be anyone's squire, much less his."

"You think too little of yourself," she said.

He said judiciously, "That's true," and she laughed.

"Look, over there, a barber pole outside that pavilion," she said, pointing. "Is that period? Do you suppose he really cuts hair?"

"That's Master Petrog. He's a medic in the Society and a surgeon mundanely. The SCA word for media is 'chirurgeons,' which is actually an earlier spelling of 'surgeon.' A barber pole is very medieval. It symbolizes the bloody stick held by people being bled. The white is for the bandages and the brass knob is the basin to catch the blood. Barbers were bloodletters and surgeons in the Middle Ages."

"Oh. There's so much I don't know," she sighed.

"You're far ahead of lots of others," he said. "You were studying medieval history before you knew there was a Society."

"Yes, I'm good on dates and reigns. It's the trivia I'm bad on."

"And it's the trivia that makes our game real," he agreed. They came out of the lane and stood on King's Road, looking around.

Katherine said, "Oooh, look at her!"

The young woman's long cream dress was covered with dragons, cut and woven from gold, green, red, blue, and copper ribbons. "Midrealmers!" she was calling. "Show your loyalty with a dragon! One hundred pence for a dragon!"

"Oh, lovely!" said Katherine. "Shall I?"

"Why not?" said Stefan. He stopped the young woman and after careful consideration Katherine selected a copper dragon with an extra-long tail. The little creature had a tiny safety pin through its back feet and Katherine was soon wearing her new pet on a shoulder.

"Shall we look for the Fat Cat first?" she asked.

"How about we stop by the Horde camp first, since it's just up the road?"

"Oh, I don't know—"

"Come on, live dangerously," he teased.

"I thought you said Anne exaggerates how awful they are," she said, teasing back. "All right, lead the way."

The road was crowded with pedestrians, and once they had to get out of the way for an elderly Chevy with six people inside and an enormous bundle fastened with rope to its roof. "Texas plates," said Stefan. "That must have been quite a trip."

As they approached the Horde entrance, Katherine said, "The pink kimono is gone. That should make Lady Anne happy."

"Wait till you meet this one before you say that," said Stefan. The rabbit-skin chair was occupied by a barefoot barbarian in a ragged white homespun shirt. He was playing something sad and reflective on a set of panpipes.

"My lord Sulu," said Stefan politely. "May we enter the camp of the Great Dark Horde?"

The music broke off. "The home of the free in the land of the brave," he said. "She's your wife, isn't she, Steffy?" He leaned forward to look at Katherine, who was standing a little behind her lord. Sulu's hair was dark and wild, and so were his eyes.

"Lady Katherine," said Stefan, "this is Sulu the Loon. M'lord, this is Lady Katherine of Tretower, who is my wife both mundanely and in the Society."

"Not giving her any slack at all, are you?" said Sulu approvingly. "I guess you know what happens if you give someone enough rope. Who are you here to see, m'lady?"

"Roc—Lord Roc," said Katherine. "Or is he still on duty at the gate?" She would not have minded postponing this visit.

"And Lord Sabas, and the Khan, if he's at home," added Stefan, naming members of the Horde he knew she'd like.

"Fine. Go on in. Roc's making the fire laugh." He began again to play his pipes.

As they passed through the gate, Katherine asked, "Is he one of the crazy ones who doesn't wear enough armor?"

"No, he doesn't fight at all. His craziness is totally benign. He's got a sideways mind, and speaks in riddles. He's got what I think is called an echo memory; he can repeat verbatim anything he's heard, even if it's in a language he doesn't understand."

"What does he do mundanely?"

"God knows. I don't even know where he's from. The only place I've ever seen him is here at the War. Look, there's Lord Roc and his dog."

Lord Roc, seen earlier guarding the entrance to the campground, had added a grimy yellow tunic to his balloon pants. The red-and-black braided cord of the household was around one sleeve. He was tending a big fire that crackled within a circle of stones in the center of the Mongol encampment. Near him was his dog, a handsome golden-retriever type, which wagged its tail tentatively at the visitors as they approached.

"Hey, Steffy," said Lord Roc, holding out a hand that was filthy from his work.

"Lord Roc," said Stefan, taking the hand. "I'd like you to meet Lady Katherine of Tretower."

Roc frowned. "I've met your lady."

"But I don't think she's met you. Katherine, this is Lord Rocco the Italian."

Roc flapped his arms against his sides in an embarrassed way. "Yeah, well, one of these days I've got to change that name, since I don't look too Italian anymore."

"We are well met, my lord," said Katherine politely, then, seeing Stefan expected more of her, she went on, "What's your dog's name?"

Roc smiled. "Buu. C'mere, Buu, and say hello." The dog came to sit by its master's knee and look intelligently at Katherine.

She liked big, friendly dogs, and she held out the back of her hand for this one to sniff. "Why do you call him Buu?"

"Old-time hoboes call friends Boo. And in Mongolian, Buu—B-U-U—is the imperative 'no.' He's a good watchdog."

"Hello, Buu," she said, bending toward the animal, which held out its paw. She took it. "Thou faithful dog of an infidel," she added.

Roc laughed at this unexpected display of wit from a lady known for her cool demeanor. "That's good. I'm sorry I didn't introduce him to you sooner."

"Me, too." She looked up at Roc. "Perhaps I've been missing some good company by sitting at table instead of in doorways during feasts."

"Plenty of room, m'lady," said Roc, spitting on the ground to hide his pleasure. "And despite rumors to the contrary, Buu is not related to a donkey. Steffy, Sabas said if you came by, he wants to see you, but you'll have to wait a couple more minutes. He's talking to our favorite bad boy."

Stefan frowned. "I thought Thorstane was being sent home."

"Wulffy tried, but Thorstane talked him out of it. He promised he'd behave. He'll be all right, if people just don't pick on him. While you're waiting, I think the Khan wants to say hi; he's right over there.''

''All right. Come, *fy'n galon.*''

''Good-bye, Lord Roc.'' She dropped another curtsy.

''M'lady,'' replied the young man. He bowed deeply and she felt herself blush.

''Who is Sabas?'' she asked as they walked away.

''He's a shaman, what they call a 'truth-teller.' He's an interesting type and a good friend to have. He's been adviser to a lot of khans, including Wulfstan.''

Katherine had never met a khan, and was wondering if she should address him as respectfully as she would a king. This new khan, Wulfstan, was spoken of as a man of honor, even by Anne—who had added that it was too bad he was a Hordesman.

Wulfstan was standing outside his striped tent. He had been knighted some time back, but because he refused to swear fealty he was called a master at arms, rather than a knight. His white belt was worn as a baldric across his chest, his household cord buckling the ends together with an elaborate knot. He was wrapping the padded end of a six-foot rattan pole with silver duct tape, but put his work aside to hold out a hand to Stefan as they approached.

''Stefan, my friend.''

''Wulfstan, well met. May I present my lady wife, Katherine of Tretower. My lady, this is Wulfstan the Fearless of Iceland, Khan of the Great Dark Horde.''

''Well met,'' said Wulfstan, with a slight bow. He was shorter than Stefan, but stood with that same self-assured air. His brown eyes were keen, and had laugh wrinkles around them. With the long-ended mustache, he looked like a charming Mongolian bandit.

''I am honored to meet you,'' she said, dropping her curtsy.

Wulfstan said to Stefan, ''I hear you got authorized as a fighter.''

''Yes. Have you decided whose side you're on this year?''

''Not yet. I have a meeting with King Oswin this evening. His Highness Prince Thomas gave six of us a wonderful dinner last night. If you're fighting in the Woods Battle, perhaps we'll meet there.''

''If you're with the East, look for me hiding behind Sir Geoffrey.'' Stefan could not prevent a quick revealing glance at his red belt.

Wulfstan followed the glance and raised a surprised eyebrow. ''That's his?''

''Yes.'' Stefan picked up the long end to show Wulfstan the miniature of Geoff's arms near its tip. ''See? Or, a pale gules, a *Fratercula arctica*—puffin—statant, proper.'' Squires' belts were marked by the arms of the knights presenting them. The miniature shield at the end of Stefan's belt was gold with a red vertical stripe, in the middle of which stood a fat black-and-white bird with a broad, brightly striped bill.

''Why'd he pick a funny-looking bird like that? Geoff always struck me as a proud one.''

''He had asthma when he was a kid.''

Wulfstan blinked, then laughed. ''Very nice! Puffin'! What's yours, so I'll know you?''

''Sable, a lit candle.''

''Nice and simple.''

''I'm Stefan von Helle. Von Helle means 'the illuminated.' I was the only one with a flashlight when we had a power failure at an event a few years back. Before that, I was Stefan Shutzmann and my arms—'' Stefan thought briefly and recited, ''Argent, a wild man's head, couped, affronté, proper, overall five pallets sable.''

Wulfstan, heraldically illiterate but unfailing in courtesy, said, ''Interesting. Too bad it was turned down.'' Coats of arms in the SCA had to go through a hierarchy of approval, which resulted in their being registered as ''personal devices'' for the sole use of the individuals submitting them. The toughest level currently was near the top, at kingdom level. Sir Ignatius had a disapproving eye for florid design, incorrect colors, raunchy puns, and designs too close to others already registered.

''Oh, it passed; every device I submit as my shire's herald is approved. It was just too evocative of my job.'' His wry smile appeared and he relented. ''It looks like a jailed felon. So I'll know when to duck, what does your shield look like?''

Wulfstan turned and picked up a round wooden shield. It had

been edged with a bicycle tire which in turn had been covered by a strip of leather laced in place. Though its red paint was new, the metal boss in the center was dented in several places. A circle of daisies was painted around the boss. "How do you say red in heraldic?" he asked.

"Gules."

"Gules, a daisy wheel proper," recited Wulfstan, adding, "I sell typewriters and computers mundanely." Stefan chuckled appreciatively, but Wulfstan complained, "It took me three tries to get a device approved. You'd be welcome if you ever decide to move to my barony."

"Where's that?"

"Brewton—Milwaukee. Our current herald has a nice loud voice for oy-yeas, but doesn't know pale from chevron and thinks sable is a fur." Wulfstan's eye was caught by something, and he looked over Stefan's shoulder. "Sabas will be free to see you now; here comes Thorstane. Have you met him?"

"Never had the pleasure." There was a distinct note of irony in his tone and Katherine turned to see what this troublesome person looked like.

She saw a tall, beefy man, wearing a fake-fur diaper and desert boots, though the hairiness of his body made him appear less naked than he was. He saw them looking and changed direction to come their way. He looked grumpy and tousled and the skin around his eyes was puffy. One eyebrow was permanently uplifted and set in scar tissue, as if it had been torn off and replaced carelessly.

He said to the Khan, "I ain't drunk," a patent lie. Then he focused on Katherine. "Hey, who's the pretty lady?"

"I am Katherine of Tretower," she said, retreating into her frostiest air.

"Very nice. You available?"

"No, this is my husband, Lord Stefan von Helle."

Thorstane's attention shifted to Stefan. "Yeah? What does he do for a living? Clean toilets?"

"He's a policeman."

"She means you'd better behave, Thorstane," warned Wulfstan with a smile.

Thorstane, looking Stefan up and down, said, "Scrawny cops they're hiring nowadays."

"If he's like most cops, he's bigger than he looks," said Wulfstan.

Thorstane made a noise of contempt.

Stefan said to Wulfstan, "I'd appreciate it if neither of you spread the news of my mundane occupation."

"Why not?"

"You'd be surprised at the number of people who want to argue civil rights, search and seizure, police corruption, or capital punishment with a cop."

"I know more about that than you think," Wulfstan said with a smile. "My wife is an auditor for the IRS."

"I'm gonna tell, I'm gonna tell," murmured Thorstane in a drunken singsong.

"No, you aren't," said Wulfstan, and Thorstane made his noise again, but stopped the singsong.

"My lords," said Stefan, "if you will excuse us, I don't want to keep Lord Sabas waiting." He bowed, his lady curtsied, and he took her hand to lead her away.

There was an open space in the middle of the Horde encampment, about forty yards across. They were nearly on the other side when Thorstane suddenly appeared again, to block their way. "I hadn't finished talking to the pretty lady," he said, reaching out to touch her cheek with a large, dirty forefinger before she could flinch away. "What you doin' here at the War without any man to protect you?" He looked at Stefan to see how he took the insult. Stefan said nothing, but smiled up at him with both sides of his mouth. The barbarian didn't see it for the dangerous sign Katherine knew it was. He reached for her again. "Got some wine in my tent," he offered.

Katherine took a step backward. She kept her personal boundaries well marked and liked them honored. "My lord, I don't believe I know you well enough to accept such an invitation," she said. "And I believe we are expected elsewhere."

"You know me; I'm Thorstane Shieldbreaker!" The barbarian jabbed himself in the breastbone with a thumb. "Everyone knows me! Let the skinny guy go keep Sabas company while you and me talk.''

''Let us pass,'' said Stefan quietly, stepping to his right.

But Thorstane was drunk and unwilling to give up his game easily. He moved to block their way again. ''Letcha go by for a kiss,'' he said.

''No,'' she said.

''Well, then—'' he said and, very abruptly, he bent and lifted her by her middle, to hold her straight-armed over his head. She gaped in surprise and he roared with laughter.

''Thorstane Shieldbreaker, put me down!'' she ordered.

''Price now is a kiss and a feel!'' he said.

''Put her down, you jerk!'' ordered Stefan. But the barbarian only chuckled and gave Katherine a little shake. From her new high-up position she could see almost the whole Horde camp. People here and there stopped what they were doing to come watch. Lord Roc abandoned his fire and came toward them with Buu. Wulfstan followed, carrying the long polearm he'd been working on.

''Thorstane, you are holding up my guests,'' said a self-important voice, and the barbarian looked down over his shoulder at a short man with a paunch and crew cut, wearing a silver-trimmed vest and black balloon pants.

Thorstane said, ''Only one of 'em, Sabas! She a friend of yours?''

''He is. Put his lady down.''

''Sure, when she meets my conditions. You ready to do that, sweetcakes?''

''No.''

''I also order you: Put her down!'' said Wulfstan, coming up behind Stefan. There was a murmur of agreement from the small crowd of spectators.

''Aw, I ain't hurtin' her,'' said Thorstane. He was beginning to look less sure of himself, but wasn't about to let himself appear to be a loser. ''We got to teach the chauguas not to be so unfriendly.'' ''Chaugua'' was an insulting Horde term for an outsider, and Wulfstan's mouth pulled thin. He nodded very briefly at Sabas.

Sabas asked, ''Is he hurting you, my sister?''

"Not very much," she said. In truth, he was pinching her ribs painfully, and the discomfort showed in her voice.

"Let her go!" called one of the bystanders, and the others agreed. But Thorstane only looked up at her and grinned.

Wulfstan touched Stefan on the arm and, when he turned, offered him the polearm. Stefan smiled that dangerous smile and took it.

"I will ask you only once more to release the lady," said Sabas, more to distract the barbarian's attention than in expectation of compliance.

"What're you gonna do if I don't? Put a hex on me?"

Stefan shifted his grip on the polearm to near one end, took two steps back and assumed a baseball stance.

"You are headed for a hard fall," said Sabas, and Stefan came around in a mighty swing that caught Thorstane at his heels with the padded end. The barbarian was swept off his feet and landed with a large *whump* that knocked the wind out of him. Katherine landed hard on his belly and scrambled off. By the time she had turned around, Stefan was in front of her, taking her by the arms. The bystanders cheered and laughed.

"Are you hurt?" he asked.

"No, he makes a good cushion to land on. Is this what you meant when you said I should live dangerously?"

"I didn't mean for this to happen," he apologized.

"I know," she said; "it's all right."

"I warned you, Thorstane," said Sabas.

She looked at the big barbarian, who had rolled onto his stomach. He was making hicking sounds. "Should we do something to help him?"

Stefan studied the barbarian with a professional eye. "No, he'll be all right. But he won't be in any shape to bother anyone for a while." There was savage satisfaction in his tone.

"You were scared!" she said, surprised.

"Weren't you?"

"No—well, a little nervous that he might drop me. He's a tall one; it was like being on top of a tree."

"Brave lady," said Sabas approvingly.

"And she was just learning to like us," said Roc disgustedly to Wulfstan.

Katherine leaned sideways around Stefan's shoulder to say, "But I still like you, m'lord!"

He said, "Thank you, m'lady. I was gonna sic Buu on him. Maybe I still should?"

"No, he's got enough problems, I think," she said. Thorstane was now on his hands and knees, but still very self-absorbed.

Wulfstan said, "That was nice work with the polearm, Lord Stefan. I would have gone for the kidneys."

"I wanted him to land on his back, not on top of my lady," said Stefan.

"Watch for him in the Woods Battle tomorrow. He may try something—he's a tricky son of a bitch. Your pardon, m'lady."

"That's quite all right," said Katherine.

"Thanks for the warning," said Stefan.

"I have tea brewing in my tent," said Sabas. "If you will come this way."

. . .

Sabas had a conventional tent, but a large one with a big porch. The porch was sided with mosquito netting, and he sat them there on beautiful mismatched pillows and served them small porcelain cups of fragrant tea.

Sabas was a square-faced man with a heavy beard shadow and an enigmatic smile. He spoke slowly, giving even his ordinary statements significance. "Your bruised ribs will recover," he said to Katherine. "And, I trust, your bruised feelings."

"I'm not angry," she said.

"You are behaving like a Christian," he said, speaking as one not of that faith, but approvingly.

"Well . . ." she said, and paused to choose her words. The incident had shaken her more than she was willing to admit, and she gave herself away by a lapse into disclosure. "For a long time I've been unjust toward the single Horde member of my shire. That was wrong, and I never gave him a chance to prove it. Perhaps what happened just now is a way of balancing the scales."

Sabas studied her, then asked Stefan, "Is this why you fell in love with her?"

"No, I went for the icing; the cake I found out about later."

"Yes." He cocked his head at her. "But there is something—" he stopped. "Your dragon becomes you," he said, which is not what he had started to say.

"Thank you," she said, touching the woven ribbon on her shoulder. "This is an interesting tea. What's it made of?"

"Chamomile, jasmine, and red clover. Would you like some honey to put in it?"

"No, thank you; it's lovely just as it is." Her control was back in place and she concentrated on sipping the beverage.

"Remember when you read the runes for me four years back?" asked Stefan. "You said that I would save a life, and take a life and watch a life be taken."

"I remember the reading," the square little man said, nodding.

"Pooh, anyone who knows your occupation might have felt safe making that prediction," said Katherine.

Sabas looked at her and she expected him to say he hadn't known Stefan's mundane occupation, but he said, "Have you been a member of the Society long, my lady?"

"No, not very."

"Do you find everything always as you expect it?"

"No, of course not." She wondered what he meant by that.

Sabas said to Stefan, "She intrigues me. Would you permit me to read the runes for her?"

Stefan said, "We'd be honored."

• • •

On the way out the gate Katherine asked, "What's a rune reading?"

"It's a truth-telling session. He uses blocks printed with the runic alphabet to make a statement about some secret inner conflict or problem you may have. It seems to work best when he knows nothing about the person he's reading. He's very good, and has surprised a number of people with his insight."

"I don't like the idea," she said.

"Why not?"

She looked uncomfortable. "Maybe—maybe because God said, 'Thou shalt not permit a witch to live'? Oh, don't look at me like that; I'm not suggesting he should be hauled off in a tumbrel and burned! But if he's real, he may say something true and private about me which is none of anyone's business—and if he isn't, he may say something untrue that's at least equally embarrassing. Can't we just say no?"

"Sure. I'll tell him you've changed your mind. He'll understand."

"Thanks." She took his hand and they went up the road together.

5

T*HIS* time Wulfstan brought Lady Freyis and two k'shaktu —bodyguards—with him. Thorstane was lying on top of his sleeping bag in his cluttered tent. Wulfstan lowered himself with a grimace onto the dirty Indian blanket. Freyis, a middle-aged woman whose dark brown hair had not a trace of gray in it, knelt beside him, her green eyes cold and angry.

The k'shaktu, sturdy men in loose black pants and knee-length black tunics, knelt just inside the entrance flap, leaning on short staffs and feigning indifference to the Khan's words.

"You swore as a brother you would cause no more trouble," said Wulfstan.

"Can we do this later?" asked Thorstane. "If I'd known you wanted to bawl me out, I'd never of told you to come in. I'm sick to my stomach and my head hurts."

"That's not surprising, and less than you deserve. But you will listen to everything I have to say."

"Hell. Well, get on with it."

"Lord Stefan is a friend of the household. His lady is young and very inexperienced. She does not like strangers grabbing her, much less picking her up or insisting on a kiss."

"Well, how was I to know that? She comes wandering in smiling at everyone—how was I to know?"

Lady Freyis said, "Frankly, I can't think of a single woman who enjoys being pawed against her will."

"Aw, what do you know about it?" growled Thorstane.

Lady Freyis chuckled low in her throat. "What, indeed?" she asked, and Wulfstan could not help smiling, for her affairs were numerous.

Thorstane said, "No, I mean, you weren't there. She wasn't screaming or anything. For all I knew, she was having the time of her life. Then that chaugua slams me one in the heels and she lands on top of me! Talk about chivalrous—!"

Wulfstan said, "The lady, the lord, and Sabas—all three asked you to put her down. I consider that more than adequate warning."

"Good for you. I didn't."

"Very well, Thorstane. These two k'shaktu are going to stay with you the rest of the War, day and night, everywhere you go. They will physically restrain you, if necessary, to keep you from bringing further shame on the household. There is to be a Kurultai meeting on Sunday before we all go home, and I am bringing this matter before the assembly. Whether or not you are allowed to remain in the Horde will be determined by a vote. I recommend you be on your best behavior until then. Do you understand?"

"You can't set a guard over me! That's illegal!"

"I am permitted to take any necessary steps to prevent a brother from causing physical harm or bringing dishonor on the household."

Thorstane grinned. "It's gonna be damn crowded in the Porta-John."

"You'll manage."

"And what about if I meet a lady who's willing?"

"You'd better find three willing ladies, or one exceptionally sharing. And further, for you, the War has just turned into a dry site."

"Aw, now, that's really pushing it!"

"Complain about it at the Kurultai, if you like. But you'll be sober when you do. I will leave you now with your k'shaktu." Wulfstan and Lady Freyis left the tent.

Thorstane dropped a heavy forearm over his eyes. After a minute he lifted an elbow and peered under it at the two men watching him. "I don't suppose you'd be willing to let me supply the drinks for all three of us?"

"No," said one of them, "and you better bring your armor out to the road. Inspection's going on now."

Thorstane rolled over. "What the hell," he grumbled. "Give me a hand here, will you?"

"Sure," said the other k'shaktu. "And then you can give us a hand with ours."

. . .

Sir Ignatius came up King's Road to see how armor inspection was coming along. Although William was often late himself, he liked everyone else to be prompt and orderly. He didn't realize, reflected Ignatius, that whatever drew people to the Society for Creative Anachronism, it wasn't a passion for order or timeliness. The inspection had been going on for half an hour, and there were still people just bringing their gear to the roadside.

Knights marshals were here and there, turning over shields, testing the padding inside helms with a thumb, bending the joints of gauntlets. At home, knights marshals were responsible for all matters concerning fighting in their local groups, which is how those present at the War had volunteered—or were offered by their barons—to make sure the armor to be used in the coming battles met the standards set by the Society.

"I can't pass this helm." A good-looking man with auburn curls, his short gray joupon exposing a white rump, bent over a Hordesman's battered helm. "Look, this ding has lifted an edge of the eyeslot, opened it up a little. Give me your sword."

Recognizing Sir Geoffrey of Brixham, the royal herald stopped to watch. Sir Geoffrey had a reputation for courtesy, and Ignatius wanted to see how firm he was on matters of safety. The Hordesman silently handed Geoffrey a big rattan "broadsword," whose duct-tape wrapping was badly notched and scored. Geoffrey easily fit the tip of it through the damaged eyeslot. "That happens in combat and you could lose an eye," he said.

"But I didn't bring another helm with me," objected the Hordesman, a hirsute man in what appeared to be a bearskin diaper. Ignatius didn't need to look at the brown shield with its painted black crack to know this was that troublemaker, Thorstane Shieldbreaker. He went over for a closer look. Geoffrey stepped aside, a gesture of professional courtesy—Ignatius was himself a fighter, and a former knight marshal—but he added a bow in recognition of Ignatius' position as a Great Lord of State.

"This helm is an old one," noted Ignatius. It was a heavy, solidly constructed helm, but dented and rusty.

"This is its fourth War," said Thorstane. "It's my lucky helm. It's never failed inspection before."

"If it's had that ding awhile, that surprises me. I don't think it should pass."

"Aw, come on, Iggy!" groused another Horde brother, one of a pair squatting nearby. "You saw how he had to twist that sword to get it through the slot! Nobody hits you at an angle like that!"

"The inspector says it doesn't pass, so it doesn't pass!" said Ignatius, disliking the man's casual use of his name. "If you people would look your armor over before putting it out for inspection, you could save us a lot of time." He gave the helm back to Thorstane and stepped back onto the road.

He heard the marshal say quietly, "Hammer it out at the forge. And rivet a band of metal around the slot to reinforce it; they've got steel for sale. I'll be here another hour at least. If you bring it to me before I finish, I'll look at it again."

"Thanks, Geoff," said the barbarian, and he set off down the road at a trot. To Ignatius' surprise, the other two got up and trotted after him.

Ignatius envied Sir Geoffrey for his casual, kind offer to the Hordesman; the stories he'd heard were not exaggerations. Of course, Thorstane didn't deserve such treatment. Thorstane deserved to be thrown out of the SCA so hard he bounced. Ignatius set his mouth in a firmer line and continued up the road.

• • •

Katherine helped Stefan arrange his armor on the narrow grass verge beside King's Road. "Have we got everything?" she asked anxiously, looking over the display. Arm and leg harness, breast and back plates, helm, the quilted undercoat called a gambeson she'd sewn new for the War, shoulder and neck protection, kidney belt, athletic protector, elbow and knee pads, three swords and a shield, and, lastly, the beautiful stainless-steel gauntlets Geoff had made for him. Geoff knew Stefan valued utility over authenticity: Stainless steel has more strength per ounce of weight than ordinary steel, and Stefan, because of his job, could not afford an injury.

"That looks like all of it," he said, turning one of the legs over to show its inside.

Stefan's armor was roughly late-fourteenth-century in style, when the shift from mail was nearly complete. It was made of jointed steel plates, with a glitter of stainless on the knee and elbow cops, and a brief skirt of mail at the waist. Rather than a visor, his helm had thick steel bars riveted across its face. This provided better vision than mere eye slots, and he could also suck in gulps of air more readily.

Katherine asked, "Do you want to put out your old mitten gauntlets, too? We brought them."

"I'd feel better if I had them for a spare."

"I'll be right back," she said, and turned to run up the path.

She found the gauntlets in a corner of their tent and was on her way back down when she literally ran into someone.

"Oof!" she said, rebounding. "I—I beg your pardon, m'lord," she stammered, looking up into the friendly face high above hers, his golden hair standing out around his head. He looked like a Renaissance archangel.

"Quite all right, my lady," said the man, brushing his sky blue tunic where she'd poked him with the gauntlets. "A pleasure, in fact," he added, his eyes sweeping down her.

She blushed. "I must get these out to the road, to be inspected," she said, holding out the gauntlets and taking a sideways step to get around him.

"No need to hurry," said the man, still smiling. "The inspector's way up the road, yet. I saw him."

"Good," she said, relieved. Then, "Should I know you? I'm new, and I don't think I'd even know the King if I saw him."

He laughed. "I'm not the King. In fact, I'm not much of anyone."

"A knight is definitely someone," she said, glancing at his white belt. "I am Katherine of Tretower, from the Shire of Appleby, a day's journey from Talltower." She curtsied.

The knight took her right hand and raised it to his lips. "I'm Sir John de Capestrano," he said. "Deeply honored to meet you. If you like, I can introduce you to the King." He lowered her hand, but did not let go of it. "Unless you're tied up with someone? You must be; I'd never get lucky enough to meet someone who looks like you who hasn't got a lord." But his blue eyes gleamed hopefully.

"Lord Stefan von Helle carries my favor," she said.

"Never heard of him," he said. "And not even a knight? You deserve at least a knight!"

"He is the herald of Appleby and a squire to Sir Geoffrey," she said crisply, pulling her hand free.

He laughed. "And therefore a paragon, right?" Then he saw the ice in her gray eyes and he dropped to one knee. "I am but dust in his wind; I have no talent but fighting."

"Rise, Sir John," she said, melting into a smile. "Would you like to meet him? I'm taking him these gauntlets."

"I would, but another time, perhaps; I've still got my own armor to put out for inspection."

"Then I look forward to seeing you again," she said, and hurried down the path with the gauntlets.

Despite his assertion of business elsewhere, he stayed to look after her until she was out of sight, his expression that of a man who thinks he smells dinner.

• • •

"What took you?" said Stefan, seeing her approach. "The inspector's almost finished with me."

"He is? But Sir John said he was a long way up the road!" She handed her husband the old gauntlets and he put them beside the new ones.

Katherine came to sit beside him, her gray eyes troubled, and he took her hand. ''It's all right,'' he said.

''Yes, but that man lied to me.''

''It mightn't have been on purpose,'' said the man bent over Stefan's armor. ''I'm a fast worker.'' He glanced up at them, and his look was so pleasant they were charmed into smiles.

He was well into his thirties, muscular in a rumpled and comfortable way. The Celtic embroidery on his rust-brown tunic had faded until it nearly matched the fabric which it decorated. His white belt was broad and scarred, but clean, and his gold chain and the spurs on his motorcycle boots were brightly polished.

''My lady,'' said Stefan, ''this is Sir Humphrey—''

''—the Vigilant,'' she finished. ''I remember him.''

''And I remember a feast made yet more pleasant by your presence at our table,'' said Humphrey. He picked up one of Stefan's rattan swords and bent it gently to see if it was broken inside the duct tape. The merit of rattan is that under stress it dissolves into fibers rather than shattering into dangerous fragments, but that means a well-wrapped sword may break without the fact being immediately apparent. He nodded and put the sword down again. ''Your name is Katherine, and you, m'lady, are a Celt.''

She looked down at her violet dress. ''I didn't know this was a particularly Celt color.''

He laughed. ''It isn't. I mean mundanely. Black hair, gray eyes and fair skin—pure Celt. But not Irish, not with that nose. Scots, perhaps?''

''Half,'' she said, reaching for the stray wisp of hair that had escaped her wimple, tucking it safely away again. ''My maiden name was McLeod-Price.''

''Price—the other half English, then?''

''No.'' And when he waited expectantly, she said, ''Welsh.''

''There's your medieval connection; the Tudors were Welsh, weren't they?''

''Not that it matters; my rose is white.'' In the final battle of the War of the Roses, Plantagenet fought Tudor; Katherine supported the Plantagenets.

Humphrey picked up a breastplate to check the buckles. "Henry the Seventh's son was half York, wasn't he?"

"Yes, but half of that was Woodville."

Humphrey put the breastplate down. "We'll have to talk when I have time to listen. I like people who know their history."

"Me, too," she said, and squeezed Stefan's hand.

"These are nice gauntlets," said Humphrey, snicking open and closed the jointed fingers of one of them. "Sir Geoffrey takes good care of his squires." He picked up the arm harness. "But Geoff never made this."

"No," said Stefan humbly.

Humphrey grinned. "There's nothing wrong with them, m'lord. Just a little green in the execution. Geoff showed you that trick of curving back the edge of the vambraces just a little, to save wear on the gambeson, I bet."

"Yes, m'lord."

"Your gambeson is nice and thick and you've got especially good padding inside your helm. Do you have any problem acknowledging blows?"

"I've never been called on it."

"How long have you been fighting?"

"Just over a year."

Humphrey nodded. "Fine. No problem here I can see." He pulled a round green sticker from the paper around his wrist and put it on the breastplate to show the armor had passed inspection. "You're fighting with Geoff for the Middle, I assume?"

"Yes, m'lord."

"I'm going to ask Geoff to join my small ambush-laying party in the woods tomorrow. I'd be pleased if you'd come along with him."

Stefan blinked in surprise and, torn between the honor and the responsibility, was unable to decide how to respond.

Humphrey tore two six-inch lengths of red tape from the roll on his belt and put one down the front and the other down the back of Stefan's helm. "To keep you from being attacked by your own people in the fighting," he explained. He stood. "You *are* taking part in the Woods Battle tomorrow?"

"Yes, m'lord."

"Good. Leave any spare equipment at Resurrection Point, so you can get at it. If you have to come to your tent for it, they won't let you back into the woods. See you there."

• • •

It was dark, and people were gathering around campfires. Wine bottles were being passed, old songs sung, stories exchanged, plans laid for the morrow. Geoff, Anne, Taffy, Stefan, and Katherine were nibbling cheese curds and sipping mulled wine around a fire that had been reduced to glowing coals. Eight kerosene torches on poles encircled them. Distantly, the anvils were still ringing, and not so distantly, voices were raised in song: "We are the worm in the wood. We are the rot at the root. We are the taint in the blood. We are the thorn in the foot."

"Ugh!" said Anne. "More wine, quick!" She held out her wooden goblet and Geoff filled it.

"What is that they're singing?" asked Katherine. "I keep thinking I ought to know it."

"It's from Kipling," said Anne.

"Then it's not period," Katherine said.

"Medieval is where you find it," said Taffy. "That Kipling poem is called 'A Pict Song,' and is against the Roman invasion of Britain."

Stefan chuckled. "No, that's out of our period, too—but in the other direction."

"I wish someone would declare the Horde out of period," said Anne. "They're making my life impossible!"

"What are they doing, beyond the usual stuff?" asked Geoff.

"Everywhere I go, one turns up to leer at me."

"Maybe it's a plot," suggested Taffy.

"It's enough to make anyone paranoid, the way I cannot find a place in this whole camp where there is not a half-naked barbarian hanging around, picking his teeth with a knife and making sucking noises at me!" agreed Anne.

"You know, I think she's right," said Stefan. "Look, here comes one now." He pointed out to the lane, where a dark figure loomed. It was well wrapped in a long cloak and wore a floppy hat.

The figure spoke. "Gentles, may I approach?"

Geoff stood. ''Approach and be welcome, Your Majesty,'' he called.

The others stood then, too, and bobbed as the figure opened its cloak and came near the fire. ''Forgot to disguise my voice,'' King William said. He was a little drunk, and his gait was uncertain. ''Is this the Appleby camp?''

''Yes, Your Majesty,'' said Anne. ''Have a seat. We're drinking hot spiced wine.''

William dropped heavily onto a camp stool, which creaked but held. ''Thanks.'' He fumbled at his belt and produced a leather mug. ''Just half a cup. Got to be up early tomorrow.''

''Yes, sir,'' said Anne, picking up the metal pitcher with a hot mitt and pouring. She nodded toward a second figure still out in the shadows. ''Shall we ask your friend if he's thirsty?''

''Naw, it's only Petty. I tol' him to go home, but he thinks I may 'faw down go boom' and he wants to be there to help me up.'' William made a go-away gesture toward the figure, which did not move. ''So let him freeze his be-hind off if it makes him happy.''

''Cheese curds go very well with that wine,'' offered Geoff.

''Thanks,'' said William, holding out a big hand for Geoff to fill.

Katherine, reminded by the lonesome shadow of Lord Roc, took a wooden goblet off the table, filled it with wine and drifted quietly off into the darkness to give it to the man, who was also huddled into a long cape.

''I thank you, Lady,'' he murmured, taking the cup and sniffing at it. ''God, it's a hot drink; thank you!'' He took a big swallow. He, too, sounded as if he'd had too much to drink.

''Why do you follow the King if he doesn't want you to?'' she asked.

''Because when he's drunk he becomes very friendly. He could end up sleeping anywhere, in the Horde camp or even in the tent of some likely Eastern lady. He's a War Point and as of midnight the East will be looking to capture him.''

''Then I'm glad he's got such a good friend.''

Master Petrog drained the cup. ''I'm not feeling friendly. His Majesty did me a big favor earlier this evening, so I owe him one in return. It's not only the knights who know how to be chivalrous.'' A golden medallion with a laurel wreath silhouetted on it was caught by a momentary flicker of light as he handed the empty goblet back to her. Petrog was also a peer, but of the Order of the Laurel, for accomplishment in some medieval art or science. ''If your name is Katherine, you'd better get back there; he wants to talk to you.''

''Me? Yes, m'lord.'' Katherine took the goblet and hurried back to the fire.

''. . . and I'm trying to find out just what happened,'' the King was saying.

''Well, here she is now,'' Stefan said. ''Katherine, His Majesty wants to talk to you.''

''Yes, Your Majesty?'' she said, coming to curtsy before him.

''I hear Thorstane waylaid you today,'' said William.

''Yes, Your Majesty.''

''Would you like to tell me about it?''

She looked at Stefan, who nodded, so she explained briefly, ''When I wouldn't give him a kiss, he held me over his head until my lord knocked his feet out from under him with a polearm.''

''Would you like to make a formal complaint about him?''

She shook her head. ''No, I think he got his comeuppance on the spot.''

Taffy asked, ''You're thinking of a Court of Chivalry, aren't you, sir?'' He sounded approving.

''The Middle's never had a Court of Chivalry,'' said William, waving dismissively. ''But I am thinking of ordering him thrown off the campground.''

''Would King Oswin back you?'' asked Geoff.

''Thorstane's from Strange Sea, which is in my kingdom,'' said William, conveniently forgetting the Dark Horde considered themselves citizens of the Known World, not any particular kingdom.

''The Khan's set some k'shaktu on him,'' said Stefan. ''They'll make sure he behaves the rest of the War.''

William looked at Stefan. ''You're not Horde,'' he said.

''No, Your Majesty; but I have friends among them.''

''You're the man who swung the polearm.''

"Yes, sir."

"And they're still your friends?"

"Wulfstan handed me the polearm. And no one complained about what I did with it."

William nodded. "They've finally run out of patience with him. Good; if they put him out of the household he'll quit the Society. They're holding a Kurultai Sunday, aren't they?"

"So I hear."

"Maybe they'll do it then." William drank his wine. "What do you do mundanely, Lord Stefan?"

Stefan hesitated and Geoff said, "He's a detective sergeant on our police force."

"No kidding," said William.

"But that's not for general consumption," said Stefan, wondering why he bothered, and if it mattered.

"Sure," said William. "Does your chief know where you are this weekend?"

"No, but my captain does, sort of. I mean, he knows I'm a member of the Society for Creative Anachronism, but he thinks it's mostly research. He saw Geoff in armor one time. Thought he was a lunatic."

"Typical mundane response," said His Majesty. "I was a volunteer fireman until my chief saw my picture in a newspaper. I was in Tudor garb, complete with codpiece. He said he was pretty sure I wasn't a fag, but none of the other guys wanted to work with me anymore. How about your lady? She's a cool head; is she a cop, too?"

"No, sir. She breeds and trains horses."

"Yeah?" William smiled at her. "I've always wanted to turn up at an event on horseback. Suppose I wanted to buy your best-looking stallion. What would it cost me?"

"My stallion is not for sale. But we've got a beautiful bay mare who'll be three in February. No bad habits, should top out at fifteen hands, a steal at seventy-five thousand dollars."

"Jesus Christ!"

She cocked her head at him. "No? Well, if you want to do some work yourself, we've got a chestnut colt, a yearling, shows promise. I'll let him go for eighteen nine."

"What the hell do you raise, racehorses?"

"Arabs. It's just a small ranch, but we specialize in quality stock. You'd probably like a bigger horse than the Arab; perhaps you should arrange for a quarter horse or thoroughbred mare to be brought to my stallion. Copper Wind's stud fee next season will be seven thousand, with the usual guarantees."

William laughed uncertainly. "How does a cop afford to give his wife that kind of hobby?"

Stefan said, "He doesn't. The ranch is hers, was hers before I met her."

William looked at her, then at Stefan, obviously doing some rethinking about them. "If he ever does something dumb and she divorces him, will someone please let me know?" He held out his jack for a refill. "Geoff, you're in the Woods Battle tomorrow, aren't you?"

"Yes, sir."

"Want to be one of my personal guards?"

"I'm honored, Your Majesty, but I'm afraid I've already asked Stefan to fight with me, and he's never fought in a War before. I was hoping the two of us could link up with Taffy and Sir Humphrey."

"That's right, Humph mentioned you to me. Anyone here know Odo's squire, Dismas the Ruffian?"

Geoff said, "He killed me at Queen's Ransom this summer. A good fighter, and a chivalrous man."

"I'm glad you think so. I told him to hold his vigil tonight."

Taffy said, "About time. I know him, too."

William looked at him. "Yeah? Maybe. After our last king, I decided to be very conservative about making knights." William stood, draining his goblet. "Well, I've got other places to go. Thanks for the wine. Oh, by the way, the Horde fights with the Middle this year."

"All *right*!" cheered Taffy.

"The Woods Battle is ours, then," said Geoff.

''Don't count your chickens,'' said William. ''The East is fielding some terrific fighters this year. See you tomorrow.'' He walked back down the lane, hauled a figure out of the shadows, threw an arm across its shoulder, and the two vanished into the night.

• • •

A loud noise jolted Katherine awake. It was thunder. She lay back and listened to it rumble away. The tent was being pelted with rain and the nearby trees were hissing in a strong wind. Lightning flashed, and for an instant she could see the rumple of sleeping bag that covered her, and the green tent wall beyond. It had seemed swollen, as if she were inside a balloon, and the next flash confirmed the impression. But the flash after that showed it collapsing. The tent was doing deep-breathing exercises—just as she was. This was not mere rain; this was a proper thunderstorm, and all that lay between her and it was a paper-thin layer of nylon.

She rolled onto her side and pulled the sleeping bag up over her ear. No good, the lightning was so bright it went right through her closed eyelids, and the thunder had an edge to it no bundle of goose feathers could keep out. She opened her eyes and by the light of the next flash saw her husband sleeping peacefully, and felt a stab of anger. He was such a sound sleeper, it would take a tree falling on him to wake him, which would serve him right. She rolled onto her other side so she wouldn't have to look at him.

''Fy'n galon?''

She rolled back again, penitent. ''Peter? I'm sorry, did I wake you?''

''In all this uproar? Don't be silly. Are you scared? Let's put our sleeping gear together.''

She climbed out of her sleeping bag, cringing in the chill, and unzipped it hastily while he unzipped his. They rezipped them into one, climbed in shivering and hissing air through their teeth, drawing together and chafing one another's back to draw the blood to the surface. A sharp crack of thunder made them both start, and they both laughed.

Then warmth set in and they relaxed. He kissed her. ''Ummm,'' she said.

He kissed her again, more warmly.

"No," she whispered, "not here."

"Yes," he whispered. "Here." And he persisted, telling her it would take her mind off the storm.

She told herself that it was the night before battle; he needed this reassurance.

6

WHEN Katherine woke, it was barely light. Excitement, she told herself. There was a stealthy patter of rain on the light fabric of the tent. Stefan was curled deep into sleep beside her and she snuggled against his warmth to nap a little. Then, over the sound of rain she heard quiet voices and the subdued clink of metalware—breakfast-making sounds.

Breakfast! She sat up, reached for her watch under her pillow. Six-thirty. *Oh God, it's a mile to the shower, there's no bread, and I'm supposed to be making breakfast!* She slipped out of the sleeping bag, pulled on her blue terry robe, shoved her feet into clogs, and unzipped the tent. The Charter encampment was quiet—the breakfast-makers were one encampment over. She sighed with relief, then ducked back inside for soap, towel, and her oldest daytime garb. She came out again, still in her robe, to hurry to the bathhouse. Not many were stirring, and most of the early risers were busy picking up after the storm, wringing out banners and pouring water from dinnerware left out overnight. The line at the bathhouse was short, and she got a hot shower.

She came out wearing a brown, full-skirted, ankle-length peasant's dress with a black-laced bodice and white apron. She covered this with a cloak knitted of virgin wool, whose lanolin made it almost waterproof. She still wore the clogs; in the mud of King's Road they were both medieval and practical.

She trudged up the hill, past the barn, and started down again, stopping halfway at the Fat Cat Inn, from which came the heavenly scent of baking bread. It was a huge, open-fronted army tent whose sign featured a smiling tiger picking his teeth with a bone from what looked suspiciously like the skeleton of a dragon. Behind its counter were a man and a girl. The girl, about fourteen, tousled and sleepy in an oversize apron, was building a fire with scraps of wood inside one of three big church-shaped clay ovens. Katherine frowned at her. "How can you bake in an oven heated like that?" she asked.

The girl smiled and closed the oven door. She picked up a metal pan and a small hoe and opened another oven's door. "Like this," she said, raking glowing coals out with the hoe into the pan. She put down the pan and lifted a tray loaded with small loaves of bread dough and slid it inside. "The clay retains the heat long enough to bake the bread."

"I see," said Katherine.

The other cook, who wore black monk's robes under his apron, was slipping little loaves off a tray into a basket. "May I get you something, m'lady?" he asked.

"Yes please. I need six of those loaves, please."

"Yes, m'lady." The loaves, still hot, judging by the hasty way he handled them, were dropped into a paper bag.

"Good morning, Lady Katherine," said Lord Roc, approaching and digging in his pouch for money. "I'll have an orange and a loaf of bread," he said to the monk.

"Good morning, Lord Roc," said Katherine. "I didn't know you were an early riser, too."

"I'm not. If you'll wait a minute, I'll walk you back."

He paid for his breakfast, broke a piece off the bread and tossed it to Buu, who fielded it deftly, and they started down King's Road.

"Are you fighting in the woods this morning?" she asked.

"No, scouting." He looked down at his gray-green tunic and gray pants laced with thongs. "This is my camouflage outfit."

"You've done it before?"

"This will be my fourth Woods Battle."

"I'll be water-bearing. Maybe we'll see each other."

"Maybe."

They walked in silence for a bit, then she asked, "Have you filled out your questionnaire? Telling why you joined the SCA?"

He shrugged. "The point broke on my pencil."

"When you get it sharpened again, what will you put?"

"I don't know. What about you?"

"I'll probably rattle on about the grand experiment, rediscovering old truths about honor and courtesy. Just like everyone else."

"When the truth is . . . ?"

She fell silent again. "The truth is," she said slowly, "that I like being in a group that has a lot of rules about interactive behavior. I've always been kind of stiff around people, and the SCA collection of formalities makes me feel less shy. Especially meeting new people. He bows to me, and I curtsy to him, and perhaps he'll kiss my hand. And if he adds a kindly glance up at me through his eyelashes, I can smile back or ignore it without feeling I've insulted him. I also like being looked at with culturally different eyes once in a while, building a different identity. In the SCA, I have friends who never ask where I work or how much money I have."

Roc tossed another fragment of bread to Buu. "You should go ahead and write that down. Nothing wrong with being shy. Maybe it's even kind of nice. How do you feel about the Horde, now that Stefan dragged you in to have a look at us?"

"It was an uplifting experience." She smiled at Roc's chuckle and then shrugged. "I keep hearing stories about drunken parties and casual sex among Horde folk, but certainly the way you look out for one another is admirable." She hesitated, then asked, "What's wrong with Thorstane, anyway?"

"Drink, mostly."

"Is the household going to throw him out?"

"Dunno." He took a bite of his bread, and, chewing, looked up at the sky. "Did you ever get a bad feeling about a day?"

"This one looks gloomy enough," she agreed.

"No, I mean there's trouble brewing. All the camp talks about is Thorstane. There's a kind of glee, like kids who know another kid's gonna get it. They can't wait for us to throw him out. They wish Steffy had laid into him harder. Don't they know this is serious? Someone could really get hurt!"

"You don't think Thorstane will—"

"It's not Thorstane I'm worried about; it's you kingdomers!" They stopped at the entrance to the Horde camp. "We can handle Thorstane, we've been handling people like him for years. But I'm afraid one of you may do something stupid. The atmosphere encourages trouble."

"Surely not!" said Katherine. "The Society stands for the rule of law!"

"Yeah," he said sarcastically. "The rediscovery of courtesy, another try at the grand experiment. I know. All the same . . ." He began ripping at the skin of his orange.

"Well, Thorstane seems to be against all we stand for. Why did he join in the first place?"

He looked through the gate, checking his fire. "Maybe he thought we'd rub off on him, or something. And maybe we have, some. He'd probably be in jail, or dead, if he didn't have us."

"Truly? Look, come up and have breakfast with us, and let's talk some more. Maybe there's something we can do to help him."

He shook his head. "No, if Lady Anne saw me coming, she'd throw a fit."

"No, she wouldn't. But why are your brothers giving her such a hard time?"

He shrugged. "What does she expect? We're an unruly, discourteous bunch of roughnecks—just ask her."

"Well, you aren't helping matters by leering around every corner at her."

Surprisingly, he chuckled. "No?"

"We're having sausage for breakfast," she coaxed. "Come on; join us?"

"No, I've got my fire to tend."

"Sure?"

"Yes—but thanks. And maybe I will see you in the woods."

. . .

Thorstane was pretending to read over his survey form. He had at first scribbled, ''None of your fucking buziness!'' under the single question put to him, then crossed that out. Why had he joined? Because this outfit featured a few people who gave a damn. Who weren't convinced the world was going to hell, so what did it matter? They made a ceremony out of being nice. They carried ceremony a little too far, which is why he'd joined the Horde, and in the Horde he'd found some real true-blue friends. He'd write that down, maybe. When he was feeling better.

Sabas' odd-tasting tea had helped, but what Thorstane felt he needed to get completely well was a drink. He opened his suitcase to get a change of underwear and saw that in removing his store of liquor they had overlooked a little half-pint of vodka he had stuck in a thick sock. He pulled it out, opened it, and took two big swallows before his guardians realized what he was doing.

''Hey!'' said the quicker of the two. ''Gimme that!'' He yanked it out of Thorstane's hand, spilling it generously on the tent's floor.

''Easy now, that's good stuff,'' said Thorstane, grinning, already feeling the welcome warmth spreading from his belly. ''Here, put the cap back on.'' He threw it at the man. ''I just needed a snort to set me up; I won't do it again.''

''Damn straight you won't,'' said the k'shaktu. ''Hand over that suitcase.''

''There's nothing in there now but clothes,'' objected Thorstane.

But the other k'shaktu leaned across and dragged the suitcase away from Thorstane. ''I don't care. From now on, if you want anything out of it, you ask one of us.''

Thorstane wanted to argue, thought better of it. ''Fine, I always wanted a squire. Now I got two of them. Hand me a pair of shorts, one of you.''

. . .

Master Petrog awoke with a splitting headache. He was severely hung over, a condition only to be expected after last night. He should have known better; today was going to be hard and busy enough without complicating things with a hangover.

He sat up with a groan and tenderly massaged his aching brow.

Fragments of last evening began to flicker on the flawed projection screen of his memory. Acts of hilarity, rage, silliness. He crawled out of his cot and pulled off the tapestry covering his ice chest—Master Petrog liked authenticity only to the point past which lay fleas, dirt, and food poisoning. He lifted the lid. Thank heaven there was still a chunk of ice. Ice bought by the block lasted longer than ice in cubes, a well-known campers' secret. After an aggravated search he found his ice pick where he'd hidden it under the tapestry and chipped off a mouth-size piece.

Why hadn't he found Sir Ignatius and let him take over the job of baby-sitting His Majesty? Iggy loved to go roaring drunk around the campground with the King. God, what a night. He sat back gloomily, letting the ice cool his parched tongue, recalling events that had run until very early this morning. Then a smile slowly began to pull at his lips. That bastard Thorstane would never bother him again.

He dug in his first-aid pack and took a couple of non-medieval remedies for hangover. He did not, however, further the cure by having tea or coffee with his breakfast; he could get along without them, and neither beverage was used in Europe until long after the medieval period. He drank an authentic cup of flat ale with his hard-boiled egg and knob of goat cheese, then put on a loose-fitting, below-the-knee buff tunic slit front and back, with very deep arm-holes and a broad row of red-and-gold embroidery around the collar. His hose were of red-brown, bias-cut cloth, and his thin leather shoes had a branching stripe of contrasting leather sewn from top to toe as decoration. His brown belt hung down long in front of its plain gold buckle, and the drawstring of his purse ended in gold tassles. Over this authentic twelfth-century Crusader's garb he pulled, with a grimace, a white tabard with a red outline of a cross, which marked him as a medic. He covered the offending tabard with a hooded cloak. He had long ago asked that the medic's cross at least be in the style the Crusaders wore, but of course no one had listened.

In the course of getting dressed, he found the survey form they had given him and looked it over. He had written sourly in the space provided that there was not nearly enough emphasis on authenticity in the Society. Perhaps it was too much to expect that everyone learn Latin or the language of his chosen persona, but members should at least read their adopted century's literature in translation and be able to recognize one tune composed in the century they claimed to have been born into.

Why had he joined? He had been looking for people like himself, who wanted to recreate as authentically as possible that honorable time, the formidable ancestor of today. The real question was, why did he stay? God only knew. He folded the form into quarters and tucked it into his purse. He'd turn it in sometime today.

Meanwhile, he'd better head off to Resurrection Point, to attend the medics' meeting. He shouldn't be acting as a medic, he should be judging contest entries, but they were short of medics this year, and he had allowed himself to be talked into serving. He came out of his tent, a silk pavilion, and started up the path for King's Road.

He hoped no one would be seriously hurt during the battle—he hated the noise and panic that accompanied injury in a place full of non-medical personnel.

Except Thorstane, of course. Thorstane should get a ruptured spleen, it would serve him right. He'd seen the barbarian taking the sun on the grass outside the campground store yesterday, looking sound asleep. But he wasn't; Petrog was just a little beyond him when the coarse chant began: "Patty-cake, patty-cake, baker's man, bake me a cake as fast as you can. Roll it and pat it—haw, haw, haw!"

He pulled up the hood of his cloak against the drizzle and wished for the sun to come out. A fragment of a fifteenth-century moral poem about a fox crossed his mind: "And rekleslye he said whair he did rest,/straikand his wame againis the sonis heit:/'Upon this wame set war ane bolt full meit!' " He reflected sadly that there were few to whom he could repeat the fox's gorged and sun-warmed jest: "This belly would make a perfect target for an arrow."

• • •

William's little queen and Sir Ignatius' gentle wife hovered over a mysterious glop hissing and crackling in a frying pan while King William and the Dragon Herald consulted a map of the woods. They were both in leg harness and the padded coats that go under armor—Sir Ignatius had put aside his herald's cloak to fight beside his king in the woods today.

"No, do it like we planned; let the others go for the banner," counseled Ignatius. "You cover your ass. If we get the banner and lose you, we're only even."

"Yeah, okay; you're right. How about we take that north trail? It turns east here and runs parallel to the main one, see? We can cut back to this trail here and maybe work a scissors on the Eastern king with another bunch."

"All right." Ignatius nodded. "And we send the Horde on the main trail. Straight on through and straight back, killing every Easterner they can find."

"Yeah. If I know King Oswin, he'll have most of his troops on that trail. The Horde, with that goddamn shield wall, will go through them like Ex-Lax. I remember last year—" He glanced up and saw a big, fair-haired knight listening eagerly. "Can I do something for you, Sir John?" William asked.

Sir John blushed red as his surcoat and dropped onto one knee. "I—I beg your pardon. I only came to ask if I could fight with the Horde, since they're with us this year."

"You fight polearm?" asked William.

"No, I—I mean, yes, I'm authorized in polearm, but I didn't bring one with me."

"Well, the Horde specializes in shield walls. Everyone else who fights with them uses pike or polearm and works behind their wall."

"I can help form the shield wall."

"No, they practice it together; you'd only mess them up."

John looked disappointed. "I see."

"Link up with the King of Meridies, why don't you?"

Sir John considered this, then nodded. "Okay." He rose and sketched a brief bow before hurrying off.

"Basil should do public penance for knighting that guy," growled William, turning again to the map. "Did you see how he was standing there spying on us?"

Ignatius laughed. "How could he be spying; he's on our side, remember? Why don't you like him? He's just another sword jock—which is how you started out, as I recall."

''I didn't get knighted till I learned better. Where were we?''

''Be sure to address the Queen of Meridies when you talk to the King, not just him alone. She's a fighter, and she'll be right in there with him and his troops.'' Other kingdoms coming to the War had to throw in their lot with the East or the Middle. Meridies had chosen to fight with the Middle this year, and their king and queen had come in person to assist in the battles.

''Breakfast, everyone,'' said Queen Ethelreada shyly. She was rather in awe of William when he was involved in kingdom affairs.

''Do we have enough constables manning Resurrection Point?'' asked William.

''Same as the East had last year,'' said Ignatius.

''Hey, listen up, you two,'' said Ignatius' wife. She was a sweet-faced lady with a lame foot, and she came limping over to stand behind him. He was not a tall man, and she looked over him at William. ''If you like, Your Majesty, I can bring you two your breakfast over here, so you can continue planning.''

''No, never mind,'' said William, folding up his map. ''If we're not ready now, we never will be. The only thing I'm still worried about is Thorstane.''

''How about we go looking for him in the woods?'' suggested Ignatius, as they walked away from the table. He put an affectionate arm around his wife's waist. ''We can nail him to a tree by his ears and forget where we left him until the War's over.''

''Iggy!'' said that lady.

''She's right,'' said William. ''Some soft-hearted water bearer'd hear him whining and cut him down. No, if we nail him up, it should be with a spike through his little black heart.''

7

BY nine-thirty, all the fighters were armed or arming. As squire to Geoff, Stefan helped him into his armor, making sure nothing was too tight, too loose, or overlooked. They began with a broad padded kidney belt, straps hanging down ready to support the leg harness. Geoff's leg armor was all of steel, with armadillo joints at the knees. It covered the front and sides of his legs, and buckled behind.

He put on a close-fitting cloth arming cap that covered his ears and cranium, then a padded leather collar called a gorget, which buckled around his neck and had a hanging ruff of mail.

His breastplate was of steel, with leather straps that led over the shoulders to jointed back plates that buckled to the breastplate at the waist. Stefan began to fasten on the arm harness, left arm first.

There came a snag when they got to the right arm. "Geoff, there's a rivet popped here."

"Where?"

"Here on the upper lame. Sure as anything it'll come loose and freeze up your elbow right in the middle of the battle."

"Rats! Why didn't the inspector catch that? I bet it's from that arm-shot Taffy gave me at practice last week."

"Where's your tool kit? Did you bring rivets along?"

Geoff groaned. "I forgot the whole damn kit!"

"Oh hell! Well, stay right here; I'm going to go see if I can borrow a rivet."

"We'll need a hammer, too!" Geoff called after him. "And hurry!"

Stefan didn't need encouragement to hurry; he still had his own armor to get into, and less than half an hour before assembly. But he had not been a cop for thirteen years for nothing. In short order he had commandeered three other fighters who were already armored into finding a rivet and a hammer.

It was Ignatius who came through, and very promptly. Stefan found him already burdened with hammer, rivets, and his little traveling anvil. "Where's your armor?" asked Ignatius.

"It's not mine, it's Sir Geoffrey's. Follow me."

The two found Geoff waiting anxiously for their arrival. He was holding the arm harness in his hands, flexing it back and forth. It wasn't moving properly, and there was a gap in the metal joints just above the elbow. They laid the joint over the little anvil and got the rivet, a brass-plated one, through both pivot-holes. Ignatius gave one healthy swat of his ball-peen hammer to mushroom the tip of the rivet, then switched to the ball end of the hammer and struck a dozen delicate shaping blows. The rivet rounded over into a faceted dome, and the repair, without which Geoff could not have gone into battle, was complete. It had taken less than a minute.

"God, thanks, Iggy!" said Geoff. "You're a lifesaver."

Ignatius grinned. "As I told Sir John, next time it could be me. Is that all you needed?"

"Yes, and thanks again."

Stefan fitted the arm harness back into place and began to buckle it to the shoulder pauldrons. He said to Ignatius, "Thank you for helping me squire my lord."

"You're welcome." Ignatius picked up his hammer and anvil and walked off.

"He sure was a godsend," said Stefan a minute later, buckling Geoff's shoulder pauldrons over the arm harness.

"He's got a talent for being where you need him with what you need in his pocket. I think that's why His Majesty likes him." Geoff ducked into the big, red sleeveless surcoat that went over everything and handed Stefan his white belt. Stefan knelt to buckle it. Geoff's gauntlets were put on, and he was ready except for his helm. That he would not don until the battle was about to start; it was too stuffy in there.

"There, you're done," said Stefan.

"Thanks. Now, get your gear, I'll help you into it."

"Katherine's going to squire me."

"She's busy filling water bottles. And anyway, I can do it faster. Let's go."

• • •

Geoff and Stefan walked together to the gathering place in front of the Middle Kingdom's royal pavilion. William stood before it, his brass crown glittering despite the steady drizzle. His Majesty Edmund, King of Meridies, stood beside William, and beside Edmund, also in armor, was Queen Jane. On the other side of William was Khan Wulfstan in boiled-leather armor braced with steel bars, his helm tucked under his arm like a spare head. Next to Wulfstan stood shy Queen Ethelreada, and beside her were the silver-crowned Prince and Princess, both in armor. Behind the King were his Earl Marshal, holding upright the Great Sword of State, and Sir Ignatius, who had thrown a borrowed herald's cloak over his gambeson. Ignatius was holding the stem of the shield-shaped banner of the Midrealm, white with a broad red stripe up its center, and over all a fierce dragon.

Other Midrealmers were filling the area in front of the pavilion: dukes (those who had been king twice or more), earls and counts (once), barons, knights, squires, authorized fighters, scouts, water bearers, onlookers.

Those who would fight were arrayed in gear that ranged from hockey pads and pieces of carpet to magnificent and authentic replicas of medieval and Renaissance armor. Helms, swords, shields, and polearms littered the grass. No one was striking noble poses—this was too real for that—and there was talk and laughter among the crowd.

Stefan saw Katherine. She had discarded her cloak, and plastic soda bottles filled with water hung on a rope around her neck. She was standing beside the little monk, Father Hugh of Paddington, who was also burdened with water bottles. Stefan's hand went absently to the favor Katherine had tied to his upper left arm, a black cloth on which she had embroidered a lit candle, with the flame enlarged until it represented a blazing sun, thus a combination of his and her arms.

Anne was tying a blue cloth embroidered with snowflakes onto Geoff's belt. He was as likely to go into battle without it as to forget his helm or gauntlets; a knight was supposed to offer any glory gained to the honor of his one special lady, a conceit most, Geoff among them, took seriously. Some fighters wore two or more favors—a man standing near Stefan had half a dozen hanging from his belt.

William nodded to Ignatius, who stepped forward and bellowed, "Oy-yea! Oy-yea! Oy-yea! Silence for the King!" Slowly the talk died.

"Gentles!" said William. "Soon we will be engaged in the first battle of this Pennsic War!" William's voice was strong, and it had a carrying quality. Stefan felt no envy for the Eastern fighters, currently being lectured down around the bottom of the hill by Oswin's much thinner voice. William continued, "The East has a banner and we are determined to capture it, and keep it, until the battle is over. I'm a War Point this year, but if you have to choose between taking the banner and protecting me, take the banner. I'll fight to the death, give 'em a hand salute"—he demonstrated with a finger waggle, thumb to nose—"and go get resurrected. And I'll do it as many times as necessary for them to learn they can't take me alive.

"I know I don't need to tell most of you how much fun the Woods Battle is. And I hope I don't need to remind you that this is the place where your honor is the most important. There's so much going on, in so many places, the marshals can't see and call everything. So if you get an arm taken off, don't use it. Or lose a leg, go onto your knees. And if it's close enough to a killing blow, fall the hell down and wait for a halt to get clear. And stay dead until you're resurrected. This is a game, remember? A serious game. People who don't play by the rules spoil it, take the fun out of it.

I don't care how sure you are you can get away with cheating, I'd sooner lose the whole damn War than hear one Midrealmer cheated. Anyone who thinks I don't mean it better go sit in his tent till it's time to go home!'' There was applause at this.

''We've Jane and Edmund of Meridies and Wulfstan of the Horde with us in the woods this year, which means we've got a good chance to win.'' Cheers. ''Let's go down there and show the East what we can do! We're gonna win this one, right?''

On cue, there was an outbreak of singing from some of the older knights: ''Hot dogs, armored hot dogs; Eastern knights are armored hot dogs. . . .''

William laughed his big laugh, then gestured for silence and said, ''Now before we go . . .'' He nodded again to his herald.

Ignatius bellowed, ''Members of the Chivalry, attend the King!''

Stefan stepped backward, yielding place to the knights as they came forward and dropped onto one knee, including Queen Jane, a trim figure among the bulkier men. The Earl Marshal came to stand beside William, holding up the Great Sword of State. There was a little silence, during which a strong breeze lifted and flapped the damp Midrealm banner.

Then William called, ''I summon Lord Dismas the Ruffian!''

A black man, wearing a shirt of mail under his loose gray surcoat, came forward to kneel before the King.

''My lords,'' said the King, ''is it your judgment that Lord Dismas the Ruffian has demonstrated qualities of prowess, loyalty, and courtesy, and is therefore worthy to be numbered among you?''

The knights chorused strongly, ''It is!''

William smiled. ''Lord Dismas, have you kept your vigil?'' he asked.

''I have, Your Majesty,'' he answered.

''You must clearly understand the duties of knighthood,'' said William. ''It is a sacred trust, one that marks every moment of your life. You must be a support to the crown, an honor to your lady, a shield to the weak, and a weapon in the hand of your lord. Your word must be dependable beyond all doubt. Do you understand that?''

''I do.''

"You must be strong in the faith you uphold, but have respect for the faith of others. You must love your kingdom, your king, your lord, and your lady. You must wear the chain of fealty and the belt of prowess, maintaining both to the best of your ability. Will you do this?"

"I will, to the best of my ability."

"Is your lady present?"

"She is, Your Majesty." Dismas looked over his right shoulder at a slim lady in a sari.

"You are squire to Sir Odo. Is he present?"

"He is, Your Majesty." Sir Odo, a big man wearing brown monk's robes, was standing beside the lady, looking very proud.

"Very well. Will you accept the accolade of knighthood, knowing the burdens it places on you, including the oath of fealty?"

"I will."

William took the greatsword from his Earl Marshal and raised it, an enormous, glittering, and very real weapon. He dropped it lightly onto the right, then left, shoulder of the kneeling man. "Be thou a true knight," he said and returned the sword. Then he gave Dismas a buffet on the side of the head with his fist, almost knocking him over. "Accept this blow and no other," he said. "Arise, Sir Dismas." And he helped the new knight to his feet.

Sir Dismas was greeted with loud applause and cheers. William removed the gold chain from his own neck and put it over Dismas' head. Sir Odo came forward with a white belt, and the other members of his household came forward with gold spurs, which they put on his feet. His lady buckled the belt around his waist and said, "I will remove this if you dishonor me."

Then Sir Dismas knelt again and put his hands, folded as if for prayer, between the King's hands. "I will be thy man," swore Dismas, "against all others. I will honor thy commands as the voice of my own conscience, and thy lady as my own, until I die, or the world ends, or until thou art no longer king."

William said, "Thy oath I hear, and will never forget; nor fail to reward that which is given: fealty with love, service with honor, oath-breaking with vengeance."

Dismas rose again and the king clasped him in a warm embrace, and the other knights came forward to congratulate their new member.

A bagpipe began to drone on the edge of the crowd, and when its chanter started into a rousing call to battle, the fighters roared, picked up their weapons and followed as the piper, wearing the swirling Great Kilt that takes half an hour to lay out, fold, pleat, and put on, led them off to the woods.

8

SIX young teens, four boys and two girls, all damp and bedraggled, stood silently across the river from the fighters, holding aloft a nine-foot strip of paper with MAKE LOVE NOT WAR calligraphed in crayon along its length. There were peace signs, also drawn with Gothic elaborations, at either end of the motto. The demonstrators said nothing, and it was some time before the fighters became aware of their presence. Most, busy with plotting, ignored them; others pointed and laughed.

"Marshals!" bellowed the Earl Marshal. "Marshals here!" He raised his long black-and-yellow baton with its black and yellow streamers, and over sixty people, mostly male, all wearing black-and-yellow tabards marked with crossed swords, gathered around him.

Four hundred Eastern fighters stood in clusters of varying sizes around their banner, a big, light-green affair with a snarling tiger embroidered in its center. It was raised so the Midrealm fighters could get a good look at it; then the Easterners trotted off into the woods, the noise of their armor audible for some time after they vanished around a bend in the trail. Half the marshals broke from their group and hurried after them.

The Midrealm fighters stood hunched against the chill mizzle and plotted. They had half an hour before they followed the Easterners into the woods to begin the two-hour battle.

A dozen medics, marked by white tabards with the outline of a red cross front and back, stood around the War Chirurgeon; and the motley group of water bearers, marked only by the mismatched plastic bottles of water hanging heavy against their legs, gathered near them. Stefan saw Katherine bending over a map of the woods with black-robed Father Hugh.

There were thirty-five Horde brothers ready to fight for the Middle. They stood near the front of the fighters and made aggressive noises. Thorstane was there, flanked by his two k'shaktu, all three in metal-studded black leather armor and red helms. Thorstane was carrying his round shield with the painted crack and a mace made by the simple expedient of pushing a roll of toilet paper onto a rattan stick and wrapping the whole thing in duct tape. He broke away from his brothers when he saw Master Petrog with the other medics, and came to grab him by his arm and mutter something in his ear. One of Thorstane's k'shaktu pulled him away when he saw Petrog's angry reaction to the muttered remark, but Stefan heard him add, "Will doesn't live in Strange Sea, chicken-shit; he won't be there to protect you!"

William assigned a group of eight Midrealmers to fight with the Horde and introduced them to Khan Wulfstan.

Another fifty Midrealmers were formed up under William's own leadership. Prince Thomas headed a select band, King Edmund and Queen Jane of Meridies led another. William called, "I want at least one small batch to lay ambushes and harass the enemy."

Sir Humphrey promptly called, "Follow me!" He raised his shield—yellow with a blue silhouette of a camel on it—so it could be seen and stepped to the rear. He was followed by Geoff, Stefan, and Taffy. Stefan, the only non-knight in the little group, felt badly outclassed, and began to wonder if, invitation notwithstanding, he shouldn't slip away and join the fighters gathered around the Prince or the King. But Geoff thumped him on the shoulder and said, "Stick with us, Stefan, this is gonna be fun."

When Humphrey saw none of his volunteers had a polearm, he put aside his sword and shield and picked up a six-foot length of rattan and made one padded end whistle in a few practice swings.

The groups began plotting strategy, and fighters with ideas passed among all the groups.

Sir Ignatius came by and said, "I'm fighting with the King; try to stay within hailing distance of us, will you? William can use a surprise backup party; he's a War Point, you know."

"Holler loud, Iggy," said Humphrey. "You know how easy it is to get lost in there."

The Khan walked over. His helm was painted to resemble a lion's face, its fierce countenance a marked contrast to the mild-looking man carrying it. "I think this is a year for scouts," he said. "My household is volunteering some really experienced people. One of them, Lord Rocco the Italian, lived some years in the East, and served as late as last year as a scout for them. Your little group might do some clever things if you want to use him."

"You honor me with your help," said Humphrey, bowing. "I had indeed planned to use scouts."

Humphrey turned to look for Roc, but the Dragon Herald was calling "Oy-yea! Silence for the King!" and courtesy demanded everyone stop and listen.

"Most of the trails are narrow," said William, "but that doesn't mean we've got to turn every engagement into a bridge battle. If the people up front meet the enemy, some of you in the rear break off and go around, come up behind. Just make sure the marker tape on the fighter's helm is green, not red. Let's not go killing some of our own." He saw Humphrey's little group and said, "Sir Humphrey, I'd like you to nibble around their edges, lure strays off into the bushes. Fight a war of attrition on them."

Humphrey bowed. "An it please Your Majesty, if it weren't for the snakes, that's just what I had in mind."

William grinned. "Don't worry about snakes; no one with the brains of a snake is going to come out in weather like this." That brought a wry chorus of agreement.

The leaders began to call for scouts. Humphrey called, "Lord Roc and another!"

Roc trotted over, and a lady in black followed close behind him. Humphrey knelt on the trail, and the pair squatted beside him, putting down their open-faced helms. The helms had red tape stripes on them, but they wore no other armor. Scouts could be killed, but they were not permitted to fight and carried no weapons. Humphrey spoke quietly. "I'm looking for the banner. You know the rules, I assume: They can't roll it up or lay it down. They can set as many as half their fighters to guard the thing, or they can try to hide it. I know King Oswin, and I think he'll try to be sneaky. That means he'll give it to a few knights to carry, and that means maybe just us few can take it away from them—if we can find it."

"Maybe they'll hide up a tree," said Roc, "like you guys did last year."

"Give me some shoulders to stand on and watch me make it rain Easterners," said Humphrey. "Like they did last year. Uh-uh, more likely they'll hide in the bushes and move off when they hear us coming. This rain won't cover the sound of clanking armor. But"—he grinned a jolly grin—"it will cover the little patter of a scout's feet."

"Ah," said the Mongol lady, her green eyes glinting with amusement.

Humphrey nodded. "I want you two to work together. If one of you finds the banner, send the other to tell us about it. We'll start out by going along the brook to the marsh, then taking the main trail back. And here—" He held out both hands to give each of them a tubular silver whistle about two inches long. "If the guardians of the banner catch you, instead of taking your one scream, blow on this. Keep them in your mouths in case of mutual surprise and I don't think the marshals will rule against it. But blow it only if you're caught by banner carriers, understand? And try not to get killed by anyone else."

The pair nodded and took the whistles.

Humphrey continued, "Lord Roc, your khan says you're an experienced scout, so you know the woods pretty well. And he said you used to live in the East; you know Easterners. I think you'll be doing great things for us today. My lady, I don't know your name—"

"Freyis," she said in her furry voice. "This is my tenth War. I've only been a water bearer up till now, but I know my way around the woods almost as well as Roc."

''Wonderful. These whistles are used by the London police and have a nice carrying note. Go show them around and explain my plan. Hurry, the opening cannon will go off in a couple of minutes.''

He straightened and watched them go.

''I know a nice, defensible place to take the banner if we're the ones to find it,'' said Geoff, beginning to work his head into his helm. It was comfortable once it was on, but had a tendency to catch on his ears as it slid down. ''We could hold off two dozen Easterners, if we have to, from there.''

''Yeah, but probably not for long,'' said Humphrey. He began pulling on his gauntlets. ''Did you look at who the East is putting into the woods this year? Some of its best fighters. But if we don't find the banner till fairly close to the end, maybe we can hang on to it until the cannon goes off. Everyone ready?'' He looked around and his fighters nodded. ''We'll cut off onto the first little trail to the left once we get in there, okay?'' He turned to watch the medics tramp into the woods, each carrying a first-aid kit. The water bearers were clearing off the trail; they'd go in last.

Stefan bumped his helm with his shield to adjust it and gripped his sword tightly. His heart was thumping, and there did not seem to be enough air to breathe. That would pass, he knew, once the action started. He glanced around at his companions so he'd know them in the confusion to come. Sir Humphrey, in purple, was leaning calmly on his polearm. Geoff, in red, was hefting his shield, yellow with a red vertical stripe and puffin. Taffy's surcoat was green; his shield was half green and half white, with a red tower on the white side. Stefan himself wore a sleeveless white surcoat, and his shield was black with a candle. *First trail to the left,* he thought.

There was a sharp *bam!* from nearby Archers' Field, like one of those Fourth-of-July shells that go off with no pretty stars. Humphrey dropped the visor on his helm and lifted his shield. ''Oh boy!'' he said cheerfully. ''Here we go!''

• • •

Roc and Freyis followed the fighters into the woods, then stopped to make plans.

''There's a place at the far end, near the fence,'' said Roc. ''Got lots of raspberry bushes around a little clearing, and some young trees whose leaves are about the same color as that banner is."

"Ah," said Freyis, pushing her helm more firmly down on her head. "When King Oswin was the East's Earl Marshal four years ago, they hid their banner there. You're a bright young man. Let's go see." She set off down a path to the right at a brisk noiseless walk and Roc, grinning, hurried after her.

• • •

William was leading his band northward when they ran headlong into about twenty Easterners headed by Oswin himself, coming around a sharp curve. The noise made by their own armor had covered the sounds of approaching enemy; and to judge by Oswin's start, he was equally surprised. The unarmored marshals scrambled for safety as a confused melee ensued, the louder and harder fought because everyone was still fresh.

Following orders, the last quarter of William's troops cut through the underbrush that lined the trail and came up behind the Easterners. This splintered the action, and William found himself separated from the main body, being backed through some bushes off the trail by four Eastern knights. Ignatius was beside him, and this, to William's way of thinking, made the odds rather on his side.

The four Easterners recognized the dragon on the royal shield and pressed eagerly. William and Ignatius let them crowd one another in their eagerness and Ignatius coolly killed one with a swift, sudden uppercut to the ribs. Then he stupidly stepped right into a solid blow on the helm that dropped him like a stone.

The Eastern knight who had killed Ignatius crowed in triumph and swung at William, who blocked the blow with his shield and deftly caught the man on his shoulder with a blow that would have severely damaged, if not removed, the arm, had William's sword been real. As bound by honor, the man dropped back to lay down his shield and prepare to fight left-handed.

William backed up against a big old oak to make his stand against the remaining two. One feinted at him, but he recognized the ploy and blocked the blow from the other before it could land. His own sword whistled as he aimed a killing blow at the feinter—and the tip of it caught against a tree branch, making the weapon fly out of his hand. The one-armed knight yelled, "Don't kill him, grab him!" but William ducked around the tree and went crashing off weaponless into the underbrush.

• • •

A scout reported to the King and Queen of Meridies that a big force of Easterners was headed their way. Edmund grinned his thanks, and the Easterners, hoping to surprise their prey, were dismayed to confront a braced line of shields bristling with swords.

The marshals moved out of the fighters' reach and watched.

The Easterners quickly formed an offensive wedge and charged the line. The two met with a loud smash and a rapid series of whaps and metallic crunches followed, a sound like a chain-reaction car accident. Fighters from both sides fell, though, thanks to the warning, fewer Midrealmers than Easterners. The Eastern wedge abruptly broke and several marshals shouted, "Hold!" Immediately, the action stopped; everyone froze where he or she was.

"Let's get the bodies out of the way!" ordered a marshal. Two other marshals lowered their batons across the trail between the combatants, and the living gratefully dropped to one knee to catch their breath while the "bodies" rolled free and scrambled off the trail.

One of them was King Edmund. He removed his helm and wiped the sweat out of his eyes. "Whew!" he said. He glanced around to see who else was dead and saw his queen, still with the living, looking at him anxiously. He grinned at her ruefully. "Some hot dogs," he said, and she laughed.

"I'll hold things down until you get back," she said.

"All right." He turned and asked a man in a black-and-yellow tabard, "M'lord Marshal, where do the dead go?"

"Forward, up the trail," replied the marshal, keeping an eye on the road where a medic was helping a groaning "body" to its feet. "There's a black flag on a pole to mark the gathering place. Just wait there until someone comes to take you out."

"Thanks," Edmund said. He grimaced and tried to rub a sore spot on his ribcage through his armor. "Let's head out," he said, and started up the trail. Nearly a dozen dead fighters from both sides followed, the sound supporting the lame without regard for which side they had been fighting on.

Behind them a marshal called, "Fighters ready!" and there was a clatter of armor as the living rose. "Lay on!" he ordered. The crash and slam of combat began again, but none of the dead bothered to look back.

. . .

Roc and Freyis stared in surprised delight at the five Eastern knights talking softly in the clearing. The war banner drooped over their heads and the woods seemed alive with movement—the rain was increasing in intensity.

"They can sneak almost right up on them if this keeps up," murmured Roc. "Which of us goes to tell them?"

"Rock, paper, scissors," whispered Freyis promptly, putting a hand behind her back. "One, two, three!" She brought out two rigid fingers, but Roc had simultaneously brought out a fist, and she shrugged and watched him slip away.

She returned her attention to the clearing, wishing she dared sneak a smoke. Two men consulted under the banner while two others peered anxiously into the underbrush. She frowned. There had been five men there a minute ago, she was sure of that. She put the silver whistle Sir Humphrey had given her between her lips and dropped even lower behind her raspberry bush. Suddenly, a bare twenty-five yards away, she heard a man's voice say, "You are dead," the formula for killing a scout. It was followed immediately by the shrill note of a whistle.

Oh, damn, she thought, *Roc just bought it. I'd better get out of here*. She began to back cautiously away from the clearing.

9

SIXTY pounds of armor isn't so much when it's hung mostly from the shoulders and otherwise distributed over the body—but it becomes noticeable again when one has been jogging steadily a long while. Stefan felt that if they didn't stop soon he would fall on his face and be unable to rise.

They hadn't met one other person since they had broken off and started down the narrow footpath. They were now so far away from everything, not even shouts or sounds of combat could reach them. The ground was squishy underfoot, both because of the drizzle and because the swollen sluggish brook beside the trail was nearing its terminus in the marsh.

Humphrey held up his polearm and slowed to a halt. Everyone but him immediately dropped to the ground, a fact Stefan barely noticed in his own collapse. The rattle of armor was replaced by the lesser noise of harsh breathing and the patter of rain. "It gets really messy just ahead," said Humphrey, sitting down on a tree stump beside the path to face them. He was looking very fresh. "I'll let you rest a few minutes, then we'll cut across to the main trail, about a hundred yards that way." He gestured off to his left. "We'll have to slow down on the main trail as we start back, so we won't make as much noise. And we'll listen for the sound of troops."

"Jees, do we hafta . . . slow down?" asked Taffy between gasps. "I was . . . havin' so much . . . fun!" The others chuckled faintly.

Humphrey gave them three minutes. Then, "All right, gentles," he said cheerfully. "Time to go." He rose and turned as if to step off the trail, reaching for his visor, but paused to listen. The others heard it too, and twisted to face the shrill note, not far away, of a London bobby's whistle.

"Quick, let's go!" ordered Humphrey, crashing off into the underbrush in the direction of the whistle. They had only gone a few yards when the second whistle sounded. "Shoot, they got both of them," Humphrey said, and increased the pace.

They came out of the underbrush onto the main trail and Humphrey, looking around, said, "Ha, I bet I know where they are!" He led them on a dead run up the trail, but fortunately not for long. He signaled and they skidded to a halt. There was a clatter of armor and at another signal they ducked back off the trail. Two Eastern knights came out from the underbrush onto the trail and stopped. One of them was holding two silver whistles by their chains in his shield hand.

"Find two of our scouts," the other said. "Have them separate and blow these damn things at different places. They want to play cute, we'll show them cute. I'll go back and we'll move the banner. Meet us along the brook, Location Three."

"Right," said the other, and the two parted.

They watched him go, then followed the knight heading back the way he had come, to the banner. The noise of the rain covered their careful approach, and when they stepped into a little clearing, it wasn't until Humphrey said, "My lords, we are well met," that the four guardians of the banner turned, surprised to see them.

Stefan, Geoff, and Taffy formed a shield wall and began an approach on the four. One, carrying a long and short sword instead of sword and shield, broke and ran around to flank the shield wall. Humphrey, who was standing behind the row of shields, swung his polearm out—and the knight ran into it with a grunt audible over the sound of impact. He fell and Humphrey immediately called "Hold!" He dropped his polearm and went to kneel beside the fallen man.

"You all right?" he asked.

"Yes," gasped the knight. ". . . no wind."

Humphrey helped him off with his helm. "You stay there and rest till this is over, okay?"

"Uh-huh," agreed the man, pulling off a gauntlet so he could unbuckle his gorget. "Dead anyway."

Humphrey stood and said to the remaining Easterners, "Let's move around out of this one's way, okay?"

"Suits me," said the knight holding the banner, and the shield wall moved off to the right, the three remaining Easterners shifting to face it. When they were satisfied with their new positions, the banner holder said, "Ready? Lay on!" and the shield wall began its approach again.

An Eastern knight stepped forward, shield high, but Humphrey dropped his polearm on it, forcing it down, and Taffy killed him with a blow on top of his helm. The other knight braced his shield against Humphrey's attempts to lower it and swung low at Stefan, who was on the end of the row. Stefan blocked the swing with his sword, and Geoff, standing next to him, landed a solid blow on the knight's thigh, causing him to drop to his knees. Humphrey swung at him, but the man hurriedly backed out of range, and they turned their attention on the knight holding the banner.

"I call for single combat!" called the knight hastily.

"Accepted!" replied Humphrey promptly. "Geoff, you want to handle him?"

"Thanks," said Geoff.

The shield wall broke apart, and Humphrey said quietly, "Taffy, how about you keep the one on his knees busy? But don't kill him unless you have to."

"Yes, m'lord," said Taffy. He went into a crouch and began a cautious approach on the kneeling knight, who, having less area to protect, was like a snapping turtle under his shell—and as dangerous. Taffy circled warily. Humphrey and Stefan backed off to give the fighters room.

The knight with the banner wore a very heavy leather gauntlet that came well up over his left elbow. He was using a combination of this and the banner's pole as a tricky sort of shield, and Geoff, further disconcerted by the flapping cloth of the banner, was pushed into a retreat across the clearing. The Eastern knight, pressing his advantage, began a quick flurry of blows with his sword, and Geoff had to use both his sword and shield to block. But the Eastern knight grew overconfident and Geoff's sword took advantage of a brief opening to snap in a blow to the knight's shoulder.

"Shit!" said the knight, dropping his sword. He tried to use the banner as a one-handed weapon, but the cloth now hampered him, and Geoff punch-blocked with his shield and swung his sword in sideways—missed—kept going, bringing his sword in a single swift move up, around and down to land a killing blow on the Easterner's helm.

"Whooo-hoo!" cheered Geoff as the Easterner tumbled to the ground, dropping the banner.

"Get it, Geoff, and let's go!" ordered Humphrey. "C'mon, Taffy!"

"Hey, what about me?" asked the wounded knight, and Taffy looked inquiringly at Humphrey.

"Leave him," ordered Humphrey.

"Hey, it must be a mile to where the action is!" said the wounded Easterner. "I can't go that far on my knees! Finish me so I can walk out, okay?" He lowered his shield and tossed away his sword. "Please?"

"Leave him," repeated Humphrey. "We've got to hurry!" He turned and started back for the main trail.

"Hey, don't do this to me!" called the knight. "Aw, dammit!" he added, as they kept going.

"Now, Geoff, where's that special defensible place?" asked Humphrey, as they reached the trail.

Geoff looked around. "If I knew where we were . . ." he said. "But I know how to get there from the entrance."

"Tell me," said Humphrey.

Geoffrey dropped to one knee. "From the entrance you take the third turning to the left,'' he said, beginning to sketch a rough map in the dirt of the trail, ''and go maybe fifty yards.''

Humphrey stooped to watch, and Stefan asked Taffy, ''Why didn't Sir Humphrey let you finish that knight?''

''Because you can't get healed in the Woods Battle, only resurrected. That's one less Easterner we'll have to worry about for a while. He'll have to wait for some of his own to come by and finish him, unless he wants to start walking back on his knees.''

''But—'' started Stefan.

''It's a recognized tactic for reducing the power of the enemy,'' interrupted Taffy.

Geoff, who had finished his map, added, ''They did the same thing to me at Pennsic Eleven, the turkeys. That's why the knee cops of my armor are so scratched.''

''No, I was going to ask: Can't he fall on his own sword?''

''Medieval theology said suicides go to hell, so it's against the rules,'' said Geoff.

''Poor guy,'' said Taffy. ''When they did it to me, at least I was within shouting distance of some of my own fighters.''

''Enough of the war stories,'' said Humphrey. ''Let's move out.''

• • •

The Horde shield wall had stood firm against the first attack and again in a surprise attack, but the fighters were tired now, and broke ranks to sit on the side of the road and rest.

A lady medic with the brisk air of a mundane hospital nurse came up to put a Band-Aid on a Visigoth's neck where his gorget was abrading it, and send a fighter who had wincingly removed a gauntlet to disclose a jammed and bloody thumb out of the woods with orders to find an ice bag.

Two water bearers came by, a young woman with a ribbon dragon on her shoulder and a little monk, who fed straws up under the faceplates of the fighters so they could drink without removing their helms. Right after they left, a new fighter came down the trail to join them, an unbelted fighter who said he was Lord Christopher Bridgeman, from Lone Castle. He was a big man, with a marked hillbilly accent. His blue-painted armor was new-looking, and he was carrying a polearm.

“I was just out to Resurrection,” he said to Wulfstan, “and you might like to know, we’ve killed twice as many of them as they have of us.”

“Hot puppies!” said an eavesdropping Viking, pleased. Word of this was handed around and spirits rose.

“Let’s go find us some more to put through our meat grinder,” said one of Thorstane’s k’shaktu, and the fighters laughed and began to get up.

They marched up the trail toward the entrance and found a group of eight newly resurrected Easterners on their way back in. After a brief discussion, Wulfstan decided to set a small shield wall in their way.

Lord Christopher volunteered to take part. “I’m rested more than y’all,” he said, “and I’d enjoy a chance to swing this thing at some folks.”

Wulfstan said, “All right, go on out there and show us what you can do.”

“ ’Preciate it, m’lord.” Christopher walked out and studied the forming squad briefly. There were four Hordesmen in front carrying shields. Three of them had swords, and one a mace. Three Hordesmen with nine-foot “spears” stood in practiced nonchalance well behind the shield wall. In between were two kingdomers with six-foot polearms. Christopher took up a position as the third polearm fighter, behind and to the right of the shield-bearer with the mace: Thorstane. Wulfstan sent in a man with a large two-handed sword to brace the polearms on the left.

The Easterners formed a single line and put their two pikemen behind it. When it appeared everyone was ready, one of the marshals stretched his baton out between the parties. “Ready?” he called. “Lay on!” He lifted the baton out of the way and stepped back.

The Easterners closed rapidly and there was a shock of blows landing. The shield wall, well practiced, held its position. They allowed only enough space between the shields for the spearmen in the last row to thrust their padded tips through. Most of the Midrealm blows came from the polearms and spears; the purpose of the shield wall was to defend.

Lord Christopher, at the end of his row, stepped a little to his right and skillfully swung his polearm against the helm of a great-swordman distracted by a spear thrust. The swordsman fell and rolled out of the way. An Easterner barely blocked Christopher's next swing and his effort spoiled the blow the man next to him was aiming at Thorstane's legs.

"Look at that man fight!" exclaimed Wulfstan.

Thorstane cocked his right elbow high in an oriental-style pose, his mace well forward, and Christopher, apparently reaching left-ward for an Easterner's helm, dropped his polearm onto the elbow, forcing it down. Lowering the mace meant Thorstane's shield was also lowered and one of the Eastern spearman thrust quickly, catching Thorstane solidly in the upper chest. Christopher yanked his polearm back as Thorstane dropped to the ground and he hesitated, his weapon upraised. The greatswordsman he'd been aiming at swung in hard and caught Christopher on the helm with a blow that echoed off the surrounding trees. Christopher staggered out of the line toward the edge of the trail, dropped his polearm, and collapsed.

"Hold!" called a marshal.

Thorstane, Lord Christopher, and two dead Easterners picked themselves up.

Wulfstan called, "That sounded like a tip shot, didn't it?" Killing blows come from the body of the sword, not the tip.

"Blue Boy seemed to think it was good," said the greatsword fighter, gesturing at Lord Christopher, and the Easterners laughed. Christopher looked at Wulfstan and nodded, then bent to pick up his polearm.

"Hey, Broddi, come here!" said one of Thorstane's k'shaktu. The two stepped off the trail and after a brief discussion Broddi was popped on the helm so he could accompany their charge to the gathering place.

As the dead fighters began to walk off, Wulfstan got serious and sent a dozen fighters in to rebuild a better wall.

• • •

Sir Humphrey, carrying the rolled-up banner, led his men out of a narrow path onto a broader one. They started up it, still at the relentless jogging pace he set. The trees were big and old along here, and the path deepened into a ravine that gradually rose to a height of nine or ten feet. The ravine broke at one point to allow a second trail to join up, and continued a little farther ahead. The brief continuance was flat on top and backed by a dense mass of thorn bushes and scrub. The face of it was slimy with wet clay. Sir Geoffrey called, "There it is," and the men stopped to look at it.

"Beautiful," breathed Taffy. "But how do we get up there?"

"See that little tree root about halfway up?" said Geoff. "Someone get me up on that and I'll hoist the rest of you up."

Stefan was lifted up on top first because he was the lightest. He knelt and helped the others up, Humphrey coming last and only after gargantuan effort—he was a runner, not a climber—and they were all liberally smeared with mud by the time everyone was on top. But the site was eminently defensible, even by a few. They stuck the point of the banner's stem into the wet ground and sat down to rest and wait for company.

• • •

The gathering place was marked by a black scarf fastened to a cane pole with silver duct tape. Thorstane walked sullenly away from the others and sat down with his back against a tree. Broddi, sighing, came to sit cross-legged on the ground nearby. After a minute he asked, "What's eating you?"

Thorstane squirmed against the tree to scratch a sweat-induced itch. "Did you see that chaugua?" he asked angrily.

"Which chaugua?" asked Broddi.

"The one that got me killed."

"The Easterner?"

"No, I mean the goddamn Midrealmer with the polearm."

"Thorstane, what are you talking about?"

"I'm talking about the shithead who let his weapon fall onto my arm so it trapped my mace and shoved my shield down so that Eastern pike could get at me. The bastard!" Thorstane shoved a dirty hand down the back of his leather armor, reaching for the itch.

Broddi frowned. "Which one did that?"

"That one right over there, in the blue armor."

"Lord Christopher?"

"Whoever. I think he did that on purpose."

"Why? Does he know you?"

''Does he have to? I bet he's got a thing about the Horde. I think I'll tell him what I think of him.''

''You stay right where you are.''

''Aw—!'' Thorstane rubbed a forming bruise on his elbow, then again leaned forward as if to get up.

''Hey, I told you to stay put!''

''Lay off me, okay? I'm thirsty; I'm gonna go see if there's some water around here.''

''No, you're not.''

''But I really am thirsty.''

''Fine, you sit tight; I'll go see if I can scare up a water bearer.'' Broddi got to his feet and walked off.

Thorstane turned his arm over to inspect the bruise. ''I want to apologize for messing you up back there on the trail,'' drawled a voice, and he looked up. It was Lord Christopher.

''You're supposed to take your helm off when you die,'' said Thorstane.

Christopher touched his blue metal face. ''I made this helm a little too small. It was hell getting into it, and I don't look forward to taking it off. I especially don't want to take it off if I have to put it right back on again.'' He squatted in front of the big barbarian. ''You know, by rights, neither one of us should be dead.''

''Yeah? How's that?''

''While I was deciding which way to duck out of your way, I caught that shot to the helm.''

''Too bad.''

''Hey, have a heart! I'm back from Resurrection five minutes and now I have to go out again.''

''It's your own fault,'' said Thorstane. ''Wulffy practically asked you to holler 'tip shot.' If you'd paid attention and said that hit wasn't any good, you'd still be back there fighting.''

Christopher bumped his helm with a knuckle. ''Hear that? Hollow.'' Despite himself, Thorstane chuckled and Christopher asked, ''Who's that guy with you, your squire or something?''

''Naw, he's my k'shaktu, my guardian, here to see I don't get into any trouble.'' Thorstane cocked his head and formed a massive frown. ''Do I know you?''

Christopher's accent thickened. "You-all ever been to Lone Castle in the Kingdom of Meridies?"

"Uh-uh, never been even to Meridies."

"Then you don't know me."

"The marshal's here!" called someone.

"Thorstane?" called Broddi.

"Yeah, yeah!" said Thorstane. He began getting to his feet. Christopher offered an arm and the barbarian took it gratefully.

"This is my first War," said Christopher as the two began walking toward the trail. "I didn't know much about how it was run. Like water bearers: I didn't know they had them, so I hid a six-pack of beer in the wood this morning in case I got thirsty."

Thorstane halted. "You *what*?"

"I hid some beer in the woods."

Christopher's expression was hidden behind blue-painted steel, and Thorstane laughed uncertainly. "I don't believe you."

Christopher shrugged. "I could show it to you. Didn't I hear you say you were thirsty? I guess I owe you at least a beer for getting you killed." The line had already started moving up the trail and they hurried to join the tail end of it.

"After we get resurrected, okay?"

They walked in silence awhile, then Christopher said softly, "Why wait? Like I said, by rights neither of us should be dead. We could drop out of this parade, go get us a frosty one, and then go off on our own, lay ambushes or something."

"The only part of that that's not against the rules is the ambushes."

"So what?" Three Eastern knights came back to join the end of the line, but Christopher waved them in ahead of himself and Thorstane. He continued, "What's a rule or two when it could mean winning?"

"What do you mean?"

"Listen, I heard two Easterners talking out at Resurrection about where the banner was hid. I'm going to see if it's still there and maybe organize a little surprise party. I'll be such a hero no one will remember if I was out to Resurrection Point a second time or not. Come on, we can just step off the trail and be gone."

Thorstane hesitated. "I dunno—"

Christopher clapped him on the shoulder. "All right, never mind, forget I asked. You hurry on, catch up with your baby-sitter; I'll find someone else to share my beer with. See you around, hear?" He checked the progress of the front of the line, glanced over his shoulder, and stepped off the trail into the underbrush.

Thorstane looked up the trail. The head of the line had disappeared around a bend, taking Broddi with it. His tongue was parched, and he was sick of Broddi's bossiness. So to hell with Broddi—and to hell with the Khan, too; he wasn't going to miss out on this. "Wait up!" he called softly, and, pulling on his helm, hurried off the trail after Christopher.

10

THE only problem with Sir Geoffrey's defensible position was that the trails it faced were being used frequently. They had little more than caught their breath and expressed a desire for a water bearer when a dozen Easterners came along and stopped to inquire.

"We saw three of our knights on their way to Resurrection," said one of them, a knight whose shield displayed a dog carrying a torch in its mouth. "I'm wondering if you know something about them."

"We did kill three Eastern knights a while back," said Humphrey thoughtfully, "but we didn't get their names."

"Did you by some chance get that banner from them?" asked the Eastern knight.

Geoff turned at the waist and looked at the banner as if really seeing it for the first time. "This? Why, yes, we did. I guess one of your friends dropped it." He brushed a dead leaf off its face. "It was getting all dirty there on the ground, so we brought it along."

"Well," said the Easterner, hefting his shield, "it's an Eastern banner, and we'd be willing to take it off your hands." The three marshals who had come with the Easterners laughed.

"No, I don't think so," said Humphrey. "I recall our king said something about wanting to take a look at any banner we happened to pick up, and so we better wait and show it to him first.''

''Shoot, no need to bother him about it; I hear he's busy avoiding some people who want to talk to him real bad. Come on, hand it over.''

Humphrey climbed to his feet. ''Why don't you come on up here and we'll talk some more about it?''

''You're on,'' said the Easterner. He stepped aside and waved forward two fighters carrying polearms, the only weapon that could easily reach the defenders. One walked warily up to the steep face of the clay bank and waved his weapon at Humphrey, who was standing at the edge. Humphrey sidestepped, bumped the weapon aside with his own polearm, and popped the Easterner on top of his helm. The man staggered back and fell. Humphrey gestured cordially, but the second polearm man went to confer with the knight carrying the dog-and-torch shield.

The newly dead man left his polearm behind when he walked off, and another fighter laid down his mace and shield, took up the weapon, and joined the conference.

''Yeah, this is no way to take the banner back,'' agreed the leader at last. ''Mike, go find some more fighters. Rafe, you go back up the trail and watch for Midrealmers. We don't want a rear-guard attack in support of these guys.'' The two polearm carriers hurried back up the trail. Dog-and-torch turned and studied the men on top of the cliff.

''Come on, we're ready,'' challenged Geoff.

''Keep your tunic on,'' said the Easterner. ''All in due time.''

Humphrey promptly sat back down and his men followed suit. After a minute, Stefan began whistling the Armour song about hot dogs in a seemingly absentminded way, and three of the Easterners retaliated by harmonizing a few bars of ''Storm the Hill and Kill the People,'' which brought chuckles from both sides.

A loud noise of armor announced the return of Mike, who brought fifteen fighters with him. ''This is all I could find right off, Sir Dom,'' he said.

''They'll do, for now,'' said Dom of the dog-and-torch. He called everyone into a huddle and gave swift instructions. A minute later they began a noisy attack near one end of the cliff, where there was room for only Humphrey and Geoff to defend. Taffy and Stefan stood helpless behind them.

Smack, *bang*, *whack*, *thump*, went the Eastern swords and polearms. *Whump*, *clang*, went Humphrey and Geoff in return. "Close in!" came the cry, and there were grunts and encouraging words from the Easterners as they literally lifted their friends on their shoulders in an attempt to take the summit.

"Hey!" shouted Stefan. "The rear!" Two Easterners had taken advantage of the loud battle to try to sneak up the cliff at the other end, using the exposed root as a foot- and handhold. One was in fact on his knees on top of the cliff, reaching for his partner balanced precariously on the root. Stefan did not give the Easterner time to rise, but rushed in swinging—and promptly lost his legs to an upward thrust from the quick-thinking Easterner. Taffy joined Stefan, and it was Taffy's sword that landed the killing blow to the Easterner's ribs. Stefan, kneeling, swung at the second Easterner, but he backed quickly out of range. The marshals called a halt to allow the man Taffy had killed and the four killed in the mass assault to retreat.

"Well done, you two!" said Humphrey to Stefan and Taffy. "Here, Lord Stefan, come back over here, in front of me."

Stefan obeyed, and as the Easterners renewed their attack he found his niche in fighting: defending a narrow position. Humphrey stood behind him, but never got in his way and even seemed at times to anticipate his moves. On one level Stefan was aware that he was going to be tired and bruised when this was over, but on another he was thoroughly enjoying himself. An Easterner ducked forward in an attempt to dodge Humphrey's lethal polearm and Stefan's sword landed perfectly on the man's helm. It was his first War kill, and Humphrey's roar of approval went deep into his soul. *This is why men fight wars,* he thought.

"Hold!" called a marshal, to give the body time to get out of the way.

"We've got to send for more reinforcements," gasped Sir Dom. "Mike, go see if you can find some more fighters when this hold is over."

"Won't do you any good, Sir Michael," called Humphrey from his position atop the cliff. "A dozen of you guys held off forty of us from right here back at Pennsic Ten, remember?"

"Is this the place?" asked Mike. "I didn't recognize it from down here!"

"Can't we come around from behind?" asked another Easterner.

"Not without machetes." Dom sighed. "Just take it slow, there's only four of them; we'll kill them one at a time." He asked a marshal, "How much longer do we get?"

"About forty minutes, I think," said the marshal. "Fighters ready? Lay on!"

. . .

Katherine stopped whistling to listen. The sounds of combat had faded completely, and the trail had become narrow and lonesome. She might have taken the wrong path back there. Ordinarily, walking down a narrow wooded lane, even in a light drizzle, would have been pleasant, but she was supposed to be bringing relief to hot and thirsty warriors.

The rope supporting the bottles of water was hurting the back of her neck, and she stooped to rest the bottles on the trail and rearrange the neck of her dress to relieve the pressure. Water dripped onto her head from overhead branches and she straightened to move along a little out of the way. It really was very quiet here, apart from a steady patter of rain onto leaves and soft earth.

Her bottles were more than half empty; maybe she should have gone out with Father Hugh for refills. She wished he hadn't taken the map with him. He didn't seem to be very handy with maps. She should have insisted on looking for herself, because she was beginning to think this wasn't the way to Twin Pines Fork.

She went onto tiptoe and looked around, trying to see over the dense underbrush that lined the trail. Maybe she should start back. No, wait, there was a place up ahead where the bushes were missing; maybe she could see more from there.

When she got to the place she saw it was a short, freshly broken passage. At the end of it lay a large barbarian in a battered red helm, his Horde cord wrapped twice around one wrist. His armor, made of thick black leather set with studs, covered only his torso and upper arms.

She went to kneel beside him. ''You can get up now,'' she said. ''Whoever killed you is gone.''

The man did not reply. His breathing was slow and noisy, and she wondered if he was asleep. She poked his shoulder with a slim, grimy forefinger. ''My lord?'' she said.

The man stirred and groaned, then coughed, a wet, ragged sound.

She frowned. ''Are you hurt?''

''Hurts,'' he agreed. ''Bastard!'' He groaned and coughed again, and she saw his eyes flickering inside his helm. ''But . . . it was a mundane,'' he said, sounding puzzled, ''. . . fight . . .'' He fell silent.

''Hey!'' she said. ''Is something wrong?'' But he did not reply. And the noisy breathing had stopped. Alarmed, she hurried back out to the trail. ''Medic!'' she called, and listened. ''Medic! Medic!'' she called again, her voice frightened. She started back toward the main trail. *''Medic!''*

A distant voice called, ''Where are you?''

''Here!''

''Where? Call again!''

''Here, over here!'' There came the welcome sound of running footsteps, and she was relieved to see a young woman come up the trail. She was wearing a white tabard with a cross in red outline, and carrying a black satchel. She hurried toward Katherine.

''What is it?'' she asked.

''A fighter's hurt, back there!'' She ran with the medic, pointing at the broken bushes, and the medic went crashing through ahead of Katherine to find the fallen fighter. She stooped to listen for breathing. ''What happened?'' she asked briskly, and began to pull off the barbarian's helm.

Katherine said, ''I found him lying there. I didn't know he was hurt at first.'' The helm came off to reveal the sweaty gray-blue face of Thorstane, and she sucked air through her teeth.

The medic groped in the man's neck for a pulse, and ordered, ''Get more help.''

She returned to the trail and called again, "Medic! Please, medic!" She hadn't meant to say please. "Medic!"

"Here I come!" called a voice, this one a man's, and a tall, dark medic came running down the trail. "There you are; I've been looking for you; I thought I heard someone calling for help. What's wrong?"

"Thorstane's hurt. There's a medic with him, but she needs help."

She followed this one back, too, and found the first medic pulling Thorstane efficiently out of his torso armor, which she had sliced apart with a box opener. "He's quit breathing, no pulse," the woman medic said. "Can you do CPR?"

"Yes." The male medic knelt and braced his hands on Thorstane's chest while the woman medic lifted the barbarian's chin and opened his mouth.

The man said, "One hundred one," and pushed hard with the heels of his hands on Thorstane's breastbone. The barbarian leapt flaccidly, and a large gout of foamy blood spewed out of his mouth.

The woman wiped the blood away with her tabard. "Go send for an ambulance!" she ordered.

"Get someone else to go!" amended the man. "You stay on the trail to show it where we are!"

"Yes, m'lord." Katherine, sickened, retreated to the trail. "Help!" she called. "Scout! Anyone! Help!" She listened, but heard no reply. She ran up the trail, calling, "Help! Help!"

She was nearly to the main trail when Lord Roc and a Mongol lady came running toward her. "What's wrong, Lady Katherine?" asked Roc.

"Thorstane's hurt, very badly. Two medics are with him. They said to find someone to call an ambulance."

"What happened to Thorstane?" asked the Mongol woman sharply.

"I don't know. I just found him on the ground a little off the trail. There's blood—" She gestured. "Please—"

The Mongol lady began to lead Roc away. "You go call," she said to him. "I'll stand at the turnoff from the main trail."

"Yes, m'lady," said Roc, and the two of them began to run down the path.

Katherine went back to stand near the place where the bushes were broken down. The two medics cursed and grunted as they worked over Thorstane, and there were other sounds, equally unpleasant. In about fifteen minutes they stopped, and the two came back to the trail, the man wiping his bloody hands on his tabard.

''A scout has gone for an ambulance,'' Katherine said. ''And a second scout is out on the main trail to show the way in.''

''No use,'' said the man. ''He's dead.''

''But . . . but he talked to me!'' said Katherine.

The woman medic said, ''He was conscious? When was this?''

''When I found him. I thought he was asleep, so I poked him and he sort of woke up.''

''What did he say?'' asked the woman, her voice sharp.

''He said it was a mundane.''

''Nonsense!'' she retorted. ''Mundanes aren't allowed on the campground during Pennsic.''

''How long after he talked to you did she come?'' asked the male medic.

''Just a minute or two,'' Katherine said. ''I came out onto the trail and called, and she answered very quickly.''

''Yes, I heard her start to call,'' confirmed the woman. ''I came straight to her, and it was only a few yards back to the man. Petty, do you know who he is?''

''Petty?'' said Katherine.

''Me,'' said the older medic, and she looked at him. Sure enough, he was Master Petrog, the King's drunken companion of last night. He said to the woman medic, ''It's Thorstane Shieldbreaker.''

''Oh, brother,'' said the woman medic.

Petrog asked Katherine, ''Did Thorstane describe this alleged mundane?''

''No. He was coughing and sort of mumbling. He said he hurt and he said 'bastard' and then that it was a mundane, a fight. What happened? Why did he die?''

''He was stabbed,'' said the woman medic, and both of them seemed to watch for her reaction.

''Oh,'' said Katherine, trying to swallow a sudden thickness in her throat.

Petrog said to the woman medic, "Go find a scout or a marshal, and tell one of the kings to stop the battle. And call the police."

"I'll go help her," said Katherine.

"No, you stay here with me. The police are going to want to talk to you, and I don't want you getting lost."

She stared at him. He didn't seem to recall the chilled and grateful person she'd comforted with hot wine last night. *Oh, help,* she thought. *Where's Peter?*

11

"HOLD!" shouted a marshal. "Someone dead up there?"

"Me," admitted Humphrey ruefully and his men groaned. He and Stefan had become the backbone of their defense position. But Humphrey was tired and slowing down; a fresh spearman had caught him in the ribs from below. He handed his polearm to Taffy and started to say something, then thought better of it. Dead men were supposed to be dead; they were not permitted to say or do anything to the living until they had been resurrected. The Easterners helped him—and offered a few friendly buffets to relieve their frustration—as he slid down the steep face of the slope. At the bottom he took his helm off with a sigh of relief, and at that instant there was a *bam!* from the little cannon out at Resurrection Point.

"Hey!" objected an Easterner. "You said forty minutes left not ten minutes ago!"

"Yeah, and I don't think I could've been that far off," said the marshal. He lifted a corner of his tabard, dug in a leather pouch for his watch and consulted it. "No, there should be twenty-three minutes to go." In the silence there was clearly heard the rise and fall of a siren. "Maybe someone got hurt," he said.

''So? People getting hurt don't stop a whole battle,'' said another Easterner.

A scout came careening along the trail and skidded to a halt in front of them. ''Battle's over. Everyone's to go to Resurrection Point,'' he gasped.

''Why?'' asked half the fighters in unison.

''Thorstane's been killed.''

''Well, good for him,'' said Taffy. ''So what?''

''No, really. They called an ambulance, but he's dead, for real. That's why the cannon just went off. We're stopping the battle, and the police are on their way.''

There was a shocked silence, into which a distant cry could be heard: ''Oy-yea, oy-yea, oy-yea! The battle has been called off! Fighters are to gather at Resurrection Point! Come out to the entrance at once!''

''Have any of you seen King William?'' asked the scout. ''We can't find him.''

Everyone shook his head, and the scout went running off down the trail.

An Easterner pulled off his helm, revealing a pale, sweaty face. He said in a shocked voice, ''Oh, Christ, we're in for it now.''

''Maybe he's not dead,'' said Geoff. ''Assaulted, maybe. You know how rumors swell all out of proportion sometimes.''

''Whatever, let's get out to Resurrection Point,'' said Humphrey.

Those who had not done so pulled off their helms and furtively studied one another's faces. The tall Easterner who had killed Humphrey was shown to be a woman. ''Come on, we'll help you down,'' she said, dropping her sword and coming closer to the face of the slope. Taffy and Stefan came down with her assistance. Geoff handed the banner to the lady Easterner, then accepted her arm to help him down. She chivalrously handed the banner back to him, and he rolled it up and carried it along as they began walking in silence toward the entrance.

• • •

Two uniformed paramedics and the ambulance driver stood on the trail near the broken bushes. Thorstane's death had been confirmed, but since it was a possible homicide, his body was not covered with the customary blanket. Someone had suggested they retreat to the trail to avoid disturbing the site further.

"You guys making a movie or something?" one of the paramedics asked.

"No," said Katherine.

"Think of it as a kind of costume party," Petrog said.

Katherine felt herself beginning to shiver. "I—I really would very much like to see my husband," she said. "He was in the woods, and when he can't find me, he'll wonder where I am."

"Who is he?" asked Petrog.

"Lord Stefan von Helle," she said.

Petrog seemed to take a step farther away from her, even though he didn't move. "You're Lady Katherine?" He hadn't recognized her, then.

"Yes."

"Didn't you and Lord Stefan have a run-in with Thorstane yesterday in the Horde encampment?"

She glanced at him. "Yes."

"And it was Stefan who hit him with a polearm to make him let go of you."

"Yes." The paramedics were giving her some hard looks. She said, "I didn't even know it was him until the other medic took off his helm."

"You sure? You should have seen him in armor earlier; he was at the entrance before the battle."

"I wasn't paying attention. I didn't even see Peter—Lord Stefan. I was sharing a map with Father Hugh, and we were trying to decide whether to follow the King's fighters or go look for Easterners. Please, couldn't we send for my husband?"

"No, everyone else is out at the Point. And we're staying right here until the police arrive."

• • •

Archer's Field was slowly filling with noncombatants, who were forbidden to cross the bridge by gruffly noncommunicative Mongols.

Kings William and Oswin shouted instructions to a peace demonstrator standing near the bridge, who nodded and ran off.

Rumor after rumor was sifted. An Eastern fighter was dead. King

William was injured. A fighter had been killed or injured, accidentally or deliberately, by food poisoning, by a copperhead, with a knife or gun. Wulfstan had made a citizen's arrest of everyone who had been in the Woods Battle, that's why the Horde was guarding the Point. No, Thorstane had assaulted King William, and they were holding him for the police. No, four Midrealm fighters had ambushed Thorstane and beaten him to death. No, four Hordesmen had really gone berserk and severely injured eight or nine Easterners, one of whom was dead or dying. No, Thorstane had raped and beaten a water bearer. The people drifted slowly toward the brook and stared at those trapped on the other side.

. . .

Resurrection Point was full of puzzled, angry, and frightened fighters. The wooden bridge across the brook and the way to the campground entrance were being guarded by stolid Hordesmen who were letting no one cross in either direction. Archers' Field, dotted with tents and pavilions, was filling with people.

Stefan saw Their Majesties William and Oswin conferring near the bridge. Sir Ignatius was with them, and Prince Thomas, and the plump lady marshal who had been in charge of Resurrection Point. They were soaked with rain and perspiration, and looking very grim.

Stefan turned and searched the crowd at the Point with his eyes. There was a lot of talk and even some laughter, quickly stifled. A little group of water bearers stood nearby, headed by Father Hugh, who was explaining something, gesturing nervously. A map of the campsite was in his hand. Stefan frowned. Where was Katherine?

"Look," said Geoff; "I think the kings are going to tell us what's happened."

Geoff and Stefan joined Humphrey and Taffy, and they watched the kings nod sharply and face the fighters. "Oy-yea!" called Ignatius, but without his usual volume. The cry was taken up by others and passed to the back of the crowd. A passable silence followed.

"Thorstane Shieldbreaker is dead!" announced William, and there was a stir among the fighters who had not heard or had not believed. There was an uproar from those on the other side of the bridge, and after a moment the cry for silence was passed again so William could continue. "He was murdered, stabbed!" There was another outburst, this time on both sides of the brook, and the oy-yea had to be shouted angrily to restore order. Some people in Archer's Field began at once to leave. William continued in his big voice, "Apparently a mundane did it! I want to know, did any of you see a mundane in the woods during the battle?"

There was a general shaking of heads and a murmured assortment of no's. William waited until they all died away.

"The people at the Point say they saw no one enter or leave the woods beyond the Point during the battle. That means whoever did it is either here or still in the woods. No one—repeat: no one—is going to leave Resurrection Point until the police arrive! Oswin and I have sent some people to the gate to see that no one leaves from there, either."

There was resentful murmuring at this and Oswin spoke up. "Settle down; this is serious! I want to see the earl marshals, mine and William's, and anyone who has some direct knowledge of this incident." He leaned abruptly sideways and William bent toward him, and there was a murmured exchange. William nodded, and Oswin turned toward Archers' Field and called, "Is Mistress Radegund over there? Summon the autocrat!"

Word was passed, and after a minute there was a stir near the front of the crowd. A tall, slender woman in pale pink broke free and started across the bridge. She was stopped from completing passage by the Hordesmen.

"Let her through," ordered William.

"The Khan told us to block the bridge," said one of them sullenly. "Nobody passes unless he says so."

"Goddammit, I'm ordering you to let her pass!" The men did not reply, but stood firm. "Jesus H. Christ!" said William. He turned angrily and looked out over the crowd on his side. "Will the Khan attend His Majesty!"

Wulfstan raised his hand from near the middle of the fighters. "I'll be right there!" he called. It took him some little while to work his way up. He did not apologize for the behavior of his men, but quietly told them to allow the autocrat to cross. They opened a narrow passage for her and immediately closed it again after she had slipped through.

Stefan pushed forward a little in order to hear what was being decided.

"We're in a hell of a mess," muttered William.

"Yes, Your Majesty," Radegund said.

"That's why we called for you. You're the legal representative of the Society on the campsite; you're the one the cops will talk to first. Here's what we know. A water bearer found Thorstane, still alive, and called two medics. They sent for an ambulance, but Thorstane was too far gone and they couldn't resuscitate him. One of the medics is up by the gate waiting for the police. She'll bring them down here. No one's left the woods or the Point since the beginning of the Woods Battle. So whoever did it is still here."

She frowned. "Didn't you say a mundane did it? I don't see any mundane standing around."

"He's probably hiding in the woods."

"No, don't be stupid," said Oswin. "By now he's gone over the fence."

"We don't know that for sure," said William.

"Who's in the woods with the body?" asked Oswin.

"I'm not sure," said William. "No SCA-folk, I think."

"Master Petrog is still in there," said Roc, stepping forward, Lady Freyis close behind him. "Your Majesty, we're the scouts who were sent to call the ambulance. The ambulance is still back there, with Master Petrog. And Lady Katherine is there, too. She's the water bearer who found him."

"Jesus!" muttered Stefan. He immediately turned and started working his way back into the crowd.

Geoff grabbed his arm. "What's wrong?"

"Katherine. She's the one who found him. She's in there, probably scared half to death. I'm going to her."

"No, you're not," Geoff said. "For one thing, the Horde won't let you. When the police arrive, identify yourself, tell them you're a police officer, and offer your assistance. They'll probably take you back with them."

Stefan considered this and shook his head. "No, they won't. I'm a suspect—we're all suspects."

12

HARVEY Harrison was a big man with a square, battered face and enormous hands. He was too tall to wear his ranger hat in the patrol car, but kept it on the seat beside him. His light-gray shirt looked about to split at the shoulders, although it fit perfectly elsewhere.

His wipers were set on intermittent, which kept the drizzle off his windshield with only an occasional squeak. The rain was patchy, which made driving dangerous. He'd been to two fender-benders and one serious pileup so far this morning.

"Butler, twenty-seven," said Dispatch in a cool female voice.

Damn, another one. He reached for his microphone and said, "Twenty-seven, Butler" into it.

"Ten-twenty?"

He glanced at the mile marker just going by. "Two miles east of Slippery Rock, on the turnpike," he said.

"Give me a ten-twenty-one."

"Ten-four," he said. They wanted him to call in.

A few minutes later he was on the phone. "This is twenty-seven, Trooper Harrison. What's up?"

"A body, possible homicide, at Miller's Pond Campground. See the owners, they'll be at the gate, and secure the scene. An ambulance has been dispatched."

"Yes, ma'm," he said and hung up, surprised. The Millers ran a nice, quiet campground. The only time he'd been out there all year was in July, on a report of kids throwing firecrackers. He got back in his car, checked his watch. Twelve-fourteen. He wrote a swift note on his clipboard. Then he started his engine, hit the flipper switches for his lights and siren, and pushed his large foot down hard on the gas pedal.

. . .

Mr. and Mrs. Miller walked restlessly, arm in arm, up and down in front of the gate to Miller's Pond. They were both a little below average height, deeply tanned, with salt-and-pepper hair cropped equally short—one of those couples who had come to look alike over the years. Both were in jeans and the short blue tunics that were the uniform of Miller's Pond employees during Pennsic.

The gate was closed but not locked. Three knights wearing the tiger of the Eastern Kingdom on their damp red tabards stood in front of it a little self-consciously. A few yards away two knights wearing white tabards with the red stripe and dragon of the Midrealm stood shoulder to shoulder. The knights rested the points of their real swords on the gravel between their feet and spoke to no one, not even each other. The rain had faded to a thin mizzle.

The young woman tugged at her white medic's tabard nervously. In her mind's eye she saw Thorstane's blue face, the foamy blood on his lips that meant a trauma to the lung. She remembered how blood had boiled out of the two little chest wounds, staining her tunic and warming her knee, a memory to shy away from. She remembered instead the pale, frightened face of the water bearer who had found him.

Those wounds—this wasn't an accident, someone had deliberately stabbed Thorstane, murdered him. Who? And where had the weapon come from? The fighters were asked before every fight or battle, "Bear ye any steel which may be used in an offensive manner?" To which the answer was supposed to be, "Nay, my lord." There were a lot of real knives and swords to be found at any SCA event, but one did not go onto a SCA battlefield carrying one. She looked again with her mind's eye at the young woman's shocked, frightened face. She could imagine herself striking in self-defense, then reacting in just that shocked and frightened way. But where had the weapon come from? Had Lady Katherine brought it with her into the woods? That would make it premeditated. No, it was probably what she said, a creepy mundane. But how did a mundane—?

The medic's head came up. The Millers had stopped pacing to listen, too. Yes, definitely a siren.

A minute later a white patrol car with a blue hood and the Pennsylvania keystone on its door pulled up to the gate. One of the Eastern knights pulled the gate open and the car, siren off but lights still flashing, drove into the campground. It stopped, motor running, and a very large man got out, putting on a Smokey Bear hat. He looked back a long five seconds at the knights.

Then he looked at Mr. and Mrs. Miller, nodding briefly in recognition. "What's the story here?" he asked.

The medic said, "There's a man dead in the woods. He appears to have been stabbed."

The trooper looked her up and down, taking in the long, dark-green tunic and stained white tabard over it. "Who are you?"

"I'm Fabiola the—" The young woman stopped and said, "Sorry. I'm one of the medics who tried to help the victim."

The trooper frowned at her, then jerked his head at the knights, who were again standing in front of the closed gate.

"Who're they?" he asked.

"Hobbyists," said Mrs. Miller, and the trooper looked at her. "It's a gathering of hobbyists who like to pretend it's still the Middle Ages," she went on. "There are about fifty-three hundred of them here. They've reserved the whole campground for the weekend."

"Is it a 'hobbyist' who got killed?" asked the trooper.

"Yes."

The trooper looked at Fabiola. "You a real medic?"

"Yes, back home I work with an advanced life-support ambulance."

"Where's the body?"

"In the woods. I can show you where."

The trooper said, his distaste apparent, "Get in." He got back in his car, and Fabiola hunched herself into the passenger seat, trying not to touch anything. The front-seat area was crowded with several clipboards, and exotic additions cluttered the instrument panel. A transceiver overfilled the space meant for an ordinary radio.

"Well, which way?" snapped the trooper.

"What? Oh. Follow the road around to the left."

The car started up with a little spurt of gravel and followed the road past the mill, along a row of trees, to pass on the other side of it a field scattered with tents and full of people in long damp medieval costumes.

"Jesus Christ," muttered the trooper, as much in exasperation as surprise. He drove along the road, which bordered the river, at a rate Fabiola privately thought too fast, then slowed abruptly as they approached a row of men whose fur garb showed around and under their leather armor.

One of them ordered the others to move aside, bellowing in a rough voice, "Oy-yea! Clear a path for the squad! Clear a path!" Beyond the furry ones, men and women in armor of every description, rusty and shining, rough and finished, haphazard and beautiful, began to get off the road.

"Who the hell's Oy-yea?" asked the trooper as he began to move forward, sounding as annoyed as he looked.

"No one. It's a call to pay attention. You know, like in a courtroom, when the bailiff or whoever it is calls "Oyez" to begin proceedings. We just pronounce it differently."

"Yeah." The trooper did not seem very interested in this fact.

As they came to the far side of the crowd, their way was again blocked by a line of furry barbarians.

The trooper rolled down his window and called angrily, "You want to get out of my way?" The line broke unhurriedly and the trooper accelerated into the woods. "Which way now?" he asked.

"Straight on, look for a pile of rocks, then take the second turning to the right." Fabiola remembered the trooper's expression as they drove through the line of Hordesmen and said, "It's just sort of a game. We're not crazy or anything."

"Uh-huh. This the turnoff?" Lady Freyis was standing on the main trail, pointing down the turning.

"Yes. Then take the first left."

When they turned left, the white-and-orange back of an ambulance could be seen. Three men in dark blue uniforms stood beside it, with Master Petrog and the water bearer, her plastic bottles still hanging against her long brown skirt.

The trooper stopped close behind the ambulance, shut off his engine, but again left his lights flashing. He and Fabiola got out.

"Where's the body?" called the trooper.

Master Petrog pointed to a place where the underbrush had been broken down. "In there," he said, and turned as if to lead the way.

"Hold it," said the trooper. "Let me go alone, okay?"

"Of course," said Petrog, stopping and turning back.

• • •

Harrison stood awhile and studied the scene before him. The body, that of a tall man with tangled black hair, strong-looking despite some flab, lay sprawled on its back near a tree. A chipped and battered red metal helmet had been tossed to one side, and a heavy sleeveless black leather shirt or topper set with metal studs was near it. Dry and drying blood was on the man's face and in his beard.

A number of baby trees and bushes had been flattened and trampled around the man, which might have meant a fight, but more likely was the result of the medics' efforts. Harrison approached very carefully, trying hard not to disturb the scene further. He squatted and shoved three massive fingers hard into the carotid of the man's neck. No pulse, which didn't surprise him. There was already the waxy pallor of death on the man's skin, and a stink that meant the bowels had relaxed. He looked closer. The corneas of the open eyes were just starting to cloud, which meant death had occurred more than half an hour ago, but not so long as an hour. He checked his watch. Twelve fifty-nine.

He stood slowly and looked around the immediate area. There was debris from a serious first-aid kit—little plastic covers that fit over hypodermic needles, and a tiny glass bottle labeled "adrenaline.'' He bent over the bottle, but did not touch it. He turned again to look at the body. There were two small trickles of dried blood halfway down the rib cage. Little stab wounds—*no sword did this,* he thought.

He looked around a little more, then went back out to the trail. The murmur of voices stopped as he approached the people waiting for him. He nodded at them, then went to his squad and called in, confirming the report that had been relayed to him by phone, knowing this would cause the crime van and coroner to be sent. He added, ''There's a large crowd of people present at the campground, all dressed up like it's a costume party.'' No need to let everyone walk in cold on these weirdos as he had.

He got back out of the car and took out his notebook and pen again. ''O-kay,'' he said. ''Which one of you found him?''

''I did,'' said the girl. She was young and pretty, and looked at him with frightened gray eyes.

''Who are you?'' he asked.

''Katherine Price Brichter. Mrs. Peter.''

He wrote that down. ''Was he dead when you found him?''

''No. He said he was hurt, and I went to call a medic.''

''That was you,'' he said, looking at Fabiola.

''Yes, sir, and I said to get some more help and that was Master Petrog.'' She added hastily, ''I don't know his mundane name, sorry.''

''I'm Dr. Devon Padstow,'' said Petrog. ''The injured man was, to all effects and purposes, dead when I got to him. No breathing, no pulse. I directed this young woman to have an ambulance summoned, but it was too late.

''You a for-real doctor or a dress-up one?''

''I'm a surgeon at Cleveland's Uptown General.''

''I see. Can you tell me what's going on here? Why the getups?''

''We're members of the Society for Creative Anachronism. This is our biggest annual event, the Pennsic War. It could perhaps be defined as a national convention.''

Harrison misspelled ''Anachronism'' and asked, ''You got people here from all over the country?''

"Yes, even some from other countries."

Fabiola volunteered, "We've got over five hundred Canadians in camp, and four people from Australia. I was helping troll."

"Troll?"

"Directing newcomers at the gate. There were fifty-two hundred seventy-four here as of nine o'clock this morning."

"What's your real name?" asked Harrison.

"Clare Porto."

"Clare, I want you to go back up to the gate and direct a van which will be arriving in a little while back down here. It's white and it'll say 'State Police' on it. And the coroner will be coming as well."

"Yes, sir. And I'll tell Lady Freyis, the lady who was standing on the main trail, to stay there and show them where to turn."

"Thank you. Now," said Harrison. "Katherine?"

"Yes?"

"You want to tell me about how you happened to find him?"

"I was coming along the trail—"

"Which way?"

"From that way." She pointed toward the way out. "I was looking for some fighters who needed a drink of water."

"Fighters?"

"Yes. There were about eight hundred of them in here a little while ago."

"What were they fighting about?"

"Possession of a banner. It's a war game, medieval-style."

"I see." For the first time, Harrison looked as if he understood an explanation of the purpose for this gathering of outlandish people. "Those are the people I saw just outside the woods, right? Wearing armor."

"Yes."

"So what happened? Did you hear him call for help?"

"No. I took a wrong turning somewhere and got lost. I had about decided to turn back when I looked through where some bushes were broken down and saw him lying under a tree."

"Was he unconscious?" Harrison was taking swift notes.

"I—I'm not sure. I thought he was asleep. The fighting was so far away that it was quiet, and I could hear him breathing. But when I spoke to him, he didn't answer, so I poked him, and he roused."

"What did he say?"

"He said he hurt and—" She glanced at Petrog and stopped.

"What else?"

She replied with an odd air of defiance, "He said it was a fight with a mundane."

"Mundane? What does that mean?"

"A mundane is someone not in the Society," explained Petrog.

Harrison frowned. "Did he say any name?"

"No."

"I think," said Petrog, "I ought to tell you that only Society members are permitted on the campgrounds during the War. No 'mundanes' allowed."

Harrison thought that over. "How would he know a mundane from one of the rest of you?"

Petrog said, "It's against the rules to take part in an event out of costume. People arrive in street clothes, but are supposed to change as quickly as possible. There wouldn't be anyone in the woods in mundane clothes."

"I see," said Harrison. "Do either of you know of anyone with a grudge against the deceased?"

The young woman looked down. Petrog drew himself up with a sigh and said in an unhappy tone, "I . . . If someone had told me someone was going to be murdered at the War, I'd have picked Thorstane as the most likely victim."

"That so?"

"Yes, most of us have had run-ins with him. Including myself—and including Katherine here; her as recently as yesterday."

She glanced at him but said nothing.

He went on, "Thorstane grabbed her, and her husband had to hit him with a club to make him let go."

"That right?"

She frowned at Petrog. "My husband knocked Thorstane off his feet with a polearm. It was more funny than serious. I wasn't frightened. Thorstane was just being drunk and stupid."

"I see." Harrison wrote that down while she watched, still frowning. He asked the doctor, "You said he was beyond help when you got to him?"

"Yes. He didn't respond at all to CPR, even when I injected adrenaline."

He looked at Katherine. "How long was it between the time you found him and the time you called for help?"

She thought. "Just a minute or two, I think. He wasn't talking very clearly. As soon as I saw he was really hurt, I came out on the trail and called for a medic. Lady Fabiola—Ms. Porto—answered almost immediately. I told her someone was hurt and she went to see. She told me to get more help, I went back and called again, and Master Petrog also came very quickly. They told me to send for an ambulance and I found two scouts and sent them."

"Why didn't you go yourself?"

"Master Petrog said I should stay on the trail to mark the place."

He asked Petrog, "How long after she called for help did you arrive?"

"Not more than a minute; I had heard her call before, and was trying to locate the trouble spot when she called again."

He asked Katherine, "Then what happened?"

"It was sometime later, I'm not sure how long—probably not more than fifteen minutes—and they came out and said he was dead and that the police should be called."

"That was before the ambulance came?"

"Yes."

Harrison asked Petrog, "You say he never regained consciousness? Is it possible he didn't know what he was saying when he talked to Katherine here?"

"Well—I don't know. I'm afraid it isn't likely that he'd be able to say anything at all so shortly before he went completely beyond any recall. It would be more likely that he was dead some time before she found him."

Harrison wrote that down. It was his experience that since the discovery of CPR, anyone down for even as long as ten minutes could be resuscitated, at least for a while. He asked the paramedics, "Did you try, too?"

''Yeah, but nothing,'' said the taller one with a shrug. ''Flat line, not a wiggle.'' That meant they had hooked up a machine that recorded heartbeat.

Harrison said to Katherine, ''But you say he talked to you.''

''Yes.''

''Did he say your name or otherwise show he knew who you were?''

''No. I saw his eyes open inside his helm, but I don't know if he recognized me. He—he was groggy. I asked him if he was hurt, and he said 'hurts' as if he were agreeing with me—but he didn't say 'I hurt,' or 'I am hurt.' He just mumbled, 'Hurts.' Then he said 'But it was a mundane,' as if he were puzzled by that. He said 'Fight' and then he fainted, so I ran out to the trail to call a medic.''

''He fainted—or died?''

She shrugged and looked away. ''I don't know; I've never seen anyone die before.''

Harrison said to the doctor, ''But he was dead when you got to him.''

''He wasn't breathing and there was no pulse. If we had resuscitated him—'' He sighed. ''But we couldn't, so I suppose I would have to say he was dead when I found him.'' He hesitated. ''There was something funny about the way he didn't respond to CPR.''

Harrison said, ''How's that?''

''We never got a pulse. Have you ever done CPR?''

''No.''

''Well, when you press down on the chest, you squeeze the heart. This forces the blood out, and you feel its movement as a pulse. Even a damaged heart will pump blood, if not so efficiently as an undamaged one. But that wasn't happening here at all. There was one big initial surge, then nothing after that.'' He glanced at Katherine.

''Do you have any explanation for it?''

Petrog shrugged. ''For some reason the heart couldn't be made to pump blood. A large blood loss might account for it. Or if the heart was severely lacerated. But in that case he would not have acted the way this young woman says; he would have been beyond speech. I'm afraid I question her story.''

13

THE fighters, medics, marshals, scouts, and water bearers at Resurrection Point sat or squatted or sprawled on the ground and murmured brief remarks between long silences.

Stefan and Geoffrey had taken up stations by the side of the trail coming out of the woods. One of the Hordesmen guarding the trail signaled, and the double line they had formed blocking the trail broke ranks. The ambulance came out first, without lights or siren, closely followed by the coroner's black station wagon. Then a State Police car came out, Master Petrog riding in back, Lady Katherine in front, beside the big trooper. Stefan glanced back down the trail before the Hordesmen closed it again, but the mobile crime-lab van was apparently staying at the scene.

The trooper's car stopped, and Katherine got out. She looked around for Stefan and took his hand gratefully when he stepped up to her.

"Are you all right?" he asked.

"Yes." But she was pale and her hand was icy.

The trooper bent to signal Petrog to sit tight, then came around to stand possessively beside Katherine. "Who's in charge of this shindig?" he called.

''She is,'' said several people, pointing, and Mistress Radegund came forward, with Kings William and Oswin in close attendance.

The trooper fished for his notebook. ''What's your name?'' he asked.

''Faith Klotar. In the Society I am Mistress Radegund d'Portiers, and I am autocrat of this event.''

''What's that mean?''

''It means I organized it, and I am the legal representative of the Society here during the event.''

''Okay, Faith, how do you spell your last name?''

''K-L-O-T-A-R.''

''What's your address?''

''Five-fifty France Street, St. Croix Falls, Wisconsin.''

''Kind of a long way from home, aren't you? I mean, to be running this thing.''

She smiled. ''I suppose so.''

William stepped around Radegund to say, ''You plan on keeping us here long?''

The trooper raked him up and down, taking in his heavy brass crown, the battered armor, the dirty white tabard with its red stripe and dragon. ''Who are you?'' he asked.

William leaned forward a little and said firmly, ''I'm His Royal Majesty William Rufus, by right of arms King of the Middle. Who the hell are you?''

The trooper's face reddened, but he said calmly, ''My name is Trooper Harrison. What's your real name?''

''Mundanely, I'm Rusty Anderson. And how about an answer to my question? How long do you intend to keep us bottled up here?''

The trooper said courteously, ''We're conducting an investigation into a possible homicide, and we'd appreciate your cooperation for just a little while longer, if you don't mind.''

''No sweat,'' said William, mollified. ''How about King Oswin and I start sorting out things here at Resurrection Point? We can get everyone's name and address, and maybe a statement about where he or she was during the battle, and turn the information over to you when you're ready for it. You troopers organize a search of the woods. It appears it was a mundane, and we're pretty damn sure he's still in there.''

''How about you go sit down somewhere, Rusty, and let me talk to Faith, here?'' said the trooper.

''Now look—'' started William.

''You look. I don't know where the hell you got that king stuff, or what authority you think it gives you, but it appears this lady is the one in charge of your group. I'd appreciate it if you'd keep out of the way.''

William swelled visibly. Oswin said mildly, ''Take it easy, Will.''

''Shut up, Ozzy!'' snapped William.

Stefan took two sideways steps, bringing Katherine with him out of the line of fire.

''Your Majesty, if you'll just let me explain to this man—'' began Radegund placatingly.

''Goddammit, I'm the King around here!'' said William.

''No, you're not,'' said Oswin. ''I am. You're in Eastern territory now, remember?''

The trooper made an exasperated noise. ''Shut up, all of you! This is Pennsylvania in the United States of America! We don't have any kings in Pennsylvania, and I don't want to hear any more crud from anyone about who is or is not king, got that? We're dealing with a possible murder, and as a law-enforcement officer, I'm helping conduct the investigation. Until that investigation is over, we're the ones giving orders, do you understand?''

William said, ''They issue that attitude with the badge? I don't take orders from people like you; I never have.''

The trooper turned over a page in his notebook. ''What did you say your real name was?'' he asked.

''I said,'' William replied with exaggerated and angry patience, ''that the murderer is loose in the woods, and that maybe you guys should be in there looking for him.''

''Anderson, I think it was,'' said the trooper, writing.

William backhanded the notebook out of the trooper's hand, and the trooper grabbed William's arm. William instantly swung with his other fist, narrowly missing the trooper's face—and found himself pushed up against the squad car, arm twisted far up his back and his neck in a strong grip. "You," said the trooper, as William's crown went rolling across the top of the car to fall off the other side, "are under arrest."

. . .

William's anger had cooled only a little by the time they reached the Millers' house. The trooper opened the back door, lifted him out by his manacled arms, and pulled him roughly aside so Master Petrog could get out. Petrog was looking very smooth and subdued, and would not look at William. Lady Katherine got out of the front and stood, small and frightened, on the other side of the car.

"We've set up a post inside the house," said the trooper to Petrog. "Follow me; we're going in there to talk."

"Fine," said Petrog. He shut the back door of the car and went around to Katherine, his manner more that of helping the trooper keep her in custody than of reassuring her.

The trooper looked over toward the gate, where a small group of people were staring at them, their faces shocked at the sight of William in handcuffs. "You!" the trooper called. "Clare! You come on in the house!"

"All right!" said the woman with a medic's tabard, waving.

The trooper hustled William up the walk, keeping him off-balance with a series of subtle, expert tugs. Petrog followed, holding Katherine by the arm, and the other medic ran to catch up before they climbed the steps to the porch and went inside.

They went into the dining room of the house and, with a last calculated shove, William was dropped onto a hard wooden chair beside a massive old wooden table. A second trooper was standing there, a walkie-talkie in one hand. He was smaller than the other one, trim, dark, and bald. The troopers conferred briefly, then the big one led Petrog and Katherine away into the front room. The bald trooper came to sit at the table and pull out a battered brown notebook.

"Rusty, I'm Trooper Bead, and I'd like to ask you some questions."

"Take these goddamn handcuffs off me!" said William. They had been put on very tightly, and his fingers were numb.

"If I do, will you behave like a civilized person?"

William glared at him and did not answer. Bead leaned back in his chair and made a ceremony of pulling out a pack of cigarettes, removing one, tapping it on a thumbnail, sticking it in a corner of his mouth, lighting it with a butane lighter, and blowing the smoke out in a long, thin plume. He studied the way the silver ash began to eat its way down the white paper tube of tobacco. William recognized the ploy and, with a show of indifference to it, looked around the room.

It was an ordinary farmhouse dining room. Wooden chairs that matched the ones on which he and Bead were sitting lined one wall. A double window was decorated with white ruffled sheers. The wallpaper was a pattern of ivy-covered trellises, and there was a framed portrait of Jesus as a young man. The War fell away like a dream, taking with it William's royal rage, and he was abruptly aware of his wet and dirty appearance.

The house smelled of fresh coffee. Lunch-making noises were coming from the kitchen. William's nose twitched; it had been a long time since breakfast.

The trooper put his cigarette down on an ashtray and took a ballpoint pen out of his shirt pocket. He clicked the point out and began to write something in the notebook, interrupting himself once to take a drag on the cigarette.

William watched him awhile, then sighed. The man was obviously prepared to wait as long as necessary. "Am I under arrest?" he asked.

"Yes, for assaulting a peace officer." Trooper Bead did not look up from his writing.

"I missed when I swung at him, you know."

"If you'd connected, the charge would be assault and battery."

"You gonna unfasten me?"

Bead looked up and smiled. "Are you kidding? Big as you are? You'd walk over me on your way out the door."

"Hell, I'm not going anywhere."

Bead put down his pen. "Promise?"

William nodded. "Promise."

Bead grinned. "Okay, then." He rose and fished in his pocket for the key to the handcuffs. William twisted sideways to help him reach his hands.

"A mundane killed Thorstane," said William a minute later, rubbing his wrists.

"I want to talk to you about what happened. You do not, of course, have to answer my questions. You have a right to remain silent, and a right to consult with an attorney before answering any questions. If you want an attorney but can't afford one, we'll get one for you. Do you understand, Rusty?"

"Yeah. But if you're gonna call me Rusty, I figure I should get to call you Mike or Joe or whatever your front name is."

"Vince. But I'll make a deal with you about that."

"What kind of deal?"

"I'll call you mister if you'll call me sir."

William hesitated, then nodded. "Deal."

"Good man. Are you willing to answer my questions now, Mr. Anderson?"

William grinned. "Yes, sir."

The point of the pen snapped out again. "What's your address?"

"Route two, Dedalia, Ohio."

"How old are you?"

"Thirty-nine."

"Occupation?"

"Blacksmith."

"What's a mundane?"

"Someone who isn't in the Society for Creative Anachronism."

"Is that as in anarchy?"

"No, it's as in something the wrong place in time—like us in the twentieth century."

"Why do you say a mundane committed the murder?"

"I don't. Thorstane did."

"He's the deceased?"

"Yes. He told Lady Katherine, who found him just before he died."

"How do you know that?"

"Sir Ignatius of Antioch told me. He's my Dragon Herald. He got it from my Earl Marshal."

"What's his real name?"

"Iggy? Francis Pray."

"And this Earl person?"

"Sir Jerome the Strident, my Earl Marshal, the man in charge of fighters and fighting. Real name, Leo Cardinale. He heard about it from a herald, who got it from a medic, who got it from the lady herself. I don't know her real name."

"Harold who?"

"A herald is a man who makes announcements. Heralds went around calling off the battle."

"What's the deceased's real name?"

William thought. "Randy something. Unwin. Randolf Unwin. He was from Cleveland."

"He have any relatives or friends with him here?"

"Not that I know of. He didn't have many friends."

"I take it he wasn't one of the shining lights of your organization?"

"Of any organization. He was a real bastard, both in and out of the Society."

"Care to be more specific?"

"At home he was a drunk, couldn't keep a job. At SCA events, he looked like a caveman and was rude to everyone. It's been said the Society has only two rules: At events you dress medievally and behave chivalrously. He should have been thrown out a long time ago."

"Why wasn't he?"

William sighed and shifted his weight on the chair. "We're pretty tolerant. On the other hand, I will say I'd been encouraged to think about a Court of Chivalry, which is roughly our equivalent of a court-martial."

"Do you think someone took unilateral action to get rid of him?"

"No, that's not like us."

Bead began to dab his cigarette out in a saucer provided for the purpose. "Come on, now; you've got hundreds of people running around the campground carrying weapons, and a lot of them aren't the wooden variety. Isn't this event you're holding called a war?"

William brushed his nose with a dirty forefinger. "Yeah, but the idea of SCA combat is to show how well you can behave under stress. You overcome your opponent with skill, not strength. I've seen many tournaments in which a fighter will lay down his shield if his opponent loses his, just to keep the fight even. New members look at our fighting like it's a sport, and that's one of the first ideas they have to lose.'' He sighed. ''Some never do, of course.''

''Could one of those who haven't caught on yet done this?''

William shook his head. ''No, I think it's a thousand times more likely some mushroom-head climbed over the fence, hid in the woods, and stabbed the first person who happened by. It's just a coincidence that it happened to be Thorstane.''

• • •

The small Miller living room had an elderly couch and two mismatched chairs. Trooper Harrison took the green recliner because it had a flat arm on which he could rest his notebook. He directed a younger trooper to take the medic and ''Lady Katherine'' upstairs and put them in separate bedrooms. Then he told ''Master Petrog'' to sit on the sagging brown couch.

The surgeon described again hearing ''Lady Katherine's'' call for help, his response, his request for assistance, their inability to resuscitate the victim.

''You said before there was something odd about his lack of response to CPR,'' said Harrison.

''Yes, though both of us tried, we never got a pulse.''

''What does that mean to you?'' asked Harrison.

''Maybe the heart was severely lacerated.'' Petrog said this doubtfully, smoothing his dark hair with a strong, thin hand. He added, ''But if that were the case, he would not have been conscious long enough to say anything to anyone.''

''But Mrs. Brichter says he talked to her.''

''Yes,'' he said.

''Tell me again about this encounter yesterday between her and the victim.''

• • •

Clare Porto, aka the medic Fabiola, seemed more inclined to believe the woman's story.

''Maybe it was cardiac tamponade,'' she suggested.

''What's that?'' asked Harrison.

"If you nick the heart, it keeps on pumping, but there's leakage into the pericardium—the sac around the heart—and when the sac is full, the heart can't move, can't expand, so it quits."

"Does that happen often?" asked Harrison.

"I saw one last year," Fabiola said. "The person was conscious when we got to him, but his heart quit before we got him to the hospital. CPR couldn't save him."

"What about her saying it was an outsider, a 'mundane'? Could one have sneaked in without you knowing it?"

"Over the fence, maybe," said Fabiola. "And out the same way. Someone dusted."

"What do you know about 'dusted'?"

"I told you, I'm a paramedic. Angel dust can be found in Minneapolis, too, you know. They get really nutso aggressive, right out of their trees."

"So you think she might be telling the truth."

"Why don't you let the autopsy call it? I don't know the situation in outstate Pennsylvania, but back home in Minneapolis you could get the results fast."

Mildly stung, Harrison said, "Autopsies are automatic in homicide cases. We get the results within twenty-four hours. We've got a real-live coroner, and I think there's even a hospital in the area."

"I'm sorry, I didn't mean—" said Fabiola.

• • •

Harrison asked Katherine, "Did you see or hear anyone running away as you came up that trail?"

"No."

"You sure? It seems to me a man with a hole in his heart wouldn't last very long. You must have found him right after it happened."

She said, "I didn't hear any footsteps." She considered this and added, "But it was raining, and the noise of the rain on the leaves might have covered the noise of someone running off."

"It wasn't raining that hard, was it?" Harrison turned back a couple of leaves in his notebook. "Tell me some more about this fight you had with him yesterday. Was he mad when your husband knocked him down? Did it occur to you that he might want another crack at you when your husband wasn't around?"

She saw where this was going, came to a decision. ''I don't want to answer any more questions until you let me talk to my husband.''

Harrison said, ''Do you know how it looks when you say things like that?''

She said bravely, ''You're treating me like a suspect, and I believe I have a right under that circumstance to silence. If you won't send for Peter, send for an attorney. I refuse to answer any more questions until I've consulted with one or the other.''

''Where did you learn to behave like that?'' She bowed her head and Harrison said cunningly, ''All right, let's talk about something else. When did you and your husband arrive at this shindig?''

But she kept her head down and would not reply.

''Come on, what could be incriminating about answering that?'' he asked.

''Better quit right now, Harrison,'' said a new voice, and he looked around to see the bald trooper standing in the doorway.

''What do you want, Bead?'' asked Harrison.

''I came to see if anyone in here saw King William during the fight in the woods.''

''My other two are upstairs,'' said Harrison.

Bead looked at her, but she only returned the look, so he said, ''I'll ask you again later, okay? By the way, Harve, you're breaking the rules, continuing to question her at this point, and you know it.''

Harrison said, ''She's not under arrest.''

''You mean she's free to go?''

Harrison closed his notebook. ''All right, Mr. Constitutional Rights, we'll send for her husband!'' He stood and looked at her. ''I want to talk to him anyhow. He attacked the victim yesterday; if he can't cover his movements at the time of the murder, I'll have an even better suspect than her.''

14

"YOU don't think they'll scare Katherine so bad she'll say something incriminating, do you?" asked Taffy. He was squatting on his heels near the bridge at Resurrection Point.

Stefan shook his head. "Not my lady. She'll be fine." He was leaning on the end of the bridge's railing, flexing a bruised knee tentatively. "She's got a very cool head."

"All the same, Steffy . . ." said Taffy.

Stefan stirred restlessly, remembering the trooper's outsize hands on her as he put her back into the squad car. "She'll be fine," he repeated and changed the subject. "Tell me, what are you going to give them as a reason for joining SCA?"

Taffy gave Stefan an odd look, but said, "It's a chance to have a close-up look at my ancestors. I really am Welsh, you know. My sister ran our family back to the thirteenth century, says there's a baron and a couple of knights in our bloodline. You're mundanely German, aren't you? Is that why your persona is German?"

"Bavarian. Both of us."

"What are you going to tell them on the survey, Steffy?" asked Geoff. "Why did you join SCA?" He made a word of it, pronounced *skah*.

"I'm telling them nothing. I'm not going to hand it in."

"Why not?"

"Because I don't know why they're asking."

"But it's probably just—" began Taffy.

Stefan cut him off by standing. "I think I'll take a walk; I'm starting to stiffen up."

"I'll come with you," said Geoff. "Taff, will you watch our gear for us?"

"Surely, m'lord." Their swords, shields, helms, and assorted pieces of armor had been stacked beside the road, and Taffy shifted his position to bring them into his line of sight. "See you later," he said, looking after them with puzzled eyes.

Resurrection Point, while not crowded, was generously filled with fighters, marshals, water bearers, and "chirurgeons." Some were sitting in groups; others, like Geoff and Stefan, moved in shifting patterns around the area.

"She'll be okay," said Geoff.

"If she's scared; if they hurt her in any way—"

"They won't. Do you think they'll find anyone hiding in the woods?" asked Geoff, who knew Stefan perhaps better than anyone except his wife, and knew he needed to be distracted. Stefan was a supposedly hardened cop, but his wife was young and new and shy, and Stefan was very much in love with her.

Stefan looked toward the trees. "I doubt it." The troopers had brought in reinforcements and two eager dogs, and were doing a thorough search. "What they may find is evidence someone climbed over the fence."

Two fighters came by, the limping one complaining, "I hope they let us go soon. I need a shower."

"Tell someone upwind that," said his companion.

"Look, here comes Iggy," said Geoff. The bandy-legged man was half-listening to the earnest talk of a big blond knight as he anxiously searched the crowd.

"I wasn't paying attention to who was there and not there when I was fighting with King Edmund," the blond was saying. "I don't think I've got an alibi. Does that mean I'm a suspect?"

''Don't ask me; I'm a suspect myself, Sir John,'' said Ignatius. ''Listen, have you seen Mistress Radegund or King Oswin anywhere?''

''No, I don't think so,'' said Sir John.

''Oh, never mind,'' said Ignatius, seeing Geoff and Stefan. ''You were there, weren't you, Sir Geoffrey?''

''Where is that, my lord?'' asked Geoffrey.

''You saw them take William away, didn't you?''

''No, m'lord. But Lord Stefan here did.''

''Was he under arrest?'' Ignatius asked Stefan anxiously.

''I'm afraid so,'' said Stefan. ''He swung at a trooper, a very serious error in judgment.''

''Why'd he do that? Did the trooper accuse him of killing Thorstane?''

''No, m'lord. William took offense when the trooper told him to keep out of the way while he talked to Mistress Radegund.''

''Lord, what an ass!'' Ignatius was not speaking of the trooper.

Geoff looked up at the fair-haired knight. Like everyone else, John was tired and grubby. The red tape down the front of his helm looked as if it had been pulled loose and replaced several times. ''You're Sir John de Capestrano?''

''Yes, m'lord. And you are Sir Geoffrey of Brixham. I've heard about you.'' He stuck his hand out. ''Honored.''

Geoff took it. ''Well met. This is Lord Stefan von Helle.''

Sir John looked at Stefan appraisingly, but did not offer his hand. ''You're the one with the lady named Katherine, right?''

''Yes, m'lord.''

''She been with you long? She sure is pretty.''

''Thank you; she's my wife.''

''Oh, I see.'' A little light went out in Sir John's blue eyes. ''Well, it's been nice talking to you. If you will pardon me—'' He sketched a brief bow in the direction of Geoff and Ignatius and walked away.

Ignatius snorted. ''I guess that's one notch he won't get to carve on his bedpost! God, why do the ladies go for something like that?''

''He's what they call a 'hunk,' '' said Geoff. ''And knowing what can make a man go weak in the knees, we have no right to be standing here making remarks.''

Ignatius chuckled. ''*Touché,* as they say. Well, thanks for the information, Lord Stefan.''

''You're welcome, Sir Ignatius.''

A little farther on, Stefan heard a clear and gentle voice: ''No, even if anyone had the heart for it, I don't think the police would let the War continue.'' It was the little monk, Father Hugh of Paddington. He and a Horde boy were kneeling near the spigot that grew up like a marsh plant out of soggy ground. The boy, in a fake-fur jerkin over a yellow tunic, was using a large and wicked-looking knife to cut water bottles free of their wet ropes. Father Hugh was sorting the bottles into two piles, whole and broken. The boy's fur and the front of the monk's black robe were wet and muddy, a condition neither of them seemed to mind or even notice.

Stefan squatted beside the monk and said, ''I'm Lord Stefan von Helle, Lady Katherine of Tretower's husband. May I talk to you?''

''Certainly.'' Father Hugh was a small fellow with a vague, gentle face under wispy flaxen hair, bald at the crown. He tossed a quart-size plastic juice bottle onto the discard pile. ''What did you want to talk about?''

''I was wondering how it came about that she found the body all by herself.''

The monk picked up another bottle and turned it over in his small, grubby hands. ''I fell,'' he said humbly. ''I don't feel clumsy inside, you know, but things seem to lie in wait to trip me up. I stumbled over a root or something on the trail and went down on one knee, right onto one of my water bottles. I suppose it must have split a little, because pretty soon your lady noticed it was leaking all down the front of me. So I came back here to replace it. We were supposed to meet again by the Twin Pines Fork.''

Stefan asked, ''Where did you leave her?''

Father Hugh put the bottle down and pulled a rumpled piece of paper out of his rope belt and unfolded it on his thigh to display a map of the woods. ''I left her here, just off the first southern fork.''

He pointed, leaving a smudge on the map. "All she had to do was continue along the trail a bit, then take the second branch to the right, and she'd have come to Twin Pines." He looked closer at the map. "No, it's the third branch. I wonder which one I told her to take? Oh dear."

Stefan bent over the map. The third branch off the trail would have led to a fork named Twin Pines. The second led to the southern fence of the campsite and went east along it. He frowned. She'd said something about getting lost, and no wonder, if she'd followed this silly little man's instructions. He wondered where Thorstane's body had been found.

He straightened and asked, "How long after you left her did the cannon go off?"

The monk thought. "Twenty minutes?" he guessed. "I'd gotten the new bottle and filled it and topped off my other one here at the spigot. I went back in, and was almost to Twin Pines when I heard the blast of the cannon. I continued to the meeting place, but she wasn't there, of course."

"I wish you hadn't left her," said Stefan.

"Yes, I'm sorry about that. I should have suggested she accompany me back out." Father Hugh was refolding the map—backward, Stefan noticed. It was tucked under the brown rope that served as a belt and the monk said sadly, "Of course, he had to be found, and I suppose it's good it was as soon as possible after it happened. I'm sorry it had to be Lady Katherine who found him. I wonder who—"

"It was a mundane," said Geoff. "Someone climbed over the fence. It wasn't one of us."

"My brothers aren't so sure," said the Horde child suddenly, sawing through a knot with his knife. "A lot of people didn't like Thorstane. And the troopers took that lady away, didn't they? Maybe it was her!"

Father Hugh sighed, and said mildly, "You mustn't spread ugly rumors like that. The police naturally want to speak to the person who found Thorstane." He looked at Stefan. "I'm sorry."

Stefan stood and said, "It's all right. Thank you for speaking with me. I'll leave you to your work now; if I don't keep moving, I stiffen up.''

Father Hugh peered up at him and said kindly, ''I hope you get your lady back soon.''

Stefan smiled his sideways smile. ''Thanks.'' When they were out of earshot he said to Geoff, ''That estimate of twenty minutes between leaving her and the cannon going off can't be right.''

''Why not?'' asked Geoff.

''We heard the ambulance siren right after the cannon blew, remember? It's a twenty-minute drive from Butler, even if you go full out, and you have to add to that the time it took to find Thorstane, get help, and for them to decide he needed an ambulance and go all the way up to the gate to send for it. I'd guess it was more like forty minutes.''

''Suppose the ambulance was on the freeway, near here?''

''It would still take ten minutes from the nearest exit. Add that to the time it took for everything else, and we're still well over the twenty minutes he estimated.''

Geoff nodded. ''Okay, his estimate of time is wrong. Should we go back and ask him about it?''

''No. It would have taken even longer for her to have encountered Thorstane, to engage in an argument and struggle with him, stab him, then go through the business of getting help. We may need that incongruity of time.''

Geoff grabbed Stefan's arm. ''You don't think she did it, do you?''

''Of course not. But I'm thinking about a trial. She was assaulted by him yesterday, and she was the last one to see him alive today. That may be good enough to bring a charge.''

''Damn, Pete!''

They continued their walk in a restless silence. A woman fighter in elaborate, fluted Prussian armor asked no one in particular, ''If a mundane did it, why are they holding us?''

A bearded Hordesman said cheerfully to a water bearer, ''If things go right, they'll hold one hell of a wake for him. And it won't cost anything; all they have to do is empty the drawers and cabinets in his apartment. I bet fifty people could get drunk on what they'd find.''

They wandered by a picnic table and found the lady in charge of Resurrection Point conferring with her boss, the Earl Marshal.

''No, I don't remember seeing William out here during the battle, and I'm sure I would have remembered him,'' the marshal, a heavy-set woman, was saying.

''Hilda, I wish you had thought to write down the names of all the dead who passed through,'' said Sir Jerome irritably. There were patches of red on his dark cheeks.

''Why? We never did that before. Anyway, Jerry, there's no way we can do that with as few marshals out here as we have. The best we can do is separate them into batches as they come out, keep the latest arrival in each batch fifteen minutes, then turn the batch loose again. At one point near the end we had six batches, and we had all we could do keeping some later arrivals from sneaking into earlier batches so they'd get turned loose sooner. And we had some injured fighters here, too, getting treated or trying to talk themselves back into the woods. And water bearers getting refills, and heralds with messages, and marshals asking questions or giving us lost and found stuff, and the medics getting bossy—I finally had to send Petty into the woods, he was getting on my nerves so bad. It was a real zoo.'' She tossed a fat braid over a plump shoulder.

''I hope you sent the cheaters off,'' said Jerome.

''No, I just made them join the next batch to come out of the woods. It wasn't serious cheating.''

''But you say King William wasn't out here at all during the battle,'' said Stefan, abruptly joining the conversation.

''No,'' said Hilda, looking at him, surprised. ''But he sent some other fighters to us. I heard them complaining about it.''

''Why complaining?'' asked Geoff.

''The first one said something about how he'd just been released from Resurrection Point and here he was back again.''

''When was this?'' asked Jerome.

''Maybe a third of the way into the battle.''

''He'd been disarmed by then,'' said Jerome, meaning William.

''Maybe he joined up with some other group,'' said Stefan.

''No, he didn't,'' said Jerome. ''Everyone I've talked to wonders where he got to.''

''He sent some fighters out toward the end, too,'' said Hilda. ''I was walking by and I heard someone who'd just come out complaining about the tricky King of the Middle. I didn't stay to listen; I had to go release the next batch.''

''Tricky?'' said Stefan, frowning.

''That's what he said.''

''I wonder what he was up to?'' asked Geoff.

''Let's find out,'' said Jerome. He looked at Stefan. ''You, my lord, are Sir Geoffrey's newest squire, I take it?''

''I am, m'lord.''

''And a herald, are you not?''

''Yes, m'lord Marshal.''

''Good, summon all marshals present to me.''

Stefan obediently climbed up on the table, gathered his authority as a peace officer to put some volume into his call. ''Oy-yea, Oy-yea!'' he bellowed. ''Marshals! All marshals, attend the Midrealm Earl Marshal, right here!''

Other heralds took up the cry, and a few minutes later a dozen men and women had gathered around. Jerome sat down on the table, feet on the seat. ''We know that His Majesty William killed some Easterners after he got separated from his troops early on in the woods. I want to know who he was fighting with. I was with King Edmund; he didn't join up with him.''

The marshals looked at one another and shook their heads. ''I saw him run off when he lost his sword,'' said one. ''Iggy was fighting with him, but he got killed; so William ran off alone. I stayed with his troops, but he didn't come back. Neither did Iggy, for that matter.''

''Bavo and I were with the Easterners trying to retake the banner at the cliff,'' said another. ''He wasn't up on top.'' The marshal looked at Geoff and Stefan. ''Right?''

Geoff grinned. ''Right.''

''He didn't link up with the Horde,'' said another marshal.

''Or with Prince Thomas.''

There was a silence.

''He must have been operating on his own,'' said Jerome. ''Ambushing people—the ones you heard complaining, Mistress.''

''Without a sword?'' asked Stefan.

''He had two spares,'' said Jerry. ''I saw him leave them and his crown with you before the battle started.''

''And I still have both swords,'' said Hilda, reaching under the table and producing one of them. ''He came to me after the battle and got his crown, but said he'd get the swords later. He had a sword in his hand when he came for the crown; he must have gone back to where he dropped the first one and gotten it.''

''No, he didn't,'' said one of the marshals. ''I picked it up myself and carried it around until I got a chance to bring out a bunch of dead, and then I turned it over to a marshal out here.''

''So where did he get a sword?'' asked Jerry, and there was another silence.

''I know,'' said Geoff suddenly. ''From the Lost and Found can. That's where it got put, right? In the barrel near the entrance to the woods. I put the banner in there. He was probably coming out to get a spare sword when he saw his in the can. I bet he pulled it out and began to lay for stragglers going back in from Resurrection.''

''That sounds like him,'' nodded a marshal.

''What banner did you put in the can?'' asked Jerry.

''The Eastern War Banner,'' said Geoff. ''I didn't want to carry it around, and I couldn't think where else to put it.''

''You put the *War Banner* in the Lost and Found can?'' said Jerry. ''Goddammit, there goes our proof that we won the Woods Battle!''

''The battle wasn't regulation length,'' protested Geoff; ''I didn't think it counted.''

''You put the East's War Banner into *Lost and Found*?'' said Hilda.

''You idiot!'' said Jerry angrily. ''Hildy, send someone to retrieve it, will you?''

But Hilda's head was resting on one plump forearm, down on the table. Her shoulders were shaking.

''My lady?'' said Geoff.

"Oh, ho, ho, ho, hee, hee, hee!" she said, straightening, but helpless with laughter. "In the—the Lost and F-F-F—ha, ha, ha, ha, ha!"

"Here, now, this isn't funny!" said Jerome sternly. But her laughter was infectious and the suppressed chortles of the marshals were released into laughter. The frost in Jerome's dark eyes melted, and he smiled. "Well," he said, "I guess the joke's on them after all."

They waited until Hilda regained her composure, then Stefan asked her, "Do you know any of the Easterners who were complaining?"

Hilda, still smiling, said, "No. I remember one had a deer's head on his shield. It had a cross growing up between the antlers."

"That's Placidus," said a marshal immediately, and Stefan was asked to stand up on the table again and call that Lord Placidus should come to the Marshal's table at once.

Placidus proved to be a slender young man wearing a thick brown knee-length gambeson with touches of steel at the shoulders and elbows. He carried the identifying shield with him. "Something wrong?" he asked.

"We hear you were killed by King William," said Jerry.

Placidus grimaced. "That sneaky bas—" he began, then stopped and asked suspiciously, "Who are you?"

"I'm Sir Jerome the Strident, Earl Marshal of the Midrealm."

"Oh, hell," mumbled Placidus. He bowed. "I beg your pardon," he said.

"Never mind that," said Jerry impatiently. "Tell us about His Majesty. How did he kill you?"

"I was at the tail end of the line going back in from Resurrection Point, and I was just walking along when someone tapped me on the shoulder. I turned around and *pow!* a killing blow to the ribs. I fell down, and when I got up, whoever had hit me was gone. I wondered, What the hell? and then I looked around and there he was, sneaking up on Levangelo, who was next in line. Taps him on the shoulder, and he turns around, and *pow!* down he falls. And on to the next one goes the King. Y'know, for as big a man as he is, he sure can move quiet!"

One of the marshals sniggered.

"You're sure it was William?" asked Jerry.

"Oh, yeah, he had the Royal Dragon shield and was wearing the tabard. If he'd just given me one second to get my shield up, I could've given him a fight, and the noise would at least have warned the others. But that man moves at the speed of light; I was out of it before I was even in it. Which was the idea, of course."

"When did this happen?" asked Stefan.

"I dunno, not even halfway through."

"Can you call it closer than that?" asked Stefan.

The young man frowned at him. "What's this all about, anyhow?"

"It's called an alibi," said Hilda dryly.

"Me? I never saw Thorstane in my life!"

Hilda said, "Not for you, for His Majesty. They took him off in handcuffs, you know."

"No, I didn't know." Placidus wiped his face with one hand. "Let me think a minute. Okay, I spent two fifteen-minute segments at Resurrection Point. And I was back in the woods after the second time longer than I was in before I got killed the first time. It was King Edmund who killed me, and he got killed himself in that same fight."

"Edmund died only once, early on, maybe ten minutes into the battle," said Jerome. "I was with his and Queen Jane's troops the whole battle."

"When I got to Resurrection Point there were only two other batches there, and none had been sent back in yet," said Placidus.

"And it took William a while to lose his sword, come back to the Resurrection Point entrance, and decide to lay ambushes. You must have been one of the first William caught," said Stefan.

"Some honor," said Placidus glumly.

"Yeah, but not the last to get it," said Hilda. "I remember now a steady little trickle of fighters coming out on their own right up to the cannon. Not under a black flag, which means they got killed near the entrance."

Jerry said, "So he spent the rest of the battle laying ambushes. Good enough?"

"Suits me," said Stefan. "I only hope it suits the troopers." He asked Placidus, "What's your mundane name?"

"Stacy Hunter. From Holyoke, Mass."

Stefan grinned. "Stefan von Helle, Esquire. Well met," he added, sticking his hand out.

"Funny how things work," said Placidus, taking it. "I had no intention of saving your king's ass. In fact, I was gonna look His Majesty up after court this evening and—"

"Oy-yea!" interrupted a herald, and everyone turned to listen. "Oy-yea, oy-yea! Will Lord Stefan von Helle, mundanely Peter Brichter, please come to the bridge and meet the trooper! Lord Stefan von Helle, come to the bridge and meet the trooper!"

Placidus' head came around. "That's you," he said in a surprised voice.

15

THE trooper at the bridge was only a pickup man, there to deliver Stefan to the farmhouse in a squad car. "Your wife's name is Katherine?" he asked as Stefan approached. He was a thin young man with the scars of an old acne problem webbing his face.

"Yes."

"Get in."

Stefan got in on the passenger side as the trooper slid into the driver's seat in a single fluid movement. His Smokey Bear hat was set perfectly square on top of his head, and his uniform was immaculate. Stefan began to feel even grubbier than he was. The trooper started up the narrow dirt road that led toward the campground entrance. His manner was stiff and a little wary. Hoping it was only the armor, Stefan reassured him, "It's just a game we're playing here."

"Uh-huh," said the trooper without looking at him.

"But we do serious research, too. We reconstruct historical artifacts and culture. Set up situations and investigate theories of medieval behavior. Sort of learning by doing. You're probably more familiar with the people who investigate the Civil War era. It's a hobby; we don't wear these clothes all the time."

''Uh-huh.''

Stefan sighed. ''Is my wife at the farmhouse?''

''Uh-huh.''

''Will I get to speak to her?''

''Dunno. Just sit quiet, okay?''

So he was under orders not to engage in conversation; another bad sign.

They parked and the trooper led Stefan up the walk and into the house.

King William was sitting crosswise to the end of the table in the dining room, looking very anachronistic in his muddy armor and tabard, one filthy pink paw around a delicate porcelain cup of black coffee. Master Petrog and another medic Stefan didn't know were sitting on chairs against the wall opposite, also holding cups.

''Lord Stefan,'' said William in greeting.

Stefan managed to look as if he were bowing without actually doing so. ''Your Majesty,'' he said. The thin trooper sniffed quietly.

Leaning against the wall next to William was another trooper with a broad stripe of dark hair around his bald head—not the one who had taken Katherine away. Stefan looked around, didn't see her.

''In the living room, through there,'' said the bald trooper, pointing the way, and they let him go through the doorway alone.

She was sitting on the very front edge of a rocker covered with a knitted throw, her face stiff and pale, her attention focused on the large trooper instructing her from his place on the couch. ''I'll be listening to everything you say to him, so no whispering, secret signs, or tricks, hear?''

''Yes.''

''*Fy'n galon?*'' he said, and her head whipped around.

''Hello, Peter,'' she whispered.

''Are you all right?'' he asked, feeling his temper rise.

''Yes, I'm fine; are you?''

''Yes.'' He asked the trooper, ''Is she under arrest?''

''She's being detained. What's this Vin-Gallon you're calling her? She said her name's Katherine.''

"It is. *Fy'n galon* is Welsh, an endearment. Her father was a Welshman. From Wales. That's in Great Britain."

Harrison's mouth tightened a little. "I've heard of it, Mr. Brichter."

"Don't, Peter," she said. "I told them I wouldn't answer any more questions until I spoke with you or an attorney, so please."

"What kind of questions are they asking?"

"About my finding Thorstane. I told them the truth, but Mr. Harrison said—" Her eyes flickered to the trooper and back to her lap again. "He thinks maybe I'm lying. Because Thorstane spoke to me, just a little, before he died. But the medics couldn't bring him back. And they know about Thorstane grabbing me yesterday, and that you hit him. And Mr. Harrison says—" She stopped and began to make a pleat in her apron where it fell over her knee. "Where were you during the battle, Peter?"

He smiled then, because it was not fear for herself that had her this way. "I was with Geoff, Taffy, and Sir Humphrey through the whole thing, start to finish."

She raised her head, blinked slowly, then color flooded her cheeks. "Truly?"

"Truly."

"There, then!" she said to Harrison. "There, then!" And she burst into tears.

Stefan immediately dropped to his knees and offered a steel-clad shoulder for her to cry on. She accepted, putting her arms around his neck besides; and he stroked her head. "Take it easy, *fy'n galon*," he murmured. "You're all right now. Sorry about the armor."

"I don't care, I don't care. You're safe."

"Now, maybe not," said Harrison. "I'm sure his friends will back up any story he cares to tell."

"Geoff and Taffy are friends," admitted Stefan, "but I'd never met Sir Humphrey before the War."

Katherine slowly pushed herself away from Stefan. "I met Sir Humphrey once," she said to him, wiping her eyes on a brown sleeve. "He was at a coronation in Talltower, and he sat with me and Taffy and Anne at the feast. It was that weekend you couldn't come.'' She looked at Harrison. ''But I haven't spoken to him here at the War.''

''So you say,'' said Harrison, but he was making a note of their names. ''And who are these people when they're at home?''

''Geoff is Geoffrey Collins, spelled G-E-O-F-F-R-E-Y. Taffy is David Waterman. They're both from the same town as my lady and myself. I don't know Sir Humphrey's mundane name; I never thought to ask. But you can send for him under his SCA-name and get him all right.''

''We'll do that, Mr. Brichter.''

''And so long as we're talking about alibis,'' said Stefan, ''King William has one, too—that is, Rusty Anderson.''

''No kidding. Want to tell me about it?''

''I noticed he seems to be in the custody of the trooper in the next room. I'd prefer to speak directly to him, if that's all right.''

Harrison sighed heavily, rose and walked to the door. He called through it, ''Hey, Bead, come here a minute.'' He walked back and sat down again.

The bald trooper appeared in the doorway. ''What's up, Harrison?''

''This turkey here says he can alibi Anderson for the time of the murder.''

Bead looked at Stefan with interest. ''Yeah?''

Stefan said, ''No, I can't give the alibi. But I was talking with some people at Resurrection Point, and it seems King William spent most of the battle ambushing and killing fighters just as they were coming back into the woods.''

Harrison sat forward. ''Are you saying there's more bodies in the woods?''

''No, no, no, Harve,'' said Bead. ''Pretend kill. Anderson was telling me how they fight. Go on, Mr. Brichter.''

''A Stacy Hunter, from Holyoke, Massachusetts, was among the first. I talked to him, and to Mistress Hilda, who was in charge of Resurrection Point. She says there was a fairly steady trickle of fighters who had died apparently right inside the entrance to the woods.''

''What was this Stacy Hunter wearing?''

''A brown gambeson—a quilted coat—with steel shoulder pauldrons and elbow cops. His shield is yellow and has the face of a stag with a cross standing between its antlers.''

''Wait right here.'' Bead ducked out and was back two minutes later. ''The first guy he got wore a brown padded coat and carried a yellow shield with a deer's head painted on it. He doesn't remember the cross.''

Stefan smiled. ''I'm not surprised. He didn't give the poor guy a chance to lift his shield before he hit him.''

Bead grinned. ''So he says.'' He looked at Harrison. ''Anderson was telling me earlier how he spent the greater part of this battle game hiding just inside the woods, attacking people. Here's corroboration of his story. Stacy Hunter, you said?'' he asked Stefan.

''Yes, sir, called Lord Placidus in the Society.''

''Bead, you gone soft in the head?'' said Harrison. ''We're dealing with a goddamn bunch of crazies, and you're talking like you believe what they tell you! One of them, remember, tried to deck me because I wouldn't treat him like he was a real king! Face it, one of these 'hobbyists' killed another one, and they're all gonna stick together to keep us from finding out who. The story it was some outsider is bullshit. If it wasn't this girl, it was His so-called Majesty, and if it wasn't him, it was her tin-suited hero here.''

Stefan said, ''If I were out to fake an alibi, I'd come up with one that cleared my wife, not the King.'' He looked at Bead. ''Go ahead and send for Mr. Hunter. He'll confirm the King's story.''

''Yeah,'' said Harrison, ''a story you just finished making up with him. You'll all stick together to help your king.''

Stefan shook his head. ''William is not Lord Placidus' king. Perhaps no one has explained to you that this is a war. William is King of the Middle Kingdom, which is where I and my wife live. The people King William ambushed, including Lord Placidus, are from the Eastern Kingdom, an area which includes Pennsylvania. They have their own king, named Oswin.''

Bead said, ''I think 'king' is just their name for the chief executive officer of their different groups—right, Mr. Brichter?''

''Something like that. Actually, the chief officer of a kingdom, the one with real power, is the seneschal. Our kings are largely ceremonial, with some real, but limited, powers.''

Harrison, notebook in hand, spoke up. ''What about this 'autocrat'? She said she was the legal representative of the Society here.''

''Here at the War, on the campsite,'' said Stefan. ''And only during the time of the event, which is due to end late Sunday afternoon. You met her; Mistress Radegund d'Portiers is autocrat this year.''

''Yeah, that skinny lady in the pink dress,'' said Harrison. ''But when I tried to talk to her, that guy in the brass hat came in swinging.''

Bead said, ''Maybe we should send for her. And Mr. Hunter.'' He sighed. ''This is beginning to look like it will take a while. I think I'll call in and see just how long we can hold everyone here.''

''Unless you intend to arrest us, you can't hold us at all,'' said Stefan.

Bead regarded Stefan sideways. ''What are you, a lawyer?''

''No, I'm Detective Sergeant Otto Peter Brichter, a city police officer.''

''Some city here in Pennsylvania? No.'' He grinned. ''Wrong kingdom, right?''

''Right. Look, since I know the workings of the Society as well as something about investigative procedure, maybe you'll let me help you with this.''

''No way!'' said Harrison.

Bead shook his head. ''I'm sorry, Mr. Brichter, but so far they haven't found anyone hiding in the woods, and a quick sweep along the fence behind the woods shows no sign anyone came in or went out that way. Mr. Anderson says he asked anyone gathered at your Resurrection Point if they saw a 'mundane' and no one had. Until we find some confirmation of your wife's story about an outsider, I'll ask you not to involve yourself with our investigation.''

''That does it,'' said Harrison. ''Mrs. Brichter,'' he said with extreme formality, ''you have a right to remain silent. If you give up this right to silence, you have a right to consult with an attorney, and to have any attorney present during questioning. If you can't afford an attorney but wish to consult with one, we'll assign one to you before further questioning. Do you understand?''

"Yes."

Stefan asked, "Trooper Bead, may I speak with you in private?"

"Sure. Come with me."

The place of privacy proved to be the downstairs bathroom, a fairly large one, done in aquamarine tile. Bead leaned against the closed door; Stefan sat on the edge of the tub. "She's innocent," said Stefan.

"You're not going to confess before I warn you of your rights, are you?"

"No. I'm innocent, too."

"I'll need more than that before we can turn her loose."

"They didn't find anything in the woods at all?"

Bead hesitated, then reached in his shirt pocket for a pack of cigarettes. "Do you mind?"

"Go ahead."

"Want one?"

"No, thanks."

Bead lit his, drew a lungful of smoke. "Why do you think I should tell you what we found in the woods?"

"You don't have to, but I'm hoping you will. You see, she doesn't lie. If she says Thorstane told her a mundane did it, then that's what she heard him say. You say no one's hiding in the woods, and there's no sign anyone climbed the fence. I'll accept your word on that. But there is an explanation for this contradiction of facts, and if you'll be frank with me, maybe we can discover what it is."

Bead flicked ash into the toilet. "All right, how about I tell you we found a suit of armor?"

"Pieces or a whole suit?"

"The man with the transceiver said a suit of armor. I assume he meant a whole suit. Painted blue, he said."

"In the woods?"

"In the woods."

"That's funny."

"Is it? Maybe someone just got tired of walking around in it. Armor's heavy, isn't it?"

"Yes, but it's a lot easier to carry around on than off."

''Maybe he didn't want to play anymore, and just threw it away.''

''You don't throw away something as valuable as a suit of armor.''

''They cost a lot of money?'' asked Bead.

''If you can get someone else to make a whole outfit for you, yes, hundreds of dollars. And if you change your mind about fighting, pieces can be resized, within limits, so fighters who quit will sell pieces as replacement parts, or give them to friends.''

''How much did you pay for yours?''

''About fifty dollars—but that was for the raw materials: steel, leather, rivets, buckles, quilts. I made it myself. Most of us do it that way. Then the major investment is time spent over an anvil.'' He stuck out a leg. ''That greave on my lower leg took about an hour, but the whole knee arrangement about five, including fitting the lames and riveting everything in place. There's blood, sweat, and tears on every rivet. That's just one leg. It took twenty-nine hours for the whole suit, and it's mere journeyman work. Anything fancy, like fluting, would have taken longer.''

''You use a forge to heat your metal?'' asked Bead, now interested as well as officially nosy.

''No, it's hammered out cold.''

''What do you wear under it?''

''A padded coat, called a gambeson, protects torso and arms.'' He turned a hand over to show the black quilted sleeve under the metal that covered only the top of his forearm. ''Most of us make them out of movers' quilts. They can be worn alone if you're brave, like Lord Placidus. For legs, you can buy padding, like this.'' He bent to pull the edge of a football pad around the edge of his knee cop—then stopped. ''Jesus,'' he whispered.

''What?''

''Look!'' said Stefan, standing. He began to unbuckle his leg armor. ''See?'' he said, uncovering a thigh, then bending to fumble at the buckles behind his calf. ''See?'' he said again, yanking the armor off.

''See what?'' asked Bead. ''A knee pad?''

''Under the pad—jeans! Most of the fighters wear mundane clothes under armor! That would explain it, wouldn't it? Look!'' Stefan turned sideways and raised his right arm. His black gambeson had been cut out at the armpit to facilitate movement, and he gestured toward the opening with his other hand. "Can you see it? I've got a gray sweatshirt on under there. Take me out of my armor and what do you find? A mundane!"

Bead said, "You're saying the murderer was a fighter who took off his armor and therefore looked like a mundane to his victim?"

"It could have been." Stefan sat down hard on the edge of the tub, greatly relieved. "If it wasn't a real mundane, it must have been."

Bead drew on his cigarette and considered the idea. "So why didn't he put the armor back on afterward?"

"I don't know— Wait a minute. Fighters may have moved into the sector where he left it, so he was scared to go near it. Or, if it was near Thorstane, the body was found too fast. She came along before his victim was even dead; and from then on he couldn't come back because more and more people kept coming."

"That's if the armor was found near where there were fighters, or the body," said Bead doubtfully.

Stefan said, "So pick up your goddamn transceiver and ask, why don't you?"

Bead sighed, threw his cigarette in the toilet bowl, and went away. He was gone what seemed like a long time. He came back, closed the door and said, "The armor's been brought in. It looks to me like a whole suit, except there's no pads or any 'gambeson.' Can you get along without them?"

"Not really. He's probably wearing them. He might have gotten that far in recostuming himself—or picked them up and ran with them. That might explain why nobody's reported a mundane running around. He's not in mundanes; he's in his gambeson. Where was it found?"

"About seventy-five yards from where the body was found."

"There, see?" Stefan wiped his face, dizzy with relief.

There was a silence and then Bead said, "How about, since you're so good at explaining things, you tell me why she says Thorstane talked to her and the medics couldn't get any sort of response, not even a heartbeat with CPR just a couple of minutes later?"

Stefan waved a hand dismissively. "Any severe trauma that causes a large loss of blood will make CPR ineffective. Ruptured aorta, maybe. The heart can't pump what it hasn't got." He shrugged. "Cardiac tamponade is another possibility."

Bead smiled. "Now you sound like a doctor."

"I used to be a paramedic, years back. And I teach advanced first aid for the department. Once you get the results of an autopsy you'll have your explanation, and it will fit her story."

"You sound damn sure of that."

"I am. Jesus, when you told me it looked like no one had climbed that fence, I thought, what kind of sloppy investigators have we got here? Because as I said, she doesn't lie. And I thought, they've got her for this, and they aren't really looking for another explanation." He glanced up and saw the look on Bead's face and apologized, "Sorry. I was too quick to think that."

Bead grinned in a nasty way and reached for another cigarette. "Maybe the kind of department you work for, it's natural for you to expect sloppy procedures."

Stefan's pale eyes glinted. "Maybe when they come to take your wife away, you'll offer to loan them your handcuffs."

"Maybe." Bead exhaled smoke and waited.

"Are you going to turn her loose?"

"Are you going to take her straight home if we do?"

"Maybe."

Bead sighed, flicked ash. "Can you think of anything else that could help?"

Stefan thought and said, "Those two men assigned to Thorstane. How did they lose him?"

"What two men?"

"K'shaktu. Guardians. Thorstane was a bad apple, and so the Khan assigned the two to stay with him at all times. Sort of a mobile arrest."

"Who's the Khan?"

"Lord Wulfstan the Fearless of Iceland. I don't know his mundane name. He's head of a household called the Great Dark Horde. People whose personas are traders, herders, wanderers, barbarians,

Vikings, or Mongols tend to get invited to join. Thorstane was one, of course.''

Bead's dark eyes glinted. ''Of course.''

Stefan was fitting the armor back onto his leg. He stopped and said, ''I remember a con artist who was taking morticians for a ride. They assigned me to the case because of my paramedic background. It took me two days just to understand what the morticians thought they were buying, and I've never understood why they wanted it. Those people have ideas and standards all their own.''

''Did you get a conviction?''

''No, the jury thought the morticians had it coming.''

''I'm glad you understand how we 'mundanes' might think you also are a peculiar bunch of people,'' said Bead.

''And now it looks like one of us is a murderer. But not my wife.''

16

BEAD and Harrison were sitting at the dining room table, reporting to the sergeant in charge of the investigation, a stolid type, and his partner, both in conservative civilian suits. Across from Harrison was the young trooper with the scarred face, and by the double window stood three more troopers, drinking coffee.

"I can't see how this will be easy," Bead was saying. "There were more than eight hundred people tramping around in the woods for an hour and a half before the murder. I think probably one of them is the murderer, but it isn't feasible to trace every individual's movements over that period of time, even with their fullest cooperation. I think we're just going to have to separate those who know something from those who obviously don't, and concentrate on the ones who can help us get to the bottom of this."

The sergeant nodded and turned to his partner. "Lloyd, what have you found out?"

The man sat forward and sighed. "The victim was stabbed at least twice with a very narrow-bladed weapon," he began, and pointed to a plastic bag containing an ice pick with a darkly crusted blade on the table in front of him. "Probably this ice pick, which was found on the ground a few yards from the body. No prints. It checks positive for blood. The area around the body was badly trampled, but we managed to get castings of five different footprints from there and three more from out on the trail. Not that I expect much good from them; I know of eight people who were legitimately present at the scene.''

''Does it look like a struggle where you found him?'' asked Bead.

''No. The trampling was done mostly by the people trying to save him. He may have walked or run to where he was found, after he got stabbed. We found traces of blood on some of the brush about where he broke off the trail, and some more back before that. Not a lot, but his wounds closed up after the injury and that leather thing he had on contained most of what he lost externally. It's possible his killer followed him to where he fell, but unfortunately that same place was walked over by the woman, the medics, the ambulance paramedics, and''—he grimaced—''Harrison.

''It's possible some of the blood belongs to his murderer, of course; the victim was a big, strong man, and he might've fought back. If we've got enough to type it, and I think we do, then we'll know. But I think he was stabbed on the trail, by someone who was with him or caught up with him. And the victim ran away, went off the trail, to fall where he was found.''

''You think a woman could've done it?'' asked the sergeant.

''Maybe,'' said Lloyd. ''If she was scared enough, say; if he came at her, scared her. Or if she was a big, strong girl. But that leather thing he was wearing is thick, and even an ice pick would resist going through it. I dunno; I'd prefer a man for this, Harve.''

Harrison said, ''Yeah, but we got the woman. The victim grabbed her yesterday; her husband had to swing in with a club to make him let her go. Her husband wasn't there to protect her today.''

''I'd prefer the husband, but you say he's got a solid alibi, right?'' asked Lloyd.

Bead said, ''We'll check, but it sounds good.''

The sergeant said, ''Don't let this influence you or anything, but I called their hometown and found out the husband's a cop, all right, and a good one. The wife is Kori Price Brichter, who could pay my salary out of her change purse and never notice the difference.''

''Oh, hell,'' said Harrison.

''I understand we'll have the autopsy results in the next hour or so,'' added Lloyd. ''The governor of her state is a personal friend. He made a phone call to a United States senator, who called our governor, who has spoken to our coroner.''

''Damn,'' said Bead, wincing.

''That doesn't mean she didn't do it,'' said Harrison.

''No, but let me tell you what Brichter told me,'' said Bead. ''He says no one would take armor off casually, because it's easier to wear than to carry. He says it's hard to make and expensive to buy, so they tend not to abandon it. So why was there a suit loose in the woods? How about we watch the fighters when we turn them loose, to see if they do or do not leave it lying around? Brichter was wearing jeans and a sweatshirt under his armor, he showed them to me. He says most of the fighters wear street clothes under their armor, but maybe we should check that out, too.''

''You think he's lying?'' asked the sergeant.

''I don't know,'' said Bead. ''He's out to prove his wife's story, of course. He didn't sound evasive or as if he were lying. He says some fighters wear only the padding, which could mean the murderer is right under our noses. He says someone in street clothes would fit the victim's definition of a mundane.''

''God, what a screwy case this is!'' complained Harrison.

''So look, Harve,'' said the sergeant, ''when you go up to turn them loose, ask what's under the armor. And ask each fighter if he was ambushed by King William, and if he was, stand him aside. And if he's wearing only pads, ask him to stand aside. And if his or her name inside the group''—he opened his notebook—''is Mistress Radegund, Lord Placidus—God, these names!—Broddi, Hreider, Sir Geoffrey, or Sir Humphrey, we want to see him.''

''Uh,'' said the young trooper carefully.

''What is it, Cotter?'' asked the sergeant.

''When I went down there to get Brichter, I thought it would take me an hour to find him. But one of those hairy guys guarding the bridge yelled, 'Herald!'—I thought it was a name, Harold, but it's sort of a specialty, I guess—and told this guy in a green cape who I was looking for, and inside five minutes there's a dozen of them yelling for Brichter, and inside ten minutes I'm putting him in the car. So I think maybe you can do the same thing to get hold of people. You know, ask for anyone ambushed by the king, and have them call out the names of those other people you want to talk to. It'll be faster getting hold of them that way, and Harrison won't have so many questions to ask every person."

The sergeant nodded. "All right, I like it. Got that, Harrison? You just look for fighters out of uniform and ask people what they're wearing under their armor." He looked across at the troopers by the window. "You guys finish your coffee and drive down in your cars, get these town criers to call for anyone 'killed by King William,' and for anyone on this list of names I'll give you, and ferry them back up, okay? Then if Brichter's information checks out, I suggest we look into that stray suit of armor, see if we can find out whose it is. And why he took it off."

• • •

Harrison went to release the people from Resurrection Point one by one, taking names and addresses as they went, asking an apparently casual question or two of each. The herald business had worked just fine, and four carloads of people had been run up to the farmhouse to be interviewed.

A bulky fighter carrying a pole and wearing what seemed to be a suede leather shirt said, "I'm Chance Clark, 1134 Canon Lane, Germantown, New York. Also known as Lord Norbert the Reformer."

"Lord Hubert?"

"No, he's from Atlantia. I'm Norbert, from the East."

"Okay," said Harrison, writing. "Is that what you wear under your armor?"

The man struck his chest with a fist and it gave a muffled metallic clank. "No, this is a coat of plates. The steel is under the leather."

"I see. What do you wear under that?"

He grinned. "Flannel shirt and jeans."

"Okay. Next."

"Jason Rosenberg, 327 Macadam, Lansing, Michigan." He was

a young man wearing what looked like a leather pinecone. "I'm Lord Berikjesu the Sassanian."

"You want to spell that for me?"

He did, and said he was wearing jeans and a sweatshirt under his strange armor.

Lady Mildthryth Merewald, a sweet-faced water bearer, spelled her name as well. But after three failed attempts to get Clyde Gilde's SCA name of Lord Illtyd O Llanilltyd Fawr of Glamorgan down correctly, Harrison reminded himself they had gotten everyone they were looking for by screwy name already, and decided he was henceforth taking only real names and addresses.

A barbarian waiting across the bridge stopped everyone again and handed him or her a pen and said, "Write SCA and mundane names on this paper. No calligraphy or funny alphabets, okay?"

When the last person had been sent off, Harrison walked around the grassy area. There was a pile of crumpled plastic bottles by the water spigot, and a trash barrel almost full of chemical ice packs, Band-Aid wrappers and other oddments from first-aid kits, empty Gatorade bottles, and a piece of broken sword. Another trash barrel was labeled "Lost and Found" in letters crudely cut from duct tape. It contained what looked like a padded dog collar, two strips of cloth with embroidery on them, a muddy example of what he would have called a fat lady's dress before he had seen what some fighters wore over their armor, four intact wooden swords, a jointed metal glove, and a long pole with a big piece of cloth rolled around it. He unrolled the cloth and found himself staring at a fierce-looking tiger. He rolled it back up and replaced it in the barrel.

He found a metal arm brace along the road, a wooden battle-ax with a padded blade in the grass, a padded dog collar under a tree, and a pair of rusty metal mittens near the picnic table. That was all.

All right, for eight hundred-plus people as heavily equipped as most of them seemed to be, that wasn't much by way of leavings.

And nine out of ten of the fighters he asked said they were wearing street clothes under their gear.

So give that skinny little city cop two-thirds of a point. Money or no money, Harrison would still swear his wife did it.

• • •

Stefan was waiting for Katherine when she came out of the shower. Since many people had sent all their mundane clothes out with their cars, there was an unspoken agreement that everyone would remain in garb. She was wearing a sleeveless buff-colored gown whose armholes were cut out to the hip, over a dark blue underdress. He had put on a knee-length, low-waisted blue tunic and dropped over it a buff tabard that buttoned closed at the hip. She took his hand, noticed his wince, and lifted the hand to look at a swollen knuckle and a brilliant assortment of colors, and she sucked air through her teeth. "Did you see a medic about this?" she asked.

"No, it's only bruises. It looks uglier than it feels," he reassured her.

"Didn't your new gauntlets work?"

"Very well, better than my old ones. I'd have a collection of broken fingers if it weren't for them—a polearm is a wicked weapon, even when you try to pull your punches with it."

"Maybe we should talk again about you fighting, okay? Especially against polearms. I don't think—"

She was interrupted by the cry of a herald. "Oy-yea!" he called. "Oy-yea, oy-yea!" He was standing a little up from them in the middle of the road, a stocky man in brown tunic and tights. "Their Majesties Oswin and Margaret, William and Ethelreada, and Edmund and Jane, along with Mistress Radegund, the autocrat, ask that everyone cooperate fully with the State Police!" He glanced at a five-by-eight white card in his hand, then continued, "Broadsides giving official information will be posted at the bathhouse and at the inns within the next two hours! Please do not spread rumors!" He paused again. "The Bridge Battle has been canceled! Judges are asked to turn in their results in the poetry, weaving, calligraphy, costume, and armor contests to Master Petrog at the barn!" He turned the card over. "Will Lord Stefan von Helle please come to His Majesty William's pavilion! Will the person who mislaid a suit of blue armor in the woods please claim it at the farmhouse! That is all!" They watched him march off, faint echoes of his announcements sounding from other heralds at distant points.

"I guess they turned Will loose," said Stefan.

"Why does he want to see you?" asked Katherine.

"Beats me. Come on, let's go see."

"No, I'll go back to the encampment. He asked for you, not both of us."

"So come and help me hold my tongue. I don't want you walking back to our encampment by yourself."

She stared at him. "Whyever not?" Stefan nodded over her shoulder and she turned to look. Three Hordesmen were standing across the road, staring at her in a very unfriendly way. "What's wrong with them?" she asked.

"I'm not sure."

She smiled. "Maybe they've mistaken me for Anne."

"No, I don't think so. Come on." As he took her by the arm and led her off, they followed. There was no silly tooth-sucking or leers in this trio's repertoire, and by the time they reached William's pavilion, she had been reduced to a puzzled, resentful silence.

• • •

As they approached the green pavilion with its crenellated canvas towers at either end, an entrance flap was raised in the middle and Queen Ethelreada came out carrying William's personal banner, a red cloth shield with a golden butterfly silhouetted on it. She hung it on a pole planted by the entrance, meaning William was at home, and continued on down the path away from them.

The royal pavilion was a long rectangle with a room at either end connected by a reception hall. The hall was set up like a throne room, with two beautiful faldstools at one end, a gorgeously elaborate tapestry of a dragon rampant hanging behind them. Pieces of the royal armor were scattered on the ground, along with the royal shield and tabard, all rather muddy. A man wearing the tabard of the Midrealm greeted them and vanished into the room behind the thrones.

A minute later, William came into the throne room wearing a short green tunic and no hose, his fine, strawberry-blond hair damp and ruffled, his feet thrust carelessly into pointed cloth shoes. Katherine and Stefan bowed.

"If I remember right, you're not just a cop, but a detective on your police force," said William without preamble.

"Yes, sir," said Stefan.

"How about you do some poking around for me, find out for sure what happened in the woods today?"

"I'm sorry, sir; the troopers don't want my assistance."

"Damn the troopers; I'm not asking you to be a liaison," said William. "I just don't think they know how to solve this, and I want it solved."

"You, me, my lady, we're all three suspects, you know," said Stefan.

"Hell, we all three know better. Your lady says it was a mundane. Maybe there's a way to prove that."

"My lady says Thorstane said it was a mundane; there's a difference."

"See?" William grinned a fierce grin. "Cop thinking. That's what we need here."

"We've got all the cops we need. The State Police are very good."

"Yeah, when a farmer flips his wig and does in his prize cow. This is different. For one thing, they don't know anything about us; they think we're some kind of cult. If this isn't settled, and fast, the media will get hold of it, and the whole damn Society's gonna be dragged through the mud. At the very least we'll never have another War. I'm not gonna let that happen, not during my reign. I want to know for sure it was a mundane. And if it wasn't, I want to know that, too; I want to know the name of the one of us who did it."

"I have no authority in the State of Pennsylvania to do any such thing."

"You can poke around on your own, can't you?"

"I suppose I could. But I have no authority to demand cooperation from anyone."

William said, "I'll give you the authority! Wait here." He went into his room and returned a minute later with a sheet of parchment-colored paper, a felt-tip pen, and a cutting board. He sat on one of the faldstools and began to write in a careful hand, pausing to ask Katherine, "You're sure, absolutely positive, Thorstane said a mundane stabbed him?"

"He said it was a mundane, a fight," Katherine replied.

"Was he mumbling or talking clear?" asked William.

"He was speaking brokenly, as if he were in pain, and it was just a few words; but he said them quite clearly."

"Could he have been saying someone's name and you only thought he said 'mundane'?"

She thought this over. "No, I don't think so. He said, 'But it was a mundane,' as if he were surprised or puzzled."

"Yeah, if I saw a mundane right in the middle of the Woods Battle at Pennsic, I'd've been surprised, too. What do you think, Stefan—he came in over the fence?"

"Trooper Bead told me they found no evidence anyone climbed the fence, coming in or going out."

"Then maybe he got in some other way." He continued writing. A minute later he signed the paper with a flourish and said, "Here, this should do it."

Stefan took it and read the beautiful italic handwriting. "To All Whom These Presents Come," it began. Katherine came to read over his arm, and he turned it a little to give her a better look. "We, William, by right of arms King of the Middle Kingdom, do ask and require that you give all honest assistance to Lord Stefan von Helle, as he is by Our order conducting an investigation into the death of Lord Thorstane Shieldbreaker. Done this Fourth Day of September, A.S. XXIII, sitting on Our throne in the Debatable Lands, by Our hand. William Rex Mediterranae."

"Will that do?" William asked.

"Well . . ." said Stefan.

"Look, if I have to, I'll send for Sir Geoffrey and order him under his oath of fealty to order you as his squire to do it!"

Stefan hesitated, then dropped to one knee. "An it please Your Majesty, that won't be necessary. I am your servant."

"Good. I want you to keep me advised as you go along—good news, bad news, no news. Okay?"

"Yes, Your Majesty." Stefan rose. "Do King Oswin and Mistress Radegund know about this?"

"No, but I'm meeting with them in half an hour. If you think it will help, I'll get Oswin to issue a writ, too."

"Yes, that may be helpful. Thank you."

Outside the pavilion, Katherine said, "If you really don't want to investigate, why did you agree?"

He said, "Because I do want to investigate—but quietly, secretly, not with a royal flourish. Because I'm afraid I agree with William: The troopers may not have the time or the knowledge it takes to do it themselves." He smiled. "Although I suspect they will make the time, if not now, then shortly, once they hear from Senator Mason."

She studied the way the toes of her shoes poked out from under her dress. "I don't like using political influence, but—"

"Yes, but. You were looking very good to them, and it would have made a fast, easy solution."

"Yes. So why do you still want to investigate?"

"Because political pressure does not bring expertise."

"Oh. Yes, I see. What do we do first?"

"Go purchase the detective's old standbys, a notebook and pen. Come on, the campground store is this way." He began to lead her away, then looked beyond her and saw the three Hordesmen preparing to follow. "I see your friends are still with us," he said.

She looked around, saw them, and before he could stop her, she strode swiftly across to them. "Why are you following us?" she demanded crisply.

"It's a free country," said the tallest one, shrugging. He was a strongly built man, with curly brown hair and a very short nose in a wide, pleasant face.

"We want to make sure we know where you are all the time," piped up the smallest one, a plump specimen whose round head seemed to sit directly on his shoulders.

"So we can tell the troopers if you try to leave," said the middle-size one, a bald man with a silver beard and solid-looking paunch. All three were wearing knee-length red tunics over black balloon pants. "We're going to be with you from now on," he added.

"Why? What have we done?"

"The troopers took you away," said the tall one, "then this hotshot cop husband of yours came along and now you're loose again. We know how cops stick together."

"Not when it's a capital charge," said Stefan, who had quietly joined them. "They released her when they realized they didn't have enough evidence to bring any charges against her."

"So when they find enough evidence, we'd like her to be within reach," said the middle one.

"There isn't any to find, Solly. Would it be possible for us to come to the Horde encampment in a little while and talk with you?"

"With me? Ask me any questions you've got here and now," said Solly. "But I don't know anything. I was helping Priscilla at our merchant's booth all morning."

"I want to speak with everyone in the Horde about Thorstane. I'm looking into his death myself, on orders from King William."

"Will's orders don't carry as far as our encampment," said the short one. "You know that."

"I want to come in any case."

They looked at one another. "I say no," said the short one.

"Yeah, but you never know with Wulffy," said the tall one uncomfortably.

"So come, ask if you can enter," said Solly to Stefan.

"Thanks. By the way, *fy'n galon,* this is Solomon ben Jacob the Levite, of whom even Lady Anne approves."

Katherine's bob barely qualified as a curtsy. "Do I say 'well met' under these circumstances?" she asked.

Solly nodded back. "Could be. We are also here to protect you from those more-excitable members of our household who want to carry you off, tie you to a tree, and not turn you loose—even to go to the bathroom—until you confess."

"Then I thank you," she said, a smile tugging at her mouth.

"You're welcome," he said firmly.

"We'll drop off our bath gear at our tent," said Stefan, "but first we need to go to the store."

"Lead on," said the little one cheerfully. "I want a Coke."

• • •

"You did *what*?!" said Radegund.

"I gave him a writ asking everyone he showed it to to cooperate in his investigation," said William.

"You jerk—and he agreed?" said Oswin. They were in the high square throne room of his pavilion, which was also situated on

King's Crest, about a hundred yards from William's. Oswin was sitting in his steeple-backed wooden chair, Radegund and William in director's chairs.

''Sure. Why shouldn't he?''

Radegund groaned. ''Because the troopers told him to stay out of it, and we're supposed to be cooperating with them. Because he is a police officer from someplace in Iowa or Illinois, and he can't arrest anyone here, even if he found out who it was. Because his wife is a suspect and if he comes across something that shows she did it, he may hide or destroy it. For the love of God, Will!''

''Now hold on, Rags,'' said William. ''He's a squire to Sir Geoffrey of Brixham, and you know Geoff doesn't pick any but the best for his squires. I've talked to a few people, and they all agree Steffy's so straight it hurts. In fact, he raised the same objections to me you are raising right now. I had to threaten him with his oath of fealty to get him to agree.'' He raised a hand to forestall further objections from her. ''Listen a minute. Like I told him, these troopers are mundanes; they don't know anything about us or how the War is run. You know what's gonna happen if Lord Stefan doesn't succeed? I'll tell you: (A), they'll arrest his wife and half the people in SCA will go around thinking she's guilty even if she's found innocent at a trial. Or (B), they won't arrest anyone, and only a quarter of the SCA-folk will think she did it. Some will think *I* did it. No, no way. I don't want to have either A or B happen, and the only way I can think of to prevent it is to let him try to solve it!'' He sat back in his canvas seat, his face tight and angry.

Oswin said mildly, ''I thought a mundane did it.''

''Lady Katherine insists Thorstane said a mundane did it. But the troopers can't find any indication that might be true. They're sure no one got away over the fence, for instance. Thorstane was dying when she found him, and who knows what was going on in his mind? Or maybe he was trying to say a name, and she only thinks she heard the word 'mundane.' I don't think it was a mundane, and from the way the cops latched on to her—and me—I don't think they do, either.''

Oswin sighed gustily, and stroked his narrow jaw with the back of a knobby hand. ''All right, I see what you mean, I guess. But

I'm not going to issue any writ. And couldn't you at least have warned us you were going to do this?''

''I meant to.'' William shrugged. ''But I decided to do it, sent out a message to the heralds on my way home from the showers, and Stefan turned up before I had a chance to finish dressing, before I could tell either of you about it.''

''I'm sorry, but I'm still against it,'' said Radegund. ''I think you should call him off.''

''No,'' said William. ''And I'm going to ask you not to run to the troopers with this. You can answer their questions if they come asking, but don't go to them with it, okay?''

''We're going to be in a lot of trouble if they find out,'' warned Radegund.

''They won't. I understand Lord Stefan's down in the Horde camp now, asking for their help. He's a friend of theirs, you know. They'll tell him things they won't tell the troopers. He'll solve this for us, you'll see.''

17

"THE troopers are not about to let me come look at the murder scene," Stefan said to Wulfstan, "so I have to begin with the background of the victim." They were standing just inside the entrance to the encampment, and Wulfstan had behind him almost every Horde member present. They were not looking friendly. "I want to find out everything I can about Thorstane, what he was or did that might have provoked someone into killing him."

Wulfstan said, "I'm sorry, Lord Stefan, but I don't think you'll get much cooperation from the brothers at this time."

"When would be a better time? Later today? Tonight?"

"Well . . ."

"Exactly. May I address the brothers?"

Wulfstan hesitated, then shrugged. "All right. Come stand on the stump."

The stump had once belonged to a very large tree. It grew out of a spot near Lord Sabas' tent, and the shaman politely helped Stefan step up onto it. It was about three feet high, barkless, and gray with age. Katherine stood beside it, a little to the rear, and Wulfstan stood in front, facing the people crowding around.

''I am here to seek the truth,'' Stefan began, and there was an immediate ''Oh, yeah?'' and sarcastic laughter from the crowd.

Stefan continued doggedly, ''Thorstane Shieldbreaker is dead, and it appears he was killed by a member of the Society.''

''And we know which one,'' said a woman's voice from the rear, and there was a murmur of agreement.

''No, we don't!'' said Stefan sharply. ''There is not enough evidence right now to arrest, much less convict, anyone.''

''Bullshit,'' said a man's voice, and this time the noise of agreement was louder.

''Lord Stefan is a friend, you know that,'' warned Wulfstan, but the crowd rumbled in disagreement.

''Perhaps . . .'' said Sabas loudly, and the rumble died. ''Perhaps Lady Katherine will agree to a reading of the runes.''

''Yeah!'' said someone.

''How can you seriously suggest we consult a fortune-teller on a matter this important?'' asked Katherine.

''Smart lady!'' said a young man near the front of the crowd, and there was nervous laughter, but another jeered, ''What's the matter, she scared?''

''No,'' said Stefan. ''She just doesn't believe in that sort of thing.''

Lady Freyis stepped forward and said, ''Sabas would never offer to do this if he didn't think he could discover the truth!'' She pointed at the shaman. ''The power is on him; I say we should let him try it.

''Yeah,'' muttered the crowd, and waited for Katherine to refuse.

Katherine looked up at Stefan for guidance. ''I don't like this,'' she said.

''She is not consulting me,'' said Sabas, coming around the other side, ''they are.'' He gestured toward the crowd.

''He's right,'' came the murmurs; ''Yeah,'' and ''Do it.''

Stefan held out his hand to her. ''I need you to agree; I need their help and they won't unless you agree.'' She hesitated then reached up for his hand. There were cheers, some vindictive. Stefan jumped down and turned to Sabas. ''Where do you want us to go?''

• • •

Sabas' tent was oriented to the compass, and a gray wool blanket had been spread on the floor, equally oriented. Seven witnesses stood or knelt in expectant silence against the western wall of the tent. Katherine saw Sulu and Roc among them. Buu stood between Roc's knees, panting and restless.

Sabas sat cross-legged on the north edge of the blanket, straight-backed, his pose and paunch making him look like a crew-cut Buddha. There was an unsheathed knife on the blanket in front of him. Stefan sat on the western edge, Freyis on the east, and Katherine on the south, facing Sabas. In the middle of the blanket, in two neat stacks, were eighteen wooden squares cut from one-by-six boards. Sabas selected one from the top, turned it over and gave it to her. It had a symbol burned into it that looked like a *Z* tipped onto its back and crossed with a single upright line.

''This is the warding block,'' he said to her. ''Put it in front of you.'' She did so. ''It lays the onus of this reading on me,'' he explained, ''and protects you from any harm that may come of it.'' She gave him a surprised glance.

''Cast the circle, Freyis,'' he ordered, and Freyis rose, drew a sword from a scabbard hidden in the recesses of her black dress, and walked clockwise around the blanket, holding the blade upright before her. On completing the circle, she resumed her seat.

Sabas said to Katherine, ''My lady, please rearrange the order of the blocks to suit yourself, and put them back into two stacks when you are finished.''

She glanced at Stefan, who nodded encouragement, then leaned forward, exchanged the two top blocks, and sat back again.

''Well,'' he said after a moment, as if it were an approving judgment on her action. He pulled the stacks toward himself, took the top right one, and tossed it face down in the center of the blanket. Quickly, he tossed out an evenly spaced circle of a dozen more, then, more slowly, put the remaining four at the points of the compass inside the circle. He turned the center one over. It had a vertical line burned into it, crossed with a second line from upper right to lower left. ''Neid,'' he said, matter-of-factly. ''Need, or thralldom.'' There was a sigh from the witnesses; the reading had begun.

The circling dozen were turned over and he spoke the name of each and gave its meaning, his voice closer to an ordinary tone than she had yet heard it. ''Kinda, happiness, the hearth; Wynn, comfort and joy; Tyr the Greater, power; Mina, time, or a trap; Fara, also time, the scythe; Yr, tears, fear, death; Is, that which impedes; Tak, death, terror, the unknown; Lagu, fluidity; Gilch, money or another valued possession, to have, to give; Fehe, love of another; Hagle, misfortune.'' He studied these briefly, then turned over the four inner blocks. ''Tyr the Lesser, honor; Foeh, good luck; Ur, strength; Sygil, the sun.''

He put his hands on his knees and stared at the blocks for a full minute. Then: ''You are at a fork in your path,'' he began. ''You must choose correctly; that's your need. One path leads to the hearth, to home. The other leads to misfortune. You must keep fluidity of movement; you must not allow yourself to be frozen into inaction. You may be trapped into losing a valued possession if you choose the wrong path, and the right path leads to the downfall of another.

''There is a power in your hands to cut through the terror you now feel. You must use this power.'' He stopped, frowning, and she stirred restlessly.

''You are separated from death,'' he said. ''Indeed, the two ways of saying death, here and here, are positioned in such a way that you could not grasp them without giving the wound to yourself. And even if you would reach for them, you will not, for Is, impediment, keeps you from them.'' Roc immediately slipped around the wall of the tent and vanished out through the flap, Buu on his heels. She could hear his voice speaking to others waiting outside.

''Choosing the right path will lead you to what lies in the inner circle: honor, strength, good luck. You are what you are. Your word is true, for only honor stands between you and your need. Because of this, I think you are—or were—not even aware of your choices. Otherwise, your sense of honor and love of truth would have made choice, in the true sense, unnecessary. You have the strength to make the choice, and because good luck is with you, the choice will be correct. And you will wake to the sun, and he will at last see what you say, and, and—'' He faltered. ''The hot sun. Summer sun. And the little breeze, the summer wind. The sad memories, the weighing down, the not-telling, not-asking, not-dreaming. And a horse that took away sorrow, gone, like the summer wind. There is a beautiful house, which you keep for—a candle. A penny candle, bought for a copper.'' He smiled, secretly amused. ''I am old,'' he said. ''I am finished.''

The remaining witnesses broke into excited murmurs and Freyis stood, drew her sword, and uncast the circle.

''Was I of help to you?'' asked Sabas a minute later, his voice portentous again.

''Yes, very much so,'' said Stefan. ''Thank you.''

''What did you mean by a valued possession I could lose?'' asked Katherine.

''I'm sorry, my lady, but I cannot tell you.''

''He's always the last one in the place to find out what he said,'' Stefan explained to her. ''He has no memory of his readings.''

''I see,'' she said politely, doubting that.

Sabas leaned back and extended his legs in front of him. ''That must not have taken long,'' he said. ''My knees are hardly stiff at all. What did I say? Is she . . . ?''

''She is innocent,'' said Stefan. ''You said she could not possibly have reached for death without bringing it on herself, and that she was prevented from doing even that.''

''Then I am pleased,'' said Sabas. ''Perhaps now you may ask your questions of the others.''

. . .

''He wasn't a mean or bad person,'' said Olaf thoughtfully. ''He just liked to be drunk and for every night to be a party.'' Olaf was, like Wulfstan, a master-at-arms, given the accolade of knighthood but prevented by his membership in the Horde from swearing fealty to any king. He was the man Thorstane had struck from behind during a melee some months ago.

Olaf and Stefan were sitting in Freyis' yurt, which was actually a van disguised on the outside by a giant slipcover to look like a dome-topped Mongol tent. Walls and ceiling inside were covered with foil paisley wallpaper. A large bed took up most of the space; it was covered with a black velvet spread. There was a smell of exotic perfume or incense. Two incongruous notes startled the eye: a wire stretcher was attached to one wall, and a big first-aid kit tried to pretend it was a bedside table. The yurt doubled at SCA events as an ambulance.

"Are you saying Thorstane didn't provoke fights with people?" asked Stefan, writing.

"Oh, he got onto people's cases, but it was in fun, like. You know, like the kind of fights you get into in the backyard at a really good party. You can't remember after what they were about, and you're still friends with each other." Olaf looked around the van. "This is the first time I've been inside here," he said.

"Me, too," said Stefan.

"I hinted a time or two, but Freyis always had someone lined up already or something," said Olaf dimly.

"I don't suppose Thorstane was ever invited over," said Stefan.

"Are you kidding? She only came to Strange Sea for events, and Thorstane was generally so drunk after an event he wouldn't be any use to her."

"What about when he went to out-of-town events?"

"He hadn't done any of that in a long while. People didn't like to take him along because he was usually too broke to pay his share of expenses."

"If he was so poor, how did he finance his drinking?

Olaf shrugged. "One was the reason for the other, I guess. He must've spent most of his money for booze. He sold me two six-packs for five dollars one time. He said he needed money to buy breakfast. I told him it was three o'clock in the afternoon, but he said the first time you eat in a day is breakfast, isn't it?" Olaf laughed. "He was kinda wild, y'know? But he wasn't a bad guy. Ask the people who knew him."

"All right, I'll do that. Who else is here from Cleveland besides you?"

"Narses the Great is here; his tent is behind Sabas'. Erik couldn't come. On the kingdomer side, there's Sir John, Master Petrog, Lady Winifred, Sir Ignatius, and Lord Kevin. Most are in the Strange Sea encampment, right behind the Fat Cat Inn. I don't know where Petty's camped, but Iggy's tent is near William's, as usual."

Stefan hadn't known Sir Iggy and Master Petty were from Strange Sea. "As usual?"

"Will and Iggy spend more time with each other at events than with their ladies. Tweedledum and Tweedle-even-dumber. I'm surprised Iggy wasn't backing up Will when he was laying ambushes in the woods. They fight together in melees and stuff all the time —they go back a long ways together."

"Where were you during the Woods Battle?"

"Right here, tending the fire, so Roc could go play scout. I'm out of fighting for a while; I tore a shoulder muscle at karate practice and it's not all the way healed yet."

"I understand you got Thorstane his last job."

"Yeah, I guess it was my turn. It took some doing. I asked Sir John, who runs a warehouse for Nerren's, but he said, 'Are you nuts? We're the biggest liquor-supply dealer in the city! You think I want someone like him working for me?' and I said I saw what he meant. Then I heard about this job driving a delivery van for Forham's, and I took him down and let him use me as a reference, and told him I'd break both his legs if he screwed this one up. And he didn't; he managed to hang on to it. Funny thing, too; one of the things he delivers now and then is liquor. So far as I know he hasn't stolen a drop. He likes driving, and he's good at it. Oh, a little wild, but good. He's been with them eight or nine months— I mean . . ." Olaf looked down at a clenched fist and deliberately uncurled the fingers. "This is a hell of a thing, a hell of a thing!"

• • •

Freyis said archly, "I hoped you'd save me for last."

Stefan replied, "You're Thorstane's Tar-Khan, and as such high on my list of people to talk to."

"Well, sit down then, and talk."

Stefan sat on the bed across from Freyis, which was his only choice. There was no other furniture except the first-aid kit, and it was already holding a battery lamp and an incense burner. Freyis leaned on a black silk pillow and said, "I see you didn't bring your lady with you."

Stefan said, "I find it helps affirm the confidentiality of an investigation to keep extraneous people out of earshot. I assure you that anything you tell me is confidential, unless it pertains directly to my investigation."

She chuckled, starting a warm itch low in his belly. "I like a discreet man. May I offer you something before we begin?"

"No, thank you. When did you last speak with Thorstane?"

She studied him briefly, then sighed. "You're going to be too busy anyway, aren't you?"

He smiled, relieved. "Yes, I am. When did you last speak with Thorstane?"

"Early this morning. He looked as if he'd been up all night. I asked him if he thought he should fight in the Woods Battle, and he said he'd be fine. I told him I could make him a special tea, and he said Sabas was already brewing one for him."

"Did you warn him about behaving?"

"I didn't have to," she said. "Wulfstan and I had both spoken to him yesterday, and Broddi and Hreider were going to be with him in the woods."

"What happened to them? How did he manage to lose both his k'shaktu?"

"I don't know. Wulfstan might; he talked to one or the other of them at the Point, before the troopers hauled them away with Radegund and the others."

Stefan made a notation to talk to ask Wulfstan. "Did you kill him, Freyis?"

She looked amused. "With Roc standing there watching? Anyway, why should I kill him?"

"He has a history of grabbing women. Maybe he grabbed you and wouldn't let go."

She held out her hand, and there was a knife in it, little blade gleaming. "You've watched me get called to the throne at royal courts, Steffy. It takes me five minutes to unload all the steel I carry before I go up there. It's a famous piece of shtick, my taking off my knives. Thorstane teased me about it a couple of times, saying if I ever fell in a lake I'd go right to the bottom. He knew better than to grab me."

He nodded. "Okay, maybe he was an embarrassment to you in your position as Tar-Khan."

"Now, that's really dumb! Granted, the Horde's a motley bunch; we draw more than our share of wild cards like Thorstane. But we know how to handle them. I've been in the Society—and the household—a long, long time, and I've yet to find it necessary to take a knife to anyone." She chuckled wryly. "Not that I haven't been tempted, mind you. It just hasn't been necessary. The wild cards come, and they settle down or they go."

"Which way was Thorstane headed?"

"Out, probably."

"Maybe soon?"

"You mean tomorrow? Maybe. Maybe not. It would have depended on how much of an effort he made to clean up his act before then. We're great one-more-chancers, you know."

"But in time, he would have gone."

"I think so. His drinking was getting worse, not better; and we were getting sick of him. But there was no pressing need for anyone to kill him."

"Humor me; tell me where you were during the Woods Battle."

She sighed. "All right. Roc and I went in together, we found the banner together, we got killed within a dozen yards of each other, and we went to the Point together."

"And after that?"

"We saw the knight who took our whistles out there at the Point, but he wouldn't give them back. When we got released, we went looking for Humphrey, both to report that we'd lost the whistles and because we were supposed to be scouting for him. It took a while, and when we found him, he was standing on a high place and too busy to send us on any errands."

"He didn't mention seeing you."

"No, none of you saw us. We heard the noise and came sneaking up and saw, let's see, you, Geoff, Humph, and what's his name—Taffy—all up on top with the banner, and about a dozen Easterners doing their best to get you down. You were out there in front, on your knees, and Humphrey was standing behind you with his polearm. You two make a great team."

"Thank you."

"Anyway, we decided Humph didn't need us to come trotting up, asking if he wanted us for anything. We sneaked back off and found King William's troops, who were thrilled to learn our side had captured the banner; but they wanted to know where the Sam Hill the King had gotten to, so we went looking for him. We still hadn't found him when we heard your lady call for help. I suppose she already told you about that."

"Tell me your version."

"Okay. We were on a side trail not too far off the main trail. We were walking slow, both to listen and to give Will a chance to spot who we were and maybe come out or signal us. We heard a woman's voice calling, 'Help, help, scout!' We came running and there she was in the middle of the trail, poor kid, looking scared. She said Thorstane was hurt, bad. I asked what happened, and she said she didn't know, that some medics were with him, but he needed an ambulance. I thought about the yurt, but that's for transporting broken legs and she was sounding like he needed life support, not just wheels. So I told Roc to go phone, and that I'd stand by the branch off the main trail to show the way in. I'm sorry I made that decision; it took twenty or twenty-five minutes for the damn ambulance to get there."

"While you were waiting for the ambulance, did anyone else come by?"

"Let's see. A medic came out and told me Thorstane was dead. She told me the battle should be called off, and I should help her find a king, or more scouts, but I told her I was staying where I was to guide the ambulance. I noticed there was some blood about knee level on her tabard, but not much. I've seen one or two automobile accidents with no fatalities but blood everywhere; and here she was talking dead man, and there's just these little stains. She was a kid, and excited, so I figured maybe she was wrong. She ran off yelling for a scout. Two minutes later one came by who said he heard the yelling, but he hadn't seen the medic, so I sent him back to talk to whoever was staying with Thorstane. He came out two minutes later at a dead run and took off up the trail; didn't say a word as he went by. A while later Sir Iggy came running up and asked was it true Thorstane was dead, and I said all I knew was Thorstane was hurt and an ambulance had been called, and would he please not go back there and get in the way. Then the cannon went and I started hearing the heralds calling the battle off and saying everyone should go out to the Point.''

''What was Iggy wearing?''

She blinked at this, and said, ''That ratty old blue gambeson he's been wearing for the past six Wars. Why?''

''Never mind. Did you go out to the Point with the rest?''

''No, of course not. I stayed and waved the ambulance down the right way, and waved again for a trooper in his car—though I didn't need to, he had that young medic with him—then for a van marked 'State Police,' and a black station wagon marked 'Coroner.' It was the wagon that convinced me he was dead.'' She stopped, plucked at a thread on the quilt. ''I didn't like Thorstane; I don't think anyone liked him. But no one, *no one,* has a right to murder a person just because he's a son of a bitch!'' She looked at Stefan. ''It's not what the Society stands for; it's not what the Horde is about. Find out who did this to us, Steffy, okay?''

''Yes, ma'am; I'll do my best,'' he said.

18

"WHY did you join the SCA?" asked Ignatius over his beer.

"You aren't the one who's doing that goddamn survey, are you?" demanded William. They were in the royal pavilion.

"Me? Hell, no! It's the Kingdom Seneschal, on orders of the BoD." Pronounced "bodd," and meaning the Board of Directors of the Society, a suspiciously mundane authority located in far-off California. "But why did you?"

"Sometimes I wonder," grumbled William. He took a long pull at his beer, then sighed. "God, that was a long time ago!"

"What?"

"Me joining SCA. I was already a squire at Pennsic Number One." He slouched further into his faldstool and sipped his beer. "But I can remember like it was yesterday the first time I saw SCA-folk. I was crossing the campus at State, and there were these people in costumes. Only they weren't wearing them like costumes, they were wearing them like clothes. And the guys were holding a melee, four on four, and I could see it wasn't choreographed. Man, was I impressed, but looking back I can see they were in carpet armor, most of them, carrying your basic round shields. One had a helm cut from a Freon tank, which was state-of-the-art back then and illegally dangerous now. But damn, it looked like fun! And it was, too. Still is, most of the time. You know how you can get sick of real life? Only you can't afford to chuck it—and even if you did, where would you go? The twentieth century is everywhere. Except in the SCA. That's why I joined."

They drank their beer and thought about past Wars, old courts, long-gone kings, in companionable silence. Then Ignatius put his empty can down and said, "So, it looks like you're in the clear, then?"

William shrugged. "I hope so. I was hitting them pretty steady right up to when the cannon went off. Where did you go?"

"Resurrection Point. I got killed, remember?"

"And after?"

Ignatius crossed his bandy legs at the ankles. He had spoken only to break the silence; he hadn't wanted to start a conversation. "I went looking for you. I found Tommy, then Wulfstan and the Horde, then Queen Jane and her troops. She was really shapin' them up, doing everything but counting cadence. She said she'd just seen your bunch and you hadn't come back to them."

"Did you see who captured the banner?"

"It was Humph and his little band of cutthroats. They took it up on top of a steep clay bank—remember Pennsic Ten? That place."

"I will never, as long as I live, forget that spot. I died three times at the foot of that greasy little cliff. So that's where the banner ended up."

"No, it ended up at Resurrection Point. Some clown put it in the Lost and Found can; I saw it there."

William snorted, spewing suds. "That's wonderful! Was it Humphrey who did that?"

"Him or Geoff; they share the same sense of humor. I remember the time—"

But William was not to be drawn off the scent. "So where did you end up?"

"What?"

"In the Woods Battle. Who did you end up fighting with?"

"No one. I just kept wandering around, looking for you. I knew you didn't have your sword, and Hilda said you didn't come out for a spare, so I figured you were hiding somewhere. I took my spare along for you, but I couldn't find you. Now I hear you were laying ambushes right where people were coming back from the Point. Where did you get another sword?"

"From the Lost and Found. The can was right by the entrance to the Point. I was hid in the bushes when you came back in from Resurrection."

"So why didn't you say something?"

"Because there was a string of Easterners behind you. I didn't want to let them know I was there. Iggy, are you telling me you don't have an alibi?"

The stocky little man uncrossed his ankles and sat up straight. "Well, no, I guess I don't," he said slowly, half ashamed, half frightened.

"Well, Jesus H. Christ, why not?"

"Well, how was I to know I'd need one?" asked Ignatius angrily. "Nothing like this has ever happened at a War before!"

"Did you kill him?" asked William.

"No. You know I was pissed as hell at him, and that I had good cause to be. If those troopers put two and two together— I'm wondering if I should pack up and go home."

"No, that wouldn't help. And you might start a stampede. Stick around; we'll think of something. You swear you didn't kill him?"

"I swear."

• • •

Wulfstan wasn't back from his interview with the troopers, so Stefan spoke next with Narses the Great, who was from Strange Sea and had fought in the Woods Battle. He was about thirty-three, a broad-shouldered man with a wide grin and a rolling sailor's gait. "Yeah, only the folks back in Little Rock can tell I been living up north," he said in reply to Stefan's comment on his marked drawl. "I been in Strange Sea for close on to three years."

"How well did you know Thorstane Shieldbreaker?" asked Stefan.

The grin died. "Well, he was a brother. Apart from that, I can't say I felt kindly toward him. He was a poor swordsman and a poor sport besides. He didn't acknowledge blows, and he hit too hard with that mace of his. And he aimed a little too often for the shins and the hands, which as I understand the rules, you ain't supposed to do."

"Did you attend any of his parties?"

Narses shook his head. "No, I'm an alcoholic, been dry for five years come November. I try to stay away from situations where the object is to see how fast you can get how drunk."

"Did you fight with the Horde in the Woods Battle?"

"Yeah, I was with Wulffy the whole time."

"Do you remember a kingdomer fighting with you, a man in blue armor?"

Narses thought. "Yeah, a guy with a polearm. He joined up after the battle was underway. But he didn't last long. Got killed and went off."

"The same time as Thorstane?"

"Yeah."

"What was his name?"

Narses squinted up an eye. "He told it to Wulffy. He wasn't a knight, or even a squire, but he impressed the hell out of us for a minute or two there, then he got killed, and that was that. He went off and didn't come back."

"Can you remember his name?"

"Lemme think. Wulffy sent just a little bunch of us out, not includin' me, playing chivalrous, I guess, forgetting this is the War, y'know? I was leaning on my shield, watching. This guy said he was just back from Resurrection and all rested, so Wulffy put him out in the second rank and he kills this Easterner quick as lightning. I remember Wulffy saying, 'See that man fight!' What *was* his name? Christopher! Christopher Bridgewater, Bridgeman, something like that. Yeah, from Lone Castle. He kills his man, and right about then Thorstane goes down, and Christopher, who's right behind him, takes a shot to the helm you can hear in Denver if you got your windows open, and goes flying out of the rank. And I was kind of disappointed, because I wanted to talk to him."

"Why?"

"Because he sounded like he might've been from back home."

"You mean he had an accent?"

The grin appeared. "No, I mean he didn't have as much of an accent as y'all. Maybe you've noticed how a northerner will hear some country boy talk and right away start in mockin' him? And some are pitiful at it, while others will get it almost right?"

"Yes, I know what you mean."

"Well, that's what he made me think of, the second kind. But I hadn't opened my mouth since he'd come, and I thought maybe he'd just been away from home even longer than I had, y'know, so I wanted to talk to him, only he got killed and went off."

"With Thorstane."

"Yeah, and some Easterners. Oh, and Broddi. He and the other k'shaktu, Hreider, step off to the side of the trail and Hreider pops Broddi one on the helm so he can go with Thorstane, keep an eye on him like Wulffy told 'em to do."

"Did Broddi come back to you from Resurrection?"

"Yeah, and was he mad! He said Thorstane never showed up at the Point. He and Hreider got into an argument over whether they should go looking for him; he wanted to and Hreider said no, Thorstane'd show up pretty soon. Both of 'em was purely in a sweat."

"What did Wulfstan do when he realized Thorstane was missing?"

"He took Broddi to the side of the trail and talked to him, and while he never raised his voice, Broddi looked like he was having strips of skin tore off him. Wulffy formed us back up and we went back to business, but you could see he was keeping an eye out for Thorstane, and I think he was about to send Broddi looking for him when the cannon went. Wulfstan says it must be a mistake, and then a herald come by and said we should go out to the Point, and we hear this siren, and we're wondering if Ozzy or Will got hurt, because why else call the battle off? Then this little scout come by and whispers in Wullfy's ear, an' I sincerely thought the Khan was goin' to have him a cardiovascular incident. He grabbed that scout by her arm and made her yell and he was white as a sheet of paper. But he wouldn't tell us what was wrong, just hustles us up the trail. We seen Freyis, but she was raising a hand to the ambulance comin' in, and she wouldn't say boo to us. The look on her face made me start to get a bad feeling about things. And after we got out to the Point, Wulffy says it's Thorstane, that he's been hurt, and if he dies, it's murder. He tells us to seal the Point. I run over an' join a line formin' up at the bridge, and we agree we won't listen to anyone's orders but the Khan's, because for all we know it was Will or Ozzy or even Rags did it."

"Did you notice a fighter on the other side of the bridge, or anyone crossing before you got it closed?"

"No. All I saw on the other side was those kids with the 'Make Peace' sign. I remember one of us asked if anyone had already crossed, and they said no. They asked who won, but none of us answered—hell, none of us knew the answer. I was trying to act like I knew what we were doing, and thinking maybe someone was going to come at us with a knife or maybe even a gun, and I was wondering what I'd do if that happened, and if my shield could stop a bullet. I was trying to look mean, so if the killer came, he'd try to get past one of the others, not me. I made up my mind that if he shot one of my brothers, I'd try to jump him from behind as he went on across. But I was so scared my knees was weak. Then King William said it was a mundane and I relaxed, because I knew a mundane with even a shoe-size IQ would've gone over the campground fence at the end of the woods and be long gone."

• • •

Roc put a log on the glowing embers. "I want to apologize for being rude to you this morning," he said. "Especially since you not only let it go by, you answered the same question when I put it to you." He pushed the log into a better position with the heel of his boot. "Not that it's any big deal, anyway." He looked at Katherine. "I joined the Society because my sister had joined. She seemed to think it was the biggest deal in the world. She came home from an event all glowing because some fake king had given her the right to bear and display a coat of arms she had to design herself. I just had to find out what she was so hopped up about, so I started coming along." He shrugged. "She was killed in a car accident a year later. My parents sold the house and we moved into town, and

I started college that fall. I stayed in the SCA because it was the one thing that hadn't changed, because it was a way of staying in touch with her."

"How long ago was that?" Katherine was sitting on a low stool Roc had brought for her.

"Four years." He grinned a painful grin. "You know, for the first time, telling that story almost doesn't hurt. She was a real kingdomer, full of ideals, had a wardrobe of Italian Renaissance garb. I started out the same way, but look at me now."

"But you're still in the SCA," said Katherine.

"I wonder if I'm staying because I don't want to let go of her, or because I don't want anyone to think I'm letting go."

She did not know what to say to that, and so said nothing.

He put another log on the fire. "Wood fires burn hot," he said, "but they burn fast. I'm not supposed to let it go completely out."

"How did you manage to volunteer to do this for the whole War?"

"I'm sort of paying off some favors I owe. Good thing I'm not fighting this year." He smiled at her. "I bet you're relieved about that reading of the runes. You're cleared now, right?"

"I hope so; can you see me going into court with that reading for a defense?"

He laughed. "You'd need a special kind of lawyer, that's for sure."

"I hope it doesn't come to that."

Roc put down a log to frown at her. "You don't seem to have much confidence in Stefan finding out the truth."

"He's the finest police detective in the world, but no detective solves every single case." She picked up a piece of bark and began to pull it apart. "The right person has to come forward and say the right thing. To solve a case takes time: time to listen, time to run down evidence—and time's what we don't have here. And he hasn't got access to the murder scene, or to the results of forensic lab work, or the autopsy. So perhaps the right clue can't reach him. There's an element of luck in his kind of work, but you have to give luck every chance."

"I think you're his luck, Lady Katherine. The runes said you were the one with the power to bring about somebody's downfall."

She threw what was left of the bark into the fire pit. "That's nonsense. The reason I agreed to the reading was so that you people would answer his questions, and I resent you looking to me to solve the case. I can't do it."

"Don't say that. That may be the wrong decision in the choice you're supposed to make." He turned the log into a stool.

"I wish I hadn't agreed to that reading! I've already told Lord Stefan everything I know. I don't understand what Sabas was getting at."

"That's right, too; I talked to Sulu about the part of the reading I missed and he said you were told you weren't aware of your choices."

"How can I make a choice if I don't know I have one, or what the choices are?"

"Don't worry about it, m'lady. Sabas said you'd make the right one anyway, without knowing you did it."

She stood. "I can't help worrying. It was so strange, listening to him saying things that made no sense, filling me with a kind of urgency to do or say—what? And then, at the very end . . . It wasn't all nonsense, you know. I was raised by an elderly uncle who was very strict with me. But he bought me a mare in foal to a famous stallion, and the foal was Summer Wind, who turned out wonderfully, spirited and gentle. Summer Wind was my escape from anger and sadness."

Roc said shyly, "I know you appreciate not being asked, but someone said . . . I've never seen where you live, but I hear it's a big, fancy house."

She laughed. "It is. Now that I've gotten to know you, I'll have you to dinner and show it off. I nearly sold it when it became mine, but by then I was in love with Peter, and he so obviously liked it, I changed my mind. Maybe he's the copper I kept it for—a lit candle is his device, you know."

Roc removed the log from under his rump and stood. "The way you didn't want Sabas to read the runes. I thought it was against your religion to believe in fortune-tellers."

"No, my religion doesn't say they aren't real, only that I'm not to deal with them. There's a difference."

• • •

Wulfstan, back from speaking with the troopers, courteously agreed that Stefan could likewise interview him. He sat cross-legged on the quilt, having left his shoes outside the door of the yurt. No matter how authentic his garb, he never looked like a barbarian, and Stefan suddenly realized why: He was too neat. His natural linen shirt with the Celtic embroidery was not only clean, it was ironed. So were his brown woolen trews. Even his knee-down leg wrappings were of deer hide, a singularly unshaggy fur.

"In my opinion," Wulfstan was saying, "Thorstane was a serious alcoholic, out of control. He couldn't hold a job, and he wouldn't admit it was his drinking that was causing the problem. He allegedly made a physical attack on the last man who got him fired."

"When was this?" asked Stefan.

"Ten—eleven months ago. He had his current job eight or nine months—a record, by the way—and he was out of work a month or two before he got it. Olaf found it for him."

"What was he doing?"

"Driving a delivery van. He was a good driver, and was generally on time for work and moderately prompt in his deliveries. There were no breakages and no reports of theft."

"Sounds as if you got access to a work review."

Wulfstan grinned wickedly. "One never knows where there is a ninja." In the Horde vocabulary, the Japanese word for a secret warrior had come to include spies.

"But he lost his previous job because of his drinking."

Wulfstan nodded. "He'd come to work drunk a few times."

"What was he doing?"

"Hospital orderly. I think he did better at the driving because he was outdoors and because there was no supervisor breathing down his neck."

"But he allegedly assaulted the man who fired him from his job as hospital orderly?"

"No, he allegedly assaulted the doctor who turned him in for sleeping on duty. The doctor said it was Thorstane, but it happened at night, in a dark corner of a parking garage, and Thorstane produced a friend who is pretty sure he was with Thorstane at the critical time."

"Only pretty sure?"

"They had been drinking all afternoon. The friend remembers going for a long, crazy car ride, Thorstane driving, and that the ride went on and on. But there are gaps—you know how it is with drunks. It might have been during one of those gaps that Thorstane committed the assault, but the witness has no memory of stopping other than for beer and gas."

"Do you know who this witness is?"

"Broddi. But that's not the hard part."

"What is?"

"The doctor who was assaulted is Master Petrog. Petrog caught him sleeping and insisted he be fired. And ever since Petty's had a run of bad luck. He was assaulted, then someone put sugar in his car's gas tank and slashed the tires. Two windows in his apartment were broken by vandals, the hospital administrator has been getting crank calls from someone accusing Petty of malpractice, and about once a month someone seals his mailbox shut with superglue. Petty came all the way to an event in Brewton to ask if I'd do something about Thorstane, but he's got no proof the incidents are even related, much less that it was Thorstane harassing him."

"Has he been to the police?"

"Oh, yes, but they say there's not enough evidence for an arrest."

"Do you think Thorstane was the one behind all this?"

Wulfstan narrowed his eyes and stroked his mustache with thumb and forefinger. "Thorstane's attention span was limited; it wasn't like him to carry a grudge for any length of time. Still, he was almost arrested for the assault, and he kept up this 'Patty-cake' business for months. Petty is sure it was Thorstane."

"How bad was the beating?"

"Broken nose, cracked ribs, assorted bruises. Petty said he would have fought back except he was scared of injuring his hands—he treats his hands like they're his babies, which is understandable; he's a surgeon, you know."

Stefan was writing in his notebook. "You led the Horde in the Woods Battle today?"

Wulfstan nodded. "Yes."

"Did a kingdomer come along and join your group, a man in blue armor?"

Wulfstan nodded again. "Yes."

"Will you tell me about him?"

"His name is Lord Christopher Bridgeman, and he's from Lone Castle."

"You know this for a fact?"

"It's what he told me. He joined us carrying a polearm, said he was just back from Resurrection, where, he said, there were many more Easterners than Midrealmers. He was doing really well, but Thorstane, who was fighting right in front of him, got killed and he fell in consequence. They went off to a gathering place and neither came back. I had never seen the man Christopher before, and have no idea if Thorstane knew him. He didn't act as if he did."

"Who else was killed at that time?"

"Two or three Easterners. And Hreider killed Broddi so he could go along and keep watch on Thorstane."

"Which he didn't do very well."

Wulfstan's mouth tightened. "I have spoken to him about that."

"Was Broddi a good friend of Thorstane's?"

"More a drinking buddy. He was prepared to make him toe the line when I asked if he'd play k'shaktu with Hreider over Thorstane. I'm satisfied this was nothing more than carelessness."

"Would there have been time for this man in blue armor to get to Resurrection Point and back again before the battle ended?" asked Stefan.

"Yes, if he wanted to. Broddi came back. We were on the main trail the whole time, so he didn't have to look long or hard for us. But maybe Lord Christopher rejoined his original group."

"Did he say who he was fighting with originally?"

"Not to me."

"Did you think he was coming back when he went off?"

"I didn't think anything. He was good, but we weren't short of polearm fighters, so I wasn't worried about it."

"What can you remember about him? Apart from the armor?"

Again Wulfstan stroked his mustache. "He was tall, maybe King William's height, and about as broad. He seemed anxious to get into the action, so when we were setting up for a small skirmish, I sent him in. He certainly wasn't a novice fighter, although he wasn't belted. I remember calling out that we should watch him fight, he was that good. It wasn't his fault he got killed; Thorstane took a killing blow and Christopher seemed to be trying to move back to give him room to fall when he took his."

"Did you tell him where to stand when you sent him in?"

"No, I just said he could go in, and he chose the place."

"Behind Thorstane."

"Yes."

"I've been told Lord Christopher took a shot to the helm that could have been heard as far away as Denver."

Wulfstan chuckled. "You've been talking to Narses."

"What does that mean to you?"

Wulfstan shrugged. "What I said at the time: tip."

"A tip shot is when just the tip of a sword catches its target," said Stefan. "It's loud, but is not considered a killing blow."

"Yes. But when I looked around, Lord Christopher was lying out by the edge of the trail, so it must have been good."

"You're sure Thorstane went down first?"

"Yes, it was the breach of the shield wall that got Christopher killed."

"Can you tell me anything else about Lord Christopher?"

Wulfstan, wanting to help, cast about for some other tidbit. "He had an accent."

"What sort of accent?"

"One of those hokey ones, like those guys on *Hee-Haw*."

"Anything else?"

Wulfstan thought. "No."

"Did you remain with the Horde forces throughout the entire Woods Battle?"

There was a flicker of amusement in the Khan's dark eyes. "Yes."

"Did you happen across King William during the battle?"

"No. We saw Iggy from a distance, and ran into Queen Jane."

"Alone?"

"No, with Edmund's troops. Edmund was at Resurrection, she said. We asked her if she wanted to join us, and she said no. She was on her way toward the entrance to meet Edmund, who was due, she said, to be turned loose. She'd turned down a chance to join up with William's troops, too, on the grounds that there would be too many fighters for efficient fighting in the woods. Though I think it was also because she was enjoying leading her own force. She seemed to be doing a good job; she is a very organized lady."

19

"WHERE to now?" asked Katherine as she and Stefan left the Horde camp.

"I want to see Lord Christopher Bridgeman or Bridgewater of Lone Castle in the Calontir encampment. Maybe he can tell us why neither he nor Thorstane turned up at the Point with the others."

The encampment was down King's Road, the next path along from the Charter encampment, marked by a crowned falcon. As Stefan and Katherine approached, they heard voices singing a familiar modern melody, the quick, rumbling words unintelligible, then abruptly rising into clarity:

Good mornin', Your Majesty, how are you?
Say, don't you know us? We're your rebel sons.
Calontir has come to save your ass at Pennsic.
We'll have killed a thousand foes 'fore the day is done.

Katherine smiled; Calontir had been a principality of the Midrealm before it broke free to form its own kingdom, and stories of its sassy attitude toward its parent were common in the Midrealm.

. . . All along the eastbound odyssey
The bus pulls out of Forgotten Sea
And heads toward Pennsylvania's bloody fields,
The yearly pilgrimage—

The song faltered and broke off as Stefan and Katherine approached. There were about half a dozen men and women sitting around a thin-tongued fire, roasting brats on long forks. Four more were sitting under a fly eating. A woman wearing a stiff, spangled Russian folk costume put down her guitar and came to greet them. "Are you looking for someone?" she asked.

"Lord Christopher Bridgeman or Bridgewater, of Lone Castle," replied Stefan.

The woman frowned. "I don't think I know him." She turned and said, "Jamie, you're from Lone Castle. Do you know a Lord Christopher?"

A brown-haired boy in a red-orange tunic shook his head. "No, I've never heard of him."

Stefan asked, "Is it possible he's a member of your group and you just don't know him?"

The boy laughed. "There's only nine of us in the whole group. You can ask my mom, she's at the store, but I can tell you the names of all the guys in Lone Castle: Sir Alan, Lord Patrick, Lord Einar, and me. There's no Lord Christopher, I know that for sure."

"Come over to the fire," invited an older man in gray. "We're going to mull some cider."

The Russian woman's golden headdress made an icon's halo around her head. She asked, as she sat down again in the circle around the fire, "What's your interest in Lord Christopher?"

Stefan produced King William's writ, and it was handed around. "It seems a man in blue armor disappeared about the same time and place Thorstane did. He's been identified as Lord Christopher from Lone Castle."

The older man handed the writ back to Stefan. "I thought the State Police were conducting the investigation. Are you helping them?"

"No, this is a private thing."

''Can you legally do this?'' asked the Russian woman.

''So long as I don't interfere with the regular investigation, yes.''

''Are you a private eye?'' asked the boy, awed.

''No, back home I'm a police officer.''

''Have you talked to that water bearer the troopers arrested?'' asked the Russian woman.

''She wasn't arrested,'' said Stefan. ''She's my lady; this is her, right here.''

''They cleared her, then,'' the Russian woman said, nodding.

Stefan hesitated. ''Well . . .''

''I see,'' said the older man, and half the Calontir people stared at Katherine; the other half became interested in how the bratwurst on their forks was doing.

''Have any of you gone to look at the blue armor?'' asked Stefan. They shook their heads.

''I was going to,'' volunteered the boy, ''only there were too many people crowded around it, so I didn't.''

''Do any of you know a Lord Christopher?''

''I don't think we have to answer any of your questions,'' said the Russian woman, picking up her guitar.

''Maybe if I spoke with His Majesty of Calontir,'' said Stefan. ''Where is he?''

''Forgotten Sea, I imagine,'' said the gray man. This caused a mild shuffle of amusement; Forgotten Sea was Kansas City, the King's hometown.

''There's no Lord Christopher in this encampment,'' said the guitar player. ''And I'm not sure we should tell you even that. King William was way out of line, in my opinion, giving you that writ.'' There was a murmur of agreement. ''I think you ought to leave now, okay?''

''I'm sorry you think that way, my lords, my ladies,'' said Stefan. He bowed, took Katherine's hand, and they withdrew.

''Whew,'' he said, as they started down King's Road, and a little while later, ''Damn.''

''What's the matter?''

''If we run into many people with that attitude, I'm shot down in flames.''

"Maybe we won't. Where to now?"

"The Couple Dragons. I just remembered I haven't had lunch yet."

"Are you hungry—or thirsty?" she teased.

"Hungry, but the gossip's better at the Dragons."

• • •

Trooper Bead reported, "The coroner just called. The victim died of cardiac tamponade caused by a stab wound to the heart made by a long, very thin, possibly circular blade—looks like the ice pick is it. In addition to the two stab wounds, there were assorted bruises, some of them more than a day old. His blood alcohol tested at point-oh-three, so he wasn't drunk." Bead sighed. "The coroner says it's easily possible the victim could have lived long enough to speak to someone, and that CPR won't work on a person whose heart stops because of this type of injury."

"So the Brichter woman is probably telling the truth," said Lloyd.

"Yes; do I go tell them?"

"Yeah, I suppose so. Seeing as how it was the governor of Pennsylvania who took a personal interest in the case, maybe you should even apologize for any inconvenience caused her. What's someone with friends like that doing in a flaky outfit like this?"

"Beats doing cocaine, I guess."

• • •

Bead had long ago gotten used to his uniform, and its difference from street clothes, but in the costumed depths of the campground it felt strangely ordinary.

Perhaps because he was so busy staring at the people, he missed his turn, and finally stopped a man in tights whose jacket sleeves had been slashed to display the gold satin shirt he wore under it.

"I'm looking for a man you call Stefan von Helle," Bead said. "He's camped with a man you call Sir Geoffrey of Brixham."

"That would be the Charter encampment," replied the man, who continued courteously, "You've come too far. Follow this road back—not as far as the Horde camp, with the canvas fence—"

"And the doorman on a rabbit-fur chair?"

The man grinned. "That's them. About fifty yards this side of it, look to your left for a path marked by a pair of silver oil torches on poles. They're at the end of the path."

"Thank you."

"Anytime, m'lord Trooper." The man bowed.

Bead turned to retrace his steps. He wondered if there was a name for the article of costume the man had been wearing at the point where his tights came together. It was bad enough that it was a contrasting color, but did it have to be so obviously stuffed, and draped with little gold chains?

Bead found the path marked by torches and went up it. At the end he found Sir Geoffrey, a tall lady with tawny hair, and a slender dark-haired man, eating bread spread with a hot, gooey mix of meat, cheese, and onions.

"I'm looking for Mr. and Mrs. Brichter," said Bead.

"They're not here," said the young woman, around a mouthful of food.

"Do you know where they are?"

"No, sir," said Sir Geoffrey. "Is something wrong?"

"On the contrary. We've got the results of the autopsy, and Mrs. Brichter's story of the victim speaking to her is in no way contradicted."

"Thank God!" said the dark-haired man.

"Thank you for coming to tell us," said Sir Geoffrey. "We'll be sure to let them know when they get back."

"Do you know when that might be?"

"No, I'm afraid we don't." There was a slightly uncomfortable air about Sir Geoffrey—about all of them, Bead noticed; but he merely thanked them and left.

• • •

"Lord Stefan?" called a voice. Katherine and Stefan turned to see Sir John hurrying to catch up with them. They waited, but when he arrived, he seemed not to know where to begin. "Uh," he said, his fair skin turning pink, a pretty contrast to his light blue tunic. "I heard— Is it true? I mean that you're—"

"Yes, King William has asked me to look into what happened in the woods this morning."

"Okay, well, could you come back to my tent? I think I may have something you ought to know."

"All right."

"Lady Katherine, that's a very pretty outfit you've got on. Kind of matches Lord Stefan's, doesn't it?"

Stefan thought that a clumsy effort on the part of a man reputed to be a lady-killer, then reflected that Sir John was probably unused to complimenting a lady in whom he had no sexual interest. But Katherine smiled at the knight and said, "Thank you."

Sir John was camping alone. "I forgot to tell the others to save a space for me in the Strange Sea encampment," he said. For a lone bachelor, he was surprisingly neat. His two-man tent, of yellow rip-stop nylon, looked orderly from Stefan's quick glance at its interior through the open flap. The knight had his armor laid out in preparation for the next battle, the gambeson beside it. It was new, if sweat-dampened, with a bad snag on the shoulder.

Few fighters made the effort to wash their things at the War. Most suffered the sweaty odor a second day, then sealed the clothes in a plastic bag for the trip home. There were hilarious stories about the consequences of opening that bag after it had fermented a few hundred miles in the trunk of a car.

Sir John had a second gambeson, lying folded on top of his ice chest in front of his tent. It was an older one, with a lot more of the snags and wear marks of his armor. "I'll have to get me a regular lady," he said, following Stefan's look. "That spare's getting kind of tacky."

"You should see Sir Iggy's," said Stefan. "Held together with safety pins and string."

John laughed, a friendly sound, but Stefan's stomach prodded him, so he took out his notebook and asked, "What is it you wanted to tell me?"

The uncomfortable look came back to Sir John. "I was fighting with King Edmund of Meridies," he said, "when we came across King William's troops. Only he wasn't there. He'd lost his sword and had to run off, you see. They talked awhile, invited us to join up with them, but he said no, and off we went, leaving them on the trail. I was still with Edmund when the cannon went off."

''Yes?'' said Stefan.

''Well, you see, Iggy wasn't there, either. I was told he got killed defending William, and went off to the Point. And he hadn't come back. Now I don't want to bad-mouth Iggy or anything, he's an all-right guy and a good friend of the King's, but I happen to know there was a lot of bad blood between him and Thorstane. I think it was kind of odd that he didn't come back to William's troops, especially when it turned out he wasn't helping William ambush Easterners, either. Have you talked to him yet?''

''No, I'll get to him later. I want to talk to everyone who's here from Strange Sea. Did you know Thorstane?''

John shrugged. ''Not really. I'm not much on the Horde, and he was worse than the average. I told him more than once to stay away from me.''

''Do you know what the quarrel was between Iggy and Thorstane?''

''No, and it's funny, no one did. It came on sudden; all at once Iggy stopped talking to Thorstane at events. Everyone noticed, but Iggy never told anyone what was wrong.''

Stefan, writing, said, ''I see. Well, thanks for the information. Oh, did you spend any time at Resurrection Point today?''

''No, I was kind of hanging back in the woods, didn't feel inspired or something. Figured I'd make it up later.''

''Too bad; you won't get a chance now.''

''Yeah, I was hoping to catch the eye of the Princess in the Champions battle. I'd like her to choose me Royal Champion when she's crowned queen.''

• • •

The Couple Dragons Inn was made up of three thirty-foot tents that outlined three sides of a square. ''I think someone knew the owner of a circus sideshow,'' said Katherine, looking at the expanse of worn canvas wall that faced them. They went through the door-size opening in the wall and found themselves in a small courtyard outlined by the tents. The customers in the two side tents were watching a kind of tug-of-war contest in the grassy courtyard of the inn. The contestants, a man and a woman, were each standing on a square of plywood balanced on a block of wood, feeding and pulling a twelve-yard length of rope back and forth between them. The object seemed to be to unbalance one's opponent—and not run out of rope. As Stefan and Katherine watched, the knotted end of the man's rope ran out through his hands, and he deliberately stepped off his board. As he left the courtyard the woman, a buxom creature whose several skirts were tucked up to expose bare feet and legs, coiled the rope with an expert hand and called triumphantly, "Next!"

Stefan adroitly avoided her eye and led Katherine to the left-hand tent. The tables were crowded with people eating cheese sandwiches or spooning up a soup thick with barley. The costumes of the customers varied widely, from furry Mongol and shaggy monk to Katherine's fine fourteenth-century gentlewoman and the leather-and-ruff of an earringed Elizabethan seaman. An assortment of mugs and goblets formed uneven rows down the tables.

They took seats on benches across from each other at one end of a table and studied a brief menu chalked on a board. *Soup 3 tickets,* it said, *Sandwidge (Cheese) 2 tickets, Well Water 2 tickets, Cider 1 ticket. Sandwidge (Ham)* had been imperfectly erased.

"Why does water cost more than cider?" asked Katherine.

"Because it's really a very good homemade ale," said Stefan.

"Don't try the soup," suggested the Elizabethan seaman, looking into his own bowl glumly.

"Thank you, m'lord," said Stefan.

Across the back of the courtyard, a tent was issuing kitchen sounds and smells from behind its lowered canvas curtain. There came also the rough-edged bawl of a man giving orders to lagging cooks.

"Sounds as if Baron Dur is in," said Stefan. He explained to Katherine, "He's the Dragons' owner, chef, talent scout, bartender, bouncer, and head factotum."

A fair-haired server in a violet tunic hurried up to them. "Yes, m'lord, m'lady?" he said with a brief bow.

"Two ales and two cheese sandwiches, please," said Stefan.

"Where's your cups?" asked the server.

"We didn't bring any," said Stefan. "Sorry."

"Cost you a ticket apiece for the loan of two," said the server. "And you pay me when I bring your order."

"Fine. Where do we buy tickets?"

"At the table on the other side," said the server, and he hurried off.

"I'll be right back," said Stefan to Katherine.

He'd barely gone when a chunky man in a dingy white tunic sat down in his place. His brown beard made a broad border around his lower face and he wore a floppy leather hat with a silver hatband. He leaned forward and said in a loud, coarse whisper, "Are you Lord Steffy's lady?"

"Yes, m'lord."

The man's spine straightened as he glanced around, then curved as he leaned toward her again. "Where is he?" he whispered.

"Gone to buy tickets," she said, mildly alarmed, and warned, "He'll be right back. And you're in his place."

"No sweat." The man turned to the Elizabethan seaman and ordered brusquely, "Find another seat, okay?"

To her surprise, the seaman immediately picked up his bowl and mug and left. The whisperer shifted down into the vacated place, lifted his wide-brimmed hat and yelled, "Ale, dammit!" She started, and he grinned at her. "I can get away with that; this is my place." She looked again at the silver hatband. Sure enough, there were knobs on it. He rolled his eyes upward. "Yep, that's a baronial coronet," he said, grinning. "I'm Baron Dur the Dwarph, at your service, m'lady."

The server set a large, gem-set silver goblet brimming with ale on the table in front of the baron. "Anything else, Excellency?" he asked.

"Naw—yeah. Tell 'em in the kitchen to start the chicken now; it wasn't done in time for early dinner last night."

"Yes, m'lord." The server hurried off.

"I trust you've been here so short a time you haven't yet offended my lady," said a quiet voice, and Stefan sat down on the bench.

"Steffy!" roared Dur joyously. "I've been hoping you'd come by! Listen, I heard—" The voice abruptly dropped again into the coarse whisper. "I heard Will authorized you to look into what happened to Thorstane."

Stefan smiled and pulled the royal writ from his pouch. Dur

unfolded it and read it slowly, stroking his beard. "I suppose this don't mean spit to the troopers," he said, handing it back.

"They don't approve of outsiders interfering in an investigation," agreed Stefan.

"But you're a real cop, right? A detective sergeant, I hear. They should be glad to have you come aboard."

"Your information, as always, is impeccable," said Stefan. "But look at it from their point of view: I'm the husband of a chief suspect."

"Anyone who'd think this lady here stuck an ice pick into someone has got to have several screws loose."

Stefan's attention sharpened. "Ice pick? Where'd you hear it was an ice pick?"

"I got a ninja working for me at the farmhouse."

"Did this ninja see something, or only hear something?"

Dur leaned forward and his whisper softened. "My ninja saw it. It was in a plastic bag on a table in the farmhouse, labeled and everything."

Stefan made a whistling shape with his mouth and nodded once. "Have you told anyone else about the ice pick?"

"Not even Will. I've been saving it for you."

Stefan took out his notebook and wrote briefly. "My lord, I am very grateful."

Dur grinned broadly, then asked, "Did you go look at that armor they found in the woods?"

"Not yet. Why?"

"Well, hell, that might explain why Thorstane said it was a mundane, right? I bet there's not half a dozen fighters here wear garb under their armor. It's jeans and painter's pants and sweatshirts, right?"

"Yes, I've already offered that theory to the troopers."

Dur blinked, then laughed. "Great minds!" he said. "I bet if you find the owner of that armor, you'll have your murderer."

The server came back with two thick cheese sandwiches wrapped in paper napkins and two brimming brass goblets with big Gothic *D*s painted on their bowls. Stefan offered the server ten tickets, but

Dur waved him away. ''On the house, Gib. Anything he or his lady wants from now on. Pass the word.''

''Yes, m'lord,'' said the server. He glanced at Stefan and Katherine to press their faces on his memory and went away.

Katherine, abruptly aware of sharp hunger, bit into her sandwich. The bread was crusty and good, thickly spread with butter, the cheese a rich cheddar. ''Ummm,'' she murmured.

''Thank you, m'lady,'' said Dur politely. ''Now, about this armor,'' he said to Stefan.

''I agree the armor is suspicious,'' said Stefan. ''Has anyone claimed it?''

''Not as of twenty minutes ago,'' said Dur. ''My ninja's watching it. She said there's been quite a few come to look at it.''

''What's a ninja?'' asked Katherine.

Dur doffed his hat and lifted the silver circlet to expose a second hatband, the braided black-and-red cord of the Dark Horde household. ''They also serve who only lurk and pry,'' he said. He replaced the hat.

''Have you seen the armor?'' asked Stefan.

''Naw, I haven't had time. This place has been a madhouse ever since they cut the fighters loose from the Point. Nobody wants to cook; they all want to leave as soon as the word is passed they can, so they refuse to dirty any pots. We're running out of food, and I can't make a run to buy more. Hell, I may even run out of ale—terrible thought, terrible! I'm about to organize a party to go around and buy food from people, or offer to cook it for a fee.'' His attention abruptly focused elsewhere. ''Excuse me; I'll be right back.'' He stood and hurried off.

''Is he really a baron?'' asked Katherine.

''Yes, a court baron, not a territorial one. William gave it to him when he was king some years back. He and Dur were closer friends then than they are now, and William wanted to do something for him. Dur wasn't enough of a fighter to be knighted, and he hadn't started the inn yet so he couldn't get a Pelican for service, and he wasn't a brilliant light in the arts or sciences so he couldn't get a Laurel. So Will made him a court baron.''

"Isn't it disrespectful of him to wear the coronet as a hatband?"

"He's taken some flak for that. But you'll never see Dur without it; he even wears it mundanely. I think he's proud of the honor."

The baron had gone out into the courtyard to challenge the lady with the hiked skirts. A man in a rust tunic was standing between them, holding the excess rope in a coil. Dur was holding his end with a careless air, and the lady was waiting tensely. The server dropped the coil, hopped out of the way, and the pair came to life in an attempt to garner as much excess as possible. Dur dropped into a bent-knee stance to maintain his balance on the board, and the lady assumed a ballet pose as the rope began to tighten between them. She pulled in a yard of it and he fed her a yard, then pulled it back again. Pause. He tugged gently; she fed him a little line, then braced and he instantly stopped pulling. Pause. She pulled, and he fed her a foot, and another, then abruptly stopped and pulled. She fed him a foot, stopped and pulled; he pulled back, her board tipped forward, and she stepped off. The watchers cheered noisily.

"That must be harder than it looks," said Katherine, who had turned around to watch.

"Much harder," said Stefan. "Now watch him lose to whoever challenges him."

"Why?"

"Because he went out there only to make her lose. He likes to make new champions every so often, to keep interest high. He'll ask her to come back this evening to face some of the other champions he's collected."

"I see." She returned her attention to her lunch, tasting the ale with approval. "About that armor, my lord," she said.

"What about it?"

"Why did he take it off?"

Stefan, who had been watching Dur toy with a challenger, opened his mouth, closed it again, stared at her. "What do you mean?"

"Why did he take it off before attacking Thorstane? Suppose Thorstane had fought him? Thorstane was armored, carrying a mace and shield. Why take off armor to go up against him? And, armor would have been a disguise. I can see taking it off after he attacked Thorstane, because people saw him with Thorstane. But suppose

Thorstane had lived long enough to describe him to me? Without the armor, that would have been easier to do. It seems unnecessarily risky, even stupid, to take off a perfectly good suit of armor to attack an armed and armored man.''

Stefan drank some of his ale and said, ''Maybe there was something about the armor Thorstane could identify. But then, when you think about it, why couldn't Thorstane name his attacker? He had a lot of enemies, so it seems peculiar that the one who did this is someone he couldn't name.''

There were cheers and laughter, and Baron Dur came back looking rueful. He dropped the expression as soon as he sat down, and took a large drink of his ale. ''Where were we?'' he asked.

''I was about to ask you if anyone has come into the inn acting strange, perhaps sitting all by himself, gray and sweaty, drinking more than usual without any effect.''

Dur stared at him. ''You know, I was gonna mention it: Petrog was in here a while ago acting just like that. He sat by himself in a corner, drank three pints of ale like it was water, and left again, didn't say diddly to anyone. Not speaking to anyone is like him; but drinking three in a row like that isn't.'' He pinched his eyes shut with a stubby thumb and forefinger and thought. ''And also for unusual, Will was here and bought four sandwiches to go and no ale, neither of which is like him. Lemme see, Sir John was here, too. He was laughing over War stories with some Meridies fighters, buying drinks for them. I only mention him because he wasn't hanging out with strictly chivalry like I've seen him do at other events. Broddi was here just a little while ago, looking like he'd bite the head off anyone who came in range, but that's because he's still getting over Wullfy's chewing him out for losing Thorstane. Earlier on I heard some ugly talk from the brothers about your lady, but I stepped on it, and now, since the runes got read and told them what anyone with a nickel's worth of sense should've already known, they're quiet. That's all I can think of right now.''

Stefan, writing, said, ''Thanks. Dur, I'm looking for the owner of the blue armor. Apparently it's a man who told Wulfstan he was Lord Christopher of Lone Castle. He fought for a short while with the Horde, polearm, then got killed, went off and never came back.

Lone Castle says there is no such person. Have you heard anything that relates to that?''

Dur frowned. ''No, not yet.''

''Well, keep your ears out. I also want to know who was wandering around alone in the woods forty-five minutes to half an hour before it ended—but for God's sake don't ask anyone. Just listen.''

Dur's narrow dark eyes gleamed. ''Gotcha,'' he said with a little nod. ''Dur the Ninja, that's me.''

20

STEFAN and Katherine came out of the inn and stopped while Stefan consulted his notes. "I think we want to talk to Sir Ignatius next," he said.

"Look," she said, "here comes Trooper Bead."

The trooper was obviously out to intercept them. His expression was grim, and Stefan took Katherine's hand as they waited. "I've been looking all over the place for you," said Bead, his voice hard.

Stefan said coolly, "As I recall, your instructions were to remain on the campground."

"I also thought we also made it clear that we don't want your help in our investigation. God knows what damage you've done, poking around like you did."

"Now, Bead, I think I've—"

Bead interrupted, "Let me see that letter you've been showing people."

"Letter?"

"You know what I mean—from the King!"

"Oh." Stefan dug in his pouch and produced the writ. Bead took it, unrolled it and read it.

"You think this gives you some kind of authority?" he asked.

"No, sir. I consider it a request for information. I'm acting as a private citizen, nothing more."

"Well, as a peace officer, I'm telling you to go back to your campfire and stay there, hear me?" Bead folded the writ and put it into his pocket. "Some people are upset at what you're doing, and I'm ordering it stopped. I hear one more report of you going around interviewing witnesses, and you're under arrest for interfering with a police investigation!"

"Yes, sir. Do you want to tell His Majesty, or shall I?"

Bead smiled grimly. "Let me; I'll enjoy wringing his tail. Now get on out of here, both of you." They started away, but Bead said, "No, wait a second." They turned back and he said, with some exasperation, "We got the results of the autopsy, and we no longer have any reason to question your story of him talking to you, Mrs. Brichter."

"I'm glad to hear that," she said quietly.

"And . . . we're sorry for any distress our detaining you might have caused," he added stiffly.

"That's quite all right," she said, looking down so he wouldn't see her smile.

"But that doesn't take away from the reality of what I told you, Mr. Brichter."

"I understand," said Stefan. "We'll go back to our encampment now, and we'll be there if you need to talk to us again."

• • •

"Fascists," muttered Taffy when Stefan and Katherine got back to the Charter encampment.

"No, I warned William this might happen," said Stefan. "Dammit, I don't like fellow cops moving in on an investigation I'm conducting, either; and if it was a civilian I'd be tempted to yank him downtown for a short scare."

"Still," said Geoff, "does that mean we're down to hoping they can get a handle on this?"

"Yeah," sighed Stefan.

"Are they close?" asked Anne.

"God knows; they aren't telling me anything," said Stefan. "Any of you heard a rumor?"

"They're still talking to people who took part in the Woods Battle," said Taffy. "And they're watching the people who come to look at the armor real close."

"Did you go look?" asked Stefan.

"Uh-uh."

"I did," said Geoff.

"What did you see?"

"It's a full suit, vaguely fourteenth-century Italian, eighteen-gauge, no pads or gambeson. Simple and undecorated, except for the paint, which is a spray-can job, done after it was put together. A hurry-up job, but whoever made it knew how to make armor."

"Eighteen-gauge?"

"Yeah, the helm is sixteen, I think, but the rest of it is eighteen."

"That's awfully light."

"I know, but when your shears are dull, like it seems this guy's were, what you remember is, eighteen's legal. The regrets come later, while you're banging out the dents and waiting for your bruises to heal."

"Do you think it's possible the inspecting knights marshal would remember it?"

"It's possible—but it wasn't inspected. It didn't have a sticker on it. Or the strip of tape on the helm."

"Maybe it failed inspection," suggested Anne.

"I doubt it," said Geoff. "I'd've held my nose and passed it."

Stefan said, "And you don't pass everything. What else?"

"Well, it was new. No chips in the paint or any sign of repair or repainting—except one."

"What's that?"

"A brass rivet. On the left knee cop."

"You sure?"

"Oh, yeah. The repair job was done after it was painted, because the rivet isn't painted; it sticks out like a sore thumb." There was a little silence.

"No, it can't be Iggy," said Geoff.

"You don't know what I know. He had a long-standing grievance of some sort with Thorstane."

"So why didn't Thorstane say, 'Iggy did this'?" asked Taffy. "Why lie and say, 'It was a mundane'?"

"I don't know." Stefan frowned. "Freyis saw him after the murder wearing only a gambeson."

"So did we," said Geoff. "Remember? He fights that way, gambeson and leg harness."

Stefan said, "I wonder what he had on underneath. I wish I could go talk to him."

"It can't be Sir Ignatius," said Anne. "Any man that fond of his wife can't be a murderer."

"Woman's logic!" jeered Taffy with a laugh. "I bet you think it couldn't be a woman who killed Thorstane."

Geoff said, "Well, it would have to be a woman even bigger than that Easterner who was at the cliff, and I don't think we've got one of them in the Society."

Stefan looked over at his wife, who had said nothing in some while. "Have you anything to contribute?"

She sighed and clasped her hands restlessly. "No. But I keep thinking about what Sabas said, and I wonder if I forgot something, or if I'm not making myself clear. I go over it and over it, finding him—" She shuddered.

"She needs not to think about it at all for a while," said Anne. "Come on, Katherine; you should lie down."

Taffy said, "Anne's right. Go take a nap, let go of it for a while."

"I don't want to go to sleep."

Stefan said, "Then don't; just rest for an hour. You'll remember more detail if your mind is refreshed."

She yielded reluctantly. "Yes, all right. Just for an hour."

Anne helped her to her feet and took her away.

"Poor kid," said Taffy softly.

"She'll be all right," said Stefan. "She's tougher than she looks."

Geoff said. "I hope you're right. We need people like her."

Stefan said, "Most people don't realize what she is until she's gone, because she's got the quiet virtues: she's brave, gentle, kind—"

''Clean, reverent!'' interrupted Taffy in a low, angry voice. ''What the hell do you think you married, a Boy Scout? Good Christ Almighty! She's smart, she's funny, she's beautiful, she pretends being the major suspect in a murder case is hardly worth fussing over!''

''Shut up, Taffy,'' said Geoff.

''Why? That's the second time today he's made that crack about how tough she is. Tough, my Great Aunt Sadie! She's scared sick, and he's so busy playing cop he can't see that!''

Geoff said with great emphasis, ''You don't know the first thing about it.''

Taffy looked at the adamantine expression on Geoff's face, and said, puzzled, ''I don't get it.''

Stefan said, ''I know better than anyone what she is. I'd crawl from here to Ganymede if doing that would convince the troopers she's innocent. But it won't, nor will braying to the world about how concerned I am over her present state of terror help her, or me, or anyone. So I say what I hope is true, that until I solve this, she'll be able to tough it out.''

Taffy sighed, blowing his cheeks out. ''Ever since she let me start teaching her Welsh, I've been thinking no one but me appreciates her like they should. I apologize.''

Geoff said, ''Come on, it's time we started dinner.''

• • •

Katherine was asleep; Anne sat with her in case of nightmare. The men gathered around the picnic table and scraped, peeled, washed, and chopped vegetables.

''My lords,'' said a familiar voice, and they turned to see King William approaching, Sir Ignatius beside him.

The men bowed. ''How may we serve you?'' asked Geoff.

''I'd like to speak to Lord Stefan for a couple of minutes,'' said William. ''In private,'' he added.

''Use our tent,'' said Geoff.

''Thanks, m'lord,'' said Stefan.

Ignatius, William, and Stefan sat on cushions placed on a goatskin rug in the small anteroom of the pavilion. ''First, what did you find out?'' asked William.

Stefan dug out his notebook. ''Thorstane was a drunk, probably a serious alcoholic. He was losing the support of his household, who may have been on the verge of throwing him out."

William nodded. "Any suspects?"

"Some eliminations. I talked with Lady Freyis, because I wondered why she decided not to send for the yurt to take Thorstane to the hospital; but she explained that, and anyway she was with Roc the whole time. Wulfstan was with his troops, you were laying ambushes, Olaf wasn't in the woods at all. Freyis told me, on the other hand, that you, Sir Ignatius, came by while she was waiting to show the ambulance in, and that you asked about Thorstane. And I also have a report that you had some sort of quarrel with the victim."

Ignatius, who had been looking ill, wiped his mouth with the edge of his hand. "Yeah," he said, "I was there. I was looking for Will. I went to the Point about the time William lost his sword, and I didn't rejoin the troops when I got released. I thought maybe he'd been captured, but I couldn't find him. I was thinking to maybe organize a rescue, or just find him if he was wandering around in the woods. I took a spare sword with me for him, but I couldn't figure out where he was, and the more I looked, the madder I got, and the more determined to find him."

"Tell me about the quarrel you had with Thorstane."

Ignatius mumbled, "It was about Germain."

"Your wife?"

"Yeah." He shrugged. "I've been trying not to be so protective of her, y'know? I mean, it's not like she's crippled all over, she's just got this weak leg. She was born with it, and they've operated on it half a dozen times, but she still limps."

Lady Germain's face rose up in Stefan's memory. It was a gentle face, marked with the look of a pain-filled childhood. He nodded. "Go on," he said.

"Well, I pushed her until she got her driver's license. And I bought her a car, a nice little secondhand Datsun. And one day, coming out of a parking lot, she gets hit by a delivery van. Thorstane comes boiling out of the van and runs up to her screaming it's her fault. He yanks open her door, drags her out and says she's got no business driving a car, that he's gonna lose his job because of her, on and on, swearing, creating a scene. But he doesn't call the cops; he just slams back into his van and drives off, leaving her there with a crumpled fender. And the upshot is, she won't drive alone anymore. She cried for three days before she told me what happened. I took her back to the place, made her show me how it happened, explained how it wasn't her fault, but she only halfway believed me. The goddamned lying filthy bastard took away all her confidence, all her pride. I wanted to kill him!'' He stopped, wiped his mouth again. ''I don't care, I wanted to kill him. I didn't, but I sure wanted to. I never spoke to him again. Germain made me promise not to bad-mouth him to anyone, not tell anyone why I was mad, but she couldn't make me promise to be nice to the bastard. I hope the guy who shoved a knife into his gizzard hated him as much as I did.''

''Iggy,'' said William, ''take it easy.'' He looked at Stefan with pained eyes. ''When Iggy told me about it a month ago, I tried to get Germain to go to the cops about it, or his employer, but she refused. And she was mad at Iggy for telling me.''

''I'm sorry this had to come out,'' said Stefan. ''And I'm sorry for your lady. How long ago was this?''

''Six or seven months, I guess. If it had been anyone else, even if it had been me, I wouldn't be one-third as mad. But Germain . . .''

Stefan made a note. ''My lord, did anyone else see you today while you were looking for William?''

Ignatius shrugged. ''I suppose so. I talked to King Edmund out at the Point. After, in the woods, I got a drink from a water bearer.''

''Can you describe the water bearer?''

Iggy pursed his lips and thought. ''A little guy, in monk's robes. He was looking at a map like he was lost.''

Stefan made a note. ''Was that before or after the cannon went off?''

''Before. Just before.''

''How tall are you, Sir Ignatius?''

Ignatius blinked. ''Five-seven. This monk was at least five inches shorter than I am.''

"Okay, thanks."

"I saw him too, you know," said William.

"The water bearer?"

"No, Iggy. Coming back from Resurrection. I'd just borrowed a sword from the Lost and Found can and was looking for a good ambush spot when he came in. There were some Easterners behind him, so I let him go by."

"I see."

"He didn't do it, you know."

"I can tell you really believe that."

"Goddammit, Stefan, I'm telling you what I know to be a fact!"

"Are you telling me he was with you at the time of the murder?"

William began to get up. "I don't have to sit here and listen to this!"

"No, my lord, you don't. But I can't conduct a fair investigation if you forbid me to inquire into the actions of people who happen to be friends of yours."

On one knee, William stopped. "Hell," he muttered and sat back down. "No, I guess not. But just be damn sure before you make any accusations, hear?"

"Yes, sir. I'd like to speak to Master Petty, if you could have him sent to me."

"Why, what about him?"

"I understand he had a long-standing quarrel with Thorstane, too."

William grinned. "I think we fixed that. Petty and I got drunk together, and he told me his sad story. The two of us went off and found Thorstane. I always wanted to do that scene from *The Godfather,* so I told Thorstane, 'This here's my friend, and I look out for my friends. And if one more bad thing happens to him, even if it's an accident, even if you can prove it's an accident, I'm gonna come after you and yank your filthy arm off and beat you to death with it.' Or something like that. It was late, and I was pretty drunk. But I remember Thorstane backing off the whole time I was talking, and his two k'shaktu making nice at me." William showed his teeth. "If nothing else, I made a believer of Petty. Unless Thorstane got his nerve back this morning and said something, Petty had no reason to kill him.''

. . .

William and Ignatius went up King's Road together. ''What do you think?'' asked Ignatius.

''Oh, I wouldn't worry. I bet that water bearer remembers you.''

''I hope he does. But it was just before the cannon went, you know. I bet I could've done it and gotten back to the main trail in time to get a drink from him.''

''You're your own worst enemy, Iggy. But Stefan's in trouble, because he can't go out and talk to people. Bead jumped all over him just like he did over me.''

''How can we help him? Any second I expect a big hand coming out of a gray shirt to land on my shoulder and say, 'Mr. Roman, you have a right to remain silent and a right to a lawyer.' Maybe now you'll agree I should go home.''

''You should never run from the cops. They take that as an admission of guilt.''

They continued up the road in silence, and were almost back to William's pavilion before William snapped his fingers. ''How about we get others to do what he asked us to do with Petty?''

''What was that?''

''Go talk to Stefan. Bead says he's confined to his encampment—okay, we'll send people to him.''

''Who? We can't line the whole damn camp up along the road, and we don't know who he specifically wants to talk to.''

''When we send Petty, we'll ask him to find out who else he wants to talk to. And we can put out the word that if anyone has anything of value to contribute, they should maybe go see if Stefan's at home.''

''The troopers—''

''Damn the troopers! You go see if you can find that water bearer you saw, and send him, too. I'm going to talk to Petty.''

. . .

''No, no way!''

''What do you mean, no way? I'm ordering you to go!''

"You can't order me to do anything! I'm not going, and that's final!"

"How dare you say that to me!" William's anger was rising to a dangerous level, and Petty unexpectedly laughed.

"Sir Ignatius was right, sometimes you think you're really a king!"

"Who told you he said that?" demanded William.

Petrog waved a hand. "Sir John was telling the story to someone, and I overheard it. But that's not the point. The point is, the War is over. When Thorstane died, we all turned back into mundanes."

William was silent a few seconds, then he shrugged. "All right, all right, maybe I do get a little high-handed. I apologize. Will you please go see him?"

"No."

"Why not?"

"You are asking me to walk into a cage with a lion who is very, very hungry."

"Stefan? He's no lion!"

"He's a lawman with a wife to protect; for someone in my position, that's the same thing."

"Bullshit; I told him about how you and I went and talked to Thorstane last night, told him to lay off you or else."

"Did he believe you?"

"Why shouldn't he?"

Petty sighed. "I don't know . . ."

"Why are you so scared? Stefan's not the type to frame someone."

Petrog looked away, but William waited, and Petrog sighed. "I went down to look at the armor, the blue armor they found?"

"Yeah?"

"And I saw this man coming out of the house with something in a plastic bag. The murder weapon."

"And, so?"

"Well, it was an ice pick."

"Ah! Still, there are a lot of people who have ice picks."

"And this was a common type of one—just like mine, in fact. Which I bought brand-new in Cleveland two days ago and brought with me. And which has gone missing. I've looked every place I can think of, but it's gone. I had it this morning, but it's gone now."

"So you mislaid it. If it's a common type, as you say, maybe someone saw it and mistook it for his own. Have you asked around?"

Petty stared at him. "Have you been fighting without your helm? Of course I haven't asked around. Do you think I want to be arrested?"

21

STEFAN sent Taffy to the Horde camp to see if Thorstane's k'shaktu Broddi was available. Geoff said, "It isn't like you to violate the spirit of the law and keep just the letter."

"You say that because you've never seen me at work," said Stefan with a sideways smile. "Did you ask Anne about my lady?"

"She says Katherine is still asleep. Shall we wake her up?"

"No, leave her be awhile longer."

"All right. Here comes Taffy."

He'd brought Broddi with him, and Lord Roc. Roc said, "Maybe it will save time if you tell me who else you want to talk to, and I'll go get him."

"Baron Dur, in about half an hour, if he can come. Thanks, Roc."

Stefan took Broddi into Geoff's pavilion and sat down with him. He pulled out his notebook, glanced up and saw Broddi's frightened expression. "Relax, Broddi," said Stefan. "I'm not going to arrest you; I'm just trying to find out what happened."

Broddi's quick grin came and went. "Yeah," he croaked, then cleared his throat. "Yeah," he repeated, "that's what you cops always say."

Stefan laughed. "I'm going to have to learn a new line one of these days. Look, I'll be up-front with you: If you had gone directly to Thorstane as soon as you were released from Resurrection Point, you might have gotten there in time to keep my lady company as he whispered his last words. And that's assuming you knew where he was.''

''And I didn't. Anyhow, I went back to my brothers.''

''Yes, Wulfstan said that. So, all I need from you is a witness who can put you at the Point when you say you were there.''

Broddi, relieved, became voluble. ''Hey, there's a whole bunch of 'em!''

''Master Petty, for instance?''

''No, but a lot of others; I was askin' everyone at the Point if they'd seen Thorstane or this Lord Christopher.''

''Did you think the two of them had gone off together?''

Broddi said, ''I wasn't sure. I think Thorstane was mad at him.''

''Mad at Lord Christopher? Why?''

''When we were first at the gathering place, he wanted to go give the guy a piece of his mind. He said Lord Christopher had dropped his polearm on his shield so the Eastern pikeman could kill him.''

''Lord Christopher did this to Thorstane?''

''Thorstane said so, said he did it on purpose. I said did he have a reason to do this to you, and Thorstane said no, but maybe he had a grudge against the Horde. Which is crazy, because if he did, why did he come along and volunteer to fight with us? And why open up a shield wall when it would only get him killed?''

''Did Thorstane go talk to him?''

''I told him not to. But before we moved on to the Point I saw Lord Christopher had come over and was talking to Thorstane. They weren't yelling at each other, so maybe they straightened it out.''

''Would you know Lord Christopher if you saw him again?''

''Not out of his armor. He had his helm on, even at the gathering place. Which, come to think of it, was wrong. I wonder why he left it on?''

''Me, too.'' Stefan was writing swiftly. ''Can you name anyone you saw at Resurrection Point?''

Broddi thought. ''Roc and Freyis. They were in the group ahead of us. They came back to talk to this Easterner about some whistles he was carrying, but he wouldn't give them up."

"Did you ask Roc and Freyis if they'd seen Thorstane?"

He said, abashed, "No. I didn't want Freyis to know we'd lost him, so I kind of stayed out of their way. She's worse than Wulffy when she's pissed. I wanted to ask Roc by himself, but they stuck together. Then they went back to their group, which was ahead of mine, and I couldn't go talk to them. The constables don't like you going up to a group for any reason; they think you're cheating."

"Who else did you talk to at the Point?"

"Couple people. The constable in charge, for one. A big lady with fat braids." He made a circle with his thumb and forefinger to show their thickness.

"Mistress Hilda of Whitby?"

"I dunno; is that her name? She said she hadn't seen Thorstane."

"Would she remember you asking her?"

"I think so. I remember saying something to her about the numbers of Easterners and Midrealmers evening up, and she said they'd always been about even, which isn't what Lord Christopher told us when he joined us."

"Anyone else?"

Broddi shrugged. "The ones I came out with. I remember asking an Eastern knight if he'd seen Thorstane cut out. He was at the back of the line with them. But he hadn't."

"Were you mad at Thorstane for running off?"

"Hey, I didn't know for sure he'd run off! I just couldn't find him. I was watching to see if he'd come out; you know, maybe he stopped at a Porta-John. Even when he didn't turn up, I wasn't that mad. I was gonna yell at him when I found him, but I wasn't mad at him, not mad enough to kill him."

"How did you get along with Thorstane?"

"Great, we were friends. Till Wulffy made me his guardian, of course; then he did everything he could think of to make both Hreider and me mad at him. Called us names. Asked us forty times a minute to give him something out of his suitcase, or put it back. Told everyone we were picking on him." Broddi grinned. "But we just stuck in there, and when he saw he couldn't make us quit, he settled down, or pretty much, for him."

"Can you tell me the names of some people Thorstane might have considered enemies?"

Broddi looked puzzled, then nodded. "Oh, I get it; you think *Thorstane* was the one with the knife, don't you? That he went looking for someone, who took it away from him, right? Well, I'm telling you right now, and Hreider will back me: Thorstane wasn't carrying any offensive steel when he went into Phillip's Forest. We watched him dress—hell, we handed him his underwear!—and we helped him arm up. No way could he have slipped something by us, 'cause we were watching for that."

"Okay. Who hated him enough to do this to him?"

Broddi sighed gustily. "Well, who can tell what makes you mad enough to do something stupid like that? I mean, you hear about people who take all kinds of garbage and others who will murder you for looking at them funny in an elevator."

"Still," encouraged Stefan.

Again the gusty sigh. "All right: Petty. He told everyone Thorstane was doing some really bad things to him."

"Like what?"

"Making phone calls to the hospital to get him in trouble, for one. Slashing his tires, for another."

"Did you believe him?"

Broddi frowned. "Well . . . maybe. Some of 'em. I saw Thorstane at an SCA business meeting watching for Petty to arrive, kind of laughing, y'know? Waiting for him to say something had happened. Like he knew Petty was gonna come in all mad again. And he did. So I think Thorstane did some things. Not everything. It got to where if Petty opened a bag of potato chips and it was stale he thought Thorstane did it." Broddi grinned. "But Petty sets himself up for some of that stuff. We had a seminar one time on 'Speaking Forsoothly,' and somehow Thorstane got himself signed up for a lecture. It was on period insults, and the teacher went into history going way back. She said even the Romans had insults and graffiti, and she gave some examples. And somehow one of 'em stuck to Thorstane. He saw Petty at the feast that night and he says, 'Hey, Petty, check out my Latin,' and he starts in, 'Patty-cake, patty-cake, baker's man,' and I thought Petty was gonna bust a blood vessel. 'Cause he speaks Latin, y'know, and he knows Thorstane is callin' him a faggot. Petty gets that look on his face, and we all crack up. Then Thorstane starts in on him again here at the War. If Petty had just turned around and laughed, that would've been the end of it. But he doesn't know how to take a joke, I guess, poor guy. I saw him at an event putting a Band-Aid on this man's finger like the finger smelled bad. I guess he prefers his patients unconscious in the operating room."

"Anyone else?"

"Sir John. I don't know what that was about—in fact, I didn't even know John was mad at him until our last Feast of Flowers."

"When was that?"

"Mid-July. Me and Sulu were carrying in trays of meat pies for the feast and John was coming out of the john—" He stopped to laugh. "Anyhow, Thorstane was right behind him, and John says to him—" Broddi, aware of the notebook, stopped to think before he repeated it. " 'You don't come near me again, you hear? That's it, I've had it with you!' Which is kind of weird, because I hadn't noticed Thorstane trying to be specially close to him before. But that's what he said, his exact words. Then he saw us, and he walked off without saying anything more."

"How did Thorstane take what Sir John said?"

"He saw us, and he made like 'so what' at us without saying anything, and he walked off, too."

"Was he angry? Hurt?"

"No, not so's you'd notice. Just 'so what,' y'know? Sulu said, 'I wonder what that's about,' and we went on bringing in trays."

Stefan made a note to ask Sulu to come by and then asked, "Was there anyone else?"

Broddi sighed. "This could take all night. Thorstane had a way of ruffling up people's feathers. Let's see, there was Iggy. I don't know what that was about, either, but Iggy looked like he wanted to murder Thorstane for a long time. Months. Wouldn't say why. Wulffy tried to talk to him when he got elected Khan and we told him about it, but he wouldn't even tell Wulffy what the matter was. It got on Thorstane's nerves a little, we could see that. But he kept out of Iggy's way. I mean, Iggy's not as big as Thorstane, but when he gets really mad, you don't push him."

"All right. Anyone else?"

"I think they're the serious ones. Lots of people would be mad at Thorstane off and on for stuff he'd do. But those're the only serious ones."

"So," said Stefan, "we've got Sir John, Sir Ignatius, and Master Petty. Is that all?"

"Like I said, lots of people were mad at him off and on."

"Who was currently on?"

"Well, Wulffy and Freyis. Wulffy told him to stay home and he came anyhow. And Freyis told him to stay home, too. Wulffy's Khan; he likes people to do what he says. And Freyis is—well, Freyis, and she's Thorstane's Tar-Khan."

"I see."

"What can you tell me about Thorstane's drinking?"

"What do you want to know?"

"Did he drink a lot?"

"Oh, yeah. One of those kind keeps booze all over his apartment. But he was generous, and lately he gave a bunch of great parties. He liked good stuff, too. He had Chivas, Smirnoff, twenty-year-old Scotch, and imported ale in his place. He sold me a quart of Smirnoff for three bucks one time, and I asked him how he could do that, and he said he could get anything he wanted for cheaper than wholesale, but he wouldn't tell me where or how. Maybe because he bought it by the case, I don't know. He didn't sell it too often, just once in a while. I tried getting him drunk one time to see if he'd tell then, but I woke up in my bathtub the next day and couldn't remember whether I even asked him."

That was all Broddi knew of value, and Stefan sent him off with a request that Sulu come by when he had time.

• • •

Stefan barely had time to go check on Katherine—she was still asleep—when Lord Roc came back with Baron Dur. "I'm glad to see some people around here aren't afraid to dirty a few pots!" he said when he saw Taffy and Geoff at the campfire. "Well, here I am, Steffy; I hear you want to talk to me."

"Just a few questions; I know you're busy. Come on, Geoff and Anne are letting me use their pavilion."

When they were seated comfortably, Dur said, "You asked me to tell you if I found out anyone was wandering around the forest all alone. Someone saw King Edmund alone, running hell-bent for election down the main trail. Had his sword and shield with him, so he hasn't got Will's excuse."

"Which way was he running?"

Dur thought, then brightened. "Okay, the guy telling it says he was coming out to the Point, and he whipped his finger toward him and over his shoulder when he told the story—both times—so I'd say Edmund was heading in."

Stefan smiled. "That's a clever piece of observation, Dur."

Dur swelled visibly. "Thanks. Iggy was also in there alone. Looking for Will, I hear. He's hiding out in Will's tent, scared green as his herald's cape, because he heard the troopers are looking to arrest him, poor guy."

"Then that would explain the cheese sandwiches His Majesty bought."

Dur blinked. "Yeah, it would, wouldn't it? Also, for strange behavior, I found out more about Sir John. He was not only hanging out with unbelted fighters, he was listening to their War stories."

Stefan raised one eyebrow. "So?"

"Steffy, the guy doesn't do things like that! He's always tooting his own horn, worse than me. All his War stories feature him as hero: 'No shit, there I was. . . .' You can hear him boring the pants off anyone from a knight up, especially if the guy's a friend of the King. Or a good-looking woman. He's at the Couple Dragons now. Her Majesty Jane came to the inn a while ago with Edmund, and John came over and said real loud how much he admired the way she was leading Edmund's men after he got killed, and she thanked him; and Edmund said afterward, 'Who was that?' " Dur snickered. "John was letting us know he fought with them, and now Edmund says, 'Who was that?' Jane said he was the guy who offered to carry her helm when they were coming out of the forest after the cannon went off.''

Stefan said, ''Maybe he'll reform. People do that, you know. I've done it myself, any number of times.''

Dur grinned. ''Me, too. But it never lasts.''

''Are many people leaving the campground?''

''A few. People with kids, mostly. They're scared.''

''Can you find out their names for me?''

''Wulffy put a brother at the gate to take names. All you got to do is ask and he'll give them to you.''

''Thanks. Anything else to report?''

''I hear the troopers are on to Petty. They must've got a dozen reports about him and Thorstane; Petty bitched to anyone who'd listen.''

''He's not a fighter, is he?''

''Him? No, but he was in the woods as a medic.''

''I know. He was the one who responded to my lady's cry for help when she found Thorstane.''

''Yeah, him and another one, Fabiola. She's a nurse mundanely.''

''When did King Edmund get killed?''

Dur thought. ''Early on; he was talking about it, but I was kind of listening on the fly, if you know what I mean. He didn't mention seeing Petty at the Point, at least that I overheard, but why should he?''

''I wonder where Petty is; William said he'd send him to me.''

''You'll have to wait until the troopers finish with him—if they ever do.''

''Did they arrest him?''

''No, just asked to question him. God, they don't begin to know where the handle is on this one.''

''Neither do I, Dur; neither do I.''

22

FATHER Hugh, both honored and nervous, came to see Stefan. "King William said you wanted to see me," he said.

"Yes, I want to think back to that period after you left my lady. Did you by some chance see Sir Ignatius?"

The little monk thought. "The Royal Herald? No, I don't think—oh, yes. He was alone, and asked me for a drink of water. I wanted to ask him the way to Twin Pines Fork, but he left before I could even say you're welcome for the water."

"Do you remember when that was?"

"A little before the end, I think. I remember I was walking along lost, but I'm lost most of the time. Maps confuse me. The top is supposed to be north, but when I'm going east, should I then hold the map sideways? Except then you can't read it. Have I helped you in your quest?"

"Yes, you have. Thank you."

. . .

King Edmund Redbeard was a powerfully built man, well over six feet tall, with light-green eyes and a grin that glinted in the curly recesses of his beard. He was wearing a blue velvet houppelande lined with white silk and a delicate gold wire crown set with garnets. "How may I help you, m'lord?" he asked.

''Do you remember when you got killed?''

His grin turned rueful. ''In our first action.''

''Do you remember seeing Sir Ignatius at the Point?''

''Yes, in fact we were put into the same batch out at the Point, and we got released at the same time.''

''Did you go back into the woods together?''

''No, I was in a rush, and I just took off running when they said we could go.''

''Do you remember seeing a man in blue armor out at Resurrection Point?''

''No.''

''How about Lord Broddi?''

''I'm afraid I don't know him.''

''A member of the Horde, a large man; he wears black leather armor set with studs.''

''No . . . no, I don't think so. But I wasn't really looking; I was anxious to get back to my fighters.''

''Before you were killed, do you remember seeing Sir John among your fighters?''

''He's a big man, right? My size?''

''Yes, that's him.''

''I remember him joining up at the Point, and he says he fought with me and my lady, but I don't remember seeing him again until almost the end. I was killed just as we got started, it was a short battle, and he says he was in the rear, so that would explain it. He offered to carry my lady's helm after the cannon went off, I remember that. I can't say for certain he wasn't there the whole time.''

• • •

Sulu the Loon came in wearing a big dark cloak. ''Suspicion is a cold emotion,'' he said. ''I'm prickling all over.''

''Were you in the woods this morning?''

''Not me. I bruise in sympathy. Why'd you want to talk to me?''

''I understand that you and Broddi overheard Sir John tell Thorstane to stay away from him at your last Feast of Flowers.''

Sulu nodded. ''I remember everything, you know that.'' He thought. ''Sir John said, 'Don't come to Nerren's again, you hear? That's all you get; I've had it with you!' '' Sulu's voice had even altered timbre and rhythm in imitation of Sir John, and Stefan wrote the words down.

"What did Thorstane say back to him?"

"Nothing."

"Did he act upset or angry about it?"

"No."

"Do you remember any other conversations between Sir John and Thorstane?"

"Uh-uh. Sir John never talked to him that I heard before. He thinks the chivalry doesn't like the Horde, so he doesn't either. That's a horse on him, right?" Sulu giggled at his abstruse pun—knights in a body are referred to as the chivalry, from "chevalier," a horseman; and a man who has a horse on him instead of the other way around is the loser in a dicing game.

Stefan riffled through his notebook, now almost full, looking for an earlier reference, found it and asked, "Do you know anything about Olaf finding Thorstane a job?"

The wild-eyed fellow nodded. "Driving a van. Thorstane was a good driver, but he went fast. 'I'm king of the road,' he said."

"When did he say this?"

"At Dragon's Day."

"This year?"

"Uh-huh. He was laughing, he said he yelled at a lady who ran into him. 'No one runs into me,' he said. I told him he better watch out, and he said, '*They* better watch out!' I didn't like him, he was crazier than me."

• • •

Stefan went in to wake up Katherine. She came groggily out of a heavy sleep, confused and unhappy. "Bad dreams?" he asked.

"No, I'm okay," she murmured, putting her tousled head on his shoulder, her forehead warm on his neck. "Wha' time is it?"

"Going on seven. The sun's broken through, just in time to set."

"Dumb weather," she grumbled.

"Supper's almost ready. Would you like something to eat?"

"No, I'm still full of cheese." She yawned and said pettishly, "Why'd you let me sleep so long? I feel all gritty; I hate sleeping in my clothes."

He kissed her temple. "It's all right, you needed to get away for a while. Take your time waking up."

"I'm thirsty; is there anything to drink around here?"

"Don't go away; I'll be right back."

He returned a minute later with a cup of water, to find her tangled in her clothes, evidently from trying to take both dresses off at once. She was making cross sounds from inside them. "Hold still; I'll help you," he said, putting down the cup. He pulled loose a sleeve that was caught inside-out at her wrist and untangled the hem of the underdress from the laces of the overdress, pulling one off, and then the other. When she was reduced to a chemise, he said, "Now, sit back," and handed her the water.

"What's this?" she asked, looking at the cup absently a moment, then handing it back to him.

"I thought you were thirsty."

"I changed my mind."

"Would you like something else?"

"No . . ." She consulted inwardly. "No." She rubbed her eyes, yawned and sighed. "Is this how you feel in the morning?"

"Yes." He was the grumpy, clumsy one in the morning; she was always up fresh and eager.

She frowned. "No wonder you hate mornings. Is anything happening?"

"Some patterns are beginning to emerge. But so far the only people who hated him enough to kill him are people who knew him well, people he would hardly mistake for strangers, much less mundanes."

"Maybe I'm wrong, then. Maybe I only think I heard what he said."

"Tell me again."

Yawning, she lay back on the sleeping bag. "Let me think a minute." She shivered, rubbing her upper arms, and he picked up her knitted cloak and tucked it around her. "Um," she said, comforted. "Okay, I thought he was snoring. You snore sometimes," she added, her good humor beginning to return. "But this was more full of bubbles. 'You can get up now,' I said. 'Whoever killed you is gone.' " She stopped to think, to be careful she got it right. "He didn't answer, so I poked him. My hand was dirty, I saw that when I poked him, in the arm, where his armor ended. It was black leather armor, with silver studs all over it. 'M'lord?' I said. He moaned when I poked him, and I thought it was funny, that he was hung over. Then he coughed, and it sounded like the worst chest cold you ever heard, with lots of phlegm. And he didn't try to get up. So I asked him, 'Are you hurt?' " She stopped, as if listening to him reply.

" 'Hurts.' " She was watching Thorstane, in pain, confused, dying. " 'Bastard!' " She stopped, then continued slowly, puzzled, " 'But . . . it was a mundane . . . fight.' "

"What?" Stefan asked sharply.

"That's what he said. 'It was a mundane . . .' sort of mumbling. And his eyes were moving inside the helm."

Stefan said, "No, listen to what you're saying. Thorstane said, 'But it was a mundane *fight*'?"

Her eyes were closed, and she nodded. Then they opened, wide. "No, he—" She stopped. "Well, yes. But there was a pause."

"A period kind of pause?"

She thought. "No. He was breathing funny. He was hurting. He was talking in little pieces of sentences, with no period kinds of pauses. 'Hurts—bastard—but—it was a mundane—fight—' Like that."

"He could have been saying, 'But it was a mundane fight'?"

"Well, yes, I suppose so." She was wide awake now. "Yes, I think that could have been it. That makes a difference, doesn't it?"

"Oh, yes."

• • •

Stefan stopped at the pay phone at the campground store and made two long-distance calls to Cleveland, one to the police and another to a liquor wholesaler to confirm they were investigating a theft. Then he and Katherine went to the farmhouse. The blue armor was laid out on an old blanket on the porch, and Stefan bent to handle pieces of it under the suspicious eye of Trooper Harrison. "Did someone send for you?" Harrison asked.

"No," said Stefan, with rude shortness. There was a sticky smudge on the front of the helm. He put it down, rubbing his fingers together. He felt the thinness of the breastplate and, turning it over, he rapped it with his knuckles. He noted the hasty, clever way the shoulder pauldrons were attached to it.

"Is this your armor?" asked Harrison abruptly.

"No."

"Do you know whose it is?"

"No."

"Then quit playing with it."

"All right." Stefan stood up, dusting his hands. "I'd like to speak to the man in charge, please," he said.

"Why?"

"I have some important information."

"Tell me first."

"No."

Harrison studied him, then asked, "Have you been going around talking to people again?"

"No."

"Then bug off."

"But he may know—" began Katherine.

"Look, Mrs. Price Brichter," said Harrison heavily. "I don't care if you can buy the whole goddamn state of Illinois or if you keep the governor in your hip pocket. Get out of here; we've got enough to do without this husband of yours trying to poke his nose in where it don't belong."

"I don't think you're capable of deciding what does and does not belong to this case," said Stefan.

"I know an arrest I'm capable of making if you aren't off this porch in *five seconds*."

"Can't count as high as ten?" said Stefan. "Never mind; is Trooper Bead inside?"

"No. And your time's up."

"Very well. Come on, *fy'n galon*."

. . .

It was almost dark as they walked down King's Road, and she took his hand. "Um, Peter . . ." she said.

"I know, I know. If I'd only use a little patience and courtesy, I'd do better with people like him."

"Geoff says—"

"Never mind what Geoff says right now, okay?" He stopped, turned her toward him and said, "I'm sorry."

"That's all right." She took his hand and they continued up the road.

The campground was abnormally silent for this early in the evening. The air was full of tension and unhappiness. The murmur of voices was low, the anvils silent. "Is this the way it's going to be from now on?" she asked. "Is our wonderful game over?"

"I hope not," he replied.

A lute began a lament and a very pleasant tenor voice began to sing. Once they realized what the subject of the song was, they stopped to listen:

We say that we kill, we say that we die,
We say that we murder, but don't really try,
For our glory's in honor, not just in the fight,
And if we killed our foes, who'd we drink with at night?

One less-than-loved man of the great Mongol Horde
Was found cruelly stabbed by a cold misericord.
We may never know why, but we all must abhor
The fact that Black Thorstane was killed at the War!

Katherine and Stefan slipped up a side path toward the sound of the voice. They found seven or eight people sitting around a campfire, one with a lute. A tall and very fat man in a black cassock with red buttons all the way down its front was standing in the firelight, singing. A dark-haired woman with large and beautiful eyes was watching the singer with an admiring intensity that marked her as his lady.

It's stolen our mock battle's murderous mirth,
It's taken our dream of Valhalla on Earth,
Our faces are solemn, our joys have all fled,
For Thorstane the Shieldbreaker's dead—truly dead.

Weep or keep silent, but share our intent,
Drape banners of black on pavilion and tent,

Pray ponder life's meanings, and what this man's meant,
And join in our mourning—in Thorstane's Lament.

The lute repeated the last phrase and stopped, and there was a little murmur of approval from his audience. Then the doe-eyed lady saw Stefan and Katherine. "Hello," she called. "Who is it?"

"Just passersby," said Stefan. "And, with your permission, we will go away now. That is a wonderful song, my lord," he added.

"Thank you," said the big man, bowing. "It just came over me, and I wrote it."

"Who are you, m'lord?" asked Katherine.

"Friar Bertram, m'lady. And you?"

"Katherine of Tretower. Good-bye."

Back on the road, she said, "Why does hearing that song make me feel better?"

"Because writing songs about something turns it into history. History's easier to deal with than current events."

"Yes, you're right. But this isn't over, is it?"

"No, not yet."

"Peter, what are you going to do now?"

"Take you home and send for William."

But when they got there, His Majesty was already waiting. "I wanted to see if you're talking to everyone you want to talk to," he said. "Geoff said you came out leading your lady by the hand and went up the road without saying anything to anyone. Where did you go? I thought the troopers put you under house arrest." He sounded annoyed.

"I went to talk to the troopers; I think we've got a breakthrough here."

William's face changed. "What kind of breakthrough?"

"I finally listened, really listened, to what Katherine was saying Thorstane said. I'd been wondering if she didn't hear him right, since I couldn't fit a mundane into the picture. But she heard him just fine. Let me explain."

23

PETROG was badly shaken. He'd managed to convince the troopers that they didn't have enough evidence to hold him, but he could only hope nothing happened to make them change their minds before morning. Their ignorance of the Society was abysmal. And they were angry, the way men used to authority get angry when human complexities thwart them. He recognized it; it was the same kind of anger he, Petty, felt on occasion. What was it King Gregory had said to him a couple of years ago? "It's no fun being a missionary when all you can offer the heathens is work and plenty of it. But keep it up, we need people like you." Then he had given him the Order of the Laurel.

Petrog reached for his medic's tabard. He was on his knees in his pavilion, packing things into his wooden chest. His hands were trembling—he, who was famous for his steady hands. He'd stay overnight because it would look suspicious if he left now, but he wanted to be ready to leave first thing in the morning.

The only good news he'd gotten from the troopers was indirect: They hadn't mentioned his missing ice pick.

Murder was a terrible thing; but on the other hand, he had never liked Thorstane, and was glad he was dead. Patty-cake to you, too, fella.

As he closed the lid of the chest, he heard it: "Oy-yea . . ."

. . .

Sir John sat alone at a table in the Couple Dragons, his goblet in front of him. He didn't want to be alone right now, but he also hoped no one would come by and start talking to him.

The War was a fantasy, and a big dose of reality had torn the fantasy into shreds, never to be mended. His garb felt like a costume worn too long after the play was over.

Should he go see this Lord Stefan person? No, he had nothing of value to tell him. He'd hardly known Thorstane, really. The thing to do was wait it out and go home.

A server came to the table and looked at John's empty goblet. "Cider, please," John said, and the server took the goblet away. John reached into his pouch for tickets, and with them came the survey form. He'd forgotten all about it. "Why did you join the Society for Creative Anachronism?" it asked. Because this great-looking woman had been a member, and joining was one way of getting close to her. He was no longer sure of her name, but he'd been glad to be introduced to the game. That's what the Society was, a game. A game he was surprised to find himself good at. Like softball, another game he was good at. As with softball, he had learned the rules, obtained a couple of uniforms, and played to win.

He looked at the large blank space under the question. Why bother? The game was over. He crumpled the paper up and dropped it on the ground under his table. As if everyone had noticed, the noise of the inn died, and without looking up to see how many were staring at him, he began hastily to grope for it. Then he heard the voice of the herald: ". . . oy-yea . . ."

. . .

Ignatius was pretending to check the names on award scrolls against a master list, and trying to avoid the sympathetic glances of his wife, who was embroidering by the light of a lantern in the opposite corner of their tent. It was quarter to eight; Court would begin in forty-five minutes. The troopers had let Petty go. Maybe that meant they had a better suspect. How plain did I make it at events that I'd like to throttle Thorstane? I never said a word—but I looked mad enough; Germain called me on it a time or two. And I've got no alibi. Oh, damn, are those footsteps? Yes, but they aren't stopping. Just get me through tonight, God, so I can go home in the morning. He rolled up a scroll with a loud crackle. "What's that?" he asked, turning his head.

". . . oy-yea!"

• • •

Katherine sat moving stew around in a bowl. Stefan had gone off with Geoff and Taffy. Anne was making polite conversation, little of which she heard. They turned their heads at the cry of the herald.

"Oy-yea! Oy-yea! Oy-yea! Will the peerage of all kingdoms please attend Their Majesties in the Couple Dragons Inn at eight o'clock! Peerage of all kingdoms, come to the Couple Dragons at eight! Court has been postponed one hour! Court will now begin at nine-thirty!"

24

THE assembling peerage—knights, Members of the Laurel and Pelican, barons and baronesses, earls, countesses, dukes, duchesses—jammed the little courtyard of the Couple Dragons and spilled over into the east room of the inn, filling it as well. Late arrivals overflowed into the kitchen area and Baron Dur hurried to tie up the canvas that separated the kitchen from the courtyard so the peers holding it up with careless hands and shoulders wouldn't pull the place down around their ears. There was a generous sprinkling of crowns and coronets among the gathering.

Dur had already put additional lanterns in the west room, setting them in rows on tables at either end and suspending two from the ceiling. The empty room glowed like a stage whose curtain had just gone up. Three director's chairs—borrowed from King Oswin—had been set up against the back canvas wall, and a space in front of the chairs had been cleared of tables and benches. The inn buzzed with nervous talk, which faded and stopped when Lord Stefan walked out into the empty space. A squire is not a peer, and they waited for him to explain his presence. When he didn't, the talk began again, louder.

After a minute, Sir Ignatius marched out in his green herald's cape and called, ''Oy-yea! His Majesty William, King of the Middle!'' William came in from the side wearing a long, loose red tunic under a shorter cream one with gold trim. His white leather belt was tied around the buckle and angled stiffly downward. His crown gleamed in the light of the lanterns, picking up reddish glints from his hair. With him was Sir Jerome, his Earl Marshal, in a short white tunic and faded jeans, over which he had hastily pulled a black-and-gold tabard marked with the crossed swords of his office.

William's manner was imperious, his mouth drawn up tight and his eyes hot. After a startled pause, there were bows from the peerage. William walked to the nearest chair and stopped, the Marshal stopping beside him. They did not sit down.

Ignatius gave the murmurs time to die, then said, ''Oy-yea! His Majesty Oswin, King of the East!'' Oswin entered, going to stand before his chair, bringing with him a knight in a mail shirt made of copper wire, a purely decorative article that marked him as Earl Marshal of the East. Oswin was wearing black tights and a short, black velvet bag-sleeved cotehardie. The crown of the East was the only trace of color about him, and he was without his usual grin.

''Oy-yea! Mistress Radegund d'Portiers, Autocrat of this Pennsic War!'' announced Sir Ignatius, and the lady entered. She curtsied gravely to the two kings as she passed them, and went to stand quietly in front of the last chair. She was wearing a simple floor-length green dress. Her Laurel medallion on its green ribbon caught the light and flashed as she looked nervously out at the crowd.

William sat, Oswin and Radegund sat, and the room again broke into whispers. Ignatius glanced worriedly at Stefan, then went to bend into a whispered conference with William.

William waved him away after a minute and addressed the crowd. ''Oy-yea, already!'' he ordered impatiently. ''I called this meeting because I want to clear this mess up. As most of you know, I asked Lord Stefan von Helle here''—he gestured in Stefan's direction—''to look into things. He's a cop, a detective, and I was hoping he'd find out what really happened this morning. And he thinks he has. So His Majesty Oswin and Mistress Radegund and I called you all together—''

"One minute, Your Majesty," said Wulfstan, raising his hand from near the front of the crowd.

"What?" asked William, displeased at the interruption.

"If this man is going to present us with some kind of evidence, shouldn't at least one of the troopers be present?"

"No. Lord Stefan went to the troopers first with his story, and they sent him away flea-bit. They don't want to know anything they don't find out themselves. So he came to me, and I'm asking you to just shut up and listen."

Jane, Queen of Meridies, stepped away from her place near the west end of the kitchen and said, "If you will pardon me, Your Majesties, Mistress: I don't believe this is a legal proceeding."

"This is a voluntary gathering," said Oswin. "You are here to listen to some information and to give advice, at the request of King William, and with the agreement of myself and Mistress Radegund. Anyone who wishes to leave may do so—and should do so now, before we get underway." His dark eyes searched the crowd, but no one moved except Queen Jane, who only went back to her place.

"I won't put up with any more interruptions," warned William. "Pray silence for Lord Stefan."

Stefan bowed to the kings and Mistress Radegund, then turned to address the crowd. "Gentles, I ask your patience while I cover ground you are already familiar with. Later, I may ask some questions, even make some accusations. You are all reminded that you have every right not to answer me. I want the right to silence clearly understood from the start." He paused to let that sink in, his expression serious, and there was an uneasy stir. He waited for it to subside before he went on.

"Lord Thorstane Shieldbreaker, known mundanely as Randolf Unwin, was stabbed twice with an ice pick during the time of the Woods Battle. He was found within minutes, still alive, but died almost immediately, and resuscitation efforts were unsuccessful. The State Police were called and have been conducting an investigation.

"Thorstane was found by my lady wife, who was acting as water bearer during the battle. She reported to the medics, the troopers, and later to me that he was semiconscious and only somewhat responsive to her inquiries about what had happened to him. His last words, to the best of her recollection, were: 'hurts, bastard, but it was a mundane,' and 'fight.' The words were mumbled with some effort, but clear enough for her to understand them. They set off a search for a mundane, maybe a person on drugs, who climbed over the fence looking for a victim, any victim, and who just happened across Thorstane.

"But it was soon proved that no mundane was or could have been in the woods at that time, so we moved on to speculate that someone stripped off his armor and went after Thorstane in the mundane clothing he wore under it.

"A suit of armor was found in the woods not far from where Thorstane had fallen, blue armor, brand new. It was suggested that this armor was discarded by our mysterious attacker. Baron Dur told me that when I found the owner of the armor, I would have my murderer.

"Master Wulfstan remembered a fighter wearing blue armor. He was, he said, an unbelted fighter with a southern accent named Christopher Bridgeman, who joined them after the battle had begun, and distinguished himself fighting polearm. Lord Narses the Great also remembers seeing Lord Christopher. Both agree that Lord Christopher was killed the same time Thorstane was, and that the two went off together, but neither showed up at Resurrection Point. It was shortly after this that Thorstane was found stabbed. Lord Christopher has not been seen since he was with Thorstane at the gathering place. It looks very much as if Lord Christopher is our man. But why would he take off the armor, which was both protection and a disguise, in order to attack a large, strong, armored and armed man? Why couldn't Thorstane name him? And where is he now?

"What do we know about Lord Christopher? Well, he's a big man. And perhaps a southerner. He spoke with a marked Arkansas accent, but that accent is one of the easiest to fake—listen to anyone who has ever owned a CB unit—and Lord Narses, whose accent is genuine, thought perhaps Lord Christopher was mocking him, or at best had been living away from home for a number of years.

Lord Christopher said he was from Lone Castle—but there is no one named Christopher from Lone Castle, and no one in the Calontir encampment has ever heard of him.

"Now, if one's intention were to establish an alibi as a completely different person, what better means than to construct secretly a new suit of armor? I submit, 'Lord Christopher' does not exist outside that blue armor. Someone made the armor, brought it with him to the War, and hid it in the woods before the battle. He came to the Point in his own armor, then dropped out of his group as it went into the woods, and changed into the new armor. He joined Wulfstan and the Horde forces as an ostensible returnee from Resurrection.

"He positioned himself behind Thorstane in the Horde shield wall, choosing the place deliberately, because from that place he could easily interfere with Thorstane, causing him to be killed. The wall being thus opened up, he could himself take a blow from the enemy. Then, on the walk to Resurrection Point, he lured Thorstane off and stabbed him. Afterward, he changed back into his own armor and quietly joined his original fighting group."

"You're doing a lot of theorizing there, it seems to me," said Prince Thomas.

"Will you shut up for just two more minutes?" said King William, and there was a chorus of agreement.

"Perhaps I am," said Stefan. "But the speculation fits the facts: No one remembers seeing Lord Christopher at Resurrection Point, and his statement to Wulfstan that the number of Easterners waiting there far outnumbered Midrealmers was untrue. Thorstane told Lord Broddi that Christopher deliberately dropped his polearm onto Thorstane's arm, forcing his shield down and thereby permitting an Easterner to kill him. And this same Christopher took what may well have been a tip shot as a killing blow, and later vanished with Thorstane on the walk out to the Point. The blue armor was found abandoned near Thorstane's body. There is no inspection sticker on it, and the tape that marked the owner's allegiance as a fighter has been removed.

"Lord Wulfstan has supplied me with the names of all the people who have left the campground since the murder, and none of them took part in the Woods Battle. Between the constables manning the

Point and the peace mongers along the river, I am sure no one entered, or left, the woods after the battle began. It is therefore certain the killer took part in the Woods Battle and is still among us."

"But if he didn't take the armor off until after he stabbed Thorstane, why did Thorstane say it was a mundane?" asked Oswin.

"Yes," said Stefan, "what about Thorstane's dying words? Let's look at them again. He was surprised or puzzled by something, my lady says. 'But it was a mundane,' he said, 'fight.' " Stefan's left eyebrow lifted and he repeated, " 'But it was a mundane—fight,' " and someone said quietly, "Son of a *bitch*!"

Stefan continued, "Thorstane was surprised the attack came at the War, because his killer had been involved in a purely mundane quarrel with him.

"In going through my notes, I find only three people who had a mundane quarrel with Thorstane. All three took part in the Woods Battle."

"Here, now!" said Petrog, stepping forward from the front of the crowd. "You'd better be very sure of your facts before you go making any accusations!"

"I am sure, very sure," said Stefan calmly. "And you are not obliged to respond in any way, either now or after I finish. But you are a surgeon at Cleveland Uptown General Hospital?"

"I fail to see any connection with my profession and this matter."

"It was you who found Thorstane sleeping off a drunk in a linen closet at the hospital and had him fired. He swore he'd get you, and since that time you've been severely beaten, you've been subjected to harassment on the job and at events, your car has been tampered with, and there have been other, lesser, incidents. You have complained to several people, including the police, that Thorstane is responsible, but nothing has been done. Thorstane has been seen gloating over your misfortunes. For a man with a high temper, that might seem more than sufficient provocation."

William said, "Now, wait, Steffy; I told you I went and scared the piss out of Thorstane last night about this. We solved the problem; Petty had no reason to kill Thorstane."

Stefan said, "When you told me that you added, 'Unless Thorstane got his nerve back and said something this morning.' And this morning at the Point I saw Thorstane whisper something in Master Petrog's ear, adding audibly words to the effect that you didn't live in Strange Sea and couldn't always be on hand to protect him."

"I won't have this!" yelled Petrog, coming forward to shove his face up close to Stefan's. "I'll have your badge if you accuse me of murder! If you press it all the way to an arrest, I'll slap you with a lawsuit so fast your head will spin! You cops—you're all alike! Can't arrest the man we all know mugged me, because he didn't leave his driver's license behind to prove he did it! But now, when your reputation's on the line, watch you bust the first man who just looks like he might've committed a murder!" Petty held his arms up, wrists together. "Come on, where's your handcuffs? Put them on, and see how sorry I can make you be!"

Stefan had stood calmly while Petrog raged at him. Now that the man had stopped, waiting for him to do something, Stefan took a step back and made a brief bow.

"My apologies, m'lord. I have no intention of arresting you, or of having you arrested. While it is true that you had a serious mundane fight with Thorstane, there is one very solid reason why I don't believe you're our murderer: You're not a fighter. It's been made clear that you have too much respect for your surgeon's hands to risk them in combat. You could not have turned up in the Woods Battle wearing a suit of armor you made yourself, much less fought polearm well enough to impress a man whose fighting skills have brought him the accolade of knighthood."

Petrog stood frozen a moment, then dropped his arms. "Well, that's better," he said gruffly. He took two steps back, seemed about to turn away, then hesitated—and bowed. "I beg your pardon for my harsh words just now," he said. "It was very discourteous of me."

Stefan bowed again and said, "I'm truly sorry for the scare I must have given you."

"Pooh-bah!" cheered someone quietly. Petrog turned and gave his face a wipe as he went back to his place in the crowd. A countess moved over to make room for him, reached up and punched him lightly on the shoulder.

Stefan turned to look at the herald. ''Then there's Sir Ignatius.''

Ignatius looked frightened and held up both hands against the accusation he was sure was coming. ''Now wait, now wait. It's true I was mad as hell at him, and I can't say I don't think he had it coming. But I didn't do it; I swear.''

''My lord, if you had gone to look at the armor, you would realize you have a perfectly good excuse: your body.''

Ignatius looked down at himself in surprise. ''How's that?''

''The armor was made for a man much bigger than you. It would have been impossible for you to wear that armor; you're much too short, especially up and down the legs.''

Ignatius' mouth fell open, then he grinned in bright relief. ''I never liked my legs before,'' he said, ''but God bless 'em forever!'' There was laughter at this, but it quickly died as Stefan turned next to look out over the crowd.

''The third man is here, I saw him.'' Stefen rose onto his toes. ''Sir John de Capestrano?''

Sir John replied from somewhere in the middle of the courtyard, ''So what?'' and there was another brief spate of nervous laughter at his laconic tone.

''You are the manager of Nerren's Warehouse, is that correct?''

''So what?'' Sir John repeated, but his tone was just a little harsher, and this time no one laughed.

''Do you want to tell us about your fight with Thorstane?''

''I didn't have a fight with him, mundane or otherwise.''

''Not exactly a fight, perhaps; more a matter of blackmail.''

Sir John had not stirred from his place in the crowd, but a narrow path was opening from where he stood to where Stefan was standing. He hesitated, then asked, ''Why would I blackmail Thorstane? He was a drunk and a loony; who cared why he did anything?''

''Thorstane was blackmailing you.''

''For what?''

''I don't know. But he wasn't collecting money, he was collecting liquor. I have been told repeatedly of Thorstane's large and bottomless store of liquor, of its being good, expensive stuff. Nerren's is the largest liquor distributor in the greater Cleveland area.''

''Prove there's a connection.''

"We could send for Sulu the Loon, who overheard you tell Thorstane to stay away from Nerren's and that he'd gotten enough out of you."

Sir John laughed harshly. "You believe what that crazy told you?" He began thrusting himself shoulder-first along the narrow opening.

"Sulu has a strange memory. When he repeats something he's heard, he repeats it verbatim, inflections and all."

"That's correct," said Wulfstan, and there were several murmurs of agreement.

"Well, so what?" Sir John broke clear and stopped, defiant and wary. He was wearing a dull-green tunic and wine-colored hose and shoes.

"Did you keep underlining the danger of snakes in the woods to keep people from wandering off the trails and perhaps finding the armor you hid?"

"I don't have to answer any of your questions, you said so yourself."

"That's right. But may I go on?"

"Talk all you like."

"You told me you were with King Edmund when he was asked to link his forces with King William's troops."

"So I was mistaken. It was Queen Jane; Edmund was at Resurrection. It's easy to get the details wrong when someone comes up all snotty and starts asking questions."

"You stopped me on King's Road and asked me back to your tent in order to be asked questions. And you discovered your mistake when you returned to the Couple Dragons and uncharacteristically sought out unbelted fighters and listened to their stories."

Sir John's face reddened. "You think you're gonna stick me with this? I'll sue you for false arrest even faster than Petty!"

"Did you borrow a brass rivet from Sir Ignatius?"

Sir John threw a glance at Ignatius, and cleared his throat. "Yeah, but I didn't use it. Check my armor; there's no brass rivet in it."

"There's a brass rivet in the blue armor. Which shouldn't surprise anyone; Sir Geoffrey said it appears to have been made in a hurry. Sir Geoffrey also told me that the armor was cut out with dull-bladed power shears. Maybe you'd be willing to let someone back home look at your power shears."

"People borrow them all the time. They may be dull, I don't know; I haven't used them in some time."

"When I looked at the armor I found a metal splinter on the right shoulder pauldron. When I saw your gambeson outside your tent, there was a nice new snag on the right shoulder. And I noticed earlier, at Resurrection Point, that the tape on your helm looked as if it had been pulled off and been stuck back on. Would you be willing to let me go get your helm and gambeson?"

John hesitated, then burst forth, "This is a setup! If I say yes, you'll see to it the tape is loose and the gambeson has a snag!"

"I'll go," said Prince Thomas. "I'll bring his armor, too; so we can see if its pauldron has a splinter that could have snagged the gambeson."

"I'll go with him," said Wulfstan.

John shouted, "*No*! None of you touches my gear, none of you!" There was a shocked silence.

"You big piece of shit," growled William.

"What do you know about it?" asked John, whirling on him. "God*damn* you, Your so-called Majesty!" John turned again and gestured at the crowd of peers. "Goddamn all of you! Grown people, playing at being honorable!" He spat. "Nobody's honorable when he's in a trap! I had to do something about Thorstane! Any one of you would've done it too, if you'd been in my position—" He stopped, took a deep ragged breath, turned to Stefan. "All right, what do we do now?"

"Would you be willing to come with me, to make a statement to the State Police?"

John sighed and wiped his face. "Sure, why not?" he said. He looked down at himself. "Could I change out of this stuff first?"

"If you like."

William cleared his throat. "If it's all the same to you," he said in a carefully careless tone, "would you mind taking off the belt, chain, and spurs before you leave here?"

John stared at him, then shrugged. "I don't mind. They don't mean a thing to me, never did." He took his heavy gold chain off and dropped it on the ground.

"I was hoping you'd feel that way," said William.

John began pulling off his belt. He would have dropped it, too, but Stefan, who had retrieved the chain, took it from him, and handed both to William.

John, whose hands were trembling in the silence, had trouble unfastening his spurs, but Stefan waited patiently. He did not offer to help. When they were off at last, he took them and gave them to William.

Then another path opened for him, and Stefan followed him up it and out of the inn.

25

THE merchants' booths in the great barn had been dismantled and removed, and rows of benches replaced them. A flatbed farm wagon had been put at the front of the room to form a dais, and six thrones were set on it. SCA-folk in Renaissance garb aglitter with gems and metallic embroidery rubbed friendly elbows with splendid barbarians, beautifully draped tenth-century gentlefolk, and the steadfastly lowly monks. Stefan escorted Katherine, resplendent in a lush red-and-silver Elizabethan dress, to their seats near the front, saved for them by Taffy, who was sharing his section of bench with a young woman in a wired headdress aflutter with veils. Geoff and Anne waved from three rows back.

The troopers had been seen taking someone away, and the room was buzzing with gossip. It was nine-forty before a herald's big voice called, ''Oy-yea, oy-yea, oy-yea! All rise for His Majesty Oswin, King of the East, and Margaret his Queen!'' A trumpet fanfare began, and Oswin, still in the black costume he had worn at the inn, walked forward with his lady, who was also in black velvet. Behind them were the Crown Prince of the East and his Princess, in white; they did not follow the King and Queen up onto the dais, but took chairs beside it.

"His Majesty William, King of the Middle, and Ethelreada his Queen!" cried the herald, and a different fanfare began. It faltered, to titters from the audience, then picked up again strongly. William also was in the red-and-cream garb he had worn at the inn, and his Queen wore a form-fitting cream dress and a flowing cream cloak lined in red. Crown Prince Thomas and Princess Godeleine wore red-orange and white. They stopped beside the Prince and Princess of the East.

"His Majesty Edmund, King of Meridies, and Jane his Queen!" Edmund wore the dark blue houppelande he had worn when he came to see Stefan, and the Queen was in a virtually identical costume. Meridies' Prince and Princess had not come to the War this year.

When the third fanfare died away, the royalty sat down and the audience followed suit. Then William stood again and said, "I think the first matter of business is an announcement that an arrest has been made in the murder of Thorstane Shieldbreaker. The person arrested has made a statement, and the troopers consider the case solved."

He stepped back and was about to sit again when a voice called out, "Who did it?" There was a chorus of assent to the question.

"As of this point, no one is guilty," said William firmly. "The person under arrest is John de Capestrano." This time he ignored the cries for more information and sat down.

"Oy-yea!" called Ignatius warningly, coming up to the dais with a fat roll of parchments, followed by another man, also in a green herald's cloak, carrying a similar roll. Ignatius went to stand slightly behind William.

The second herald took center stage. "Oy-yea!" he bellowed in a voice as big as Ignatius', although he was a slim man, and shorter by half a head. "The Court of His Majesty Oswin is hereby declared open!" He unrolled his parchments, looked at the top one and called, "Will the members of the right honorable Order of the Laurel come before His Majesty!"

A dozen or so people rose and came to kneel before the dais, including Master Petrog and Mistress Radegund. All were wearing a brass medallion with a green laurel wreath inlaid or painted on it, no two alike. Oswin looked over the group and said, "I don't think all of you are present."

A very thin man with a prominent Adam's apple rose and said, "I believe you're right." He looked out over the audience and said, Lord Simeon Barsabba'e, come here!" and there was an immediate joyous whoop from several people.

Oswin's herald repeated, "Will Lord Simeon Barsabba'e attend His Majesty!"

Simeon Barsabba'e wore a Persian costume of light purple, complete with turned-up shoes. He stopped halfway up to draw his scimitar and hand it to a friend—one does not approach the throne armed. He dropped onto one knee before the dais with a proud air and a pleased smile.

"Is it your wish that this man be enrolled in your number?" asked Oswin, looking amused.

"It is, Your Majesty," chorused the Order.

The herald handed Oswin a large scroll and the King read from it: "Be it known that We, Oswin, being by right of arms King of the Eastern Kingdom, and Margaret, Our Queen, desire all who witness these letters to know that it has pleased Us to enter Simeon Barsabba'e into the Order of the Laurel by reason of his distinguished service to Our Society, specifically for his accomplishments in the teaching of Near Eastern music and his skill in the making of steel weapons.

"We confirm and acknowledge to him the right to bear or, a setting sun gules by letters patent within the Society for Creative Anachronism without let or hindrance from any person, and the right to all titles, insignia, and privileges conveyed by his elevation to this rank, from this day onward.

"Done this Fourth Day of September, A.S. twenty-three, sitting on Our thrones in the Debatable Lands, at the Pennsic War. In testimony whereof We have placed Our hands and seals."

Oswin turned the parchment around to show its gorgeous illumination and decorative border, and the audience made in unison the "Oh! Oooh! Aaaaaah!" of approval common in the East. He handed it to Master Simeon, who looked it over before rolling it up. The tall, thin Master rose once again, took his medallion off, and slipped its green ribbon over Simeon's head, and the others crowded around to congratulate him as people clapped and whistled.

When they returned to their places, Simeon's head was high and his smile proud as ever, but Katherine noticed tears streaming down his face.

Two shy young women in identical gabled headresses, twins, were made Pelicans for their editing of *Tournaments Illuminated,* the Society's official publication. Pelicans, less formal than Laurels, saluted the newest peers by tucking their hands into their armpits and flapping madly.

Oswin's herald was about to make another announcement when Oswin caught his eye and signaled him back. He bent to listen, then turned with a startled look toward the nearest entrance to the barn. All eyes followed his look, and there was a murmur when two uniformed State Policemen came up on the dais.

William, Oswin, and both heralds conferred with the troopers briefly; then nods were exchanged. Oswin's herald turned and called, "Oy-yea, silence for an official announcement!" This seemed to amuse a number of people, including the troopers.

One stepped forward and removed his hat, and Katherine recognized Bead. He said, "As you have already been informed—" but was interrupted by cries of "Louder!" from the back, so he raised his voice and repeated, "As you have been informed, an arrest has been made in the matter of Randolf Unwin's death! I'm here to thank you for your cooperation during what must have been a trying time for all of you! And to say we have no further reason to detain you, so consider yourselves free as of this time to go to your homes!"

"God bless you!" called someone, and there was a smattering of applause. The two troopers left the stage, and the Eastern herald, consulting his next scroll and looking uncertain, went to talk to Oswin.

A minute later he stepped to the front of the dais and called, "Lord Aloysius Costiglione, attend His Majesty!"

Lord Aloysius was a good-looking fair-haired youth with burning blue eyes. He wore a hooded mail tunic and soft boots. Oswin stood and said, "Lord Aloysius, I was going to ask you to hold vigil tonight, but in view of the fact that we've just been told we can go home, perhaps there won't be time or a proper representation of the chivalry present in the morning to do this right."

Aloysius bowed his head and said, "It will be as Your Majesty wishes."

But Sir Geoffrey stood and said, "An it please you, Your Majesty, I'm sure Taffy and I can delay our departure in the morning long enough to be present."

Sir Odo and Sir Dismas stood; then, slowly, six, eight, a dozen, twenty, fifty, a hundred stood. The King and Queen of Meridies stood. Somebody started to applaud, and all of a sudden the room was thundering with it, a noise that went on until, for sheer pain in the hands, it slowly died away.

Oswin, his lean face glowing, said to the young man, "Go, hold your vigil. And come to my pavilion at seven tomorrow morning." The man stood, bowed, and left.

Oswin's herald said, "Is there any more business to be brought before this Court?" There was a silence, and he said, "I hereby declare this Court closed!"

There was a brief interval of talk and laughter, then Ignatius stepped out and called, "Oy-yea, oy-yea, oy-yea! King William's Court is now in order! Will the members of the Great Dark Horde come before the throne!"

There was a stir from the rear where most of them had gathered; then a Viking Stefan recognized as Hreider led them forward. He was carrying a long pole topped by a crossarm from which hung streamers of feathers and horsehair, with a yin-yang emblem in black and red in the center. He stopped about halfway to allow his brothers to disarm themselves, a process that took a considerable amount of time and left piles of various sizes in the aisle. Lady Freyis, of course, took longest and had the largest pile.

Lord Roc was left behind to watch the weapons—some joker had included a hand grenade and a .45 automatic, and it wouldn't do to have a child wander by and pick something up. The parade continued forward. Lady Anne, to her embarrassment, was again the object of some leers and kissing noises as they went by, but they arrived at last at the dais in a semblance of order, although none went to his or her knee and not all of them bowed. Wulfstan came to the front of the group—there were about forty of them—and bent his head to William. "You rang?" he said loudly, and everyone laughed.

William came to the front of the dais. "Khan," he said in his big voice, "you and I agreed that your brothers would fight on the side of the Midrealm this War. In return, I promised you some things: five yards of red silk and five of black velvet, two cases of Baron Dur's well water, a new dagger for Lady Freyis, and your pick of the litter when my champion setter whelps next spring. I have everything but the pup here—but . . . The War is over, and your people fought for me only once. I am paying what I promised you, on one condition."

"The Great Dark Horde does not like conditions," said Wulfstan. "But because we are courteous, we will listen."

"I don't want you to take Thorstane's death into consideration." There was an angry buzz from the audience. William's face tightened into an angry glare, and it faded. "Thorstane didn't die in Phillip's Forest today. Randy Unwin, of Cleveland, Ohio, was murdered in a wooded area of a campground by some jerk. He was killed as a mundane, for mundane reasons. The fact that his murderer was a member of the Society is a shame, but not important, except as a lesson to the rest of us how not to behave. Those interested in studying courtesy, chivalry, honor, and the disciplines of the crafts can continue to do so. I speak not only to you, but to every person in this room, every person who hears about what I am saying right here and now. The Society as an institution, as an ideal, cannot be damaged by the failure of any of its members to live up to its standards unless we let it. And I ain't gonna."

Wulfstan held up a hand and replied, "Nor I." He grinned. "But if you let your bitch get mixed up with that Airedale like you did last year, the deal's off!"

The cheers and applause that greeted this were somewhat out of proportion, augmented as they were by relief and joy at what William had said.

The gifts were brought forward by Prince Thomas and Princess Ethelreada and borne aloft by the Horde members back to the middle of the room, where weapons were quickly picked up. By the time they were back in their places, Ignatius had to oy-yea several times to restore order.

"I summon Lord Stefan!" called William.

Startled, Stefan rose, worked his way over the feet of those sitting between him and the aisle, and came forward to go down on one knee. "Lord Stefan," said William, taking a scroll from Ignatius, "we decided, Oswin and I, to keep the courts short tonight. So I'm going to forgo all the other things I meant to do, except this." He unrolled the scroll and read, "We, William, by right of arms King of the Middle Kingdom, and Ethelreada, Our Queen, desire all who witness these letters to know it has pleased Us to grant Stefan von Helle an augmentation to his arms, to wit, a mullet argent in sinister chief, to be borne without let or hindrance, for extraordinary service to Us at this Pennsic War. Done this Fourth Day of September, A.S. twenty-three, et cetera, et cetera." William turned the scroll around so Stefan and the audience could see it. One half of it was taken up by a large representation of Stefan's arms: sable, a lit candle—with a silver five-pointed star now glowing in the upper right corner. Stefan recognized the beautiful italic writing on the other side as William's own. He rose and came to claim his scroll. William stooped and murmured, "Ethelreada painted your arms. Be careful, I'm not sure the ink on your tin star is dry yet."

"I will. Thank you, Your Majesty." He stepped back, bowed deeply, and returned to his seat, and was not aware of the applause until it stopped.

Ignatius called, "Is there any more business to be brought before this Court?" When there was no response, he recited the Midrealm formula, "This Court is out of order."

"Whoo!" shouted someone in a falsetto. "Let's go pack for home!"

• • •

On the way back to their encampment, people kept interrupting their conversation to shake Stefan's hand and say, "I wondered if you were the one who solved it."

To which Stefan would reply only, "The State Police made the arrest."

Master Petrog came up to them and said, "Well, another piece of the mystery is solved."

"What's that?" asked Stefan.

"My missing ice pick. I carried it outside my tent this morning and stuck it in a tree. It fell and my neighbor saw it and put it away in his tent for safekeeping—and forgot to tell me about it until just before Court this evening."

Stefan stared at him. "My lord, if I had known about that ice pick, you would at this moment be calling your attorney from the Butler jailhouse."

Back at the campfire, they gathered for mugs of cocoa or coffee or tea. "All right, you're among friends," said Taffy. "Want to talk about it?"

Stefan pulled an ear. "I didn't catch on until almost too late. Once I had the right piece of information—which was under my nose the whole time—it was simple. It was a mundane quarrel. No mundanes were on the site, so it had to be a mundane quarrel with an SCA member. Since Thorstane lived and worked in Cleveland, it had to be a mundane quarrel with someone from there. And he'd had serious mundane quarrels with only three SCA-folk from Strange Sea: Petty, Iggy, and John. Petty wasn't a fighter, Iggy couldn't wear the armor, and so it had to be John. Simple."

"So why couldn't the troopers solve it?" asked Taffy.

"Maybe they would have, eventually. But they were handicapped by a lack of knowledge of the Society. Mundane, for example, is an adjective as well as a noun."

"What will happen to John?" asked Katherine.

"If he recants his statement to the troopers, he'll stand trial. I hope he doesn't do that; this case will sound damn strange in a mundane courtroom."

"Is there enough evidence to convict him?" asked Geoff.

"Oh, yes, I think so. The snagged gambeson will match the metal splinter on the armor, he was heard warning Thorstane, there is a liquor shortage at the warehouse he worked in, and I'll bet money his power shears are dull. And even after Sergeant Foster warned him again, John said very calmly that he'd done it and wasn't sorry, but was glad it was over."

"Why did he do it?" asked Taffy.

"He said Thorstane caught him stealing, putting two cases of champagne into his trunk, and threatened to turn him in if he didn't share what he'd stolen. And once he agreed, Thorstane just kept coming back. The more he gave Thorstane, the tighter the hold Thorstane had over him, and the less able he was to refuse his demands, which Thorstane kept escalating. The amount stolen had long gone over the value needed to bring felony charges—and Nerren's prosecutes thieves."

"Did you know beforehand what it was about?" asked Anne.

"No. But I suspected either blackmail or extortion. Thorstane was getting hold of a lot of very expensive liquor, in amounts he couldn't have bought on his salary. And he wasn't stealing it from the deliveries he was making. When I called Cleveland, I got hold of John's boss, who told me about the losses, and that, as manager, John knew they were investigating. But Thorstane wouldn't lower his demands, and so John simply couldn't see any other way out from under. As he put it, Thorstane was scum anyway."

" 'M, 'm, 'm," said Geoff softly. "Nasty."

There was a sound from the path, and Lord Roc came up to the campfire. "What do you want?" asked Anne sharply.

"Two things," said Roc. "First, to thank Lord Stefan for solving this for us. And second—" He turned and dropped to his knees before Anne. "I want to ask your forgiveness."

"For what?"

"Well, if we'd had the whole time of the War, it might've worked," he said. "But we're going home tomorrow morning and I don't think you've caught on yet."

"Caught on to what?" she asked, frowning.

But Stefan started to chuckle and was joined an instant later by Geoff. Taffy and Katherine looked as puzzled as Anne. "What's so funny?" asked Anne.

Roc said, "You see, Solly said maybe if we acted like you think we act, you'd see we don't really act that way. Only maybe we didn't lay it on thick enough, and for sure we didn't have time to do it enough. Though I admit I wasn't looking forward to tending that damn fire the whole War!''

''What's the fire got to do with it?'' asked Anne, bewildered.

''From there he can see when you leave our encampment,'' said Geoff, laughing openly.

''Yes, and signal a brother or two to follow and leer at you,'' agreed Roc. ''But it didn't work and now you've really got cause to be mad at us. And I'm sorry. We'll lay off, I promise. And I'll keep out of your way back home, okay?''

Anne studied the penitent on his knees before her, then gently touched the tangled hair. ''Am I as awful as that? So awful you'd actually organize to teach me a lesson?''

''Well, they know how hard it is being alone like I am. And you carry a lot of weight in our shire. So they figured if we could turn you around, the others would follow suit, and I could enjoy my status as loyal opposition.''

Anne sighed. ''All right, you're forgiven. And I guess now I'm going to have to go along with you and apologize myself.''

Roc looked up at her, touched and amused. ''Would you do that?''

''Of course. Do you think my lord and his squire are the only ones with class?''

As she and Roc went down the path together, Katherine turned to Stefan. ''I think we're going to be okay, don't you?''

''I think we are okay,'' he said, kissing her lightly. And from one encampment over, the Calontir bunch could be heard singing.

Homeward bound, amazing we survived it,
We all look like we've just been through a war.
Tellin' tales and swappin' brags about the battle,
We'll be reveling a thousand miles and more.
And all the knocks and bruises seem
To fade into a fighter's dream
Of plans to build a better helm and shield.
Next year we'll be back again

For revels' sake and glory gained
With tactics that are sure to sweep the field.

Good night, Your Majesty, we'll see you,
Now you know us, we're your rebel sons.
We've always done our share—and more—at Pennsic,
And we'll have gone a thousand miles 'fore the day is done.